PLAYS WELL WITH OTHERS

LAUREN BLAKELY

Copyright © 2023 by Lauren Blakely

Cover Design by Kate Farlow, Photo by Ren Saliba

All rights reserved. No part of this book may be reproduced or transmitted in any form or by any means whatsoever without express written permission from the author, except in the case of brief quotations embodied in critical articles and reviews. Names, characters, places, brands, media, and incidents are either the product of the author's imagination or are used fictitiously. The author acknowledges the trademarked status and trademark owners of various products referenced in this work of fiction, which have been used without permission. The publication/use of these trademarks is not authorized, associated with, or sponsored by the trademark owners. This is a work of fiction. Names, characters, business, events and incidents are the products of the author's imagination. Any resemblance to actual persons, living or dead, or actual events is purely coincidental.

ABOUT

Am I fake dating my best friend? Hear me out...

So I'm throwing myself a breakup party, a glittery fete where I envision I'll lift a glass and celebrate being free and single again.

What I actually do: Drink too much champagne and blurt out to my best guy friend that I'd really like to get back on the horse.

But what I truly don't expect is Carter's answer - he volunteers as tribute.

With his sinful brown eyes and too-good-to-be-true body it'd be no hardship for me to say yes, though I certainly don't want him to feel obligated to, um, service me, just because my failed, loveless marriage was a s-e-x desert.

But since the charming and confident pro football star owes five public dates to his dating app sponsor, we make a deal to help each other out.

Pretty soon, our public *how to date* lessons turn into, ahem, very private ones. And I'm a star student, graduating quickly from flirty banter and lingering looks to toe-curling, sheet-grabbing, mind-blowing hours of physical education.

The problem? Turns out learning to date again feels a lot like the real thing. Can our friendship withstand all these late-night bedroom sessions?

Especially since I'm suddenly longing for my best friend and there's nothing fake about my feelings...

DID YOU KNOW?

By Lauren Blakely

To be the first to find out when all of my upcoming books go live click here!

PRO TIP: Add lauren@laurenblakely.com to your contacts before signing up to make sure the emails go to your inbox!

Did you know this book is also available in audio and paperback on all major retailers? Go to my website for links!

PLAYS WELL WITH OTHERS
BY LAUREN BLAKELY

A Standalone in the How to Date series

AUTHOR'S NOTE
BY LAUREN BLAKELY

Hi! Sometimes authors like certain names a lot. Like the name Rachel. Some eagle-eyed readers might recall that in The Boyfriend Comeback the character of Beck had an ex-girlfriend he remained friends with and her name was Rachel. When I went on to write The Good Guy Challenge, Two a Day and My So-Called Sex Life, I introduced a new Rachel as a sidekick of the various heroines. Now it's *new* Rachel's turn for her romance. But she's not the same Rachel who was in The Boyfriend Comeback. I just forgot I'd used the name recently! Oops! In any case, enjoy Rachel Dumont's romance! You don't need to have read any of the other titles to enjoy this standalone.

Also, Carter plays professional football and the team names are fictitious and so is the name of the biggest game of the year.

1

DID I JUST FLASH HIM MY BOOBS?

Rachel

Where are my lucky spatulas? I swear they were in *this* box in the corner of the kitchen. The one marked *Very Important Things*.

Because my baking supplies are vital. They're therapy, dammit.

Wait.

There's a box next to the stove labeled *VIP Things 1* and a box on the counter designated *VIP Things 2*.

Which one has my spatula in it? And why didn't I label any of these things specifically?

Oh, right. Because I fled Los Angeles faster than a twelve-year-old could stack plastic cups on social media. That, too, was a Very Important Thing.

Now, I'm scrunched in with the boxes in the itty-bitty kitchen of my new townhome in San Francisco, hunting for the necessities of life—spatulas. How can I bake lemon cheesecake blueberry bars for my breakup party tomorrow night without them?

Think, Rachel, think.

I close my eyes, remembering the packing frenzy last week in my Venice Beach home, seeing clothes flying, hearing the screech of packing tape, feeling the skittering of my pulse. The ink was finally dry on my divorce papers, but the news of the birth of my ex's newest child was still fresh in my head. I couldn't spend any more time in Los Angeles with those painful memories chasing me wherever I went.

Ah! I remember now. I jammed the spatulas into the underwear compartment of my carry-on, in between my new Valentina lacy bra-and-panty set and the scorching-hot burgundy bustier, the one I've vowed to wear…*someday.*

Because *someday soon* is a fool's wish.

I rush to the bedroom, unzip the suitcase, and grab the pretty little kitchen darlings from their place of honor next to the pretty little bedroom darlings.

"There you are," I say, relieved, then I return to the kitchen and set the spatulas down on the counter, pushing aside *Badly Labeled Box 2*. I head to the pantry and grab the flour, sugar, and baking soda.

Thank you, Elodie, for stocking the pantry for me. You're the best friend ever.

I'll bake tonight, but I want to make sure I have everything I need ready now. Carter is coming by soon to help me move heavy objects.

Every gal should have a muscular and helpful guy

like Carter to call on to lift things, move things, and carry things.

Also, his shoulder is quite nice to cry on. I'd give it a five out of five for sturdiness and absorbency.

As I sort my baking supplies, I review the day ahead. We'll rearrange the living room so I can have a better view of California Street, and after that, I'll spend the afternoon in my jewelry shop. Fable has been handling the shop while I've been absent, and while she's great, business hasn't been smashing while I've been flying up and down the coast of California, managing two shops. This evening, I'll shut myself off from the world and devote the night to baking and, well, wine.

My shrink will be so proud. She's always advocating self-care, and that sounds like baking and merlot to me.

Now that I have a plan for the day, my pulse starts to settle a skosh—then the doorbell rings.

Oh, shit. Is Carter here already? I glance down at my outfit and cringe. Three-day-old yoga pants and a white T-shirt with a red splotch design that says *Of course it's wine, Officer*. The shirt is courtesy of my friend Hazel. But when I sniff myself, I find I'm desperately in need of a shower, and that's courtesy of me.

I race to the window in my slippers, dodging a peace lily to peer from the second story to the stoop below. Oh! It's the delivery guy from the wine shop.

"Coming!" I shout, even though he's already trotting down the steps to the street. But wine gets lonely quickly, so I leave my townhome, rush down the stairs, and hold open the front door of the building to grab the box.

Tucking it under my arm, I spin around, when my feet go out from under me—

Buttplant.

I wince. There must be grease, or powder, or something on the foyer floor. But I make a quick scan and the floor is pristine.

Great. I slipped on my own enthusiasm for discount wine. But hey, I shielded the wine from harm. The box is still safe and sound in my arm, so I get up, precious cargo in hand, and head up the stairs and back to my townhome, ass aching the whole way.

I set down the goods on the kitchen counter and check my phone. Twenty minutes. Just enough time to look presentable.

Note to self: add showers to your to-do list.

As I hightail it to the bathroom, the device vibrates with a text.

> Elodie: Guess what I got for you?

That's such a trick question. I don't even want to play her guessing game, since I'll get it wrong. But I do love gifts from all my friends fiercely. As I strip off my stinky shirt, I reply.

> Rachel: A pony?

Plays Well With Others

> Elodie: You're close. Think horses.

Hmm. Does my chocolatier bestie know any hot cowboys to set me up with? A gal can dream. With my phone in one hand, I shimmy off my exercise pants, dictate a reply, then hit send.

> Rachel: A date with a hot cowboy who'll ride in on a stallion?

> Elodie: *writes down idea for next year's Christmas gift.* Anyway, not that, but you can definitely ride this stallion.

I'm simultaneously excited and terrified as I toss my panties into the nearby hamper.

> Rachel: Tell me the make and model!

> Elodie: I'd better show you. I'll come by later. Gotta go. Customer here.

And I'll have to add *See Elodie* to my to-do list, but she'll be a bright spot for sure, and after a terrible year (or five, but who's counting), I do enjoy my bright spots. I set the phone down on the vanity, then turn on the water in my spacious rainfall shower—another bright spot in my life. As it heats up, I loop my hair into a bun.

Ten minutes later, after a scalding shower that steams up every surface in the bathroom, my butt no longer aches and I'm fresh as a coconut.

With the tropical bodywash scent filling the little room, I grab a towel. While I dry off, my phone buzzes again. I peer at the device, but the glass is steamed up.

Looks like Elodie's texting again.

I'll write back in just a second. Gotta dry my legs first.

The phone rings.

I sigh, but I'm laughing. She's so impatient. I swipe up, answering the call without looking as I dry my back. "I solved your riddle. You got me a ten-speed vibrator. It's called the Cowboy. And yes, I will test it tonight."

Silence.

Nothing but crickets for five long seconds. Then a throat clears.

A masculine throat.

Carter's handsome face looks out at me from the screen. "If that's a hint, I can leave right now and pick that up for you," he says, and when I look closer, I see my street behind him since he's on my front stoop.

I freeze, all my dignity evaporating with the shower steam.

I'm naked, and I just flashed my best friend my boobs.

2

THE WORD OF THE DAY

Carter

Earlier this morning as I was brewing my coffee at home, I ripped off a page in my word-of-the-day calendar in the kitchen.

The word was lachrymose.

Another big-ass word no one uses in daily life.

But I'm committed to the learn-a-new-thing-daily resolution I made this year, so as I measured the beans into the grinder, I read the definition of the ten-dollar word—it's an adjective used to describe someone who cries often.

Now, I'm pacing around Rachel's block, giving her time to get dressed, and I've got a use for the fancy word all right. No, I don't even try to put lachrymose into a sentence. No one can do that and mean it.

Instead, I repeat it—*lachrymose, lachrymose, lachry-*

mose—in a desperate attempt to drown out the other word echoing through my brain.

Boobs. Boobs. Boobs.

Rachel's boobs.

My best friend's boobs.

But c'mon, *lachrymose*. You can do it.

When I reach Fillmore Street, I pause, take a deep breath, and then soldier the hell on.

One foot in front of the other.

But the flashing billboard of perky beauties is too powerful.

As I walk down the busy shopping street I jerk my gaze right, then left. There has to be something on this block of Fillmore that'll work like a time machine. Not that I want to forget the flashing. But I *have* to forget the flashing.

I spot my favorite place for coffee. More caffeine would be a bad idea. But An Open Book is a block away. I could get a new book.

Except...look over there. Like it's a beacon of hope calling out to me, I follow the light of the quirky new gift shop across the street. Dubbed Effing Stuff, it's like the universe's answer to my help-me-forget-tits prayers.

I'll get Rachel a mug.

Yes!

We have this ongoing mug-gifting game, and it's probably my turn. If it's not, I can use the distraction anyway. I'll find one that says we're friends and always will be, whether I've seen her in the buff or not.

Half-buff, to be precise.

Hmm, what does the other half of her look like in the buff?

Stop. Just stop.

Rachel's beautiful—sure, I'd have to have been blind not to notice that before. And she's funny, and smart, and kind. She also doesn't take herself too seriously, which I like. But those are great best friend qualities— and that's what I need in my life right now.

Plus, I'm pretty sure the last thing she needs in her upturned life is for her dude friend to suddenly perv on her.

With blinders on, I march into the quirky gift shop. "That one," I say to no one in particular when I spot the perfect mug.

As in, perfectly innocent. There's a unicorn shooting rainbows from its ass.

I grab that bad boy from a shelf and head straight to the counter. "One rainbow-tooting unicorn, please," I say to the nose-ringed woman working there.

"So cute. My little niece loves unicorns." She gestures to the shelves behind her with bags on hooks. "Want a gift bag?"

Yes! That'll cement the goal of this gift for sure. "That one, please," I say, picking a pink bag.

Pink is innocent.

I take ten more minutes and another lap around the block and then head back to Rachel's place. On the way, my alarm beeps. *Haircut later.* I hit snooze. If I don't, I'll forget it again.

When I reach Rachel's stoop, my mug sleight of hand

has done the trick. Now the tricky bit—walking into her home like nothing happened.

And since I can learn from my mistakes, I call rather than FaceTime.

She answers with a chirpy, "Hello!"

That's promising. She sounds like herself. The Great Flashing Incident must not have bugged her at all.

"Good morning, Sunshine." There. Using the nickname I gave her back in high school will also help the reset. "Want to let me in?" I ask.

Wait…Does that sound dirty? *Want to let me in*? Or does it only sound dirty *today*?

"Of course," she says.

The buzzer blares, and I bound up the steps. She's already opening the door when I get there. Her chestnut hair is swept back in a ponytail and she's wearing jeans, a black T-shirt, and the most awkward grin ever.

Eyes up, I thrust the bag at her. "I got you a mug. A housewarming present."

"Oh." She takes the mug from the bag, but before I can see her reaction, I peer around her place, looking for something to focus on other than *my* dirty thoughts.

Ah, perfect. Her windowsill is covered in tiny plants. I didn't notice those last time I was here. I point at one with leaves and shit. "Hey, is that…a cactus?"

"No. It's basil. But close."

"Cool, cool," I say, and I'm pretty sure basil has nothing in common with desert plants, but that's good of her to be so chill. I beeline for the windowsill, stopping to pick up a pot from the floor. I set it with the rest of her plant family, keeping myself busy.

"That's the rosemary," she says, bright and cheery. Maybe more cheery than usual?

I scratch my jaw as I stare at the plants, then check out a taller one on the floor next to the windowsill. "Is this a fern?" I ask, though I've no idea what ferns look like. Green, maybe?

"No. But good guess. The tall one is a ficus. I call him Bob the Ficus. Well, Juliet named him. She gave it to me. Said it's a starting over plant." Like me, Rachel is talking a little faster and chirpier than usual.

"Smart move on your sister's part." I touch Bob's waxy leaves. "I've been meaning to get a plant," I say, and that's a lie. But the more I talk about plants, the less I'll think about tits. "Do you have to, um, water Bob a lot?"

"I do. Bob gets thirsty. I could use this mug to water him," she says, extra upbeat.

And hey, if she's not weird, I don't need to be weird. Besides, we've got plants to discuss. Slowly, I wheel around, successfully keeping my vision locked on hers in a straight line. "That's perfect because the mug, you know, holds water."

"One of the nice things about mugs," she says from across the room.

"Or you can use it to drink coffee, or wine, or really anything. Tea, soda," I say, then pause to think about more beverages so I don't think about breasts. "Juice maybe."

"I don't like juice. But wine could work," she says in the same spirit.

It's like the incident never happened. "Want to break it in?"

"With wine? I mean, sure. I got a delivery."

I shake my head. "No. I meant to water Bob?"

"Oh, sure. Or you can. To practice for your own Bob," she offers.

Right. Yeah. I'm getting a Bob, evidently.

She turns into the open-plan kitchen. Since I'm doing well at not staring below her neck, I follow her, stopping at the counter full of boxes while she fusses around with the faucet. She heaves a sigh, then another, finally lasering me with a no-bullshit look. "Carter. This is a mug that says I'm going to pretend I never saw your boobs, right?"

I blink.

"What? No. No way," I say, sputtering as images rush back to my brain—my lifelong friend, naked on camera, steam rising around her like she's a goddess. Pale skin that invites kisses. Curves that should be worshiped. Flesh, so much gorgeous flesh that I now know exists under her clothes.

Yes, I've always known she's a woman. But I've never thought of her as a *woman*. A sexy, sensual woman with water sliding down the valley of her breasts. A woman with lush curves and dips and places for my lips to travel.

I am a bad man with a very dirty mind.

But I'm relieved, too, that she's dealing with the elephant taking up all the space in the tiny kitchen. She's a better human than I am.

I exhale deeply, admitting…everything. "You're right. I've been making bullshit small talk."

Chin up, she gives me a tough-girl grin. "So then this is now officially the commemorative I-saw-your-breasts mug."

I laugh as she plays our mug-naming game. "Exactly. And who cares? We're friends. It's fine."

She shrugs like it's all no big deal. "It's totally fine. Let's water Bob."

I take the offered mug and head to the thirsty plant. When I'm done, I square my shoulders like I've accomplished something amazing. Well, in a way, I have. "I'm ready to be a plant daddy now."

"There comes a time in every man's life when he can take that next step. I'm proud of you, Carter."

You know what? So am I.

It's taken a mythical creature on a mug, a thirsty plant, and a whole lot of superhuman willpower, but I'm almost free from the new word of the day.

* * *

Rearranging her living room helps me even more. Using my body has always calmed my mind. Hell, I could move her couch all day long if I had to. Turn it ninety degrees. Turn it again. Move it here. Move it there. Doesn't matter. I like to stay active however I can.

As much as I possibly can.

But there's nothing left to move now that she's finally got the couch where she wants it, situated with a view of California Street and the city of San Francisco beyond.

She sinks onto the cranberry-colored cushion, patting the seat beside her. "I do love a good sit," she says.

Sitting is not my speed, but since she's urging me to join her, I flop down next to her.

Not too close though.

We both stare out the big bay window, drinking in the city that's always been my home. Even when my parents moved to Los Angeles for a bit—then moved back—this city with its hills and fog, its crooked streets, and impossible-to-keep-up-with restaurants has always called to me.

To Rachel, too, it seems, since she's returned here.

She sighs happily as we watch the city roll by.

"Perfect," she says, looking my way with gratitude and a legit smile that I haven't seen much of recently. When I smile back, she squeezes my shoulder. "It's completely different from my view the last several years. Which means, it's what I want."

"I'm glad you're here. I'm not glad about what happened, but it's good you came home," I say.

She nods resolutely. "Yeah, me too."

There's sadness in her voice, but something like possibility too. Maybe a shred of hope. Then she shakes her head, as if she's shaking off that dangerous emotion. She spins around, her smile real now. "And you're coming to my breakup party tomorrow. I need it. It's the real starting over."

"Of course," I say. "I wouldn't miss it."

"The Tata Incident won't change things, right?" she asks, a touch of worry in her tone.

I scoff. "Hell no."

"Good," she says, then moves closer to me and gives me a half hug.

I try. I swear, I try to be good. But my eyes. Those naughty fuckers. They steal a peek at the top of her shirt.

I tear my gaze away before I can undress her again mentally.

I am going to have to run six miles tonight to undo the incident.

But I can forget it. It's what I need, and it's clearly what she wants since later that night after a haircut and an eight-mile run—overachiever that I am—there's a delivery waiting for me at my home.

I'm not good with plant species, but I recognize this one for sure. It's a forget-my-tits ficus.

The note from Rachel confirms it—*Meet Jane*.

It's like the incident never happened. This is for the best, but it also makes me a little…lachrymose.

3

HAVE YOU CONSIDERED A GEORGIA O'KEEFFE FOR YOUR UNICORN DICK?

Carter

There's nothing like having free therapy living next door.

The next morning, I'm emptying the dishwasher and getting my neighbor Monroe up to speed on the Rachel situation.

He's parked on a stool at the kitchen counter, listening as he savors one of my best-ever cortados, courtesy of this brand-new Slayer single boiler I am obsessed with.

"And then she sent me a plant," I say, finishing the story.

"Let me rewind to my favorite bit. You actually got her a unicorn mug?"

I shoot him a *duh* stare as I stack plates in the open cupboard. "Was that not clear, doc?"

With a chuckle, he shakes his head. "I think what's quite clear is you were thinking with your dick."

"Have a little sympathy here. It's that thing where you care what happens to other people."

"Thanks. I'm in short supply lately."

"I've noticed," I say.

He waggles his cup at me. "But I will compliment you on this drink. It's like sex in coffee form."

"Right?" I say, proud of my newly acquired espresso skills. Taught myself. It's like a puzzle, making coffee that tastes as good as coming. "I'm a fucking rock star barista."

"We need to work on your confidence, Carter," he says, then takes a drink as my phone's alarm blinks with a notification—*Do NOT forget you're playing golf with your agent tomorrow morning, you time lord.*

I groan. I don't want to deal with that one. I do like golf, but I also know I need to talk to my agent about Date Night, one of my sponsors that I owe some appearances to. I've been putting off that convo as long as I can.

I silence the alarm, then turn back to Monroe. "So? What do I do?"

Monroe fixes me with a serious stare. "You want to know how to get past the *incident*," he says, sketching air quotes.

"Yes," I say emphatically. "Her party is tonight. I need to be there as her friend. Her longtime buddy. Not the pervy bastard whose mind is elsewhere. Ever since it happened, I'm like—" I gesture to my head, then make a scrambling gesture. "I don't need more things going haywire upstairs."

He nods, with real sympathy this time. "I understand," he says, then takes a very psychologist-like weighty pause. "But you may want to consider if you've got some subliminal things going on with you...and, well, her."

I scrunch my brow. "Speak English, Freud."

"When I said you were thinking with your dick, I meant it. You have dick on your mind." He takes a beat, then in his classic, droll style, he adds, "You got her a unicorn, man."

He makes a rolling gesture, waiting for me to connect the dots. When I do two seconds later, I drop my head on the counter and bang it a few times. "A unicorn has a dick on its head," I mutter.

When I raise my face, Monroe is slow-clapping. Asshole. "Good job, buddy," he says. "But let's not forget the symbolism of the pink bag either. You put the unicorn mug in the *pink* bag."

"Pink is innocent, Jung," I protest, but it dies on my tongue. He's so right. How did I miss it? "Is giving a woman a unicorn in a pink bag some new dating lingo for you want to bone her? I do not want to learn any new dating codes," I say, then sigh heavily.

He raises his empty cup in anti-dating solidarity. Dude's been burned too. As for me, I still have the tire tracks on my back from Quinn's peel-out-of-town-with-the-engagement-ring act a year ago. "I hear ya."

I shove thoughts of my ex and the ax she wielded to

my heart aside, flashing him a cocky grin. "Though, to be fair, I do have a unicorn dick."

Monroe stares blankly at me, like he's not even going to dignify that with a response. Fair enough. "Let's rewind to thirty seconds ago, please. The part about your brain going haywire."

That's the real issue. Even with the eight-mile run last night, even with the new plant—that reminds me, I need to water Jane, so I grab a water bottle and fill it—I'm still thinking about Rachel in new ways.

Wildly inappropriate ways.

I had a dirty dream about her last night, and I don't need a dating code or a shrink friend to decipher it. I put her on her hands and knees on a raft in a stormy sea. I don't think the dream means I want to visit a beach with her so much as show her the motion of the ocean. I woke up far too hot and bothered for a workday. "Seriously, how do I get these thoughts out of my head? Do I have OCD now too?"

From someone else, that might sound like a joke. But I mean it genuinely. It's a legit worry, given what I deal with every damn day.

Monroe knows where I'm coming from, and he must read the seriousness in my tone, because his shifts too. This is the voice he reserves for patients. "I'm not your therapist," he says, giving me his familiar caveat, "and I can't diagnose you, but I don't think you do. I do, however, think there are encounters in our lives that we can fixate on. That *anyone* can fixate on, regardless of brain chemistry. Like, when a parent walks in on a teenager masturbating."

I shudder. "It's taken me years to get over that day."

"That's my point."

I set the water bottle down on the counter, then I return to the dishwasher, grabbing the utensil basket. "All right. I'm going to go work out some more," I say as I snag the forks and set them in a drawer. "Round up a few of the guys for some extra practice. Find a new hobby. Take up kayaking. I bet my contract permits that. Maybe woodworking. I already aced espresso-making. So I need something new anyway."

"Relax, Carter. The best thing you can do in these situations is to acknowledge them. You did that already with Rachel. It defuses the awkwardness. If it's still weighing on you tonight at her party, just make a joke, have a laugh, then move on for her sake. She's probably way more embarrassed than you are. And then, focus on all the reasons you like being friends with her."

That's brilliant. I smack the counter like I'm nailing an answer on a quiz show. "She was my jigsaw puzzle club partner in high school," I point out excitedly. "We could start a jigsaw puzzle club again. That'll be friendship vibes for sure."

"Great. Maybe get her a puzzle before the party," he says, then checks his watch. "My first client will be here soon. I need to go dispense *paid* wisdom."

I point at the gleaming silver espresso machine. "Oh, I paid for that wisdom."

"True," he says with a smirk, then pushes back from the stool, standing. "But here's some free advice for you. Try a Georgia O'Keeffe puzzle."

I make a mental note as I put the spoons away. "New puzzle brand?"

"Yes, Carter. I keep up on puzzle brands," he says dryly. Then he leaves for his office in the townhome next to mine.

I swivel away from the open drawer. I'll finish putting these dishes away in twenty seconds. Just need to know more about this puzzle maker. Grabbing my phone from the counter, I google Georgia O'Keeffe.

Fucking Monroe.

She's that artist who painted flowers that look like vaginas.

The downside of a neighbor who's a therapist is there's someone right next door to mock you.

I click over to my texts and fire one off.

> Carter: Look for a delivery later. A book of Georgia O'Keeffe paintings. Think of it as a map. I know dinosaurs roamed the earth the last time you were up close and personal with a real one.

> Monroe: Pot. Kettle.

Dammit. He's too right.

But I still like the puzzle idea. I hop over to my to-do list and add *Look for non-unicorn, non-Georgia O'Keeffe, non-pink puzzle.*

Then, a new calendar item pops up. An invitation from Rachel. I open it. *Water Jane, you badass plant daddy.*

Damn, see inside my soul, woman.

I hit accept, grab the water bottle I'd forgotten about, and feed Jane. When I'm done, I head to the bathroom. As I brush my teeth, I pick up my day-of-the-week pill container to confirm what I suspect. Yup. I took it this morning right on time. I can't take Adderall since it's a banned substance in pro football, but I've been taking non-stimulant meds for years.

They help.

Mostly.

I'm sure Quinn would say they don't, but whatever. She might not have liked that I was late now and then to pick her up for dates, but I'm not the one who ran off to join the circus after saying yes to a marriage proposal. A few weeks after posting her *look at my ring* pics, she skipped out of here with her diamond, leaving only a goodbye text that said *Got a gig with Cirque du Soleil! Maybe we can date another time.*

So, maybe the demise *wasn't* about my occasional tardiness.

Still, I know what I was like without these, and I didn't enjoy myself then. The meds don't solve everything, but they make it easier for me to be present at most everyday moments.

Like this party tonight, when I will be all friendship all the time with Rachel. And, as Monroe suggested, I'll try to find a moment to joke about yesterday.

After brushing my teeth, I take off to pick up our kicker on the way to practice. Thank fuck for the game.

Football is one of the few times everything goes quiet and comes into focus. My brain settles down on the field and knows its place—working in synchronicity with my body. Another thing happens, too, when I play ball. Time makes perfect sense. The clock is my friend, not my enemy. When I play football, I can feel the passing of every single second and experience every glorious moment.

The sport is a little like magic.

And, after the last twenty-four hours, I'm craving the tricks football plays on my mind.

4

AND THE DRESS CODE TONIGHT IS...

Rachel

I should call it off.

I'm not a throw-myself-a-party person. It's a little self-indulgent.

I'm pacing behind the counter of my jewelry shop on Friday evening, seriously weighing my decision to let Juliet talk me into this *fête*. It's just me here, handling the shop solo since I sent Fable home early to work on her own jewelry designs.

Alone with my thoughts, I'm second-guessing tonight big time. Is an extravagant party really the best way to start over? Maybe I should stay home and find a new recipe to tinker with. I discovered a great new baking blog earlier this week. I bet there are all sorts of fun treats I can make. Maybe give out to my neighbors as I get to know them.

I grab my phone from my back pocket and tap out a

quick text to my friend Hazel, who's in town for my official divorce party. The one I might be canceling. We can all just grab drinks at my place instead. Maybe my friends can help me bake too.

> Rachel: On a scale of one to ten, how much would Juliet kill me for canceling the party she insisted on throwing me?

> Hazel: One hundred. Also, why, why, why?

> Rachel: I should just focus on my shop. I'm here to grow Bling and Baubles, not call attention to my pathetic-ass self.

Lord knows, I inadvertently called enough attention to myself yesterday with my impulsive phone answering. The only reason I'm not suffering from next-day mortification is that Carter was a total darling about the eyeful. He handled my embarrassment so well.

Ten out of ten, I recommend accidentally flashing two of a kind to a man who's a perfect gentleman.

But a party where I'm the newly single and kicked-to-the-curb-by-her-ex-husband guest of honor?

That's a real look-at-me event. I never threw parties while I was married. I never let loose. I never wore flashy clothes. It's all so...*not me*.

While Hazel's typing—the dots tell me so—I add another text.

Rachel: I probably have more wound-licking to do anyway. I should do it with the lemon cheesecake blueberry bars, some Amelia Stone breakup tunes, and a binge of the new season of F Boys And Girls. I can even bake some butterscotch brownies. Get a good night of sleep for the first time in a while. I haven't been sleeping great in my new place. Then I'll take a HIIT class in the morning.

Hazel: First, friends don't let friends binge-watch bad reality TV alone, so if you choose to do that, I'm coming over with my jammies to join you.

Rachel: Do they have pockets?

Hazel: Obviously. I refuse to acknowledge the existence of jammies without pockets. But here's my second point—there are literally studies showing that surrounding yourself with friends is the best medicine after a breakup. Better than butterscotch brownies.

Rachel: Someone studies that?

Hazel: Someone studies everything. And I've researched everything ever studied—I've googled it for a book at some point.

Hmm. She probably has. She's written a lot of romance novels, and all her characters have serious shit to deal with. But I feel guilty celebrating my failure in love. Is getting divorced really something to throw a party for?

Oh hey, my ex kept a secret second family for years! Have a glass of champagne!

> Rachel: Maybe I should stay in the shop and do…inventory. Research some new looks. Work on a marketing campaign.

> Hazel: That's Edward's voice talking. Shut. Him. Down.

I peer around at my empty shop, needing to do *something* to prop up my baby. It's been a rough few weeks here. Heck, it's been a rough few months, ever since I decided to return to my hometown and open the shop here in San Francisco. Until a few weeks ago I'd been flying back and forth from Venice, trying to manage both stores. Now I'm living here, and the Venice one is still swimming along, with my manager there running it.

But this store hasn't found its footing yet. I know it takes time, but the only amazing days have been when the spa owner up the street has sent bachelorette parties and groups of pampered and massaged friends here. I haven't even met her. Maybe I should make her some brownies. Yes, that's what I should do tonight.

I reply again to Hazel.

> Rachel: I haven't had a customer in twenty minutes. Hence I'm at my store, texting my friend, and contemplating baking brownies for the spa owner up the street to bribe her so she keeps sending me business.

As she's replying, a text from my mom pops up too, but the bell above the door tinkles.

Hurrah!

With the enthusiasm of a marching band, I put down my phone and focus on the customer—a handsome man with some gray in his beard. He wears a tailored suit and sports an expensive watch and a platinum wedding band. I can read him from a mile away—he's here to buy something for his wife.

Hey, big spender. Come to mama and open your wallet.

"Welcome to Bling and Baubles. Let me know if I can help you with anything," I say. I'm closing in five minutes, but I don't mention that. I've never understood why some shopkeepers make customers feel unwelcome even if they come five minutes before closing time. Last time I checked, five minutes before closing time was still, you know, *open*. Why make someone feel bad, especially if they might buy something from you?

He walks to the counter with the commanding stride of a man who gets what he wants. Like Edward does. "I'd love some help," he says. "I need a little something for my wife. I missed her birthday last week."

Like Edward did when he was visiting his other family.

"Oh. That's too bad," I say, trying to strip the *how the hell did you miss her birthday* from my tone.

"It happens. I was out of town," he says with an *I can't be bothered* shrug.

That was what my ex told me too.

Dick.

"That happens," I say breezily to cover up my irritation.

"I had business meetings that ran unexpectedly long."

Sounds so familiar. *Does she believe you? Has she believed you for years, like I did?* I want to shout. But I don't, asking instead, "What would you like to get her, then?"

He waves a hand airily, a man who can dismiss his indiscretions with money. "Something that says I was missing her. And I'm so sorry."

How about half your worth in the divorce you'll be getting?

"I'm sure you're very sorry. Perhaps a lovely necklace with a dollar sign on it?" I ask brightly. Or was that sarcastically?

He blinks. "Excuse me?"

Shoot. "I apologize," I say, meaning it. I can't take my hurt out on a customer. "Let me show you some necklaces," I say, then I steer him to a display shelf. "Here's a pretty pendant with a flower on it."

"She likes lotus flowers."

I touch my naked neck absently, remembering when Edward gave me a similar one more than a year ago—with a rose on it. *Your favorite flower*, he'd said. But those aren't my favorite flowers. I love wildflowers. His other woman must have liked roses.

I grit my teeth and try to fight off the memories. "These do wonders for smoothing away the *little things* that happen when husbands travel. You know?"

The customer jerks his gaze to me, sneering. "Like meetings? I had meetings."

"Yes, meetings, of course," I say, trying to correct my mistake, but did that come out as bitter as the memories?

"They were meetings with my marketing partner," he adds, then stares at me like I'm a piece of gum on the bottom of his shoe. "I think I'll shop elsewhere."

The horror of what I've said smacks me in the face, but it takes me a few seconds to recover. "I'm so sorry. The necklace is on me. Consider it a gift," I call out, trying to fix my mistake.

But with a huff, he turns on his heel and leaves, without the necklace.

With him gone, I lock the door, then slump against it, groaning in misery. I can't believe what I just did. I sabotaged my own business over a stupid memory.

Pull yourself together, girl.

I head to the counter and grab my phone. I was wrong. I absolutely, positively need this party.

I text Hazel to tell her I'll be there. I reply to my mom's *have fun at the party* text by promising ***I will have***

so much fun, then I text Carter and ask if he can give me a ride home from the fête. He only lives five minutes from my place. He replies right away.

> Carter: A ride home? Do you mean a ride there?

> Rachel: Nope. A ride home. I will need a ride home since I'll need an extra-large glass of champagne to erase what I just said to a customer.

> Carter: Then I am definitely picking you up, too, since I need to hear this.

He's such a sweetheart. He's not even thinking about yesterday. He's moved on. Let that be a lesson. I can move on from my shitty marriage.

Divorce party, here I come.

I send him a calendar invite to pick me up. There. It's official now.

* * *

Burgundy lace bustier or the light blue one with embroidered red flowers? I'm in my bedroom an hour later, weighing the underthing choices post-shower.

The answer? Whatever will make me forget what I just said to a customer.

Did I really say all that *marriage sucks and so do you* stuff? Yes, yes, I did.

Fuck burgundy. Fuck light blue. I need black lace to match my black heart. I ditch the bustiers, grabbing a new black bra-and-panty set.

They won't be seen by anyone but me, but that's fine. Clearly, I shouldn't be near people this week. This month. This lifetime.

I march—no, stomp—over to my phone and crank up the volume on Amelia Stone's new tune blasting in my earbuds. It's a breakup anthem, and that's what this gal needs.

I blast it loud enough to drown out the last hour of my life as I slide into the panties, then snap on the bra. When I yank open my closet door, I see red.

So much glittery red hanging in front of my other clothes like a diva taking center stage, outshining the chorus girls behind her.

But...how did that get here?

Did I drape that red dress over my other clothes and then forget about it? Do I even own that postage-stamp-size number? I step closer and spot a card with my name on it dangling from the hanger.

I grab it, take it out, and open it.

There is one rule for what to wear at your divorce party—something smoking hot. I took care of an outfit for you, you beautiful single goddess, you.

. . .

Juliet must have used her code to come inside and leave this for tonight. Sister's rights and all, to burst in and leave gifts.

And it's not just any dress.

It's a ruby red, sparkly, sequined body-con dress that leaves nothing to the imagination.

This looks like what a teenager would wear to a fuck-me-at-homecoming dance. But I don't have a teenage-girl body. I flick the card against my palm as I consider the outfit. Then I spot my sister's P.S. on the other side of the card—*Body-con dresses aren't just for the teens. Women in their thirties with women's bodies can wear them and slay them.*

She can read my mind. She's always been able to. I run my fingers along the sequined look-at-me dress. "I am not worthy," I confess to the dress. "I was a supreme asshole today."

I go on, telling the dress everything, every terrible detail, until they're all out of me.

And you know what? After what I've been through, the fact I didn't try to garrote him with a necklace is absolutely miraculous.

I *am* worthy of this dress.

First, though, I've got to ditch the bra. I free the girls, then slingshot the black lace across the bedroom. It lands on a lamp, and that feels like a statement—the statement is *I can wear whatever I want. Commando up top? Hell, yeah.*

I tug on the dress, pulling up the spaghetti straps. The neckline plunges deeply.

And...hello! Is there a breeze down there?

I peer at the hem. Hmm. Do we call this mid-thigh length or butt-cheek length?

I shrug. Whatever.

I head to the mirror and...whoa. Is that me in this tiny thing? I'd never have worn this with Edward. He likes his ladies classy. He likes his women subtle. I am not subtle tonight. I am a billboard for Fun with a capital F.

I take out the earbuds and set them down on the bureau.

"Fuck him," I say to my reflection, then I do my makeup, slip on some heels, and grab a purse and the lemon cheesecake blueberry bars.

Carter calls me at eight-thirty-five, five minutes after he said he'd arrive, but exactly when I figured I'd see him—Carter time. "On my way," I say, then head down the steps of my townhome and swing open the front door. I'm so damn ready for this party.

Carter's standing on the stoop, wearing dark jeans and an untucked slate-blue button-down that is form-fitting in all the right ways. It hugs his big biceps and snuggles against his strong chest. Bonus—with the cuffs rolled up, it shows off his forearms. In short, the shirt makes my handsome friend look even more handsome.

He's just a good-looking guy, empirically and all.

"Hey, you," I say.

"Hey," he says, but it comes out strangled, like all the air has left his lungs.

"You okay?"

He clears his throat, blinks, then he manages a nod that looks a little uncomfortable. "You look...wow."

"Aww. That's sweet." I lean in and kiss his cheek, taking that wow. Needing that wow.

When I let go, his eyes linger on me a little longer than usual. Well, he's not used to seeing me in sparkles, so it makes sense that he'd want to make sure it's really me under all this bling.

"It's sparkly, isn't it?" I say with a jut of my hip.

"Yes, just a little," he grunts, then reaches for the plate of bars. He takes them as I hook my arm through his on the other side.

"Let me tell you what I said to a customer tonight."

As we walk to his car, I tell him what I said so I can put my bad behavior behind me.

"I'm sure he didn't think twice about it," Carter says, exonerating me as he holds open the passenger door.

"Like us, with yesterday," I say with a smile, sliding in.

"Yes. Exactly. We can even laugh about it," he says once he's in the car. "And we can laugh about it while we reinstate our puzzle club. Because I had an idea."

"Oh! Tell me, tell me."

But as he drives away, my phone buzzes with a notification that I have a new online review. I stop smiling.

I brace myself as I click it open.

The woman who owns this store is a big-mouthed, stupid bitch who should mind her own business.

5

HELLO, CHEESE GRATER
RACHEL

Repeat after me—*don't ruin your mascara.*

I say that over and over in my head as Carter drives to the party in the Marina, where all my friends will be gathered.

Suck back those sobs.

I fight off the lump in my throat that's threatening to unleash a fire hydrant of tears. I won't walk into the party looking like a crying banshee at Halloween.

"And I googled some new puzzle brands earlier today," Carter says, chatting amiably as we pass the Palace of Fine Arts. This is helping, too, his warm, rumbly voice talking about all the regular things we like. "There's this new puzzle maker called Florence and Arlo—how hip is that name, right?"

"So hip," I say, trying to contribute something to the conversation while I let his voice soothe my shame.

"I bet she wears a beanie and he's got a beard. But let me tell you, their puzzles do not suck," he says as he slows at the red light near Chestnut Street. "No five hundred red jelly beans or one-thousand-piece boring gray castles. I can order one online, or even better, I found a shop in Noe Valley called Puzzle Nerds. They have this puzzle with caricatures of raccoons digging through trash cans. The name of it is *One Mammal's Trash is Another's...*" As he turns to me, the word *treasure* dies. "What is it, Sunshine?"

I shake my head, embarrassed by this stupid, utterly stupid, reaction to a bad review. It was all my fault anyway. "Nothing," I mumble.

"You look like a kid holding her breath," he says.

The lump grows so big it's like a thrashing monster in my throat. I slam my hand to my mouth as my shoulders shake. "I'm fine," I say, gulping in air.

"You're not," he says. The light changes, and with a lightning-fast assessment, he makes a right turn instead of going straight, then maneuvers the car along the curb and into a just-vacated spot. That's no easy feat in a city where parking is harder than completing a thousand-piece puzzle.

He turns off the car and sets a hand on my shoulder. "What is it?"

"My mascara," I blurt out, wobbly. But it's too late. The lump wins. My eyes are faucets.

"Your mascara's fine," he says, then wraps his arm around me, pulling me against his shoulder.

"It's not fine," I choke out.

"Are you still upset about that jackass who clearly cheats on his wife?"

"That jackass left me a one-star review," I say in a strangled breath as I push my face against his shoulder.

I don't want him to see me. I don't want anyone to see me. I'm so ridiculous.

His hand slides over my hair in a comforting move. "That sucks," he says, and I'm so grateful he didn't try to Band-Aid over the awfulness and tell me it's nothing. It's not nothing—it's something. And it's my mistake.

"It's all my fault," I say as tears rain down.

"Still sucks," he says, stroking my hair softly.

"I deserve it," I add, pressing my face hard against him.

"You *don't* deserve it. You had a bad day."

"This review will ruin me. I'm already struggling with my business. My shop here isn't taking off like the one in Venice because I'm the idiot who thought it would be smart to flee town and just open a new shop in a new town and trust that everyone would come."

"Hey," he says, firm this time. "Would you talk to your friends that way?"

"What way?" I mutter into the dark cave of his comforting shoulder. I don't ever want to leave. I will burrow here and hibernate.

"Would you let them call themselves idiots?"

"Well, I was one," I say.

"It happens, Rachel. You had a moment. You said something you regret. You just have to pick yourself up and keep going. It's like when I miss a big catch. Which, ahem, I did in last week's game against the Pioneers," he says, regret seeping into his tone.

"And I was so mad when the other team's fans cheered you for missing it. I stomped my feet and flipped them off on the TV screen," I say.

He chuckles, and his easy approach makes me lift my face a tiny bit, but not enough for him to see my mascara streaks.

"That guy who came into my store? He called me a stupid bitch in his review," I confess, and it's embarrassing to admit that out loud even though it's in black and white and living forever online.

Carter seethes like a bull in a ring. "And he's a cheating asshole. Want me to track him down and tell him he fucked with the wrong jewelry store owner?"

The image of Carter marching up to that slick man's fancy home amuses me so much that the tears slow, then stop.

"No thanks. But I feel better now."

I finally raise my face and, judging by Carter's quickly hidden horror, I might feel better, but I can't say the same about how I look.

* * *

Thank god for Sephora's world-domination strategy. Five minutes later, Carter's miraculously found another parking spot on this street and pulled up at the nearest makeup shop. "Tell me what kind you need, and I'll get it. I love errands," he says, rubbing his palms like he's excited to track down a new tube of eye makeup.

"It's from Mia Jane. It's called Evening Shade. I need it in black. But not Jet Black. Be sure to get Studio Black. Not the volumizing one and not the waterproof one, but the curling, conditioning one," I say.

He repeats, "Evening Shade. Studio Black," but his

warm brown eyes glaze over a bit, and it's pretty clear what I need to do. I can't let him save me every second of today.

"I'll brave it," I say, then dab at my cheeks again with a tissue I found in my clutch.

"I'll go with you," he says.

I take one more soldiering breath, then I step out of his car and join him on the sidewalk. I try not to freak out. Truly, I do. I hold my head high, and we stride into the shop, where a woman with electric-blue hair gawks at my clown face, then quickly course corrects. "Oh, honey, let's take you to the makeup triage center."

"Thank you," I say.

Ten minutes later, I look presentable again with my makeup redone thanks to the electric-blue makeup angel.

Trouble is, there's a new problem. I didn't spot it before, but under the bright lights of the shop, I point at Carter's slate-blue shirt, covered in my Jackson Pollack tears now. "I ruined your shirt," I say, and maybe I do need waterproof mascara after all.

He glances down at the ink splotch the size of a sandwich on his shoulder. "Yes, you did, Dumont," he says, but he's sort of amused, maybe even proud.

My turn to save the day. "Gap to the rescue," I say. There was one on this stretch of Chestnut when I grew up here, but when I scurry outside, there's no Gap nearby. There's no Target or men's shop I can see either. I speak into my phone, asking where the nearest Gap is since those things are like Starbucks. But I shake my phone when I read the answer: "Google said the nearest Gap closed down."

"I'm still in mourning. But I can just wear this," Carter says, plucking at his horribly stained shirt. "I literally walk around with mud on my shirt on Sundays."

"But it's a Friday," I say, energized by my new mission—to help him. He's done nothing but help me since I made the official move to town, from lifting the couch, to giving me a ride, to letting me slobber all over his shoulder.

And dammit, I need a victory. If there's one thing this broken down, hot mess of a divorcee can do, it's shop.

I speak into the phone again, asking where the nearest men's shop is when my attention snags on a thrift store at the end of the block. Daisy's Duds. "Oh, I know that place. There's another one in Haight-Ashbury. My yoga teacher Katie went to it one night and told us about it. They have a lot of costumes but clothes too."

"We're going to be late though," he says, chagrined. "I'm late for too many things in life."

I smile sympathetically. "You've got that under control, though, with all your alarms. You were bang on time yesterday at my house, after all."

See? I can make light of the boob flashing. We have so returned to the normal zone, no problem.

His brown eyes darken, then he jerks his gaze away from me for a second. "True. I was."

"And besides, this tardiness is on me. Okay?"

After a beat, he acquiesces. "Let's do it," he says.

"Yay!" I text my sister that I'm running a few minutes late, then we fly inside the shop teeming on one side with sequined dresses and feather boas alongside cop, doctor, and fireman uniforms. The other side of the shop is stuffed with everyday clothes, including rack after rack of short-sleeve button-down shirts. "Look! It's like the holy grail of thrifting. Utility worker shirts," I say, grabbing his arm and tugging him to the X marks the spot, where most of the shirts were clearly donated from men who work in blue-collar jobs—their names are sewn into patches on chest pockets.

Carter gawks at the selection of shirts. "I don't know how to choose between Jim the Plumber and Chet the Electrician."

From the counter, a voice calls out: "Let me know if I can help you, darlings. I'm Angel."

I turn to a muscular man with stunning emerald eyeshadow and a fabulous feather boa. "I'm good for now," I chirp as I flick through the racks quickly, hunting for just the right shirt. "The Texaco one is cute, but it's a medium, so that won't fit."

"How do you know what size I wear?" Carter asks.

I toss him a *what do you take me for* look. "You play football for a living. You're a brick wall. You're not just a large. You're an extra large," I say, quickly surveying the strapping guy in front of me. "How tall are you? Are you six-six?"

"Only where it counts," he says with a wink.

And I'm a little flustered. Is he saying what I think he's saying?

Of course he is, you dingus. He's a man.

Show me a man who doesn't crow about the size of his dong and I'll show you a leprechaun.

I snap my gaze back to the racks, hunting feverishly for an extra-large dick—I mean, an extra-large shirt.

I need a shirt. That is all.

Ah! Bingo. I spot a gray auto-repair shop shirt with a patch that reads *Magnus*. "Well, Mister Six Six, this one seems perfect for you," I say, then thrust it at him.

"I'm actually six three," he says, lifting his hand to the top of his head to indicate his real height, then he peers at the name on the shirt. "The name does fit."

Does Carter moonlight as a dildo model?

Stop, you dirty perv.

"It's only a large though," I say, trying to stick to the task at hand. Sizes of shirts, not rods. I call out to Angel, "Any chance Magnus left a shirt in a large and an extra large?"

He chuckles, a big, booming, baritone laugh. "Magnus is one of a kind, but I might have something else for you. Be right back, darlings."

"Try this on anyway," I say to Carter, staying in full bossy shopping mode. "Let's hope it fits like an extra large."

Carter smirks at me, then takes his time before he says, "That's what she said."

Am I sweating now? I hope not. Boob sweat is not a good look in a body-con dress. "Go, go, go," I say, searching for a dressing room. Shoving him into one and out of sight might similarly hide his naughty comments from my suddenly filthy mind.

I spot a booth a few feet away and push him toward it. "Try it on now."

Carter ducks in and starts unbuttoning his blue shirt. I know this because...that curtain barely covers the stall. It may be the smallest curtain ever. It doesn't hide anything.

Like...

The breadth of Carter's pecs.

The smattering of chest hair over them.

Or that hair trailing down, down, down and...

His abs.

He has abs for days.

For months.

They go on forever, and that brown hair is the happiest trail I've ever seen.

My throat is dry.

My chest is hot.

My skin is tingling.

"How about this one?"

I jump at the sound of the deep voice. Maybe I shriek, too, as I tear my Peeping Tammy gaze from the dressing room curtain to Angel, who's standing next to me.

"Sorry to scare you, darling."

"I'm fine," I squeak out right as Carter steps out of the dressing room...and, dear god, I'm not so fine anymore.

I'm having heart palpitations as I stare shamelessly at his chest. I can't look away from all that muscle, all that golden skin, all that masculine hardness. Everywhere.

Angel whistles approvingly. "Well, hello there. Let me just go get some cheese for that grater you've got, thank you very much."

Carter laughs. "I work out a little."

"Understatement," Angel says, then hands Carter the shirt. "This is your fine-ass size, darling."

My friend turns back into the dressing room. I still can't move. I can't speak. I am officially stuck here.

There's a tap on my shoulder then a *psst* in my ear. "*Your jaw is open, darling,*" Angel mouths.

As red seeps into my cheeks, I shut my hungry mouth, stat, then try to bleach my mind clean.

I think of things like traffic lights. And deviled eggs. And week-old moldy bread.

There. That'll do. I'm all good.

But when Carter steps out of the dressing room with the new shirt buttoned up, I can't stop looking at the name tag.

I'm pretty sure it can see inside my soul right now.

Randy.

6

A SHIRTLESS-NESS HANGOVER

Rachel

I've always known Carter had a strong body. He's played football since forever. I went to his games in high school.

But when we sneaked off with our friends to midnight bonfires on Stinson Beach senior year, and he went for late-night dips with the other guys, he was leaner, lankier. His abs weren't quite so defined. When I crashed in his dorm one night during college and woke up to him wandering in from the showers, towel slung low on his hips, I wasn't awake enough to take mental pics.

Now I know what was missing from my memories, and I hate every shirt for coming between that view and me.

I'm still in a man chest daze twenty minutes later when we arrive at the boutique hotel on the Marina.

The valet's eyes widen when I step out, then they linger on my very visible cleavage, but in a flash, Carter is by my side.

"Thanks, man," he says to the guy, slapping the key fob into his palm then ushering me away.

It all happens so quickly, I'm honestly not sure if the guy *was* staring too long, but I do like Carter's surprisingly possessive side as we walk into the hotel.

Quickly, we head to the garden level and find the private suite.

With her blonde hair curled like a pinup, my friend Elodie stands outside the door of the suite, tapping the toe of her comic-book-styled three-inch pumps.

"You're fashionably late, Rach. And your sister is dying to make a toast," she chides as she takes the cheesecake bars from me. "Were you playing with the Girl's Best Friend toy I sent you? You do look a little sweaty."

Is it that obvious? Also, she needs to stop talking about vibrators. While staring at Elodie, I glance sideways at Carter, jerking my head, telling her without words not to discuss sex toys in front of him and his cheese-grater abs I want to lick.

Elodie rolls her eyes. "I'm sure Carter is aware of the existence of the Girl's Best Friend. It's only the most popular vibe on the market. Remember when vibrators used to have names like the Man-inator, and Deep Thruster?" She adopts an overly masculine tone as she says the names. "Or better yet," she says, her eyes on his name tag, "The Randy."

"I hope there's not a vibrator named the Randy. Or

the Dicky for that matter. Or Peter," he adds, rolling with the sex-toy talk so much more smoothly than I am.

"I hope not either," I say, even though it doesn't matter what the vibrator is called. I'm breaking out Elodie's gift and using the Girl's Best Friend tonight. Several times.

Well, since I can't use one now and all.

"Anyway, I need to steal the woman of the hour away. Okay with you, Randy?" Elodie asks Carter as she offers me her arm.

"I'll allow it," he says playfully.

Yup. He has no clue I'm suffering from a sudden onslaught of weirdly misplaced lust.

Thank god.

Besides, it's just temporary, surely. Like a shirtlessness hangover.

Elodie guides me to the front of the packed room where my sister presides over twenty or thirty people here at the event. Juliet is a breakup party planner extraordinaire and she's surveying the glittery scene while standing next to a grand piano all while looking effortlessly fabulous in a black dress that hugs her curves.

The spacious suite she's booked is both classy and sexy at the same time, with dark wood walls, green banker's lamps, and card dealers in old-timey costumes manning green felt tables filled with chips and cards for poker and blackjack. On a few high tables are stacks of Elodie's chocolates from her shop, and my mouth waters at the sight of the robin's egg blue boxes holding truffles, caramels, and dark chocolate decadence. Sugar, come to me, sugar.

"You can have some later," Elodie says, reading my mind.

"How ever did you know?" I tease.

"I've learned to recognize the signs of a chocolate trance. God, I love it when people go into chocolate trances," she says as we reach my sister.

A banner hangs on the wall behind Juliet with the words *Celebrate chances* written on it in a silvery font. "You're here," she says, then hugs me before she quickly slides back into party-boss mode. "Take this," she says, handing me a glass of champagne from one of the coasters on the gleaming black piano where a woman in a dapper suit tickles the ivories, playing pop music.

My sister grabs her own glass of champagne, lifting it high, then clinks a fork against it. The crowd quiets. The pianist plays more quietly, a background tune, giving the attention to Juliet.

I try to catch my breath as I scan the room.

Hazel's here with her arm draped around her boyfriend, Axel, who is Carter's half-brother. Elodie has slinked into the crowd, hanging out with some of my friends from Venice Beach, like my TV writer pal Ellie who flew up to celebrate tonight with her fiancé, Gabe, a retired football star. My friend Brooke is here too, along with her quarterback husband, Drew. My brother Sawyer's not here but he's been working in New York a lot recently, and I'll get to see him soon when I visit our parents in Petaluma.

It's overwhelmingly wonderful to see all these

friendly faces. But it's weird too. They're here because I failed at marriage. Thank god there are other uncoupled people here as well, like Elodie and Juliet and Carter and others. I paste on a smile I try desperately to feel.

"Thank you all for coming," Juliet begins. "I just want to say it wasn't easy to convince my fabulous sister to let me throw a party for her. Rachel resisted more than a few times. But I'm used to winning her over.

"When we were kids, I always had to convince her to take me to the beach, to bring me to the mall, to sneak out for ice cream. And I won her over this time, too, but it's not just because I grew up doing it." Juliet turns to me, her expression heartfelt, her green eyes full of affection. "I threw this party because I love you, Rachel. And I'm pretty sure all of us do. We want you to know we're here for you as you embark on this next phase. Let it be the best part of your life. Let's celebrate the awesomeness of divorce!" She lifts her glass, and everyone erupts into cheers as she shouts a hearty, "Congratulations!"

In one bold word—congratulations—all my misgivings slink away.

I am glad I got out of my marriage. I'm glad I found out the truth before more time went by. I'm glad I'm living a real, true, authentic life now.

Not a lie.

I lift my glass. "To family. And to friendship," I say, and for a few seconds, my eyes lock with Carter's across the room, and it's as if everyone else melts into the background.

He holds my gaze with a fierceness that means the world to me. A tenderness too. And it's kind of hard to look away from him since tingles are rushing down my skin.

I jerk my gaze back to Juliet. "Thank you so much. You put the pushy into pushy little sister, and I love you for it."

"Love you," she says, then kisses me on the cheek, and it's sweet and stirs up all my emotions all over again.

The piano player kicks into a poppy Stone Zenith tune as the guests head to the casino tables. Juliet pulls me into a corner of the room, calling over Hazel and Elodie too. When it's just us chickadees, Juliet gives an impish grin and says, "And we have another surprise for you."

"What is it?" I ask, equally excited and worried. My besties give good gifts—like vibrators and sassy T-shirts and hot, hot, hot dresses—but they also push me out of my comfort zone.

With a nod to Hazel, Juliet says to me, "*Someone* might have told me you were dreaming of pajamas earlier."

Hazel shrugs coquettishly. "Me? That was me? Okay, fine. It was so me."

"Is this going where I think it's going?" I ask, a frisson of hope whisking through me.

Juliet nods quickly. "We rallied. We heard your cries for help. And when this party ends at midnight, a limo is picking us up and taking us back to Elodie's place where we're having…a pajama party! Girls only."

I gasp. "I haven't had a pajama party in ages."

"I know. Your ex was a dick for many reasons, but

partly because he hated fun. You're back home now, and life is going to be extra joyous," Juliet declares like she's going to make it so.

I glance at the sequins hugging my body. "But all I have is this dress. And Carter was going to take me home," I say, and I'm a little bummed I won't get to spend more time with him, but maybe it's for the best I'm not in close quarters with his...well, his whole entire freaking body.

"I'll tell him," Juliet says breezily. "Also, Hazel picked up jammies for you and they're at Elodie's home."

"Do they have pockets?" I ask eagerly.

Hazel rolls her eyes. "Do I look like a monster? Obviously, they have pockets. And we have wine there too."

"We'll save the cheesecake bars for the after-party," Elodie says.

"What about Amanda?" I ask, since Elodie is raising her little sister all by herself.

"She's having a sleepover at a friend's. The place is ours," Elodie says.

Wow. I get to have a divorce party here, then a pajama party there.

Maybe it'll be enough to erase the sexy thoughts of Carter that are rapidly occupying my brain.

Maybe.

* * *

It's kind of hard though. I've been to parties with Carter before. Picnics, barbecues, friendsgivings, and countless brunches.

But I've never, ever been so aware of where he was in a room until tonight. I've never been so aware of where another person was, *period*. Even as I say hi to all the guests, I can't help but steal glances at Carter.

While he's chatting with his brother.

While he's talking to Drew.

While he's grabbing a drink with Gabe at the bar.

And now, while I'm standing near the piano, drinking champagne and catching up with Ellie on her life in Los Angeles writing a popular TV series, Carter is talking to Gabe—and they're four feet away from us.

"Gigi and I miss you so much," Ellie says to me with a playful pout.

"I miss you too." Leaving the new friends I made in Venice over the last few years was the hardest part of taking off. "How is the little darling?"

"My mother is obsessed with her *granddog*. Yes, she's actually started calling her that," Ellie says.

"Well, obviously."

"Which also means I have the world's best dog sitter right in the family. And I'm trying not to miss Gigi too much while we're gone."

Gabe leans into the conversation, clearing his throat. "Sweetheart, you called the dog sitter four times today."

I crack up. "I'm not surprised."

Ellie snaps her gaze to Gabe. "You're one to talk. You made Mom put Gigi on FaceTime."

"Busted," Carter says, with the glee of catching a friend in the act. "You're like a helicopter dog dad."

Gabe snarls at Carter then grumbles something about playing poker with Drew.

When Gabe leaves, Ellie waves Carter closer, and he joins our circle, making me even more aware of him and…wait…What is that yummy smell? Is that his bodywash? And has the ocean always been so smoking hot?

No time to linger, though, since Ellie's steering the convo, and she looks like she's ready to issue a declaration as she sets a hand on my arm. "I'm glad you're remaking yourself here with friends and family, Rachel. San Francisco looks good on you." She turns to Carter, her boss mode activated. "And you're looking out for my girl?"

Carter's all resolute as he nods. "Absolutely."

"Good. You'd better be my eyes and ears. I want you bringing her soup if she gets sick. I want you to binge-watch TV shows with her at least once a week," she says, and I roll my eyes. I simultaneously love Ellie looking out for me and want to tell her to stop. I'm not *that* broken. Except, soup and TV does sound nice, even when I'm not sick. Maybe especially when I'm not sick. "And I definitely want you to do that nerdy thing you two always did," Ellie adds.

"Puzzles," I say in unison with Carter, then I continue, "Don't worry. We're on that."

Ellie smiles at us like we're adorable. "Seriously. You two are like brother and sister," she says with a smile.

I cough-laugh while Carter snorts.

Did he catch me staring at him salaciously earlier?

Does he know I had very un-brotherly thoughts about him?

Oh, shit.

Oh, hell.

He was so gracious about the incident. I should be the same.

After Ellie rejoins Gabe, it's just Carter and me again, hanging out by the piano. I sip champagne. He takes a pull of his beer. For a few seconds, we're just quiet, listening together as the woman at the keys taps out a tune that sounds vaguely romantic. I look into Carter's warm brown eyes, and I feel a little fizzy.

Not at all how I feel when I look at my brother.

But Carter *is* my friend, so I swallow past the awkwardness, and say, "Thanks again for offering to take me home later. But it turns out I'm being girl-napped for a pajama party at Elodie's."

"Juliet mentioned that earlier. She marched over to me pretty much right after the toast."

That's so Juliet. "She likes to be in charge. Of everything."

"She picked the right profession then," he says, giving me a secret little smile. "Now, this pajama party —will there be a pillow fight?"

I laugh, shaking my head. "No pillow fights."

"Too bad," he says, then adds a little apologetically, "And no problem. I have an early bedtime anyway."

He's disciplined with his sleep. More than most athletes, and I get it. "Yes, you do," I say, wagging a finger. "You need to leave by eleven. In bed by eleven-thirty."

"And since I'll be solo, that means I get to blast Taylor Swift as I drive home."

"You and your Taylor obsession."

"What can I say? She just knows me," he says, shameless in his devotion to the pop star.

And I know this man too. As a friend. That's what we are. "We should definitely go to Puzzle Nerds. Whenever you're free," I add.

There.

"We have a Monday night game. So I need to get into game-mode tomorrow night. And all day Sunday. Obviously, Monday is out," he says, then scratches his jaw, lined with one-day stubble. Or is that two days? Maybe more? Maybe even the start of some yummy scruff. How would that scruff feel to the touch? "But Tuesday could work."

To touch his scruff?

Oh, right. Puzzle acquisition.

"Perfect," I say. We were going to restart our puzzle club. That's safe. It's not like puzzles are sexy. You don't set up candles and play soft music and feed each other strawberries as you slide puzzle piece into puzzle piece.

"Just you and me. Like old times."

Before all the flashing incidents. "Let's do it. And thanks again for earlier in the car. And the makeup. And everything. I owe you big time."

"You don't. But it's no problem."

However, I do want to get one thing out in the open. "And, um, I guess one good flashing deserves another," I say. His expression is blank for a second, almost confused, so I sputter: "In Daisy's Duds. When you were all…you know…man-chest-y."

He smirks. "Man-chest-y? Is that what we call it?"

I raise my chin. "Yes. But I can't promise it's a Scrabble word."

"Maybe someday." He lifts his beer bottle, takes a drink, and I stare at his lips. His full, lush lips.

I blink away thoughts of them and focus. I am a laser. "Anyway, I was just thinking how it's sort of the same thing. I mean, not exactly. Not entirely the same. One will get you an R-rating in a movie. The other just makes you want to, well, gawk."

Okay, maybe I wasn't a laser.

His lips twitch. "Gawk, Rachel?"

Gah. I'm making this worse. "I'm just saying—"

"—I know what you mean." He lets me off the hook. "It's good we can joke about it. Maybe we'll even need a commemorative Man-Chest-y mug."

"Yes, for when we do our trash puzzle."

He tips his beer bottle against my champagne flute. It's a friendly enough moment, sealing a deal. But I'm studying his jaw, and his eyes are lingering on my face, and I swear, there's some new charge between us. I hardly know what to make of it.

It's a little thrilling, but a little terrifying too.

* * *

As the clock ticks near eleven, I've had a few glasses of bubbly. I've won a few hands of poker, or maybe blackjack. Possibly both.

Carter's hanging with his brother at the table next to ours, and he gives me a chin nod as he checks his cards.

I smile back, then I up the ante in my poker game, sliding another chip into the pot. I shimmy in my seat, my free-range boobs shaking under my sparkly get-up. This dress is like magic. I feel better after my fiasco of a day.

"I'll raise myself by another chip," I declare.

The dealer—a square-jawed guy with a mustache that might be sexy in an "are mustaches sexy" way but also might not—laughs gently. "I'm not sure poker works that way."

"Aww, c'mon, Scotty. Let her," Juliet encourages him. Or, more like demands.

The dealer slowly shifts his gaze back to me, licking his lips as he says, "Sure, I'll let it slide for you," he says, keeping his eyes locked on me.

Oh.

Is he flirting with me?

It's been a while, but I'm pretty sure that's flirting.

As he deals, I tuck my face closer to Juliet's. "Is Scotty flirting with me? And…do I like him?"

She laughs. "I don't know, Rach. Do you?"

I shrug. Hard to say. The bubbly in me likes the flirting, that's for sure. "Flirting is enjoyable," I say.

She high-fives me. "See? I told you the party would be fun."

"It is dirty, flirty fun," I say, smacking back. Everything is fun. Everything is festive.

Elodie meets my gaze from next to Juliet. "Speaking of fun, you never answered my question from earlier…"

I arch a brow. "Oh, you want to know how the Man-inator is?"

Juliet snort-laughs. "Yes, do tell us. But please use its proper name. The Man-inator is seriously gross."

I square my shoulders, acting all proper. "If you must know, I was going to break out the Girl's Best Friend tonight."

Scotty's gaze snaps back to mine. He looks away to deal, but I think he's still listening. A perk of the job, I suppose, dealing cards at a party full of the buzzed and horny.

"So we're cramping your style with the PJ party?" Elodie asks with a cute little grin. "Or wait. Were you going to slip into my bathroom and use it?" She lets her jaw fall open, comically wide. "Rachel, you bad girl. Did you smuggle it here in your purse?"

"Shut up. I am not going to diddle myself at your house." Primly I add, "I have standards."

Scotty smiles, then waves a hand in front of his face. Oh yes, he is definitely listening.

"Only home diddling for this classy babe," Elodie chimes in as Scotty clears his throat.

With a nod at my card, he asks, "What have you got?"

An ache between my thighs.

Oh, right. He means in my hand.

Honestly, I've lost track of what game we're even playing so I set my cards down face-up and ask, "Did I get twenty-one or a full house?"

"Or both," Elodie offers hopefully.

Maybe we've all lost track of the game.

"Looks like you're winning," Scotty says, then as he pins his gaze to mine, he adds, "Rachel."

And did he say my name a little sensually? A little invitingly? I really need to figure out soon if I like mustaches.

I don't have the answer yet, so I flash a grin, then return to the important topic with my friends. "Tomorrow night. I have a date with wine, my dirty imagination and *the Man-inator*," I say, then add a roar for effect.

I giggle.

We all giggle.

"Or," Elodie says, tapping her red nails on the felt, her impish soprano tone saying she has a clever idea. "Hear me out. Maybe you could get back on the real horse."

My first instinct is to scoff and laugh. Me getting back out there for a hookup is a ridiculous notion. But my very next instinct is to tilt my head and consider her suggestion. *A lot*. I raise a glass. "You know what? That's not a bad idea," I say right as Carter comes up to the table next to me.

With the champagne in hand, I turn and stare, perhaps a little salaciously. Maybe even enough to bite my lip.

Because…Carter and his chest. Carter and his abs. Carter and his happy trail.

"It's getting late. I need to take off," he says, setting a hand on my arm. "Just wanted to say goodnight."

He squeezes my shoulder. It's friendly-ish. But it makes me tingly, too, right between my thighs.

And since I'm full of good ideas tonight, I raise my glass of bubbly, look him straight in the eye, and say, "You know what? I think I'd like to get back on the real horse after all."

Juliet hoots. Elodie claps.

And Scotty clears his throat. "I'd be happy to help."

I freeze.

I was not expecting someone to volunteer as tribute.

I snap my gaze to the flirty dealer, but I don't even know what to say. It's been years since I was hit on. How do I respond? I turn back to Carter, and he's watching me carefully, studying my expression, perhaps asking if I need backup.

I swallow. *Gulp.*

I'm...at a loss.

Carter holds my gaze for a long, weighty beat, then says to the dealer, "Thanks, but the position is already filled."

The table is quiet for a few seconds until Elodie breaks the silence by doffing an imaginary hat and shouting, "Giddyap, Carter!"

With a smile, he bends closer. "Need anything else, Sunshine?"

A Girl's Best Friend, like, right now? Your saddle?

"I'm good," I croak out.

Before I can say another word, he turns and walks away. I stare at him, slack-jawed and shockingly turned on, until he exits the bar and my sight.

7

BRIGHT IDEAS

Carter

During my run the next morning, I replay the scene at the party. But I am not second-guessing myself.

I'm making sure I did the right thing.

I peel off the miles a little after dawn, jogging down Divisadero Street, then through the Presidio before I curve up to the majestic bridge. Fog rolls across the Golden Gate Bridge, typical for most mornings here, but especially the ones in late September.

I try to outrun it, a game I play in my head. As I race the fog, every slap of my sneakers on the pavement brings me to the same realization—I offered because saving Rachel from the mustache man was the right thing to do. Hell, Ellie told me to look out for Rachel. Gotta follow orders from the pack. After all, that's what friends are for.

With that settled, I turn back toward home, upbeat

music from my sister's favorite playlist blasting in my ears.

Along the way, my phone flashes a reminder—*The meeting with Maddox is TODAY, you stud. In 1.5 hours.*

When I near Alta Plaza Park, I'm a block away from my street, so I slow my pace to a walk. My heart pounds and sweat slides down my back, making my T-shirt stick to me, and my thighs scream with a good burn. The post-workout feel is the best. There's nothing—except sex—that I enjoy as much as exercise.

When I reach my home, Monroe's standing on his terrace next door like a stern daddy, tapping his watch, the tats on his forearm visible with the sleeves rolled up. He's a man of contrasts—he wears a cardigan like a professor but his arms are covered in ink. He's also in his mid-thirties but unfairly looks like he's still in his twenties. The dude has gotten carded on two or three occasions when we've gone out with the guys. It's ridiculous, especially since the fucker has an MD.

"You're like a dog now, aren't you?" I call out.

"I can tell time by my need to caffeinate," he says.

As I bound up the steps, I hold up a finger. "Gimme two minutes to fire up the Slayer. Need to stretch the hammies first."

He makes a show of setting a timer on his phone. "Fine. You've got two minutes to tell me about the party."

Oh, boy. Here goes. "So, I guess there was a little role reversal in a thrift shop," I begin as I bend my right leg and reach for my toes.

"Now, by role reversal do you mean she was wearing

the secondhand PJ bottoms and you were wearing the tops?"

With my free hand, I flip him the bird. "Anyway, I needed a new shirt for...reasons," I say, glossing over Rachel's tears. Monroe raises an eyebrow, but he lets it slide, and I rush on before he changes his mind. "I was changing and stepped out of the room when I didn't have a shirt on."

"How thoughtful of you."

"And it became this thing," I continue. "You know how you said to joke about what had happened? Later at the party, she joked about it, and then I joked about it, and everything was defused...well, for a while."

His eyebrows lift. "Sixty seconds. Keep going."

Might as well skip to the good stuff. "And to make a long story short, right before I left the party, she said she wanted to get back on the horse, so I volunteered."

Monroe straightens then just stares at me like I've lost it. "Well, that's not really putting things behind you, is it?"

I hold up a hand. "Now wait a sec."

"Sure. You've got forty-five more seconds on the clock." He crosses his arms.

"I had to help out. This dealer dude was hitting on her. She clearly wasn't into him. But when she said she wanted to get back out there, he threw his hat in the ring." I sneer at the thought. *That guy.* How dare he. "And I was like *no fucking way.*"

"Ah, I see. You were simply white-knighting."

Now he gets it. "Rachel was giving off serious *save me* vibes. It was the only thing to do."

He sets a hand on his heart. "How very noble, offering to bang your hot bestie."

"Relax, doc. I'll see her soon and sort it all out." Once I'm inside making him a cortado, I turn over his last words. Does Rachel think I was trying to get with her?

Shit. I'm going to need to fix this sooner than Tuesday. But first, I have to have a talk with my agent about Date Night. Too bad I can't forget this meeting.

Before I hustle out of there, I rip the word of the day from my calendar. *Jouissance*. French origin, meaning pleasure or enjoyment.

Even my calendar is calling me out.

* * *

I don't usually wear my rings. They're big and tend to draw attention. Which is the point of winning the biggest game of the year, I suppose.

But there are two places where I like to wear the twins. One is when I meet my football buddies at the gym because my team, the Renegades, has won more Big Games than our cross-town rivals, the Hawks, and I'm friends with guys on both teams.

The other is on the golf course because I might run into the team owner there. And since he owns the golf course, too, there's a better than even chance of our paths crossing.

Wilder Blaine likes to see the bling on his players' fingers. Totally his prerogative. The man pays our very pretty salaries, hires the best coaches and trainers, and makes sure his GM drafts the best players.

The Renegades are a well-oiled machine, and I'm damn lucky to play for them.

When I pull up to the course—on time, thanks to my matrix of alarms—I say hi to the valet then tip him well on Venmo. I head straight for the clubhouse to look for Maddox LeGrande. My agent is always early. It makes me a little jealous, how easily time management seems to come to him.

I'm pushing open the door when a high-pitched voice calls out, "Mommy, that's Carter Hendrix! Number eighty-eight."

I spin around to find a girl—maybe nine or ten—pointing at me from ten feet away. "You're my favorite Renegade!"

"And you're my favorite fan."

A woman in khakis and a polo sets a gloved hand on the girl's shoulder. "Grace, what did I tell you about the members? Give them their space, honey."

"I don't mind," I say as I walk over to the mom, who I'm pretty sure is the club's new golf pro. "You work here, right?"

"I do. I'm Alice," the woman says, then squeezes her kiddo's shoulder. "And this little troublemaker is tagging along today."

"I like to make good trouble," Grace declares. "And I'm going to hit a hole in one today."

I offer her a fist for knocking. "I like that attitude," I say as she knocks back.

"Can I have a pic for luck?" the girl asks.

Alice gives me an apologetic look. "We're not supposed to ask members. You don't have to."

I wave a hand to dismiss that worry. "But I want to," I say, then I bend to kneel next to the confident little kid as her mom snaps a shot with her phone.

"Carter, since I'm going to hit a hole in one, can you make a big catch on Monday? That only seems fair," Grace says intensely.

Damn, this kid would make a great agent. She's a helluva negotiator. "I think that can be arranged," I say. This convo is more fun than facing the music about my sponsorships, so I chat a little more with Grace about the upcoming game.

A few minutes later, I say goodbye and head inside.

Maddox stands by the counter, and I'm relieved he doesn't seem to be waiting for me. He's busied himself chatting with the man who pays the team's bills.

Wilder Blaine looks every bit the badass billionaire who came from nothing and made his money in Vegas real estate. Even his golf clothes seem custom-fitted, but they're not preppy. He wears black slacks and a dark gray shirt. It's like they say *do not fuck with me*. The dude has ink on his knuckles, too, like he rode through the night in a rebel biker gang before he took a wrecking ball to the sorriest properties on the Strip and built new beauties instead—buildings that have funded the team.

As I near them, he turns to me. "Morning, Hendrix," he says, with a casual chin nod.

"Morning, sir." I can't *not* call him sir.

"You can call me Wilder."

"No, I really can't," I say honestly.

Maddox laughs, then meets Wilder's dark gaze. "I'm

afraid you're not going to win this battle with my client."

"But I'll keep trying. I'll leave you two to your business," Wilder says, clapping Maddox on the shoulder, then looking me in the eye. "But I hope to see *you* around more."

Why is he directing that comment at me? "Here at the club?"

"More like…around town. But only if it works out." He gives a smile that says *it*—whatever it is—better work out. On that vague note, his attention lasers on a little sprite racing toward us from the ladies' room, wearing golf pants and a polo.

"I'm ready, Daddy," the kiddo calls out as she rushes over to him.

"Let's do that lesson, sweetheart," he says warmly, then wraps an arm around his daughter.

"And Grace is going to help teach me too. Along with her mom," Wilder's daughter says.

"You're going to devastate me on the links soon, Mac," he says with parental pride as he calls her by her nickname—short for Mackenzie. Then the man in charge gives us a chin nod, his gaze landing on my hand. "Rings looking good, Hendrix."

"Thanks, sir," I say before he leaves with his kid. When he's out of earshot, though, I turn to Maddox, a little thrown off. "What's that all about?"

"I presume you don't mean his daughter's golf lesson."

"I do not."

My agent nods to the driving range. "Let's talk."

I hate those two words. I feel like I'm in trouble, like I was nearly every day in school.

It's not a comfortable flashback.

* * *

I only have thirty minutes to spend on the driving range. At ten-thirty, I'm due at the Renegades facility for our final red-zone game-plan practice before tomorrow's walk-through, then Monday's game.

"So, we've got an issue with Date Night," Maddox says as we walk.

I knew this was coming, but I still dread it. "They want the videos I owe, right?"

He nods, resigned but resolute too. "They do, buddy."

I drag a hand down my face, groaning. "Well, I'd love to, but there's that little issue of Quinn twirling on ropes or sheets or a fucking hula hoop from the ceiling."

My ex and I were supposed to do a bunch of videos together on great dates for Date Night, a dating app that shot up in popularity recently. The quarterback on the Hawks hooked me up with the app a couple years ago, since he knows the founder, Zena Palladium. I'd already been using the app on my own and loving it, so it was a perfect fit for me sponsorship-wise. I love dating. I love getting to know women. I love spending time with a special someone and figuring her out. Women are wonderful puzzles. Talking up Date Night was easy, since Zena wanted someone who actually went on dates via her app. I've been the spokesperson ever since then, and the partnership has been gold.

For my bank account.

For the team.

For me.

A few months into the deal, I met Quinn on the app, and damn, did that make Date Night look good. Like a gold mine for real romance. The pro baller and the acrobat—two athletes who discovered true love online, just like the app promises with its *Find the One* tagline. As part of my contract with them, Quinn and I posted pics and videos of our dates on the app, which they then used in their social media marketing.

You, too, can find the real thing on Date Night.

It went so well Zena inked a deal with Wilder, too, becoming one of the official marketing partners for the team. And when I proposed to Quinn, Zena forked over more dough. She upped my contract and basically said she'd love me forever if Quinn and I showed off some great date locations around the city for couples to enjoy.

Except, all love stories end.

Mine with Quinn, and mine with Date Night.

After Quinn and I split, I had zero interest in getting back on the app. Zena was chill at first. "Take your time. No worries. There's no rush for you to start dating again," she'd said over dinner with Maddox and me a year ago.

Now, I'm getting the impression time's up. But

dating again? Putting my heart on the line? That sounds worse than getting pummeled by a bloodthirsty pass rusher. "I am so not into dating again. I honestly don't know when I will be. Can I just pay back the fee for the additional videos?" I ask Maddox. I have the money. I could bow out gracefully.

"You *could*," he says tactfully. "Though Zena would rather not go there."

Code for *don't piss off a powerful woman*. But I get it. I signed a deal. She waited while I was off the market. Just because I'm not interested in dating again doesn't mean she's lost interest in me.

"Pretty sure Wilder would prefer to keep her happy too," Maddox adds.

Yeah, it's clear now why he said he wants to see me around more. Around on the app. Around the city. Around in general.

"So, to fulfill my contract, I need to find someone on the app and traipse around the city looking like a happy couple?" It just sounds painful, the idea of showing off five great dates for you and your special someone.

"Look, I can tell you're not ready for a relationship. I respect that. But you do owe them these videos, so here's a thought—instead of finding one person you want to do these dates with, would you be willing to do five first dates?"

I let that soak in, but it doesn't take long. First dates are easy. No commitment. No promises. "Probably."

"No one is saying you have to meet your wife," he reassures me.

"Good. Because that won't happen."

"So then if I can get Zena to reframe the contract around five first dates, you'd be willing to hold up your end of the deal?"

I don't have any leeway; I can't say no. And I don't want to piss off Zena or let Wilder down. Plus, Maddox has come up with a pretty decent compromise. I can fake it through five first dates. "I would. Because...you rock," I say.

He flashes me a professional grin. "I do. Just reactivate that profile *today* so Zena sees you making the effort, all right?"

I can do him one better. I whip out my phone from my back pocket, toggle over to the app that's gone unused for so long it's got digital cobwebs. Then I fire up my profile—my screen name is Plays Well With Others—showing the proof to Maddox on the screen. "There you go."

My agent lifts an eyebrow in a way that says he's impressed. "I'll call Zena when we're done."

We reach the tees, and Maddox hands me one of the two clubs he's been carrying. I line up, take a big swing, and look at that. The ball soars, and as it flies forward, so does my mind.

I'm ten paces ahead.

Wouldn't it be easier if that *first* first date was with someone I already know? Because I'm pretty sure there's someone I could ask to go on a first date with me—platonically, of course. Last night, Rachel said she owed me a favor. Does she? *Hell no.* But would she help me?

That's a hell yes.

All I need to do is convince her to make a profile for the sole purpose of swiping right...on me.

8

SWEET UNBANGABLE ME

Rachel

It's a good thing I'm not hungover. But the flip side is I can remember everything I said last night at the card table.

As in this bon mot…

I'd like to get back on the real horse.

Oof.

And I can't even blame a couple of glasses of bubbly for my megaphone mouth.

I was buzzed light. I was sober adjacent. I wasn't even drunk enough to blame the liquor for the way I bit my lip or eye-fucked Carter when he was just trying to say goodnight.

Where is the rewind button?

But on the bright side, at least I have some customers in my shop on Saturday, so I can't stew in the what-do-I-say-to-Carter zone. Options include but are not limited to: *Thanks for saving me and the horse my libido rode in on,* and...*yes, I am a bad girl who's having very dirty thoughts about you.*

Fable is chatting with a couple of tourists, vehemently discouraging them from setting foot on Fisherman's Wharf, while I help a couple of teenagers pick out a gift for one of their boyfriends. The one with a rose-pink midriff-baring top and jet-black hair peers at the display of thick gold chains, tapping her chin. "Do you have any in silver?"

"I do," I say, then reach into a drawer and show her a silver chain designed for a guy. "What do you think of this one?"

Her redheaded friend—the one wearing a dark pink midriff-baring top—gasps in excitement. "Yes. Get that one, Soph."

The girl named Sophie, I presume, nods sagely, then meets my eyes. "My boyfriend has been checking out gold chains online. But I don't like gold, so this way if *I* get a silver chain for him, I can make sure I like what he's wearing. It's what I call a selfish gift."

That is delightfully underhanded. "Brilliant plan," I say with a smile. "I wish I'd been that smart when my college boyfriend wore cargo pants."

"So cringe," they say in unison.

"Want me to wrap this for him?" I ask.

"That would be great. Thank you," Sophie says, then her gaze catches on a small, delicate chain with a sparkly heart on it. She urges her friend over. "Oh, Aud, come see this."

While I wrap the not-selfish-after-all gift, the tourist

ladies leave with a wave and one of them gives a final, "I solemnly swear I won't go to Fisherman's Wharf."

Fable punches the air. "Victory."

I shake my head at her in amusement while the girls try on the heart necklaces. I'm surprised, though, when they turn to me rather than their phones, with Sophie asking, "How do we look?"

"Like friendship goals," I say, grateful to have been asked.

Sophie wraps her arm around her friend—Audrey, I'm guessing—and squeezes. They remind me of my friend group. I might have lost all skills at interacting with adult men, but I can hang with the girls no problem.

"I'll get these too," Sophie says. "On me."

"Oh my god," Audrey says, then throws her arms around her friend. "Thank you."

"Now that is *not a* selfish gift at all," I say.

While they keep the necklaces on, I enter their purchases in my tablet and swivel it around for the phone swipe.

"Enjoy," I say, and once they leave, they snap selfies outside in front of the store.

Hurrah!

Maybe I can turn my fortune around with teenagers leading the way. Let that be a reminder that I should always behave with customers.

It's just Fable and me in the store now. "They're adorbs," Fable remarks from the counter. "They almost make me want to be seventeen again."

I shudder as I head to a display shelf to tidy up some

bracelets. "Nothing could make me want to be seventeen again. I'd have to go through my marriage a second time. No thanks."

But Fable stares dreamily out the window of the store. "If I were seventeen again," she muses, "I'd bet Calypso would play me in the movie of my life. *The Badass Jewelry Designer Makes it Big Time.*" She likes this game, and she whips her gaze to me, appraising.

"Better give me someone good," I warn her. "Last time we played this, you gave me Brynnie, a woman best known for selling vagina-scented candles. And you just gave yourself someone at least ten years younger than you who won an Emmy at age seventeen."

"Shhh. Don't give my age away," she says.

My phone buzzes from my back pocket. I grab it. Carter's name flashes across the screen, and my cheeks flame. That's a weird reaction, but the weirder one is the flip in my stomach. Talk about seventeen again—I feel like I'm back in high school. "I need to take this call," I say to Fable, then I duck into the tiny office in the back of the shop and answer as I shut the door.

"Hey," I say, trying to sound cool, like I'm not replaying last night's hot mess moment. I've had enough hot mess moments to make a reel lately.

"Hey there," he says, and I try to read into his tone in those two words. Does he think it was weird when I bit my lip? Like I qualified for an Internet meme of mockable lip-biters?

I need to fix things, stat, especially since I can't read his tone. "Listen, Carter," I say, just diving in, unrehearsed. "About what I said last night at the party. I was just having fun, and I don't want you to think—"

But, now that I'm here, I don't know what comes next. *I don't want you to think I was undressing you all night long? Oh, and this morning, too, when I returned home from the pajama-party-kidnapping and finally took care of the ache between my thighs while picturing you?*

I squirm over that memory.

But it's such a good memory that my mind goes blank, and my body feels a little melty.

"I'm glad it worked out. I could tell that guy was putting the moves on you and you didn't want him to," he says.

Ohhh.

He was simply superheroing last night while I was going all vampy. I really messed up. "I mean, it was just the champagne talking," I say quickly. "That thing I said." God, why can't I repeat it in front of him?

Because he's the reason you've been low-key horny for twenty-four hours straight.

"Champagne filter," he says. "It's a thing."

I laugh, grateful for the humor to defuse the tension. "Better than champagne goggles."

"Definitely. And listen, I hope I didn't come across as…um, crass," he says. "Like I was trying to…ba—"

He can't even breathe the awful words. *Bang you.*

Great. Just great.

"Sweet Unbangable Me" is going to be my new anthem. "Please. You were so gallant. Like a prince riding in on a steed," I say, and what's with the horse analogies? "A unicorn," I say, trying again to make, well, hay. "A unicorn saving the day. You were a unicorn who shot rainbows from his butt."

"Yeah, maybe not *that* kind."

Okay, perhaps that wasn't the best compliment. "I bet you're more like a fire-breathing unicorn, only you breathe rainbow fire. So thank you for your rainbow fire," I say, and can someone just shut me up?

"No problem," he says, then takes a beat to clear his throat. "And…I need saving now."

Thank god. I'm more than eager to move on and put this awkward moment behind us. "Hit me up."

With a heavy sigh, he says, "I owe Date Night some videos."

He dives into the problem with one of his big sponsors and when he's done, I want to throat-punch Quinn. I hate her more than I did before. "Want me to find Quinn and burn all her underwear on the Strip?"

He laughs, but then it fades. "Nah, but maybe instead would you go on a date with me?"

That tingle I felt last night turns into a hot spark.

9
I CAN BE DELIGHTFULLY UNDERHANDED

Rachel

There's no way I heard him right.

After all that terrible lip-biting last night, he couldn't possibly be asking me on a date, right?

Also, do I even want to date my best friend?

No, no, and a hell no.

Because then what would happen when the date went south? I'd be left alone all over again. No, thank you.

"A date?" I ask, a little uncomfortably.

"A platonic date," he quickly corrects, and I breathe a very audible sigh of relief. Thank god. But now that he's said *that,* I feel the tiniest bit let down. Yes, a date with Carter would have been a terrible idea, but for a few dangerous seconds there I felt…wanted.

And it was nice to feel wanted.

Warm and kind of woozy in my chest.

But I shake off the foreign sensation. Obviously I don't need to be wanted by my friend.

"Sure," I add, upbeat.

"You're a goddess," he says. "I don't want to go anywhere near a real date, so my agent is getting it all sorted for me to do five first dates. And it'll be way easier for me if you and I could do the first one. As friends. So I thought maybe we could do the Puzzle Nerds thing and record some of it."

"Of course," I say, even though I've already agreed, both to Puzzle Nerds and helping him. "I'll get my profile up tonight."

"You're the best," he says, then adds, "I should go to practice."

"I need to get back to the store."

"Thanks again, Rachel."

"Anytime."

I hang up, relieved things aren't weird with us after last night, even though I still feel a little kernel of disappointment as I leave my tiny office.

I return to the front of the store right as the bell tinkles. A woman in a flowy cream blouse and with the most perfect complexion I've ever seen floats in like Aphrodite rising from the foam.

She's the picture of serenity. She even smells calm too. It's like lavender is wafting off her, lulling me into a sense of peace and harmony.

"Welcome to Bling and Baubles. We're happy to help you with anything you need."

She steeples her fingers together. "Wonderful. I definitely need some help."

"Let us know what we can do. I'm Rachel, the owner. And this is Fable. She works here and she also designs a number of our necklaces."

Fable nods toward the Venus on the Half-Shell lady. "You'd probably look good in anything with your dewy complexion," she says.

The woman smiles, clutching her chest like she's so touched. "Thank you." She turns to me, her smile widening. "I do have a question for you."

"Sure," I say.

"Are you unhappy?" she asks with a placid smile.

That's a strange thing to ask. Confused, I say, "No, I'm not unhappy. Why?"

"Then, why are you raining on other's happiness?"

I steal a glance at Fable, who looks just as perplexed as I feel. "I don't know what you mean."

"You should apologize for your negative energy," she says to me, never raising her voice, never changing her tone. Just holding my gaze with an eerie serenity.

"I'm sorry?" I say, but I'm not. She's freaking me out.

"Your negative vibe is affecting this whole block, Rachel," she says, then sweeps her arm behind her to the window. Saturday traffic streams by—joggers and walkers and families happily heading to lunch, to yoga, to kombucha. But in here, I'm getting lectured for my... bad energy.

Fable clears her throat. "Excuse me. Who are you?"

"I'm Ava. And the negativity from this quadrant is so strong, I can feel it all the way up the street at my spa. I own Haven Spa." Then she raises her hand, finding the chain at her throat, tugging it from her blouse, and revealing a rose-gold lotus pendant, similar to the one I sell, but not exactly the same.

I gasp.

No, please no, please don't let this woman be who I think she is. "My husband bought me this for my birthday. *From another store.*"

The hair on my arms stands on end.

Apologies form on my tongue, but they're so tangled, so messy I don't even know where to start.

She's the wife of the man who called me a stupid bitch in an online review.

But that's not the worst thing.

She's also been my secret benefactor, sending friends here to shop after their facials and hot-stone massages.

"I'm so sorry," I say, feeling like a chastened child.

Ava presses her hands together and says, "I'll be sending you healing energy, Rachel." Then with a steadying breath, she lifts her face, resolute, like a warrior. "But I can't, in good harmony with the universe, send my clients to you anymore."

She turns and sails away into the San Francisco afternoon.

* * *

I twirl the book-shaped charm on my necklace and stare at the snow-covered cabin in the painting behind my therapist's cushy chair. It's homey and warm in here. The opposite of my barren heart.

It's Monday morning, and I still haven't recovered from Ava's spot-on assessment of me two days ago.

"The worst part is…I think she's right," I confess, slumping deeper into the welcoming couch.

Elena Alvarez is my therapist, and we started in-person sessions recently, but we'd been zooming while I was in Venice. When I'd learned the terrible truth of Edward's secret life, secret girlfriend, and secret family, I'd been so devastated, so broken that I hadn't known what to do. Elodie had swooped in and asked for an appointment on my behalf. *"I've seen her over the years, and she's helped me with some tough things. You can trust her,"* Elodie said.

That sold me. I mean, I do have trust issues the size of Alaska.

"Is she right, Elena?" I ask.

Elena's older than me by a couple of decades, with silver in her hair and passion in her voice that says she's always listening. She misses nothing. "Do I think your negative energy is affecting *her* spa? God no. That's ridiculous, and she's the one responsible for her spa's energy," she says with an eye roll. "But obviously the encounter has stayed with you. So I think the more important question is this: is your outlook affecting your job and your life?"

I scoff. "Clearly."

"So, how can you change that? What's one thing you can do differently this week to change your attitude?"

"I take it the answer isn't 'indulge in more wine and sugar,'" I say with a wry grin. Or maybe it's a hopeful one. Because that'd be a fabulous solution.

She smiles but shakes her head.

Elena waits for me to come to a real answer. What

can I do this week to change? Because Ava the Queen of Serene was right. I need to do better. I need to interact with the world as well as I do with cool teens.

But how?

Well, tonight is Carter's football game and I'm going, of course. Tomorrow is our platonic date.

Oh, I know, I know!

I'll be a fucking ray of sunshine every time I see him. Including on our date. No crying, no talk about bad reviews, no more wallowing.

I'm about to say that, but something stops me. I'd have to divulge that I have a platonic date with Carter, and I don't want to tell Elena that. It would raise more questions that currently lack answers.

So, I sidestep that part, just for now. "I'll get Carter a mug," I declare.

But Elena's not the best for nothing. She doesn't let clients dodge the hard stuff. "How will that help you change your attitude, Rachel?"

Dammit.

I stare at the painting till the snow gets a little blurry, but I keep a lock on the wildly inappropriate thoughts I've been having about Carter lately. I don't want to give them voice. My fervent hope is that they'll vanish if I double down on friendship.

And, well, if I stop getting off to fantasies of him doing bad things to me, that *would* probably help.

I tear my gaze away from the painting, meet my therapist's warm light blue eyes, then answer truthfully. "It'll help by focusing on others. By doing something nice for someone else. *That* could bring positive energy maybe to *this* one-foot radius," I say, gesturing to me, then giving her a hopeful look, like *did I get the right answer?*

"Well, there you go," Elena says proudly.

And look at that—I've aced the self-care pop quiz.

* * *

I am a new woman at the football game on Monday evening with Elodie. From our seats on the fifty-yard line, I holler like I'm entering a cheer competition in Texas.

As Carter flies downfield deep in the third quarter, chasing a long spiral, I shout till my throat is raw. "Go, go, go, go!"

When he closes in on the ball, he jumps for it, and with outstretched arms he catches it...on his fingertips.

"Yes! That's how you do it!" I cry out.

Hauling it close, he spins out of bounds to dodge the coverage, and Elodie cheers with me. "Yes, eighty-eight!"

With the game play stopped, she turns to me, her bright eyes sparkling with questions. "Someone is extra excited tonight."

"Well, did you see that play?"

"Yes, he has magic hands," she says, but her eyes stay locked on mine. She's a determined bumblebee. "Do you still want to ride his horse?"

"Shut up," I say.

"Well, do you?"

"Elodie," I chide.

"I'll take that as a yes."

I don't answer her. On the field, the Renegades get back in the huddle, and I put all my positive energy into the game.

My brand-new vibe must be some kind of good luck charm because the good guys win.

After the game ends, Elodie and I make our way out of the stadium and find Carter outside the players' entrance. He's all relaxed and upbeat in his post-game suit as he shoots the breeze with Malik Hamlin, the team's running back.

When Carter spots us coming toward him through the turnstiles, his grin widens. He smacks Malik on the shoulder in parting then ambles over.

Malik tips his chin toward me. "Hey, Rachel," he says before he waves and takes off.

"Good game, Malik," I call out.

When Carter reaches us, he says hi to Elodie and then lifts me into a hug. A warm, friendly hug. I refuse to think bangable thoughts about it or him.

When he sets me down, I reach into my purse for the gift I got him. I hand him the mug with a cartoon of a cheese grater on it, captioned: *"Don't you look grate."*

"Aww, it's the commemorative I-saw-your-man-chest mug," he says.

Now he'll never know I wanted to bang him. See? I can be underhanded in my gift-giving too.

10

HOW TO SABOTAGE A FIRST DATE

Carter: I'm up late. Don't tell anyone.

Rachel: Your secret is safe with me.

Carter: Thanks. Appreciate that.

Rachel: Are you cleaning the floors? Organizing the cupboards? Or using that amazing mug I just gave you to water Jane?

Carter: Jane! Fuck!!! Be right back.

Carter: Okay, she's satisfied now. She appreciates you hearing her cries for help, since I'd snoozed that alert like a bad boy.

Rachel: I have a special gift for sensing bad plant daddies.

Carter: I like to tease my ladies. Make them beg for it. Also, my cupboards were organized yesterday. Thank you very much.

> Rachel: Come do mine then please. Or should I beg for it?

Carter: I'm not opposed to that.

> Rachel: Please, Carter. Oh god, please come sort my pantry.

Carter: Good girl. You've earned a very big reward.

> Rachel: Someone else to do chores! Yay!

Carter: Is that what you'd like to do on our first date instead of Puzzle Nerds? You want me to straighten up?

> Rachel: Considering the state of my cupboards, that sounds like an amazing first date! I'm also fond of massages and napping. So a nap date works for me too.

Carter: How about you nap while I put away your plates? Bet Date Night would let me out of the rest of my contract if I did that.

> Rachel: I'm up for sabotage! We could even try a date at the dentist. Want to get cleanings together?

Carter: Then we'll have the tires rotated on my car.

> Rachel: And we can go to some government office to renew our passports.

Carter: Well, that's actually dirty. Don't you know?

Rachel: Because no one fucks as well as the government?

Carter: I mean, I do. But that's beside the point.

Rachel: I don't know, Carter. That sort of seemed like it was the point.

Carter: Now that you mention it, a sex date at the passport office would definitely get mega views on Date Night. We'll skip that.

Rachel: Fair enough. But in all seriousness, I thought we were doing Puzzle Nerds?

Carter: Do I look like an underachiever? Of course I don't. Which is why I'm up late after my game, diligently researching first date ideas since I refuse to simply piggyback off our existing plan and retroactively assign the word 'date' to it. We'll do a two-parter— Puzzle Nerds and something else. But do you have any idea how many options there are for quote great first dates end-quote?

Rachel: This may shock you, but I do not. Been off the dating market for a millennia.

Carter: Let me enlighten you then. The Internet says dinner and a movie will get you blackballed. A bar is a Very Bad Idea. And coffee is so yesterday. It's like the first date is now some reality-show competition for cleverness. Take her kayaking! Bring her to a paint-and-wine studio! Shop for antiques! Pretend to be tourists!

Rachel: Please promise you will never, ever take a date on a pretend-to-be-tourists date. Live-action role-play sounds like way too much work.

Carter: The only role-playing I want to do is in the bedroom.

Carter: And it's been brought to my attention the above text may have been inappropriate.

Rachel: And the 'fuck like the government' one was not?

Carter: Hey, that's on your conscience, Sunshine.

Rachel: I'll try to repent for it. Or…idea! If you're really into sabotage, maybe the first date gimmick should be to see how many inappropriate things you can say before the end of it. We're already on a roll.

Carter: I'm getting the sense that inappropriateness, napping, and massages are actually the way to your heart.

> Rachel: Pedicures too. Which might explain why I have no clue how to date.

> Carter: Then it's a good thing I have access to the Internet since the number-one dating rule is to do something she enjoys…while you get to know her.

> Rachel: I'm so excited you got your pedicurist license!!!!!

11

THE BEAST AND ME

Carter

So this is what surreal feels like.

I leave my home the next evening on time and absolutely ready to take Rachel out on a first date. One that I researched just for her. One that I'm actually kind of excited for.

Hell, I even broke out my best Henley.

This navy blue one is my good luck shirt. From the planning to the aftershave to the special clothes, tonight with Rachel feels like a real date.

But it's not.

And that's the point.

The mission is to settle the bill with Date Night one first date at a time.

I shut the front door of my home, then steal a final glance at my reflection in the glass.

The perfect amount of scruff. Nothing in my teeth. My breath is minty fresh.

You're not kissing her.

From mere feet away, a familiar voice interrupts my thoughts.

"And now, spotted in his natural habitat, we have a rare sighting of the North American variety of Clueless Male as he ventures into the wilds of modern dating. Watch as he preens. Observe as he partakes in the traditional mating ritual of checking out his ugly mug."

With an aggrieved groan, I turn to Monroe, who's on his terrace, his phone held up in my direction, the red light from his video on. *Are you kidding me?* "You recorded that?"

"You can thank me later for my contribution to your Date Night commitment."

"Unlikely," I say.

"You'll come around," he says then lowers the phone, switching it for a glass of what looks to be scotch. "I hoped to catch you on your way out to wish you luck and my efforts were rewarded with wildlife nature photography." With a satisfied sigh, he knocks back some victory scotch, savoring the moment.

I can't do anything but cede victory. "We will meet again on the battlefield, doc," I say, then bound down the steps to my car. I parked it on the street after practice today. I could have parked it in my garage, but there was a spot exactly two inches longer than my car calling out to me. I had no choice but to show off my parallel parking prowess to anyone who happened to be walking past or driving by. I like to perform under pressure, and in one try, I got the car all the way in.

It's almost a shame to give up the glory of this spot, but I hop in my wheels and head off, driving to Bling and Baubles. Rachel closed a few minutes ago and said to pick her up there.

I pull up, acing another parking job, thank you very much. I head to the shop. Rachel's at the counter, her back to the door, spraying the display cases then wiping them down.

I rap on the door.

She spins around.

My breath catches.

She's *Date Rachel*, and holy shit.

Her chestnut hair is swept up in a twist, a few strands framing her face. She's wearing a bright pink top that clings to her skin and makes mine sizzle.

She sets down the cleaning supplies and comes to unlock the door. "Come in. I just had a new idea for the pre-date video. But you need to shoot it. I tried doing it myself, but I need to use my hands."

I want to use *my* hands. On her.

"Sure," I say roughly, trying to adjust to how unfairly sexy she looks tonight. What the hell did that boob sighting do to me? It unlocked some inner beast, and I need to wrestle the monster back into its cage.

Once she locks the door behind us, she guides me over to the main counter then points. "Stand here," she says.

Simple directions. Good. That's about all the beast in me can handle right now.

"And shoot it on your phone. Since you'll be editing it for Date Night. Or giving it to someone to edit. Or however you do it," she says, easy breezy. She's clearly into the whole help-a-friend aspect of tonight. I should follow her lead.

"Right," I say as I grab my phone from my back pocket and hit the camera icon.

But when I look up, a rumble nearly escapes my lips —a bestial rumble. She's letting down her hair and shaking out her locks. Have I walked into a shampoo commercial?

If so, I have a new dream. To live inside a shampoo commercial.

"You're wearing your hair down?" I ask, my voice a rough scrape.

"No," she says with a bright smile. "I'm wearing it up."

Up, down, it's all good. I'll just watch her do things to her hair all night long. That sounds like a great date to me.

"Just hit record," she adds. "I'll show you."

I comply, positioning the phone to shoot. "Ready. Go."

She flashes a smile at the camera. "Hey, there. So my date is picking me up from work, and you know what that means, ladies? It means you need to go from business to night like that," she says, snapping her fingers. "So, the first thing I do to get ready is this—I sweep my hair into a simple updo."

She grabs the hair clip, then twists her hair back up on her head, exposing her neck.

My throat goes dry.

"Then, I throw on some fun date jewelry," she says, grabbing a necklace from the counter, and quickly clipping it on. "And for the final tweak? I adjust my top from day to night," she says, then shimmies the sleeves off her shoulders, wriggling them down, showing off more gorgeous flesh.

More kissable skin.

More bare inches of her body.

Monroe was right about one thing—I am definitely in the dating wild tonight.

"There you go," she says, then takes a pause, before adding, "You can stop shooting, Carter."

Oh, right. "Of course," I say, then end the video and put my phone away.

When I look back, I see her wincing as she tugs at the delicate chain. "Ouch. Can you help?" she asks. Then she spins around, showing me the nape of her neck. "I think my necklace is caught in my hair. Can you undo it and redo it?"

I step closer, catching a dangerous hint of her perfume. It smells like orange blossoms and the kind of desire that clobbers you from out of nowhere. It's dangerous and seductive all at once. I undo the clasp, gently freeing the wisps of hair from it.

"Thank you," she says, seeming relieved.

"No problem," I mumble.

But I don't redo the clasp right away.

The thing is—I have good hands. Great hands. It's my job to use them to pull footballs from thin air. To have complete control.

My hands are even insured.

Right now, though, they don't feel steady at all. I'm dying to run a finger down the back of her neck, then along her shoulder blades, to learn how she responds to a gentle touch.

And to a not so gentle one too.

To all sorts of touches from my curious hands.

I close my eyes, fight off the images, then find the will to clasp the necklace.

I don't deserve an award for not kissing the back of her neck, but I'm giving myself one anyway.

12

SHINY OBJECT, DO YOUR THING

Carter

Walking into a chocolate shop is almost as good as exploring a new hiking trail or trying out a new pass route.

Shiny object, do your thing on my ADHD brain.

And oh hell, do the options here at Elodie's Chocolates tractor beam my attention their way the second we walk into Rachel's friend's shop in Hayes Valley.

As the sensual aroma of decadence floats through the air, it throws me off the scent of orange blossom and onto the scent of dessert.

Win-win.

"Too bad it doesn't smell good at all in here," I deadpan.

"I was thinking that very same thing," Rachel says dryly as she lifts her nose in the air, then sniffs.

We're enrobed in chocolate, and even though I didn't

pick this place for the sensual assault, it's working on me in ways I need. I'm in the chocolate zone now.

We check out the countertop displays of little chocolate squares, truffles, and wildly colorful bonbons, some in red with champagne, some in green with fleur de sel, some in purple with praline. Elodie loves colorful chocolates, and it's one of her signatures in her creations.

The shop is bustling, even on a Tuesday evening. Elodie's young sister works behind the counter, her twin blonde braids tucked under a pink paisley bandana as she rings up gift boxes. With her hair swept back in a matching black paisley bandana, Elodie answers a customer's question about the difference between chocolate from Ecuador and Guatemala.

When she's done a few seconds later, she spots us, then scurries around the counter, dusting her hands on her cherry-red apron.

"Your table is ready, Mr. Hendrix and Ms. Dumont. May I show you to your seats?"

Rachel blinks, then with a confused smile says, "Why, yes, thank you."

Elodie gestures for Rachel to walk in front of her, then she shoots me a private smile. I return it, grateful for her help. She guides us to the small café in the back of the shop, steering us to a plush red booth set for two. A white card on the table says *reserved*.

Elodie snatches it and tucks it in the apron's pouch. Rachel sits, giving me a *what is going on* look. I shrug innocently though I'm so not.

Playing the part perfectly, Elodie squares her shoulders and says, "I've been told you're quite the chocolate connoisseur, Ms. Dumont. And I've prepared a chef's selection of chocolates just for you," she says to the woman in pink across from me.

"Wow. Thanks," Rachel says, still seeming a little bewildered. "I kind of like sweets."

"You came to the right place. Now, can I get you a chocolate drink while you wait? You might like our Dark Chocolate with Cayenne Pepper. It comes with a splash of tequila."

Rachel's amber eyes sparkle with a gleam that says *sold*. "Yes, please."

Elodie gives a conspiratorial nod. "Someone told me you like it...hot," she says, then shifts her attention to me, rattling off more spiked cocoa options. I pick one that has whiskey in it, since why the fuck not combine two of the best tastes ever?

"I'll be back shortly." Elodie spins around and takes off. And even though the shop is bustling, we're tucked away so it feels like just Rachel and me in this section of the little café. We're right beside an older couple, quietly doing a crossword puzzle together on a tablet, while nibbling on a chocolate bar.

With her friend gone, Rachel stares at me, baffled. "You planned all this? Set this all up?"

I lean back in the chair, feeling pretty damn good about myself. "You didn't want to pretend to be tourists, so I had to find something else to impress my date. And the big takeaway from my research last night was to focus on what your date likes." I count off on my fingers. "You like sweets. You like spicy things. You like your friends. So I thought a little chocolate tasting at Elodie's shop would fit the bill. Called the owner and asked her to save us the best table in the house."

Rachel brings her hand to her mouth then shakes her head. "I can't believe it," she says, and though I like her date disbelief, I'm a bit mystified. Pulling out the stops doesn't seem like such a big deal to me. Planning tonight was fun, and frankly, what a dude should do.

"Really?" I press.

"It's so...*thoughtful*." It's as if she hasn't spoken the word in ages. Like it's unfamiliar to her tongue. She bites the corner of her lips then waves a hand in front of her face, her eyes shining.

Oh, shit. Is she going to cry again?

Instead, she takes a steadying breath. "It's more than I expected tonight."

Does being nice to her make her cry? No clue. Probably best to make light of the whole situation. "I told you I wasn't an underachiever."

She shakes her head vehemently. "I know you're not, but that's not what I mean, Carter," she says, soft and vulnerable.

Her sincerity neutralizes my need to make her laugh. "What do you mean?"

She exhales shakily. "When Edward wanted to impress me, he'd always pick the hot new restaurant that a finance buddy had told him about. He'd usually have missed something I'd planned. A dinner at home. Or a birthday. Or a night out with friends. So he'd make it up to me with these fancy meals. A shabu-shabu place in Silverlake where you had to know someone who knew someone who had the secret handshake to get you in. An Argentinean steakhouse in Santa Monica run by a chef who'd escaped the country, one with a long waitlist Edward could bypass with money. A dessert shop in Los Feliz that was opened by a woman who'd studied under the next Gordon Ramsay, but then defected to do her own thing."

"Okay," I say, carefully, waiting for her to go on. I need to make sure she's not suggesting that I'm doing *that*.

"And I'd go with him. Put on pearls. A simple black dress. The sommelier would bring over a bottle of wine and uncork it, and Edward would swirl it, and say it'd be my new favorite. Then he'd tell me about his business trip to London or Singapore or Milan, and the deals he'd struck, and the stories he'd heard. The endless stories from the road. The international banker he'd met who'd just trekked across Nepal in a *life-changing journey*. The financier who'd climbed Kalymnos in Greece and experienced god," she says, with a derisive twist in her tone. "It was all just part of the deception."

Don't go there. Do not put me in the same breath as that scum. "That's not what I'm doing," I say, a warning in my voice.

"No, god no," she says, flustered, then she sets a hand on my forearm, wrapping her soft fingers around me—skin against skin since my cuffs are rolled up. "I know that's not what you're doing. This is so different. This is…" She dips her face, shakes her head. "I feel so selfish saying this."

"Say it," I urge.

She lifts her face, holding my gaze. "This is about me. All the things he did were about him," she says, a little awestruck.

"Good. This *is* for you. *This* is about you," I say. It saddens me that Rachel sets the bar so low. That she doesn't realize that considering your date's wants and wishes is a minimum standard.

But that's easy for me to say. I wasn't the one married to a cheating charlatan who kept another family on the side. Rachel already beats herself up for having been bamboozled by him. The least I can do is show her what respect and decency look like.

And how it feels, too, to sit across from a man who listens to a woman.

And, most of all, that she deserves that.

She squeezes my forearm harder. "I don't even know what to say except…thank you," she says.

"You're welcome," I say, hazarding a glance at her hand on my arm. Her eyes are a little glazed, as if she's a million miles away, but she strokes her thumb over the muscle. It's a dangerous path her fingers are traveling. She's zapping my body with endorphins, so I put on my game face, maintaining some stoicism even as my body crackles.

She lets go.

I miss her touch.

But it's probably for the best that she stopped turning me on with her damn thumb. Especially since Elodie has just arrived with a bright smile and two cups of spiked chocolate.

She sets the first one down in front of Rachel. "I call it Some Like it Hot."

"Nice name," Rachel says.

Elodie puts the other one in front of me. "This is With A Kick," she says. "And I'll be back soon with your special tasting."

Rachel grins again. "This is the red-carpet treatment."

"And you deserve it," I say. This is just baseline shit that a friend should do, let alone a man taking out a woman.

I lift my cup, knock it to hers, and drink up. The chocolate is rich and bittersweet, and the whiskey is good and strong. "Whoa. Elodie should, like, go into business selling chocolate."

Rachel drinks hers, then nods in agreement. "Let's tell her to open a shop."

"She might not have thought of it before, right?"

"It's only helpful to pass on a tip."

"We're like Career Doctors," I say.

I take another drink right as the guy at the table next to us looks up from his tablet, clears his throat, and says to his companion, "I heard about this new face lotion. It's made with Vitamin C. It firms up your skin."

"Are you saying I need to firm up my skin?" says his date.

"We all need to firm up our skin," he says.

With a smile she can't hide, Rachel dips her face, mouthing *he's a skin doctor*.

I whisper back, "That sounds filthy."

"Can't help it. I'm inappropriate."

"You're very inappropriate," I say.

She lifts her mug, takes another sip, then sighs contentedly. "I love chocolate."

"I know, Rachel. I know."

And I know that the feeling of being a dating king won't last. Focusing on Rachel is easy. Just like focusing on football is when I'm practicing or playing.

But that's not my issue with dating.

The issue is that the first date is just an illusion. It's supposed to feel good. It's supposed to seduce you. Then, before you know it, you're asking her to move in, and you're buying a ring, and bam. She's peeling out of town with her ten-thousand-dollar diamond and using it to start her new life.

It's not about the money. I don't need my ten grand back. But I also don't need the hassle or the hurt of a relationship.

Best to just enjoy this first-date feeling while it lasts. It'll vanish soon enough. Always has. Always will.

A few minutes later, Elodie returns with two identical sleek black trays, each with five kinds of chocolate. "Hand-selected by the chocolatier," she says, then points to each treat. "Each tray has…a pecan toffee, a champagne truffle, a chocolate square with dark caramel, an Aztec-spice bonbon with cinnamon, and an orange zest-infused square."

Rachel beams at her friend. "Can you arrange to have this sent to my home each morning? It's part of my new self-care routine. I'm going on a chocolate diet."

"Best diet ever," Elodie replies, then waves as she heads off. "Enjoy."

Don't need to tell me twice. "I think I will," I say, then reach for a chocolate.

But when Rachel grabs one too, my brain lights up like a Times Square marquee. "Stop!"

"What?" she asks, seeming worried.

More pleased than I have a right to be, I grab my phone. "Smile for the camera."

"Oh, right," she says with a laugh. "I was having such a good time I forgot."

"I didn't," I say, and when she blanches, I quickly add, "I meant I didn't *forget*. But I am having an excellent time."

"Good."

"And I'd better set a reminder to shoot a video the next time too," I say, and like that, her smile disappears, like a candle's gone out.

Mine flickers away too.

Because…my next date won't be with her.

Does she dislike that thought as much as I do? No idea, but it twists my gut for a few seconds. When I lift the phone to shoot the video, she grabs it from my hand. "No one wants to see me. They want to see the football stud falling for chocolate."

I arch a dubious brow. "I don't think that's a thing."

"Oh, it is. It definitely is," she says, a little flirty.

"Pretty sure that's not on any woman's dating profile —*Seeking pro baller who loves chocolate.*"

"Maybe it's on mine," she says.

"I'll check later and see."

"You do that. Now, eat it," she demands, and I pop the chocolate square with the caramel center into my mouth. It melts, and I moan. Obscenely. When I finish it, I breathe out a long, satisfied, "Wow."

She hits end, sets the phone down, then smiles at me like she's made a platinum jewelry sale. "It's like you had a chocolategasm."

I roll my eyes. "Yeah. That's it."

"And women will like it. You kind of made an O face."

I'd like to see your O face.

And on that wildly inappropriate thought, I try my hardest to divert all my attention to this date, not to images of Rachel's lips parting in pleasure, her back arching, her toes curling in bliss. That's way better than chocolate.

Snagging the phone, I click on the camera again, flipping it to selfie mode. "This series is all about great first dates, so let's be honest," I say to the camera. "A woman's enjoyment is the number-one thing that makes a date good."

I swivel the phone to angle on her. "Rachel, are you having a good time?"

With a seductive smile, she says, "The best." She pops the champagne truffle between those lush pink lips, then rolls her eyes in delight. "That is soooo good," she says, in pure, sensual praise. A woman aroused by chocolate.

This—right here—is peak dating goals. Not just the arousal, but the happiness gleaming in her eyes too.

As she takes another bite of the truffle, I try to remember the last time I saw her like this. Maybe before she met her husband? I don't even know. She wasn't unhappy when she was with Edward, but she was more buttoned up. More poised. When I'd see her out with the friend group during the five years that she was with him, she seemed a little like she was playing the part of Sophisticated Rachel.

Maybe that was who Edward wanted her to be. His poised, elegant wife.

Now, she's shedding that side of herself. She's a little silly, a lot flirty, and very dirty.

She's the woman who fell asleep at my place late one night after a party in our early twenties, then wandered blearily around in the early morning muttering *pancakes, pancakes, pancakes.* She said she'd been dreaming about pancakes. Then, she went to the kitchen and whipped up a fantastic batch of cinnamon-roll pancakes.

She's the Rachel who knocked on my door during my first year as a starter for the Renegades and said, "Congrats on your first reception. Now let's see if you can do the Cats with Careers puzzle in one evening."

I showed that 500-piece puzzle who was boss in two mere hours.

I record a few more seconds, but when I've got enough footage, I put the phone away and just enjoy the company.

We finish the chocolate together, praising each piece as we go. When we're done, I waggle my empty plate. "Want to lick it clean?"

"Don't tempt me. I will," she says, then sticks out her tongue and flicks it.

I bet she never did that with Edward. And since I am

a competitive fucker, I can't resist asking, "Scale of one to ten, how awesome is a chocolate café for a date?"

She taps her chin while staring at the ceiling, then says, "The Date Doctors give it one hundred."

"Better than an Argentinean steakhouse? A hot shabu-shabu place?" I ask.

"So much better," she says. "He bought me chocolate, but he never took me to a chocolate tasting."

That does not surprise me at all. But it still disgusts me. "He *never* deserved you," I say, even though I'm pretty sure she knows that already.

With a sad smile, she nods. "I know." She pauses then adds, a little resigned, "Lesson learned."

But man, that's a tough lesson all right. I wish I'd sniffed out the jerk sooner. Sensed it at the wedding and objected before she said I do instead of clapping when the happy couple walked down the aisle together, hand in hand.

Then again, even astute outsiders don't always see the signs. Monroe had thought Quinn was *good people*—those were his exact words after we all went to a baseball game together. Even Axel, who has the bullshit detector of a bloodhound, liked my ex when we all played poker on one of his visits. I loved her so much I thought I'd marry her. Then boom, see you later.

Still, an idea has sprouted in my mind, pushing determinedly up from the past. What if Rachel had never met Edward after we'd finished college? What if I hadn't ventured down the serial monogamy path several years ago? What if something else had happened six or seven years ago, the morning she muttered about pancakes when she slept over?

Settle down, man. Settle the fuck down.

Rachel's a friend and that's that. She was in my life way back when I was fifteen, and she'll be around when I'm thirty-five.

And Quinn is history. So is Edward.

There is no *what if*.

* * *

Soon we leave, thanking Elodie on the way out. We head over to Puzzle Nerds in Noe Valley to pick up the *One Mammal's Trash* puzzle.

On the drive back, I say, "Puzzle club? Next week? I'm pretty busy with practice and then we travel this weekend."

"Your game's in New York." she says, and I wonder if she knows my schedule by heart.

"It is. I can see you Tuesday though."

"It's a plan," she says.

A plan, not a date.

Too bad. That's just...a little too bad.

When I reach her home, I pull up to the curb, then cut the engine. For a split second, I debate my options—say goodbye here or hop out and walk her to the door.

It'd be easier for me if I stayed here in the car.

But it's nighttime in the city and that's douchey.

I get out and walk her to the steps. But I don't go up them. I'd want to kiss her too much if we got to the front door.

Great first dates have that effect.

* * *

Later, when I'm home alone, I'm restless. More restless than I usually am at the end of the day.

I'm wanting things I can't have.

Things I shouldn't have.

Things that could ruin this long-standing friendship.

When I flop into bed, I check my phone once more, out of habit, reviewing my calendar for tomorrow.

But something else tugs at my brain. Something more interesting. A distant possibility.

It's ridiculous, but I do it anyway, clicking over to Date Night.

When I open Rachel's profile, I smile stupidly over the words she's added.

Seeking pro baller who loves chocolate.

13

FUCK OFF, FLUTTERS

Rachel

On Sunday, I've got one eye on the TV screen as I grab the tray of nachos from the oven then set it on the kitchen counter with a loud, irritated *thunk*. Juliet and Elodie are in the living room, camped out on my couch, watching the game.

But I'm glued to it even as I move around my home.

"C'mon! That was pass interference," I shout at the officials across the country in New York. "You suck, ref."

From her spot on the couch, Juliet thrusts an arm in the air in solidarity. "You tell 'em, sis."

I stalk over to the TV screen and stab my finger at the instant replay, already showing the Leopards safety slamming an arm across Carter's chest while he tried to catch the ball. "See? PI. Big PI."

Elodie swirls her wine with a knowing look. "Yes, that was *big PI*, Rach," she parrots.

The TV coverage narrows in on the refs conferring. "Are you kidding me? This isn't brain science," I say to them. "You don't need to discuss it."

After taking five seconds too long to recognize the patently obvious, the head ref finally calls the foul. "Automatic first down," the guy in black and white stripes says.

Oh. What a surprise.

"Told you so," I say, parking my hands on my hips and…oops. I actually spat on the screen. But that's what sleeves are for. I use the end of mine to wipe it off.

When I turn around to head back to the kitchen, Elodie's still giving me those eyes as I go—the *I know what you're thinking* eyes.

"What're those for?" I ask, drawing a circle with my finger and pointing at her freckled face.

"You're just *extra-ish* today," she says as I scoop the nachos onto a plate at the counter. "Extra Carter-ish, to be clear."

Way to diagnose me.

Is it that obvious?

Well, it's been obvious to me too. Even the mention of his name right now makes my stomach flutter. My belly's been doing that a lot since that date five nights ago. My mind's been pretty busy today too. Since I woke up and went to a HIIT class at the gym down the street, it's been swirling with absurd ideas. Ones I definitely should not utter out loud. Ones I shouldn't even entertain in my head.

I vowed to focus on our friendship, after all. I've done that quite nicely this last week. I've even abstained from getting off to thoughts of him, instead using a generic Hemsworthian hottie in my fantasies. Sort of like an AI man of my dreams.

"Just like I've done since high school," I say, reminding them of the score with Carter and me as much as reminding myself.

We are friends. Just friends. That is all.

Fuck off, flutters.

I bring the plate of yummy, cheesy goodness back to my crew, setting it on the coffee table in front of the couch. The TV screen is against the wall that's next to the bay window, since I didn't want to block the view that Carter helped make possible the other week. On Boob Day, to be exact.

"Yes, everything with the two of you is *just* like it was in high school," Elodie says as the tense game goes into a commercial.

Juliet scoops some olives, cheese, and guac onto a chip, then eggs me on with a drawn out, "Sooo. What's going on with you two?"

Nothing. But lately I've been having this crazy idea about the four first dates he still has to go on...

I'm too afraid to voice my wild ideas though. Maybe I'd just sound foolish, even to my friend and my sister. I don't trust my instincts enough to know if what I've been thinking is normal or wackadoodle. Actually, I don't trust my instincts at all. "There's nothing to tell," I say.

Elodie coughs. "Bullshit."

"Need more wine, Els?" I ask innocently.

"C'mon, Rach. He rolled out all the stops for you at my store," she says. "He arranged that whole date *for you*."

This isn't the first time Elodie and I have discussed the chocolate date. She texted me the next day to say **You looked so happy last night**, then she added **Also, you two looked like a couple.**

I'd replied with **We aren't!**

"The date was amazing. But it was *entirely platonic*," I say, then bite into a chip, finishing it before I add, "Something he made quite clear when he asked me out on it. It was for Date Night. You know he has this sponsorship with them."

"Yes, I see him all over the app," Juliet says breezily while snagging another chip.

What? Like, hitting on women? A hot burst of jealousy flares through me, chased by red-hot irritation. Is he messing around with women on the app? Is he lying to me? Like Edward did?

My heart spins like a washing machine off-kilter. "What do you mean? Like you can see him flirting or something? Can you tell who he swipes on? Is he going on dates? What can you see?"

I'm desperate to know since I barely understand how apps work these days. I used them in college and for a few years after, but I didn't even meet Edward online. I was a retail buyer for jewelry at a big department store, and he was one of the company's bankers. I've been off apps for more than seven years. A lifetime in modern dating.

Juliet laughs gently. "No, grandma. You can't *see* him flirting or talking to anyone. That's not how apps work."

Oh. Right. Of course. But he *could* be talking to other women.

Of course he is. He owes his sponsor four more dates. Unless...

"Sure, right. I knew that," I say, then grab my merlot since wine doesn't make me feel stupid. I do that well enough on my own.

"But I saw the videos he did with Quinn on Date Night a couple years ago, and now there are all these 'five great first date' ads running," Juliet continues, twirling a strand of brown hair with a free hand. "And obviously there's the video of you two from the date."

Of course I knew that. He showed the video to me before he posted it a couple days ago. I even approved it. But now I can't stop thinking about him using the app to talk to women. My eye is twitching.

My sister's lips curve into a *gotcha* grin. "Oh my god, you're sooo into him," she says, then reaches for a nacho triumphantly.

"No," I say, trying desperately to cut that notion off. "Not like that."

"Then like what?" Elodie asks pointedly.

"I'm not into him like anything," I say, and I'm saved by the game, since the action on the screen returns to first down.

I stare intensely at the TV. As I crunch hard on chips, I pour all my focus into the game, only the game, as the Renegades quarterback hands off to Malik Hamlin. The running back hustles downfield, evading first one tackle, then another as Carter blocks for him. Malik's finally knocked down but after he nabs another first down. Carter offers him a hand and yanks him up, then they smack palms. I cheer. A few plays later, Carter easily sails across the end zone on a short pass.

"Yes!" I shout.

He smacks palms with his quarterback in the end zone, then he rips off his helmet as he trots to the sidelines. His grin is pure exuberance. The thrill of a job well done. A bead of sweat slides down his brow and his eye black is smudged. He high-fives his teammates.

I smile stupidly.

"You sure seem like you're *not* into him," Elodie says dryly.

"It was a platonic date," I insist. The more I say it, the quicker these flutters I get as I stare at the gorgeous, sexy, totally built stud on the screen will stop. I hope. I really hope.

"Sure," Elodie adds with a *whatever you say* nod. "I see a lot of men who roll out all the stops on platonic dates."

"For a sponsor," I add. "A sponsor. Let me remind you of what he said to me when he asked me on said platonic date." I clear my throat, then adopt a masculine tone as I repeat Carter's words. *"I don't want to go anywhere near a real date, so my agent is getting it all sorted for me to do five first dates. And it'll be way easier for me if you and I could do the first one. As friends."*

I mime dropping a mic.

Juliet frowns.

Elodie sighs.

Then my sister grabs a couch pillow and tosses it on

the floor like a petulant child. "Thanks for ruining my Sunday."

Elodie slumps deeper onto the couch. "And to think I was going to live vicariously through you."

"I was too," Juliet puts in.

"Aww, my poor little single friends. We'll just have to stick together," I say, then I side-eye my sister next to me. "But you're actually on the apps, Juliet. Why do you need to live through me?"

Her gaze sears me. "Have you seen my dating track record?"

Fair point, since I have and it's not pretty. But neither is mine. "Yes, and may I introduce you to the woman who got hoodwinked by her hubs?" I ask with a fake-ass smile. "Oh, speaking of, I really should send Edward a baby gift for his newborn. His *third* child. The man impregnated his girlfriend *three times* while he was married to me." A hot rush of shame washes over me again. I was such a fool. The day I learned he'd been cheating, I felt like I'd been hit by a wrecking ball. I was at the store in Venice, doing inventory, when a customer I'd become friends with sent me a text saying, "Looks like your husband's doppelgänger is here in Palm Springs!"

A seemingly innocent text had opened the floodgates. Only it wasn't Edward's identical twin. It was Edward and the mother of his children, enjoying a playdate in the desert on the swings. The other woman wore a T-shirt with roses on it.

That was where he'd been going on all those business trips. To see his other family a couple hours down the coast. The rose necklace he'd given me suddenly made too much sense. The rose necklace had been meant for her. She was the rose lover.

The wrecking ball doesn't wallop me like it did then, but even more than a year later, the aftershocks of heart, hurt, and humiliation ricochet through me.

I swallow down the ache and stay strong here with my sister and my friend. "I am never dating again. I am never falling in love again. I am going to marry my vibrator and have battery-operated children with it." It's a declaration of singletude.

Juliet squeezes my arm. Elodie rests her head on my other shoulder.

"I'll help raise my vibrator nieces," Juliet offers.

"Thank you," I say, pouting, but grateful. Then I try to shake it off. *It* being the shame, and the flutters.

But when the camera on screen pans in on eighty-eight again as he pulls a cap down over his hair, little brown waves sticking out, I can't shake off the wild idea that's been dogging me lately.

I just can't.

Maybe I need to give it breath.

And this is a safe space. Elodie and Juliet are my people. "I need to tell you an idea I've had," I say as the Leopards take possession.

Their gazes whip to me. "What is it?" Juliet asks, wide-eyed.

"It's a little wild. We should enlist Hazel," I say.

"Obviously," Elodie seconds, and in no time, she's ringing up our redheaded friend in New York on FaceTime.

"Well, to what do I owe the honor of the assembly?" Hazel says from my phone.

"This might be crazy…"

Hazel's green eyes twinkle. "The best ideas always start with *this might be crazy*."

But this idea also seems…smart and useful and, strangely, safe. "So, Carter owes Date Night four more dates," I say, then I tell them what I'm thinking.

To my surprise, they don't say I've lost my mind.

The answer is a unanimous *go for it.*

* * *

When I go into the store the next day, there isn't a line around the block. But there are a few more customers than I've been used to. And I could get used to this uptick in traffic.

Maybe, if I'm lucky, I can drive even more.

14

VERY BRAID-ABLE HAIR

Rachel: I'm on my way! Walking and texting.

Carter: I could have picked you up, Sunshine.

Rachel: A girl needs to get her steps in. Did you get ten million in already today?

Carter: Twelve million.

Rachel: Show-off.

Carter: Well, you asked.

Rachel: Do you want me to get food?

Carter: We'll order something when you get here. I have the puzzle, but Date Night just reached out and wants us to answer comments from the video if that's cool with you. Guess you were a hit.

Rachel: Um, you were.

Carter: Yeah, pretty sure there are Date Night fans of you. I read some of them already and there were comments about your hair thingy.

Rachel: My hair thingy?

Carter: When you did that hair-flip thing, then it was all up and clipped and kind of sexy.

Rachel: The French twist?

Carter: That. Yes. It got a lot of comments.

Rachel: They were commenting on my hair?

Carter: You have nice hair, Rachel.

Carter: You just do.

Carter: Someone said she wanted to braid your hair.

Rachel: Really? Really???

Carter: Does this surprise you?

Rachel: Do the triple question marks not make it clear how surprised I am? No one has ever said they wanted to braid my hair before.

Carter: You have very braid-able hair.

Carter: It looks nice right now too. Down, just like that, all swishing around your shoulders.

Rachel: I see you in the window next to Jane. Looking at me :)

Carter: Busted.

15

JACKASS COUCH

Carter

If you think about it, couches are the most dangerous pieces of furniture.

Take the bed, by contrast. You know what you're getting into with that one—sleeping or fucking.

Then there's the simple chair. It's commonly used for sitting, but every now and then you can bend a woman over the back of it for a good, hard banging. Mostly, it's a landing pad for clothes you haven't yet put away.

A couch though?

Man, those are the shapeshifters of the furniture world, and they mess with you. Sometimes it's a place to hang with your buds while you battle zombies at the end of the world with your game console.

But right now? It's a jackass.

I'm parked on this silver-gray couch cushion inches

away from Rachel on Tuesday night, catching the scent of her orange-blossom lotion, or shampoo, or perfume, or bodywash like it's a wave I want to ride over and over.

We're huddled together, checking out Date Night comments on my phone. Does this couch have it out for me? Is it testing me? Like, *hey, motherfucker, try to figure out what to do on me right now that you're this close to the woman you want.*

Rachel points a polished sky-blue nail at the little screen. "Look at that one," she says, and I linger my attention a second longer on her finger, even though that's not what she's drawing my attention to. But she has pretty hands, and I'm imagining how they'd look up above her head if I pinned her wrists like, say, on this couch. If I moved her underneath me.

Let me revise my description of the sofa. This couch is a demon.

I try to blink off the dirty thoughts, focusing on the task as I home in on the comments on our first-date video.

SanFranDude3 writes: ***Thanks, Carter. Really appreciate you showing us all up. Like any dude can live up to this now.***

"Aww, poor guy," I say in mock sympathy, then I scroll down to read a reply to him from a woman.

Because picking up your date, taking her to a chocolate shop, then listening to her is hard? Oh, wait. It is for most guys. You all need to learn how to date.

"Burn," Rachel says, then turns to me with a satisfied

smile. "Look at you, just showing up all the men out there."

"Not my fault that some dudes fail at romance. I am not to blame."

"Exactly," she says, then grabs the phone and shimmies her shoulders. "I'll reply."

She taps out a comment. *Is Carter showing up these guys? Or giving them the secret code for how to date?*

I raise an eyebrow at her written reply. "Is that what I did?"

"Kind of," she says, then nibbles on the corner of her lips, looking like she's weighing something. Like she's about to speak. Instead, she waggles the screen at me. "I mean, look at this comment."

OMG he's the best boyfriend.

I scoff-laugh. Not sure that's true at all. "I'd have to disagree."

"I don't know," she says then takes a beat, getting that look in her eyes again. The one that says something's on her mind. "You were kind of boyfriend goals the other night, and that got me thinking…"

"About what?" I ask, trying to play it cool while inside I'm hoping she's thinking about sex, and more sex, and still more sex, then returning to friendship.

Shit. Does that even work? Can you fuck and then be friends again?

I don't know. I should shut down those wild thoughts. They're the jackass couch's fault. Orange blossom's responsible too, dammit.

But that look in her eyes right now? A hint of

mischief mixed with hope. Maybe she's on the same sex wavelength I am.

Another beat. Another breath, then she adds, "So, the other night while I was watching your game I got this crazy idea."

Does it involve me stripping you naked and kissing you everywhere till you moan and writhe and beg for my mouth on your pussy?

I'm sure that's the worst thing possible for our friendship, but my brain is locked in on that. "Hit me up," I say, my voice rusty with desire.

She sets down the phone as if she wants to turn all her attention my way, but she's had mine from the second she walked up the block.

"I was thinking this before I read the comments, Carter," she begins. "Because I really did enjoy that date with you. And it made me realize I don't know what it's like to date. *For real*. When a man actually cares," she says, and oh shit. I need to stop the sex train since Rachel's clearly not traveling to Dirty Town. She's heading to Emotional Shores, and I respect that. I do. "I mean, everything with Edward was a lie. But then with you…it was all so new and kind of wonderful. And I was hoping that you could give me…girlfriend lessons?"

I have no idea what that is. Like, is she asking me for bedroom tutorials? A fake date? Something else? "What does that mean exactly?"

"I know it sounds crazy, but I just want to know…" she stops and takes a steadying breath, "…how a man is supposed to treat a woman when they go out. So when I said, 'girlfriend lessons,' I was going to ask if you could take me on those four additional dates you owe Date Night, as friends, and just kind of show me how a man treats a woman." Her voice pitches up, full of hope and anticipation.

I hesitate. Do I want to take Rachel out on dates as friends? Like *un-dates*? Spending more time like we're together sounds like it's going to test all my resolve.

But the look in her eyes right now is priceless. Her words from moments ago echo in my ears. *I don't know what it's like to date. For real. When a man actually cares.* And when she puts it like that, I can't say no to her. I want her to have everything good in the world. "Yes. I'd love to."

She claps. She *actually* claps in excitement. "I was even thinking maybe Date Night could call it *How to Date*. Like the comments said. It could be the How To Date series. Do you really think they'd go for it?"

She sounds so eager that I do the only thing I can. I call my agent on speakerphone right then and tell him the idea.

Maddox listens intently then asks, "Like, what to wear on a date? What to talk about on a date—that kind of thing? Where to go?"

Rachel nods vigorously. "Yes, exactly. What to do, how to have a great date. Some of us have no idea, but I can do lots of research and pick some fun places and things to do," she says, then rattles off some options.

She really has thought this through.

"Can you make that happen instead of five first dates?" I ask Maddox.

There's no hesitation from him. "I'll call them right

now. But consider it done," he says, then I say goodbye and hit end.

"Boom. I'm the date doctor," I say dusting one palm over the other.

"You're the best," Rachel says, with obvious relief and excitement. "I thought you were going to laugh at my crazy idea."

Oh, hell.

I was thinking about boning her and all she wants is someone to be good to her.

"I swear I'll be the best platonic boyfriend ever," I say, meaning it.

But I'm also cursing the couch for what it just got me into.

* * *

Ten minutes later, Maddox emails the good news. Date Night loves our plan and Zena wants to have dinner soon. Rachel and I order Thai food to celebrate—the Date Night love, not the pending dinner meeting. When the food arrives, we eat at the kitchen counter because I refuse to sit on the jackass couch with her any longer.

I am not that strong.

Not that good.

We will eat, and then I will drive her home, and then I'll jerk off, and then tomorrow I will start my first-ever cleanse.

A dirty thought cleanse.

"I came up with some ideas. Now, I hope it's okay if I

don't want to do some fancy new restaurant as a date," she says.

"Too Edward," I say. "I get it."

"Exactly. But there are so many other things we can do. Like, what if we went to a farmers' market for a date?" Rachel says as she scoops up a spicy eggplant chunk with chopsticks. "Because I was researching dates and that came up, but I have no idea how to go on a date at a farmers' market. I mean, do you?"

Well, yeah.

That's sort of a thing these days. But is it rude to say that to her? I don't want her to feel worse about her lack of dating savvy. Honesty is probably the best policy though. "Yes, I've been on them," I say. "With Quinn, and then with Sasha before. Even Izzy."

Smooth, real smooth. Why not go a little further down Ex-girlfriend Lane?

I take a bite of pad Thai to shut the fuck up.

"Good. Because I love farmers' markets, but I don't think I'd know how to go on a date at one," she says, seeming entirely unfazed by the mention of my exes. It's just part of our friendship history, after all.

But she also sounds excited, and I key in on her enthusiasm since it raises a really good question. After I finish the noodles, I swallow some water, then say, "Does this mean you're going to start dating for real? Like when we're done?"

As soon as I ask, I feel like I'm being strangled by a python.

She snort-laughs, shaking her head. "God no." She shudders too. But then, after a deep breath, she says, "I just...want to know. For someday. Way down the road." She sets down her chopsticks, her guileless eyes meeting mine. "Not now, not tomorrow, not anytime soon, but someday I really would like to be in love. For real. When it means the same thing to both people."

My heart lurches. "I want that for you," I say.

My best friend wants love. When we finish eating and she asks if I'd like to watch a show, I say yes. I'm not ready for the night to end.

She returns to the couch, and I grab my laptop and find a new episode of *Privilege* on Webflix.

At least it's not a romance. Near the end of the hour-long episode, when the broody lead, Bryan, is taking out his trash, and the shadows turn dark and foreboding, Rachel whips her gaze to me. "I bet his next-door neighbor turns out to be his new boss, who's spying on him," she whispers.

Damn, that's brilliant. But I'm good at games too, so I add, "And Bryan will say, *I didn't see you there*."

Five seconds later, Bryan startles, then says to the man, "I didn't see you there."

I laugh, then we knock fists. "Now we're the script doctors."

When the episode ends and the screen offers us another, Rachel nods. She settles deeper into the couch, and soon, very soon, as Bryan confronts his boss, her eyes fall closed and her breathing evens out.

I watch her longer than I should but exactly as long as I want to. I just can't look away. Her shoulders rise and fall gently, her hair spills around her face, and she seems content.

Like she got what she wanted tonight—girlfriend lessons from a man who can treat her right.

But I still want to slide my body against hers and kiss her every-fucking-where.

Which means…I need to take care of one more thing before I begin the dirty thought cleanse.

Quietly, I get up from the couch, put a blanket over her, then dim the lights as I head to my bedroom.

16

THE SHOWER SHOW

Rachel

Ow.

My underwire is digging into me.

I fumble around in the dark, plucking at my evil bra as I push up onto an elbow. The button on my jeans is bugging me too, and I'm about to undo it and go back to sleep, but I'm twisted around in this blanket, and…ohhh.

I fell asleep on my couch again. I've been doing this a lot lately. Conking out on the couch. But then I can never get back to sleep in my bed.

I will stay sleepy, dammit. I will successfully transfer my tired ass to my bed.

With a monster yawn—this is good, this is so good— I sit up, then shove this tangled blanket off me. I can barely keep my eyes open as I stand.

Rubbing my eyes, I trudge across my dark living

room in my socks, head to my bedroom, and push open the door. Just need to get these stupid clothes off, then I'll crash into my pillows.

Don't even care about my makeup. I'll wake up with a raccoon face. Whatever.

I pull off my shirt and toss it on the floor as I go to the bed, then I unbutton my jeans, unzipping them too. As another yawn wallops me, I stop at the foot of the mattress, peeling my jeans down, my eyes fluttering closed, when I hear falling water.

I freeze at the sound, my jeans at my ankles, my head flipped over, my hands on the denim I'm removing.

That's the sound of…the shower.

From this weird upside-down pose, I peer around.

That's…Carter's king-size bed.

All at once, everything clicks into place. I fell asleep on *his* couch. I walked into *his* bedroom. And I'm feet away from *his* en suite bathroom.

Where he's taking a shower.

Because, holy smokes, from this vantage point, with the bathroom door half-open, I can see his naked legs.

Can he see me upside down, wearing my…what the hell panties am I wearing today? Oh, great. The red lace ones. They basically scream *I want a side of sex ed with my girlfriend lessons*.

I will never live this down after Boob Day.

Not only did I flash him my jugs, I sleepwalked into his bedroom while stripping to nothing.

Real smooth, Rachel.

Carefully, so I don't faceplant, I pull up my jeans in

slow-mo. When they're at knee level, I lift my face, and...

Whoa.

That's a hearty eye-full of mostly naked man in the bathroom mirror.

The vanity above his sink is wide enough, big enough, thoughtful enough to offer me a view into the rainfall shower.

I knew Carter was built, but I didn't know he looked like he could star in an artsy sports magazine photo spread of naked athletes, the kind where you can see strong bodies in motion but no *parts*. I can't see anything truly risqué since he's turned slightly away from the mirror. As I inch up my jeans more, my eyes devour the somewhat chaste shower scene, cataloging the droplets of water caressing his golden skin, his thick thighs, his strong calves, and the side of his ass.

He has a great ass, and I can't stop staring at it. It's strong, and firm, and what would it feel like to grip that ass as he fucked me? To wrap my legs around his ass as he drove into me?

That's it. I'm officially a voyeur. A shower voyeur. I have to stop. You're not supposed to wander into your friend's bedroom, peek in the half-open door to the bathroom, and steal glances as he bathes.

Get it together.

I hold my breath as I pull my jeans up the rest of the way, trying not to peek in the mirror.

But once I find the zipper of my jeans, I realize I'm failing. I'm still staring at Carter's ridiculously sexy reflection.

I'll just grab my discarded shirt, tug it on in a hot second, then skedaddle. Quietly, I tiptoe a few feet to grab my long-sleeve top, then gasp. I slam my hand to my mouth to swallow the noise.

He's not just gloriously naked and washing up.

He's deliciously X-rated and jerking off.

Carter gives his hard cock a long, sturdy tug. I purse my lips tight to vacuum seal up all the lascivious groans building in my chest. With the shirt in my hand, I slink back against the doorframe, my spine to the wall. I'll just get dressed here and then go home.

Where I will fuck my vibrator for the rest of the night and into the eternity of my dirty thoughts.

But my gaze is still stuck on the scene in the mirror.

That's a very confident hard-on. Long, thick, and— I can't believe I'm thinking this because dicks by nature aren't pretty; they're funny-looking, dangly things—but Carter's dick isn't simply big. It's beautiful.

It's hypnotizing me. I'm some kind of cartoon character, caught in a trance.

I want that hand to be my hand so badly.

My head swims. My thighs shake.

I have to snap out of this. Quietly, I stick my left arm into the sleeve. I don't want to utter a sound. I'll be dressed in a jiff, then I'll go before...

Oh fuck. He's sliding his fist down the head, squeezing it.

I squeeze my thighs, like that'll ease the exquisite ache in my center. I pull on my shirt and turn around, jeans still unzipped. But once I take a step to go, a long, guttural moan greets my ears. Then, a panting of his breath, that unfurls into a word.

And a revelation.

It's a word I've heard my entire life, and it changes the score.

I can't move. I can't leave. I'm lit up. Crackling from that wonderfully familiar, two-syllable name. Over my shoulder, I steal one last peek.

He's fucking his left hand so ferociously that he slams his right palm against the shower wall.

This is the hottest thing I've ever seen.

He's so turned on, he needs to hold onto the wall as he jerks. His hand flies along his length in a savage blur.

He's all urgency, all purpose as he strokes, his breath coming fast.

Then, there's a bitten-off moan and that word once more as he grunts, "Fuck, Rachel. Yes…"

He shudders. Coming in his hand.

To. Me.

While I've been trying to quietly get dressed and go, he's been jerking off to me. *The entire time*.

My body ignites like a rocket about to launch. I'm buzzing with lust and longing. But when Carter reaches for the faucet, my reason reactivates. Somewhere in the midst of all these hormones, a voice says *get the fuck out*.

I spin around and race out of his bedroom, shutting the door behind me, then stop in the living room in a panic as the water shuts off in the shower.

Do I stay or go? Grab my things and take off? It's too late to walk, and I'd need to call a Lyft.

The car wouldn't arrive for a few minutes. In that

time, Carter will probably have pulled on shorts and a T-shirt, then walked out here to say goodbye to me.

If he comes out here, I'll have to see him when I'm like...*this*.

With my body vibrating with lust. With my cheeks flush with desire. With my panties soaked. And with the lie on my tongue—*oh hey, just woke up, totally didn't just watch you jerk off to me.*

I can't face him right now. But I can't leave his home either.

I'm stuck here until he goes to sleep. Then, I can slip out without him seeing how aroused I am.

I dive for the couch, burrow under the thin blanket, and zip my jeans at last. Then I curl around the pillow and get back in position.

I shut my eyes.

But all I can see is the reel of my brand-new fantasy.

Carter's hand on his cock. Over and over and deliciously over again.

I squirm.

I need to stop squirming.

I'm asleep. I'm asleep. I'm asleep.

A few minutes later, I'm still wide awake but pretending to sleep as the sound of footsteps grows louder. Then closer and inevitably closer.

Can he tell I'm faking it? Does he know I watched him get off? Is it obvious I'm still outrageously turned on?

I'm intensely aware that he's in the living room, standing by the back of the couch.

A blanket lands softly on my shoulders, then my whole body. He's covering me with a bigger comforter.

And…it smells like him.

I'm dead.

Just dead.

"Night, Sunshine," he whispers into the darkness.

His footsteps retreat, the bedroom door creaks shut, and I'm alone in the moonlight on his couch.

I faked him out.

And now I'm surrounded by the clean, soapy scent of him, and the inescapable images.

Most of all by the raspy, throaty sound of his voice reverberating in my head.

Rachel.

I count to ten. To one hundred.

I hope he's asleep.

I really hope so.

But I can't wait anymore.

I shove my hand down my jeans, desperately seeking relief. I'm ludicrously wet.

My body sings its *thank you*.

I need this so badly. Quickly, I stroke myself, my fingers rewarding my hungry clit. Sparks fly under my skin, and the relief is so palpable, I nearly cry.

I replay the shower over and over.

His hand flying. His hips pumping. His ass flexing.

But most of all, above everything else, I let the loop play of him muttering my name. *Twice.*

My orgasm slams into me without warning, shaking my whole body. Inside, I'm shouting and crying out, screaming his name. But in reality, I'm silently aching for him as I come.

It's not till the orgasm subsides and the tingles slink away that I fully register what this means.

He wants me as much as I want him.

17

LEFT-HANDED NIGHT CREAM

Rachel

The friendly, freckled woman in the tortoise-shell glasses is asking me a question. She sticks out her hands, showing me two bangles. "Gold? Or rose gold?"

I remind myself I'm in my shop, and peer at the gold on the customer's left wrist, then the rose gold on her right wrist.

Left, right.

Right, left.

Good question…

Is Carter left-handed? I'd always thought he was right-handed. He eats with his fork in his right hand, but he jerks off with…

I snap up my gaze and meet her eager gray eyes. "Left," I say quickly, then blink away my mistake. "I meant, right. Rose gold is very you. With your coloring."

"Oh, good. I was leaning that way too," she says, then nods resolutely, removing the gold one and keeping the other. "I'll take it."

"Great. I'll ring that up for you," I say, then grab my tablet, forcing my focus right here, right now, and not on last night. "Are you having a good day?" I ask, making small talk as I enter the bracelet's info.

"I am. Thanks for asking. You?"

Great, if great means I'm carrying the weight of the most salacious secret and it's driving me wild. I can barely concentrate, and I'm half-aroused as I walk around helping customers like you, AND I HAVE NO IDEA WHAT TO DO, SO CAN YOU HELP ME PLEASE?

"Fantastic," I answer with a big grin, then tell her the amount, and she taps the tablet screen with her phone. After a thanks and a goodbye, she takes off.

I breathe a loud sigh of relief. I survived another customer encounter without blurting out *the wildest thing happened to me last night, and can I tell you every dirty detail of the time I was dick-notized? We can workshop next steps together, pretty please.*

I swear it's a goddamn miracle I've been able to work at all today given the state of my mind. I've toyed with texting my girlfriends the details, but they know Carter. Sharing what I stumbled into last night with anyone feels like crossing a line, so I've been holding the secret inside all day, and it wants to come out.

A throat clears. I turn to Fable, a few feet away. Her copper hair frames her face as she fixes the clasp on a pendant with a mini plier. "You're so cheery today,

Rachel. Want me to let Ava know you've got all the good vibes now?"

I laugh to make light of my obvious extreme horniness. I mean, my extreme happiness that's covering up my extreme horniness. "Yeah, please let my former *benefactor* know."

Then, I valiantly try my best to stop thinking about last night for the rest of this—okay, let's start small—this minute.

A few seconds later, the door tinkles and a woman about my age walks in. She strides right up to me like she knows me.

Shoot. Is this a friend of Ava's sent to rip me apart? Can you say *online review PTSD?*

"Hi. Let me know if I can help you with anything," I say brightly, hoping she's not from the spa posse.

"I need something for a date," she says, then giggles like she has a secret. "The kind of thing you wore on the date last week."

I startle, then connect the dots. "Really?"

"Yes, that combo was fire," she says. "I'm going to wear my hair up too."

Fable strides over, pride in her eyes. "Rachel looked good that night at the chocolate café, didn't she? She kind of had a glow about her."

The woman nods excitedly at Fable, then turns to me. "Looks like you still do."

I lift a hand to touch my cheek. My skin feels warm. Is it obvious to her, too, that I've been thinking naughty thoughts?

"We had fun," I say, noncommittal, as I smile to hide the words threatening to burst free from my soul.

I walked in on my best friend last night, and I didn't walk away TILL HE FINISHED. Now, please buy a necklace to fund my vibrator collection.

"I hear you'll be doing it again," she says.

Watching him jerk? I'd love to. "You did?" I ask carefully.

"I saw on the app earlier today that you're doing a whole how-to series. I can't wait," she says.

Wow. Date Night moves fast.

"I'll be watching the rest of them," she adds, then studies my face for a second. "You know, you do kind of have a glow. I would love to get the name of your face cream."

"Secret cream," I blurt out.

Fable turns to me. "What? Is that a new brand?"

God, my mouth is a traitor. I need to shut the eff up. "I mean it's called Secret Night Cream," I say, but that really isn't any better. "I think the company is called Left-Handed Dreams. But let me check when I get home."

The customer quirks a curious brow. "That's an interesting name."

"Well, you know, it's hard to find an original name these days," I say breezily.

"True, that," she says, then leaves.

Fable shoots me a look that calls bullshit. "Left-Handed Dreams? What's up with you today?"

I was a bad girl last night and spied on my friend, and now I'm cursed to never stop thinking about my best friend's dick. Also, NEXT TIME I SEE HIM, WHAT DO I DO WITH MY EYES?

"Just feeling all the good vibes today," I say.

She's skeptical as she says, "If you say so."

She returns to her work, and I'm about to return to mine when my phone buzzes with a text.

I take it out and see Carter's name. My pulse spikes in excitement, and I decide I'd better read his text in the back of the store. "I'll be right back," I tell Fable, then duck into my tiny office and shut the door.

My heart races as I open the message.

> Carter: Date Night is already promoting this How To Date series. Guess we should figure out when the next date is and what we're doing? You're in charge, Sunshine.

I start to write back, but another text lands before I'm done. He's on a roll.

> Carter: P.S. I just got off the field from practice. Coaches worked us hard today. I'll be working out with the guys for a while, but I'm free tonight if you want to plan date-y things.

> Carter: Also, you're such a bad girl.

Shit. He knows. He's about to bust me.

My heart beats in a wild frenzy. But it's best to play it cool. If he's going to bring a well-deserved penance on me, I'll make him spell it out. I'm not serving up my sins.

> Rachel: I am? Any reason?

Please don't say THAT reason. It was only like a minute of bad. I swear. Okay, maybe two. BUT YOU SAID MY NAME! TWICE! I WANTED TO RSVP!

> Carter: Because you keep distracting me. We never did that puzzle. Clearly you're afraid of my puzzle prowess, so the only solution is for you to bake me some brownies tonight and I will take you on.

I let out a huge sigh. "Thank god," I mutter.

He doesn't know what I did. But it's also a good thing I opened these messages back here in my tiny office. Because I am on fire from the *you're in charge* to the *got off* to the *take you on*.

Yes, Carter, take me on. Take me anywhere. Just take me.

The thing is…he's up for girlfriend lessons but I

don't know if that means he's up for bedroom practice too.

I'm pretty sure I am. One night—what's the harm? I really want him. I don't think I can fight it anymore. Especially now that I know he thinks of me that way too.

Except I need to be certain. I need to know if he's truly into *me*. Maybe he has a spank bank of friends he cycles through—I don't know. Maybe he jerks it to lots of different ladies, and my number just came up in the rotation last night. Maybe my name moaned into the night means nothing.

Thanks to Edward, I have no clue what's normal. I never walked in on Edward whacking it to his other woman. Or to me, for that matter.

When I see Carter this evening, I won't let on about last night. I'll keep that little nugget to myself for a while longer. But maybe I *can* take the temperature of the situation. Feel him out while hedging my bets.

Hmm.

If I wanted to plan an *un*-date for tonight with an easy escape hatch, what would I do? I stare at the ceiling for a minute, running through options. I'm not a dating expert, but I've taken an immersion class these last few days, digesting dating how-to article after dating how-to article. I've learned that a gal needs an eject button.

After last night, I need to have my parachute ready to pull.

That means no wine. No dark corners. No low-lit rooms.

I've got it, thanks to his last text.

A smile forms, and I feel pretty clever. I will see his brownie offer and raise it.

> Rachel: Baking. Cookies. My place. Eight.

There is nothing sexy about milk and chocolate chip cookies. It's the perfect smoke screen.

* * *

That evening, I tie on my pink apron with black cartoon mustaches on it, courtesy of Juliet. She has a cat named Mustache, who has a mustache.

Now, I will wield this mustache apron like the disguise it is.

In my kitchen, I prep all the cookie ingredients, measuring the flour, white sugar, brown sugar, and baking soda. I set the vanilla on the counter, then two eggs, butter, the mixer, and a bag of chocolate chips. I preheat the oven. I grab my lucky spatula from the utensil drawer and place it next to the mixer.

There.

I'm ready for whatever tonight brings—cookies or cock.

But when Carter arrives ten minutes late, I'm not thinking above-the-waist thoughts.

Because I'm looking at his warm brown eyes and the

way they lock on my face. Then his mouth, curving in the slightest smile, like he's happy to see me.

I'm not thinking about his dick, because all I can think about are his soft, lush lips.

And how desperately I want to kiss him.

18

A DICK REVIEW

Carter

Call me a detective.

Rachel seems off tonight, and I'm adding up the clues.

First, when I came over to plan our dates, she was like a jack-in-the-box.

She swung open the door, then she gave me a kiss on the cheek like she was a cheerleader, all boppy and oh-so-friendly.

Now, as she slides a tray of cookies into the oven then sets the timer, she asks, "Can I get you a drink?" But she sounds like she's auditioning for the role of *bright and peppy server* on a new sitcom.

"Sure. I'm always up for a beer or a bubbly water."

She tilts her head. "Or milk? Milk goes well with cookies?"

Not sure I want to down a glass of milk. *For fun.* "A LaCroix would be great," I say.

"Great idea! Me too," she says, like she's just learned we're both from the same hometown and *OMG isn't that so cool.*

Yeah, I'm Inspector Poirot all right. Something is suspicious because Rachel likes wine, even with cookies.

She grabs two bubbly waters from the fridge then thrusts one at me. I take it then ask, "What's going on with you?"

Flicking a dollop of cookie dough off her apron bib, she looks away from me. "What do you mean?"

The question comes out pitchy.

As she pops open her can, I wave a hand at her. "You're kind of…off."

"Me?" She brings her free hand to her chest, like I could possibly be talking about anyone else.

"Yeah, you."

"I'm fine. Totally fine. Just a busy day. You know how it goes. Busy, busy, busy. Customers. Which is good. So good, right? Like yes, this is what I want. Customers!" She stops talking long enough to take a quick drink. "I mean, especially after the other week. And oh my god, did I ever tell you about that guy's wife?"

Holy shit, my head is spinning from the speed of her chatter. "The guy who left the dick review?"

She nods exaggeratedly then sets down the can on the counter with a loud clang. "Yes. His wife came in. It turns out she's the spa owner up the street, and she's basically my brand-new enemy. I told Hazel, and Hazel put her name on her whiteboard. You know about Hazel's whiteboard, right?"

What the hell? She's doing it again, spinning like a top. "I don't know about Hazel's whiteboard," I say, then lean against the kitchen counter, taking a drink as I try to figure out what's up with my friend.

Rachel motors around the kitchen, cleaning up baking supplies as she talks. She reminds me of me, keeping busy, doing something while her mind races—right along with her mouth. "She has this whiteboard where she writes down things that irritate her. People and places and events," Rachel says, and I try, I swear I try, to feign interest in Hazel's fucking whiteboard, but I don't care.

Because Rachel is not Rachel tonight.

She's like Rachel on helium. She's Rachel times ten servings of caffeine. And if there's one thing I know about Rachel, it's that she's a terrible liar.

Like that time our friend group went to a bonfire on Stinson Beach our senior year and stayed out too late. I dropped her off at her house an hour past curfew and took the fall. "My fault, Mr. and Mrs. Dumont. I forgot to set an alarm to leave on time. My bad," I said.

It was simple and believable, but then Rachel piled on. "And my phone has been like an alien lately. I swear, there's some strange Martian life form taking it over. Like, hello, alien. Why are you messing with the alarms on my phone too?"

Her parents were not fooled. They were pissed at me, too, for trying to cover for her.

What's she covering up now with her ramblings?

"So now the guy who left the dick review and the wife of the dick reviewer are on the board," she declares as she sets a mixing bowl in the sink with a flourish.

Oh, shit. I've got a sinking feeling about what's gotten into her. What if it's the girlfriend lessons? Is she getting cold feet now? I should point-blank ask her, but I need to figure out the best way to say it. Rachel's sensitive at the moment. Hell, she's always been sensitive. But she's particularly sensitive about romance stuff. I busy myself by grabbing a kitchen towel and wiping down the counter as she launches right into another tale of the whiteboard.

"And Axel was on there once," she says, then adds, "Your brother."

In case I've forgotten who he is.

But as I empty the crumbs into the sink, I'm no longer in the mood to guess. I had a hard practice. Coach worked us to the bone. Yeah, I love football, but it's also exhausting. I don't have endless energy, despite what some people think.

Besides, a good boyfriend would ask. And whether Rachel has changed her mind or not, I promised her I'd be an excellent platonic boyfriend.

Here goes.

As the timer beeps, and she removes the cookies, I run a couple of conversational plays in my head. Then, I flip a coin and pick one.

I set down the can. "Hey, Rachel?"

"Yes?" she chirps as she slides the next batch of cookies into the oven.

"Remember that time when you threw me a surprise birthday party when I turned twenty-five?"

She cringes as she sets a new timer. "Yes?"

"And you told me you were taking me to a rock-climbing gym for my birthday? You sent me a whole list of things I needed to bring. You said you even checked with the NFL and that rock-climbing gyms were allowed in player contracts?"

She covers her face with the oven mitt. "Don't remind me."

I step closer and tug on the cloth, so she's looking at me. "What's really going on? I thought we were going to talk about this whole girlfriend lessons thing and dates, and you've been going on about Hazel's whiteboard. Maybe you changed your mind. Maybe you didn't. But something's amiss, and if you want to know how a man who cares would handle that in his woman, here's how I would." I make sure she's meeting my gaze, then I add, gently but firmly, "Talk to me."

She gulps. Meets my gaze. Her lower lip wobbles as she puts the mitt on the counter.

Holy shit. Something is really wrong. I should have been more sensitive. "What is it?" I ask, a little alarmed.

She jerks her face away, toward the window in the living room.

"What happened? Did some fuckface leave another shitty review?"

She shakes her head. "No."

"Then what is it? You're freaking me out."

She lifts her face and draws a breath. "You're going to hate me. I'm so sorry. I can't believe I did this. I'm the worst friend ever," she says, her voice wobbly and worried.

And it's totally wrecking me. She *is* backing out of our four dates. This bothers me so much more than it should. "What happened? Just say it," I say, trying to be cool though I'm not.

I'm fucking annoyed.

"I watched you last night," she mutters, barely audible.

And I'm still clueless. "Watched me?"

"I woke up on your couch last night, and I walked into your bedroom. I thought I was at my home. I didn't realize I was there. It took me a minute to register that I'd fallen asleep at your place," she says, the words pouring forth like they're spewing from a geyser. "And I was taking off my clothes to get into bed, and it wasn't till I was in next to nothing and a few feet from your bathroom door that I realized where I was, and I saw…"

She stops. But I can connect the dots. Oh hell, can I connect them.

Maybe I should be embarrassed.

But I'm not.

I'm just not. Not about my body, my sex drive, my solo flights. Did I want her to find me in the shower? Now that I think about it, maybe some subconscious part of me did.

Maybe I've been wanting an opening with Rachel for longer than I've realized. Maybe this is it.

But I need her to be very clear about what happened last night. "What did you see, Rachel?"

Translation: how much did you see?

"Enough to do my own dick review."

Whoa. I thought she was going to say she walked away. But this? This is better. I'm a little hot under the collar as she powers on, adding, "I'm sorry. I had stripped down to my undies in your bedroom and was about to get in your bed, but when I realized where I was, I freaked out that you'd hear me, and get out of the shower, and then it would be the forget-my-boobs all over again," she says, and my brain is popping with delicious images—her in my bed, her in her lingerie, her, mere feet from me last night. "So I got dressed as quickly and quietly as I could, but I could see you in the mirror, and I should have just run off with my clothes. But I didn't know what to do. I was frozen, and I hope you'll forgive me, and I wasn't going to say a word, but I didn't know how to act tonight. I haven't known how to act all day."

I take a tentative step closer, wanting to set my hands on her shoulders but unsure if now's the moment. Instead, I say, "Breathe."

She takes one deep breath. Then another. "I'm so sorry," she adds.

But I'm not. I love a good mystery, and my mind will not let me do anything else till I assemble every single clue. "So you watched me the whole time?" I ask, my voice low and maybe a little dirty.

"Yes, but it was only for a minute. I'm sorry," she says again.

Fuck apologies. I want confirmation.

"You watched till I finished," I say.

"Yes," she says, sounding miserable. "The door was half open and I saw you in the mirror."

"And you couldn't look away," I say, and I do my damnedest to wipe the cocky grin off my face. I swear, I do. But it might sneak onto my face.

She looks at my face, her guilty amber-eyed gaze catching mine. Her breath speeds up. "I couldn't."

Fuck friendship right now.

I am a man who wants a woman. And that woman has revealed herself. "Why'd you watch me?" I ask, pressing, pushing.

Playing.

Her cheeks pinken. "I…liked it," she says, then closes her eyes, like she can't believe she's said that. When she opens them, those irises are no longer filled with apologies or guilt. They're flickering with sinful confessions. "It was sexy. It was hot. Really hot. I tried to look away. But I couldn't."

I'm sizzling everywhere. "What did you do when you went back to my couch and pretended to be asleep?"

She startles. "You knew I wasn't asleep?"

"Something seemed off then. You were too quiet. I didn't put it together till now." Smirking, I roll the dice. But this feels like a sure bet in this moment. "What did you do?"

She meets my gaze straight on. Squares her shoulders. Then whispers, "The same."

Yes. Fucking yes.

Rachel in the dark, under the blanket, playing with her pussy while I was in my bedroom, hard again, horny again. Wanting. Wishing.

One room away, she was touching herself.

I'm aching to haul her into bed right now. But I will take my time with this gorgeous, fragile, incredible woman. I will make sure she knows what she does to this man. That's what she signed up for. That's what she wants. Girlfriend lessons. And if there's one thing I know, it's this—a man should treat his woman right both out of bed and *in* bed.

"When you played with yourself, what were you thinking?" I ask.

"About you," she says in a feather of a voice. "All I thought of was you."

I'm more than hot under the collar. I'm a forest fire. "What else? Did you think about the way I said your name when I came?"

She gasps, a sexy sound that turns into a shudder. "I did," she whispers.

"Tell me something else, Sunshine."

"Yes?" Her voice trembles.

"Did you come hard? When you were on my couch and I was in my bed, trying to sleep but failing because I was still fucking turned on? Did you come hard thinking about me getting off to you in the shower?"

She nods savagely. "I did."

I don't fight the cocky grin now. I don't fight it at all. It takes over my filthy soul. "Can I kiss you?"

With hopeful eyes and an eager grin, she gives an answer. "Only if it doesn't stop at kissing."

That feels like a whole new kind of girlfriend lesson. And Rachel can enroll me right now.

19

PROPORTIONALISM

Carter

Since the day I moved her couch, I've thought about kissing Rachel countless times.

Hell, I've run this scenario in my head and tried to erase it from my mind too.

But not once did I imagine I'd kiss her for the first time under the bright fluorescent lights of her kitchen while she was wearing a mustache apron and smelling like vanilla and chocolate chips.

There's a first time for everything, and I am here for it. But like in a game of football, it's a good idea to read the coverage. And Rachel's a lot shorter than I am.

I back her up to her kitchen counter, grab her hips, and lift her up onto it, next to the mixer.

There.

It's a two-fer. She's perfect kissing height, and I can kiss her like *this*—between her legs.

After I nudge her thighs, I settle into the V then I cup her cheeks and drop my mouth to hers.

My head spins.

Her lips. Her absolutely delicious lips. Her incredible mouth. She's warm and pliant. She parts for me easily, inviting me to kiss her deeply. As I seal my mouth to hers, I press my hard-on against her center. A groan escapes me as I kiss her. She matches mine with one of her own, a soft, unbearably sexy sound that I eat up with another hot kiss.

A kiss comprised of lips and teeth and tongue. Of my hands holding her face. Of our bodies seeking each other.

I try to get closer, needing to feel her against me. I kiss my best friend thoroughly, with a hunger that surprises me. With a fervor that drives me to grind my cock against her while I explore her sweet mouth. She tastes like cookie dough and pent-up lust.

I've never thought cookies were sexy till now.

But they're a goddamn aphrodisiac. I clasp her face harder. I want to consume her. I want to do everything to this woman. Touch her, caress her, fuck her, please her.

Say filthy things to her all night long.

Yeah, I'd really like to tell her the truth about my dirty heart.

Images of her spread out on the bed snap before my closed eyes. Me eating her, tying her up, smacking her ass, marking her.

I've got to slow down so I don't bust a nut right now. I tap the brakes, downshifting into a slow and sultry kiss, a dirty grind. She wraps her legs around me, hooking her ankles on the waistband of my jeans.

I kiss the corner of her lips, then flick my tongue along their seam. We indulge in another impossibly sexy kiss, then I break it and meet her lusty gaze, taking a few seconds to catalog this brand-new view. Her messy hair, her swollen lips, and the glimmer in her eyes.

It's a woozy look, and I've never seen it before.

Maybe that should be a stop sign. A reminder to ask her questions about friendship, and ground rules, about expectations and what happens tomorrow.

But when her questing hand grabs my chin, tugging me close, I don't have a single question I want to ask.

"Gonna take this off you," I tell her as I play with the ties of her apron.

She reaches for the hem of my Henley. "If I can take *this* off you?"

She's coy, a little flirty with her tit for tat, but her voice rises in a question. Chased by nerves. Like she needs the reassurance that I want her to strip me naked.

"Take it off," I tell her.

She smiles, but then she tries to hide it, pursing her lips as she grabs the fabric and tugs up. I help her along, tossing my shirt on the floor.

"God, Carter," she says on a shudder, then she lifts her hands in front of my pecs.

But she doesn't touch. She just stares. Everywhere. With wandering eyes, and trembling fingers, and so much eagerness that I want to just let her do whatever she wants to me.

Since she wants to.

But I can't stand her being clothed a second longer.

In no time, I untie the apron, but as I'm tugging off her shirt, the timer beeps.

"The cookies! They'll burn," she yelps and makes a move to wriggle off the counter.

I stop her with a firm hand on her thigh. "You look too sexy to move. Stay there. I want you right fucking here, Sunshine."

I turn around, grab the oven mitt, and take out the cookies. I set the tray on the cooling rack, next to the others. Then I turn off the oven. "Next batch comes later. You come first," I say, then toss the mitt on the counter and return to her, standing between her parted legs, undoing the apron once and for all, then sliding it under her ass. I tuck a finger under her chin, make her meet my eyes, reading her needs. These *lessons* should extend to the physical. "I want to make you come harder than you did alone on my couch. I want to show you how it feels when a man is obsessed with your pleasure and *only* your pleasure," I say, and I'm not a mind reader. I'm just a good listener.

Last night, she told me her wishes when it came to dating. To discover *how a man treats a woman.*

When a man actually cares.

It doesn't take a rocket scientist to figure out that she wants the same in bed. A man who tells *only* the truth. Easy. So fucking easy. But a man should ask too. Should make sure she's one hundred percent on board. So I follow up with, "Do you want that, Rachel?"

"Please. Yes. Do that. Now," she says, and this time

she isn't unsure where to put her hands. She's one hundred percent committed to the cause of feeling me up. Her nimble fingers slide down my pecs on a mad dash for my abs, till she reaches my happy trail. When she arrives at the waistband of my jeans, I cover her hand with mine, then slide her palm over the ridge of my erection.

Her reaction is gold. A surprised gasp of excitement. Curiosity too. Maybe a touch of fear.

But there will be time to face that fear later. First, I want her to know what she does to me. I guide her hands back to my chest, and she's smiling, perhaps a little sex drunk as she explores my body.

Good. Fucking good. She can use me however she wants. "I like that. Feeling your hands all over me," I tell her.

I finger the hem of her shirt, then kiss her jaw. On a staggered breath, she stretches her neck, asking for more kisses all while she journeys over my chest, down my arms, across my abs. Like that, we explore each other with lips and fingers.

As I go, I lift up her shirt, exposing her belly inch by inch, touching her soft flesh.

But that's slow enough for now. I tug her shirt off the rest of the way, and it's like I've unwrapped a gift with my name on it.

Holy fucking lingerie.

"Look at you. Who knew you had such a sexy bra on?" I say, shaking my head in admiration. It's pink lace, with an embroidered flower between her tits, and I want to bite that off. I run a finger over the cloth petal, playing with it. "You like pretty things," I say, and I sound amazed. Hell, I feel amazed to know this private detail about Rachel Dumont.

"I do," she says but her smile disappears. Nerves take its place, and she's gone from bold to uncertain as she asks, "You like it?"

Is that not obvious? I tilt my head to study her face, but her expression answers it for me—it's not clear to her. I'm not sure why she's flip-flopped, but I'll just need to show her how much I enjoy this detail of *her*. "Fucking love it so much," I say, then I bury my face between her tits. *Hello, happy place, I am in you.* That orange-blossom smell, her soft skin, her fingers in my hair.

But, hold on.

Her fingers are tentative still.

I'm not sure if she's nervous because it's me, and we're friends, and this is a line.

Or because of what she told me last night about how a man treats a woman. I should ask what's going on. Really I should. But she tastes so good and I'm far too distracted by her breasts, and the kisses I'm laying on her exposed flesh.

"Need more," I murmur, then reach my hands around her back and unhook the bra. She shrugs her shoulders and the lace flutters to the counter.

Fuck yes.

Sure, I've seen her half-naked.

But no, I have not at all.

Because there's Naked Mistaken Phone Answering.

And then there's Naked Arousal.

The second comes with hardened nipples and a flushed chest and a woman so eager for my touch. "Rachel," I mutter, my voice a dry husk on a hot summer day as I cup these glorious beauties.

She looks down at my hands, squeezing her tits, kneading the flesh.

"You have big hands," she says, mesmerized.

"I do," I say, but I don't add *and you have big tits*. Because that's kind of douchey. This handful is real *nice* though. As I play, I meet her gaze. "You feel fucking incredible."

"I do?" she asks, and there are those nerves again. Those concerns. Maybe she's having them because this is, obvs, our first time. Good thing I can reassure her from the bottom of my heart and cock.

"God yes," I tell her.

She lets out a long sigh, maybe of relief. Whatever worries she had seem to have faded away.

Maybe I didn't need to ask what was wrong. Maybe I just needed to *show* her my desire.

I will gladly show her with my mouth, and my dick, and my hands, and my words. I spend another minute adoring her tits with my hands, rolling her nipples between my fingers, letting my thumbs travel over, up, and under till she's panting and moaning. I kiss her breasts again and again, sucking on them, caressing them with my tongue and lips till she's gasping for air.

When I raise my face, I say, "Guess Jane didn't work."

She blinks, barely focusing. "What?"

"The plant. It didn't make me forget these at all," I say, then pinch a nipple.

"Yeah?"

"Not. One. Bit," I say, and I let go so I can unzip her pesky jeans. She helps me along, lifting her hips so I can scoot down the denim to her thighs.

And…I groan salaciously. "Jesus. They match," I say stupidly, but how could anyone expect me to think *unstupidly* right now?

Her panties are pink lace and absolutely soaked. "I can't believe I never knew you wore lingerie like this all this time," I say, but then I replay that comment.

Of course I never knew what panties she wore. We've been friends for over a decade. This is the first time we've engaged in *un-friend* behavior.

Maybe we do need to make rules before we cross the next line. "Rachel," I say, seriously.

She goes stock-still. "Yes?"

"Are you sure about this? I mean, we're still friends after. I don't want to ruin our friendship," I say.

She growls at me. "Don't ruin the moment. Just fuck me. Please just fuck me. Can I make it any more clear?" she demands, and there she is again. Bold Rachel. I like all Rachels, but I do like this forward side of her in bed.

A lot.

"No, but maybe I can," I say, then finish stripping off her jeans and her panties as she watches me with avid eyes. "Since I'm gonna fuck the last shreds of doubt right out of you." I take her hands, bring them to the button on my jeans. "Take out my cock."

Then her hands are eagerly sliding down the zipper, pushing my jeans down, right along with my boxer briefs.

My dick springs free and is so fucking happy to see her.

And yeah, maybe I did want her to walk in on me last night. Because of *this*.

Her reaction. The wide eyes. The parted lips. *The moment when her mind asks the question.*

The thing is—I'm a big guy. I'm supposed to be big to do my job well. For whatever reason—call it luck, good fortune, or just proportionalism at play—I was blessed with size *everywhere*.

She gulps. "Will it...fit?"

That's so fucking hot to hear her say.

But it'll be even more fun for her to find out. I take her hand, wrap it around my shaft. "That depends, Sunshine," I murmur, then I sigh happily as she fondles me. Up, down, then over the head.

"On what?" she asks, trance-like, on an upstroke.

"How wet you are. And if I've got you worked up enough to take me all the way," I say, then slide a hand between her thighs, gliding my fingers through all that slick wetness. Mmm. Yes. She's silky and hot, but I need to get her even wetter. Drive her wild. She lets go of my dick, lifting her hips for me as she grips my shoulders.

That's it. That's the way to find out.

I stroke her eager clit till she's moaning and arching on the counter, offering me her wet pussy.

Just to be sure though...

I slide a finger inside her and she gasps. I crook it, then draw a delicious circle on her clit with my thumb as I stroke inside and out. I add another finger. She's soaked. Then I nip her earlobe. "What do you think, Sunshine? Think my cock will fit now?"

"I don't know. Maybe you could give me a lesson in size as you fuck me," she says, biting her lip.

I go up in flames. "You are a fast learner," I say as I ease out my fingers, then bring them to my lips, sucking off her taste. "Fuck, you're sweet."

"And you're dirty," she says, her lips curving up.

"I think you like my kind of dirty." I grab a condom from my wallet, then toss the billfold onto the counter. As I open the foil, I play the part of gentleman for a second, asking, "Want me to fuck you on your bed? Will that be easier?"

The woman knows her mind since she shakes her head adamantly. "I've never been fucked on a kitchen counter," she says in a whisper full of wicked delight.

My cock throbs as I cover it, eager to give her a first. I tug her closer to the edge of the counter, keeping the apron under her bare skin. I line myself up and rub the head against her slick heat. She can't seem to tear her gaze away from the place where we meet. Her eyes are locked on us.

"You like that? The way we look when we're about to fuck?"

"I do."

I take my time. Pushing in just an inch or two.

Her hands shoot out, grabbing my shoulders.

"Does it hurt?"

She winces as she nods. "But I like it."

My brow furrows. "You sure?"

She digs her nails into me. "Yes. Give me more."

Well, I won't deny her. I ease in another inch or two, and she's gritting her teeth.

"Rachel," I say, cautiously. "We can stop. We can try another—"

"—I'm in a long-term relationship with several industrial-strength vibrators. I want the real thing and I want it now."

Like I stood a chance at denying her.

I ease in more. She squeezes her eyes shut. But with her jaw set, she urges me on: "All of it. Give me all of you."

I am a torch. I had no idea my best friend was like this in bed. Eager, hungry, fearless.

And so turned on.

I slide in the rest of the way, and she sucks in a breath. "God, Carter. You're so big—"

"—You're so wet, baby. That's why you're taking me so good. You're so fucking turned on. That's how you can take my dick."

She shudders, then opens her eyes. "Yeah, I've been a little horny for you lately."

"Good. That's really fucking good," I say, then I ease back a few inches, giving her time to breathe again before I sink back into the tight, hot paradise of her pussy.

She shudders this time.

"See? It's all you."

"I'm pretty sure you have something to do with the big dick in me," she says.

I give another slow, tantalizing thrust that has her tossing back her head. Moaning. Swearing.

"Yeah, but you're taking me like a good girl," I say.

"Am I? A good girl?"

"You take my dick like a very..." I press a kiss to her throat. "Good..." I lay one on her chin. "Girl."

I cover her mouth with mine as I thrust deep into her, filling her all the way. Then I hitch her legs up higher around my ass. "Hold onto the edge of the counter, baby."

She complies, gripping it as I curl one hand around her hip then bring the other between her thighs.

As I fuck her, I take care of her. With each thrust, I caress her clit till she's arching her back, panting, and then shouting, "Yes, yes, yes."

She's trembling and shaking, then coming on my cock on a loud cry.

It's the sexiest sound I've ever heard, and it annihilates my last shreds of restraint. I fuck her hard on her kitchen counter till I forget all about cookies and friendship and dates and everything but the wild thrill of finally, finally having her.

After I come down from the high, I'm struck by a brand-new thought.

What if I've been wanting this for a long, long time?

20

UN-DATING AND ULTRA-SEXING

Rachel

My brain is hitting me with too many questions all at once, and I am not ready to traffic cop the *what happens next*, the *what does this mean*, and the *where do we go*.

I focus on practical things instead. I straighten myself up in my bathroom—it's been a while since I've done the post-sex clean-up dance, but it's like riding a bike. Well, if you needed to change your panties after a bike ride—then I put on leggings and a sweatshirt.

Next comes the cookies. I return to the kitchen solo and set some on a plate. I place the uncooked dough in the fridge. I'll deal with the final batch another time.

I'm a little sore as I bring them to the living room, and that's *all new*. This stretched-wide sensation between my legs. But I don't mind it. It's like the feeling you get after a good workout.

I set the plate on the coffee table then double back to

the kitchen to pour some milk into glasses, and I revise that estimate to *a lot* sore.

Better not walk *that* fast.

Carter rounds the corner from the guest bathroom as I'm carrying a tray of milk, a little hunched over. Staring at me, he arches a brow. "You okay?"

"Why do you ask? Because I'm waddling?"

He laughs. "Well, yeah."

"I'm a sex trouper," I say with a lift of my chin.

And that's new too. I just made a joke after sex with my best friend. Is this normal? Is this how it goes? I'm about to ask Carter, but then I shut down that notion, stat. I don't actually want to know if he's slept with other female friends. But it's too late. The dark thought is lashing through my mind like a tornado. Wasn't Izzy a friend first? He dated her a few years ago when I was in Los Angeles, but I feel like he told me they were friends before they were lovers.

And she is history now.

Oh god. My libido is an idiot. What if that happens to us? What if I'm Izzy-i-fied?

"Trouper or not, let me help," he says, sweeping in to grab the tray and carry it to the coffee table.

This is surreal. He's still shirtless and I seriously appreciate his low-clothes commitment, even though I'm freaking out now about what's next with us. Can you freak out and also admire a man's back? Yes, yes you can. I mean, those muscles. That strength. What does his back look like when he's fucking me? Or his ass? Can we have sex in front of a mirror sometime?

I really should stop perving on him. I should start adulting.

Now. I will do it right now.

I settle in on the couch and gesture to the cookies and the milk. "I have three different types of milk. Almond milk, oat milk, and two percent. We can see which one tastes better with cookies. It's a milk and cookie taste test," I say, and I'm reverting to my pre-sex plan.

I'd arranged my escape hatch so well I bought three types of milk, and planned this whole elaborate cookie taste test, so I wouldn't have to face uncomfortable moments.

Only, I didn't anticipate this one—the *what happens next* one. But here it is, awkward as hell, and I hope milk and cookies make everything easier.

With a wolfish grin, Carter grabs a cookie, then takes a bite. He moans as he chews. Then he sets the half-eaten cookie down on the plate a little defiantly. "Delicious."

I blink at him, shocked. "You took it dry."

"I'm that studly, Rachel."

"You didn't have any milk," I add.

His grin widens. "I don't like milk with cookies."

I gasp, over the top. "You savage. How did I not know this about you?"

"Guess I'm packing a few surprises," he says.

My gaze strays to his pelvis. "Packing for sure. Like your secret dick."

A laugh bursts from him. "Secret dick, Rach? Does that mean the fact that I had a dick was secret? Because you say that like it's a secret birthmark, a secret extra toe, a secret second dick."

"I guess if you have two dicks, it probably is a good idea to ease a girl into that. So secret dick works if you have another one."

"Do you think I'm hiding another dick from you?"

I shudder. "I hope not. I don't think I could handle your two dicks. The single super-size one is enough for me. The *secret* super-size dick," I say, and I'm smiling too, and then something dawns on me.

This is not uncomfortable at all. Not one bit. We're Racheling and Cartering once again. He's eating a cookie shirtless, and I'm taking one and dipping it in milk, and we're joking about his dick.

This feels normalish.

When he finishes, he leans back against the couch cushions, stretching his arms over them, so at home here. "So, was this milk and cookie tasting part of your whole cover-up?"

Shoot. He does know me too well. Earlier, I wasn't sure how to talk to him, so I protected myself by rambling. I'm still unsure, but this is also a new chance. I took a chance at sex. I should take a chance at communication. I need to know the score, and I'd rather learn it directly than dance around it.

I set down the cookie and face him. "I baked because I didn't know what was going to happen tonight—if I was going to find the guts to tell you I'd been thinking about you like this, or if it was going to scare you off, so I wanted a parachute. I thought if we had a normal thing to do, then it'd be fine if you didn't want...the same thing. The sex thing."

"You saw me jerk off to you and you thought I didn't want *the sex thing*?"

I shrug, a little helpless. "Carter, I don't really trust a lot of my instincts with men."

He's quiet for a beat, his expression turning thoughtful. "But you trust me?"

"Of course," I say instantly. "You know that, right?"

"I do," he says. "Always have. I just want you to be upfront with me."

Another thing that's new? Believing someone. Trusting someone. Not second guessing every single thing. That's a damn good feeling. "Okay. Here goes. I kind of needed some reassurance when you were touching me before—my breasts—that you wanted to, like really wanted to touch me. Because I didn't want to second-guess it all the next day."

His eyes pin me. "Don't second-guess me, Sunshine. You can ask if I like something. And I'll tell you the truth. But you need to know this—I wanted you. Only you. I still want you," he says, the intensity of his voice a reassurance too.

"Maybe that was a sex lesson I needed to learn. That it's okay to ask if *you*—your partner—likes something," I admit, feeling vulnerable but needing to say this. He could read me when we were making out. I didn't have to spell out my fears and I appreciate that. He sensed them and took care of me. But I can also ask for what I want, and what I need. That's something I've never really done before. I've never felt comfortable doing it.

"It's fun to ask for what you want. And yeah, I could tell beforehand, too, that you felt off tonight. I just had no idea if it was because, well, you'd done a dick review."

I drop my face into the couch pillow, groaning. "I'll never live that down."

A hand curls around my shoulder. "Next time, just come into the shower," he says in a low rumble. Pleasure zips down my back, and when I lift my face to his gaze, his eyes are glimmering with heat.

"I wanted to," I say, even though he knows that. But it feels good to admit the truth fully and completely this time. It feels great to say what I want and to *know*—to *trust*—that the other person isn't lying.

He runs his thumb across my shoulder, hard enough that I can feel a little buzz through the fabric of my sweatshirt. "I think I'd lose my mind if you joined me in the shower. Or if you found me in bed with my cock in my hand."

That outrageously sexy image lodges front and center in my mind. Not sure it's going to leave anytime soon. "Do you jerk off a lot? And in different places in your home?" I ask in a hushed voice. Because this feels like confession time. And I want him to serve up all the details.

"Yeah. Every day, easily. Bedroom, shower, couch sometimes. I live alone. I have a lot of energy and a very busy brain. So yeah, you could walk in on me in bed, enjoying a little *self-care*."

I swallow, but that does nothing to abate the heat flooding me. "Me too," I admit.

He licks his lips, then lets out an appreciative rumble. "I want to see that."

I want him to. I want him to find me in bed. I want him to climb over me and help me finish.

All these mentions of *next times* give me courage. He's right. I can't hide behind milk and cookies. I want a next time with him, and I want his friendship for all time. I want everything, dammit. I sit up straighter, take his hand from my shoulder, and set it in my lap, clasping it in both my hands. "What if we did this sex thing while we do the four dates?"

There. I put myself out there without overexplaining, blurting, rambling, or backtracking.

I shut my mouth and wait.

But not for long. His slow, sexy smile tugs on my heart. It's like the sun rising, warming me all over. I want to bask in its glow. Lift my face to the light. Let it heal my hurting soul.

Because I still hurt.

I still ache.

I'm still shut down.

With Carter, though, I feel safe from heartache. Shielded from pain.

"So, let me get this straight," he says. "You want to help me fulfill my Date Night contract and let me make you come over and over in every possible way?" He gestures to the coffee table. "And you'll also feed me cookies?"

Now.

I want that all now. All at once. "I'll take one of everything," I say, as I shiver from his dirty promises.

"Good. But I'll probably give you two or three. I'm generous in bed."

And out of bed since, well, he's still shirtless. "But it's not like I don't get anything out of it. I get the sex thing too, *and* you're giving me girlfriend lessons."

"I'm in," he says.

I sigh contentedly from the ease of the request.

Carter lets go of my hands to cup the back of my head and comes in for a kiss.

It's soft…and tender.

My toes curl.

My limbs feel loose. He's gentle this time. It's more like a caress. And it's a stark contrast to the way he kissed me on the counter. I want more of this kind of kiss too. The kind that has me melting in his arms.

But it ends far too soon. When he breaks it, he shakes his head, like he's trying to clear the kiss.

"What's wrong?" I ask, since worry is never far from me.

He scrubs a hand across his jaw. "I should have asked first."

I roll my eyes. "Carter, you have blanket permission to kiss me. You did just fuck me like a rock star on the counter. We've agreed to more. You can kiss me whenever."

"Yeah?" He sounds doubtful.

"Yes," I say emphatically, and it's sweet that he asked. I love that he wants to make sure I'm good with everything. But it's unnecessary.

He doesn't seem convinced though. "It just feels… like something a—"

Ohhh.

He doesn't finish. But I can guess the rest of it. His reticence wasn't over consent. He's wondering if free kisses *should* be part of girlfriend lessons.

Because kisses can lead to feelings.

My heart sinks annoyingly. I'm a little disappointed that he'd worry I might get clingy. But rationally, I understand. He doesn't want to lead me on. But that's okay since I don't want to be led. I don't want a boyfriend. I don't want someone who can hurt me. I'm not ready for real romance, and I won't be for a long time. "Carter, we're friends," I say, trying to reassure him. "I want to stay friends. Neither one of us wants more. But I think we both want sex," I say, hitting the flirt button a little harder now.

That earns me a naughty smile. "We do."

"So, you can kiss me anytime. Think of it as part of the whole sex thing and girlfriend lessons. It's like we're..." I cast about for the word I thought of earlier. "Un-dating."

His brown eyes sparkle. "That's what I was calling it in my head before too."

"And while we're un-dating we can...wait. What's the un-dating equivalent of sex?"

His brow knits. "It's not de-sexing. I don't ever want to de-sex. And un-sexing should not be a thing either."

I grab my phone from the coffee table and look up prefixes. He slides closer and we huddle together, checking out a list of prefixes online. "Oh! Extra is an option." I try it on for size. "Extra-sexing. Maybe, but that also sounds like it's beyond sex."

"What's beyond sex? Don't tell me. I don't want to know about a world beyond sex," he says, then peers at the screen, then at me with a wicked glint in his eyes. "Super," he says, lingering on that word like it's a tasty treat.

"We're super-sexing," I say, nodding too, liking that a lot. Except as we stare at the list once again, there's another prefix that feels just a bit better. I turn to him right as he's turning to me, and in unison we say, "Ultra-sexing."

"Let's ultra-sex and un-date," he says.

"Deal," I say, then I grab another cookie and make a show of dipping it into milk before I bite it. He grabs one and makes a show of crunching into it dry.

As we snack, we plan our next un-date.

When we're done, I'm glad I faced all the questions I had earlier head-on. But one issue still nags at me. I want to let it go, but I can't. So I clear my throat. "Carter?"

"Yeah?"

"Were you friends with Izzy first?"

"Huh. I haven't really thought about her in a while," he says, a little stunned, it seems, that I brought her up.

But he hasn't answered me, so I press. "Were you? I thought you said you were when you told me about her."

Something like regret flashes in his eyes. "Sort of. She's a friend of Hayden's," he says. Hayden's the kicker on his team. "And we'd all do karaoke together and stuff."

Stuff. All the stuff I missed when I was in Los

Angeles with my ex. I could have been doing that stuff with Carter. But you can't change the past, or your past choices. You can only make better ones in the present.

"And then we started seeing each other one night after we all went to Japantown," he adds, but there's a curt sort of finality to it.

Still, I need to know. "So she was a friend, but she's not in your life now?"

His jaw tics, then he lets out a long breath. There's a touch of irritation in it. He's like that every now and then when he doesn't want to talk about things. "Rachel, she's not like a *way back* friend. Besides, she broke it off when I missed a date," he grumbles, then drags a hand through his hair.

I've touched a sore spot. "Sorry I asked," I say, since no one *likes* to talk about exes. Especially Carter.

He waves a hand dismissively. "It's fine. She's an ex. That's all."

She's also an *ex-friend*, which worries me. But I'm not going to belabor the point. Because part of the point is that his exes didn't entirely understand him. That he's sometimes late. That he sometimes forgets. Maybe he didn't tell them about his ADHD. Whatever the reason, I'm not going to push about Izzy's absence in his life. "I get it," I say, trying to be as upbeat as I can about it.

"Good. Now Let's talk about something else."

"Like what?" I ask, letting him lead so I don't poke a wound again.

He smirks, then he grabs my hips and, in one swift move, tugs me onto his lap so I'm straddling him.

"Like asking for what you want. I'll go first." He

pauses, his eyes glinting with no doubt very dirty thoughts. "How sore are you?" he asks as he lifts his hips, grinding up into me. Letting me feel the ridge of his cock again. He's semi-hard.

I'm not sure I'll be able to walk tomorrow. But I didn't stop going to HIIT classes even though I could barely move after the first one.

Besides, this is what I wanted at my breakup party. So I swivel my hips, rocking against his growing erection. Time to show him what a good student I can be. "I mean, I did say a week or so ago that I wanted to get back on the horse," I point out helpfully.

He lifts a hand and runs his thumb along my jawline. "You should ride me, baby," he says, and he's all the way hard now.

I shiver and he pulls my face closer so he can kiss me again. This kiss is playful. He nibbles on the corner of my lips. Then he nips along my jawline, murmuring as he goes. When he reaches my ear, he bites the lobe.

Is Carter a biter? Do I want him to bite me?

I think I do. But do I just ask? I should, since we just talked about that. But I don't know how to say it though, and I've done enough thinking for one night. Enough asking too. I'll figure it out another time since I can't really think anyway when he presses another new kind of kiss to my lips.

This one's possessive.

And in the span of one night, I've learned Carter Hendrix can kiss hard, soft, and teasing.

He can kiss like this too—like he owns me.

And he does just that as I ride him on the couch till

I'm so far gone, I barely realize I'm tugging his face to my chest and asking for something without words.

That's new too. Trusting my body to ask. Trusting my instincts.

* * *

In the morning, with him long gone, I look in the bathroom mirror, running a hand down my throat to my chest. There's a mark above my right breast. A dark red bruise.

I love it more than I ever knew I would.

21

NICE SCARF

Rachel

The second I walk into Elodie's home on Saturday morning, my friend is all business. She points to the stools at the kitchen counter, then taps her wrist. "You've got ten minutes till Amanda is back from ceramics class."

"I gave you the headline over text," I point out coyly as I breeze over to the counter. Juliet's here too, her eyes wide and eager, already waiting for Tales from the Great Wednesday Night Banging. We're all heading up to Petaluma to have lunch with my parents today. Elodie's driving, so that's why we're here at her place. "Wasn't that enough?" I tease.

Brooking no argument, Elodie shakes her head. "Text does not count."

"We need the full story, and we need it now," my

sister puts in, then grabs the stool and shoves it at me. Bossy thing. "Sit. Spill. Share."

With a satisfied smile that I haven't been able to wipe off my face for sixty hours—that's how long it's been since my last O with Carter—I pop up on the stool, tapping my chin. "Where to start…?"

Elodie stares sharply at me. "How about with the scarf you're wearing?"

Way to read a bestie.

But despite the ticking clock, I'm going to have fun with them. Fun—that thing I haven't had a lot of till recently. I finger the soft, light blue chiffon number wrapped artfully around my neck. "Oh, this?"

Juliet rolls her eyes. "Don't act innocent. You're the one who taught me about scarves and turtlenecks."

Elodie groans, as if deeply aggrieved. "Mon cheri, please tell me you never taught your little sister about turtlenecks. I'm still hoping Amanda goes through life without learning those fetid things exist," she says with a shudder.

"I *had* to teach Juliet about turtlenecks," I say, pointing at the brunette troublemaker with my last name. "In eighth grade after the Spring Fling, she came home with a hickey the size of Texas. She spun this elaborate story about how she was drinking fruit punch at a dance, and then the red Solo plastic cup broke and it scraped against her neck."

Juliet cringes. "Uh. Shut up. I've tried to block that from my memory."

"The hickey or your terrible lying skills?" I ask.

"I wonder where I got those from," Juliet fires back.

With a sympathetic tone, Elodie turns to Juliet. "You need to learn the art of the coverup from someone more skilled. Moi."

"Yes, of course. Your years at a French boarding school taught you skills," I tease.

"Chocolate skills and life skills," Elodie says, then tugs on my scarf, like she's disarming me at a Clue-themed dinner party.

It was Carter, with the wicked mouth, on the couch.

Juliet points to the offending hickey. "Well, that answers everything about what happened," she declares.

I clasp the bruise. "It got a little bigger," I say defensively, maybe a little protectively.

Elodie hums in obvious approval. "I've been waiting for the dirty details," she says, clearly pleased with my mark. "And this is a good start."

While I still don't want to tell them about my discovery of his solo shower session earlier in the week —that's private—they both know I had planned to ask him for girlfriend lessons. They'd encouraged me when we watched the game last Sunday. They know, too, that he said yes.

But this is the first time I've been able to…indulge in details. "Well, he came over on Wednesday night, as you know, and one thing led to another. And now I have this," I say, still proud of the mark. Is it weird I'm so proud of it? I don't know why I love it so much. I just do.

Elodie glances at the clock on the stove. "Specifics. Beyond the mark. Now."

My stomach flutters as I remember the hottest sex of

my life. I stop toying with them. "He fucked me on my kitchen counter, then on my couch, and he says the dirtiest things during sex, and before sex, and after sex. He's voracious, and he kisses me like he wants to devour me. I shoved his face against my chest, and then he sucked on me with his teeth, and it was crazy hot. He's not sweet in bed. He doesn't call me a rose petal, he doesn't tell me I'm his precious love, and he doesn't say he loves me over and over. He just fucks me good and hard."

Well, that was a two-man sex review, wasn't it?

Still, I lift my chin defiantly.

Partly to hide the stupid lump in my throat that I do *not* want to feel right now. The lump that reminds me how fooled I was by Edward's style of lovemaking. The overly romantic gestures, the cooing words, the professions of sweet affection while he was inside me.

Like he thought that could fool me. Well, the asshole was right. He did fool me.

But Elodie's clearly not latching onto the Edward part. She's hooked on the Carter deets. "Damn. Clone him," she says.

"He's dirty, and passionate, and *real*," I add, then I shrug, a little sadly, still stuck in the past more than I want to be. "I kind of can't believe how foolish I was to think Edward meant any of that."

I guess I can't stop thinking about the contrast between the two men. I should. But it's too hard.

"Sweetie," Elodie says, giving me a side hug. "Edward was an evil magician. He wove dark romantic magic."

"You were caught in a spell," Juliet adds.

"All that over-the-top romance from him. The words, the deeds, the gifts," I mutter, but then I straighten my shoulders. "And then here's Carter, and boom, in one night, he's like, *let me show you how a man fucks a woman he wants.*" I touch the bruise again, feeling connected to it in a whole new way.

Now I know why I love it so much. It's evidence. It's the opposite of empty words. It's something I can trust.

"I didn't want to upset you by asking," Elodie says. She's always been forthright and tough. She didn't come by it easily. She had to lift herself up in a lot of ways. The net result is she's one of the strongest people I know and also one of the most direct. "I just wanted to hear the good stuff. It is good, right? You feel good about all of this with him?"

I set a hand on her arm, squeezing her in reassurance. "It's so good. I didn't know sex could be like this. He's very, very focused on me."

Heat travels down my chest as I think about Carter. As I recall the way he touched me.

"It's good then that he's the one you're getting your feet wet with," Elodie says.

Juliet ahems. "Sounds like it's more than feet she's getting wet."

I laugh, then try to wave off my earlier worries. "Yes, exactly. I'm just going to focus on the fact that I'm having hot, dirty, passionate sex with no commitments for a few weeks. With someone I trust."

"I always did wonder if Carter had a thing for you," she says, like she's musing on the topic.

"Me too," Juliet says.

"What?" I turn to my sister.

"Oh, you think I was too young to pick up on his vibes?"

"He wasn't into me in high school," I say, certain that's true.

But Elodie lifts a questioning brow, even though she didn't know Carter or me back then. I met her post-college. Still, she says, "Maybe he wasn't into you in high school. But you've been friends forever. It can't be the first time it's crossed his mind that you're hot."

Has Carter thought of me like this before? Like while I was married? Before I was married?

"I mean, haven't you ever thought of him like this before?" she adds, then checks the time. Amanda will be home any second.

I shake my head. "No. He dated a lot. Always dated a lot. I was just the friend," I say, a little flummoxed with the question. But now I'm wondering if I ever did think of him this way, and squashed the thought before it turned into something? Only, I'm not sure I will ever know, or if it matters. Probably best to leave that in the past too. "And we both *only* want to be friends." I add. "So this is four dates. Girlfriend lessons. Then we're done."

"And will you tell Elena?" Elodie asks.

That's a good question. I don't see my therapist for another week or so and honestly, that's for the best right now. I'm not sure I want to say something to Elena yet. Maybe because I don't want to hear anyone tell me to be careful and she'd say that surely. But I am being careful. This plan *is* careful. I'm being so goddamn careful with my heart, and I don't need any more reminders.

From anyone.

Fortunately, the door swings open before I can even answer the question, and the most fashionable twelve-year-old in the city sails in.

"Hey, bug," Elodie says, her mama voice on. Her parents died a year ago, making Elodie a single mom of sorts to her much younger sister.

"Hey, Els," her sister says as her bracelets jingle on her arms. She wears a crocheted top, baggy jeans, cuffed twice, and white Converse sneakers that she's drawn some sort of elaborate sketch on.

"Hi Rachel. Hi Juliet," she says to my sister and me, then tilts her head to the side, meeting my gaze. "Can we play Halo at your parents' house?"

I laugh. "Of course. Sawyer will be there too. He's back in town for the weekend. He loves Halo."

"I'll beat him," Amanda says, then heads straight for her room.

"Her confidence is such an issue," Juliet says dryly.

"Yeah, you need to work on that," I say, then I touch Elodie's arm. "But she's doing okay, otherwise?"

Elodie nods. "Most of the time," she says.

Most of the time seems like a good target these days given what she's been through.

* * *

When we arrive at my parents', my brother's already there, swinging open the door. After he lets in Elodie and Amanda, he stops at Juliet and me. Like he's a sentry, weighing our admission.

"Well, if it isn't my troublemaking sisters," he says.

"Right, right. As if we're the bad ones," Juliet says.

His dark eyes narrow at us. "Speaking of trouble, any new guys in your life who I need to beat up?"

"No one," I say with a roll of my eyes at his usual big-brother-type question.

Juliet scoffs at him. "As if I'd tell you anyway."

I head inside and say hi to my parents, grateful to spend time with family. Days like these are why I moved back to San Francisco.

To help Mom and Dad in the kitchen as they make lunch. To catch up on their lives. To give my brother a hard time about anything and everything. To enjoy Sawyer and Amanda playing video games.

It's only slightly odd at the dinner table when my mom asks how Carter is.

"Great," I chirp, then take a bite of the salad to shut myself up. So I don't say *I can't wait to go to his game tomorrow. I can't wait for our un-date on Monday. And I really, truly can't wait for him to come over after the un-date.*

With an inquisitive look, my brother clears his throat. "Nice scarf. Did you get cut with a plastic red Solo cup?"

22

WIN SOME, LOSE SOME

Carter

"Number eighty-eight...at wide receiver. Carter Hendrix!" The familiar voice of the Renegades announcer warbles as I trot onto the field from the tunnel, giving a wave to the hometown crowd.

The cheers are beautifully deafening. Like a dose of natural medicine right before a game. As I run past my teammates, I smack palms with them, amped up from the crowd, and from the sheer excitement of playing a game for a living in front of the best fans ever.

When I reach the end of the line, the final player's name is announced—the guy we all depend on to lead our team.

"Your starting quarterback at number nine...Beck Cafferty."

The steely-eyed missile man was traded to our team a couple years ago right after my first Big Game win, and we are the luckiest dogs in the world, since Cafferty took us to the Big Game in his first year.

Too bad we haven't gone back since. I hate to be greedy—actually, scratch that, I love being greedy in this game—but I'd sure as hell like to be the last team standing come February.

Three rings would work for me, thank you very much.

Our record is solid this season so far, though not stellar. Anything can happen, but I want to march through the rest of the season like we own it. To show our fans and the whole football world why we won two in a row a couple years ago.

After the coin toss, I jog to the sidelines with Hamlin, glancing at the fifty-yard line as I go.

Okay, it's more than a glance.

It's maybe a long, hungry stare as I hunt for Rachel. There she is with some of the crew—Monroe's here, along with Rachel's sister, and that's Rachel's brother next to him. They're all buds, and Rachel mentioned Sawyer was back in town. My parents are here too. They usually are for home games. But my gaze stays on the woman I'll see tomorrow night. She looks *good* in the stands, showing up for me.

Damn good.

Hamlin smacks my arm, snapping me out of it. "Aww, got some fans today, Hendrix? Miracles do happen," he deadpans.

"That's true. Every now and then you nab a first down," I say, then we get to work.

* * *

Down by two. Less than a minute and a half left in the game. Third and long. I'm in the huddle as Cafferty calls the play. With a quick nod, I get in position, and I'm in motion at the snap.

I fly downfield, getting open, darting away from a safety when Caff lobs the ball my way. I'm racing, fifteen, now ten feet from the end zone, and holy fuck, it's coming in hot and fast.

My arms are over my head and the ball is threatening to sail past me. I leap and grab that motherfucker with one hand.

It bobs in my palm.

Not today, football.

I haul it down, hugging it to my goddamn shoulder, then bring it to my chest right in the end zone.

That's how you do it!

A few seconds later, Hamlin smacks palms with me. "Dude, you caught that ball with your fucking shoulder."

"I fucking did," I say, then we bump chests. Some plays just fire you up. I steal a glance at the fifty-yard line. I swear, I can make her out from here. Cheering, hollering, getting hoarse from excitement. Yeah, I hope she saw that touchdown catch. I hope it fired her up like it does me.

Cafferty joins me next, high-fiving too. "Ringleader! You and your circus catches," he says.

A few years ago in our last Big Game appearance, I caught one of his passes on the side of my helmet.

"I am the End Zone Ringleader," I say, taking that new nickname and owning it.

And I'm also all energy as we head to the sidelines for the extra point. "Let's do this, D. Fucking lock it up," I say when the point is good and the kickoff return team heads to the field.

"Maybe there's *another* reason Hendrix is extra excited today," Hamlin drawls.

I shoot him a look in question.

"Your *fans*," he says with a smirk, then nudges Cafferty's arm while looking my way. "I think it's because *someone* is here."

"That so? Who is this special someone, Hendrix?" Cafferty goads.

This convo with the guys is as normal as high-fives, spotting your bud in the weight room, and talking trash in the locker room.

But for a few seconds, I'm more speechless than I'd like to be. Rachel's a friend. She's always been a friend. They both *know* Rachel. She's been a fixture on the sidelines for most of our home games this season.

Trouble is, I don't know what to call her as I fashion my comeback.

No one feels all wrong.

Someone is too much.

And *just a friend* feels like a lie.

I choose option D, sidestepping it. "It's hard, isn't it, that my cheering section is so fucking big," I say, then gesture to my crotch, since, well, size is the easiest way to tackle any trash talk.

"Like your ego," Hamlin retorts as the special teams leave and the defense takes the field.

We're all business now, focused on the game. The defense has to hold off the Wolves. But the Wolves are gnashing, and two big plays later, they've scored a touchdown.

I groan in abject misery. We only have thirteen damn seconds to get in field goal range.

We start deep in our own territory, so Cafferty goes long and hurls the ball my way. Like a hawk, I track it as I run. I can feel it in my fingers. I'm this close to hauling it in and getting out of bounds with enough time left.

But out of nowhere, a cornerback slices my path, batting the ball down before it even reaches me.

There is no out of bounds. The clock runs out, and I don't groan in misery. I curse in despair as I walk off the field, head down. It's one game, but it's not just one game. Every game matters.

After a few shitty minutes where I want to kick things, but I don't, I pull myself together to head to the stands to say hi to friends and family. First, Mom and Dad.

"Tough loss, kid," my dad says. I've always been *kid* to him. I'll always be *kid*. I don't really mind.

"Yeah, sucks," I mutter. He never expects me to be happy all the time. It's nice.

My mom ruffles my hair, and since she always looks on the bright side, she says, "But that catch was amazing."

"Thanks, Mom."

I don't say what I'm really feeling—*lot of good it did*.

I raise my face. I can't avoid it any longer. I have to see my friends. When I make my way to Rachel, I'm even more disappointed in myself. That's a weird feeling with her. But maybe it's not a weird feeling in general. I've always wanted to impress the girls I like. Knowing your girl is in the stands always adds something extra to a game. You want her to see you at the top.

Sure, Rachel's been to countless games of mine in the NFL, but this is the first game she's come to *after* we've slept together, after our chocolate café date, and after the decision to do girlfriend lessons.

I want to win for me, for my team, for my job, for the fans.

But as I close the distance to the amber-eyed woman, disappointment sinks a little harder in my gut with a realization—I wanted to win for her too.

And she's not even my girl.

"Hey, thanks for coming," I say a little heavily.

"Great game. Tough loss," she says.

"Yeah."

I say nothing more. Partly because I have nothing to say, but also because I'm overcome with the urge to wrap her in my arms. Bring her close. Tell her how much tonight sucked, then bury my face in her neck for a few seconds and inhale her orange-blossom smell.

Shake off the loss like that.

Instead, I shake off the desire. Can't act on it. That's not our deal. This thing with Rachel is temporary. It's not for post-game comfort.

I don't stay with the crew for long. Coach will want

to break down that loss. Reporters will ask questions. It's time to go so I leave, the scoreboard flashing the loss my way.

* * *

When I'm home alone that night, Rachel texts.

> Rachel: You doing okay? You didn't seem like yourself.

Carter: It's football. You win and you lose.

> Rachel: If you want to talk, I'm here.

Carter: Nah. I'm all good.

She doesn't need to know I'm in a funk. I turn off my phone and shut out the world.

23

A SEA URCHIN THINGY

Carter

A long run through the fog the next morning works wonders at putting the loss behind me.

It gives me something else to focus on—peeling off miles.

So does the word of the day. *Endemic.*

It means growing or existing in a certain place or region. As I run, I turn it over in my head to take my mind off yesterday.

Like fog is endemic to San Francisco, like ups and downs are endemic to the game I play for a living, like Monday morning quarterbacking is endemic to, well, Mondays in the NFL.

After six miles, I shower, then head to work. Along the way, I stop by Cafferty's home nearby. He lives with his husband, Jason, the rival quarterback for the city's other football team. During his first season with us, he was sneaking around seeing McKay on the down-low. When he finally fessed up to me, I wasn't pissed he was dating a rival. At the time, I was pissed he'd kept it from me for a whole season, since we're buds. But I don't hold grudges. Life's too short for that.

Besides, I like to give him a hard time for other things. Like the fact that he *never* wants to drive.

"Didn't you get a car once upon a time for this very reason?" I ask when he gets into my ride.

He smirks. "Why drive when I have a driver?"

I shake my head, amused. This is good, this chitchat. It helps distract me too.

But as I weave through traffic, I go quiet for a bit, still stuck in my mood, till Cafferty clears his throat. "So, Jason wanted me to invite you to our Halloween party."

That pulls me out of my head. "Aww, was it hard for you to say the word *party*, Caff?"

He grumbles a "no."

"Sounded hard to say," I tease, since he's not the most social cat.

"It wasn't," he says.

"You hate parties," I say.

He sighs. "I don't *hate* them."

"You hate them a little."

"No, seriously. I don't mind them," he says, but he sounds a little like he's protesting too much.

I slow at the light. "Why don't you just tell your hubs you don't like parties?"

He shoots me a deadpan look. "It was *my* idea to have the party. He likes parties. I said we should do it."

Ahh, that makes sense. He's not annoyed about the event. He's rising to the occasion. Wanting to do something for his guy.

"Then I am definitely making you a T-shirt that says...Mister Compromise."

"Thanks," he says dryly before he adds, "You can bring someone. Obviously."

The only person I'd want to bring is my best friend. "Thanks, Caff. I'll ask Rachel," I say, but then I'm quiet once again. Even the thought of seeing her tonight isn't lifting my mood. My bad mood is endemic.

I say nothing the rest of the drive. When we reach the facility, he stops me before I get out of the car with a firm "Hendrix."

I turn to him. "Yeah?"

"I've done what you're doing. It's hard, man. But don't let yesterday get to you. It was one game," he says.

The fucker knows me too well.

"Thanks," I say, appreciating his pep talk.

We go to the team meeting. Coach breaks down what went right and what went wrong. But at the end of the day what went wrong is this—the game slipped through our fingers.

Mine specifically.

* * *

When practice ends that afternoon, I drop off Cafferty at his home. As he grabs the door handle, he says, "Did you set an alarm to tell Rachel about the party?"

Oh, shit. I fucking forgot. "Thanks, man," I say, then grab my phone and set it.

"No problem," he says, then we knock fists.

I don't talk about my ADHD with most of the guys on the team. There's no need. I'm not interested in being a poster child for it. I'm not going to do commercials on living with it or succeeding at your highest level or whatever.

That's not my shtick. It's just something I have to deal with. Something I've *always* had to deal with.

But Beck's different. He's struggled with social anxiety and panic attacks. Sometimes, he still does. He's shared some of his struggles with me, so I look out for him. And he looks out for me.

Guess I needed that today. Needed someone to accept my mood. I'm so damn used to being Mister Happy, to playing the ringleader. But it's a welcome feeling, this space to be…a little off.

Not sure I can show it to anyone else though.

* * *

I really should put the game behind me this evening. It's been twenty-four hours. I need to get over the loss. It ought to be easy to stop obsessing on it once I pick up Rachel for our farmers' market date.

Especially since holy fuck, she looks amazing. "Look at you," I say as I meet her at her door with a *whoa* and a whistle, then drink her in.

Rachel flashes me a sweet and borderline seductive smile. "Thanks," she says.

And I just keep staring. She's positively edible in those jeans and that black top that not only slopes off her shoulder, but reveals a hint of white lace.

In fact, *thanks, fucking lingerie.* Now I'm going to be hard all night at the market.

"You look pretty good yourself," she says, eyeing me up and down in my Henley and jeans.

"Yeah, but *you*," I say, since I can't stop complimenting her.

A blush creeps across her cheeks. "You're too much. You make me feel too good."

Pfft. "Not a thing," I say, and yup, focusing on her is all I need. I won't think about that stupid loss anymore. Won't stew in my mood a second longer.

"Question?" I ask once I shut her door, then get into the driver's seat.

"Yes?"

"Are you trying to torture me with your lingerie?"

"Oh. Is this torture?" she asks innocently, her gaze straying to the white lacy strap that's on display. *For me.*

"Yes. It is," I say, then fuck it. I run my finger along the strap, taking my time to brush along her skin too. "Pure torture," I whisper.

Our gazes lock. Her amber eyes flicker, and they say *I meant it when I told you to kiss me anytime.*

I lean in for a lingering, start-of-the-date kiss that puts my bad mood in the rearview mirror.

Except, as I drive to the market, I'm strangely distracted. Not by the game this time. Not by the instant replay in my head of the catch I didn't make, but by the things I want to say to her.

The things I would have said a week ago. Like, *I'm bummed about the loss, I feel like it's my fault, and I wish I'd moved faster, tracked the ball better, reached higher.*

I don't say any of those things that are bubbling up in my throat.

I won't let myself. That's boyfriend or best friend territory, and here in this no man's land, we're not enough of either for me to get away with it.

* * *

Every now and then, there's a Monday night farmers' market at the Ferry Building. The stalls are teeming with crowds since the Ferry Building is the trendy place to be. It's right on the bay and boasts gorgeous views of the starry sky over the water as well as fantastic food in the booths.

When we walk in, we pass a few vendors peddling flowers. Rachel's attention snags on the buckets and buckets of buds as she slows to admire them, then sniff some.

She stops. "All right, before I get distracted by wildflowers, let's do the video."

"Let's do it," I say, then bring her to my side and hold up my phone, making sure there's a nice view of the flowers and fruit vendors behind us. I hit record. "Some people might be wondering how the hell you do a date at a farmers' market," I say.

"I know I was," she says. "But I have some ideas why it's a great first date."

"Don't keep them to yourself."

She gestures behind her to indicate the stalls. "Well, you get to walk around with your date," she says, bumping shoulders with me. "It can be easier to get to know someone as you're walking around rather than sitting at a coffee shop or a bar. Walking means there are plenty of things to see. And you can talk about all the things you see as you go."

"The whole farmers' market is one big conversation piece," I say, and this is what I need. This date will shove all these strange thoughts about what I'm telling her and not telling her out of my head once and for all. "We can even make it a game. Like, let's go find the weirdest produce here."

We hunt through the stands, stopping first at the eggplants—because how can you not make an eggplant joke at a farmers' market, and these purple veggies are big. But at the next stand, she finds a kohlrabi, a pale green bulb thing with leaves that look like they could commit murder. "Those leaves want to kill me," I say to the camera.

"Don't cross them, Carter," she says.

Next, we find a neon green vegetable that looks like cauliflower. But also broccoli. I hold it up while she shoots. "Now, let's be honest—is this broccoli's cousin or cauliflower's?"

"Or maybe it's related to a sea urchin," she says, then tells me it's Romanesco broccoli. "And it tastes good."

"I'll take your word for it," I say.

"Or you could let me cook it for you. Since that's another great thing about farmers' markets. They can be the starting point of a two-part date. Shop and eat," she says, on a hopeful note.

But with a hint of innuendo too.

Which means it's time to turn off the camera. "I do want to eat," I say in a low voice, letting her connect the dots. That shouldn't be hard to do.

Her lips part, and a greedy breath seems to ghost across them. Ah hell, I'm desperate to kiss her in public, too, but Date Night would have a field day if I did that. They'd say we're a thing, and then people would get excited, like they did about Quinn and me, and then I'd have to say we're not together.

Not for real.

Just for lessons.

And fuck that.

I don't want to explain what we're doing to anyone. It's private, and I want the rest of this night to be private too.

Starting now.

"Want to get out of here?" I ask quietly, but a voice interrupts my thoughts.

A booming voice from a few feet away. "Dude. That loss sucked last night."

I groan, but then slap on a smile. It was inevitable that we'd run into a fan.

I turn around. "Hey, man," I say to a guy wearing a Renegades sweatshirt. Don't know him but the sympathetic look on his face tells me he's a hardcore fan.

"Good game, Hendrix. But that was a tough loss. Why did Cafferty overthrow?"

Immediately, I shake my head. I won't let my QB

take the blame. "My fault, not his. I should have been farther downfield."

We talk about the game for another minute, but when the guy leaves with a *next time you'll win*, my mood is right back on the game where I don't want it at all. Since that also means it's back on what I'm not telling Rachel.

Like I was with Cafferty, I'm quiet as we stop at a few more stalls. Rachel tries to make small talk, but I mostly grunt till she pulls me to a quiet corner, away from the market, out by the dock. "Hey, it's girlfriend lessons time," she says.

I blink, confused. "What do you mean?"

"I think you're the one covering something up," she says, gently. "And maybe as part of these girlfriend lessons, you could tell me what it is and see if I can help. Because I think I know what it is."

I gulp, this close to busted. "Yeah?"

"You're still bummed about the game," she says, reading me perfectly, just like Cafferty did. Maybe I don't have a good poker face.

I wince, feeling stupid. Feeling like a fucking rookie. "It's nothing," I mutter.

She sets a hand on my arm in a reassuring touch. "It's your job. It's your passion. It's your love. It's okay if you're frustrated about the loss. It was a tough one."

My jaw tics. It was. And I should not be worked up about it a day later. "It's fine."

"Carter," she says, in a tone that makes it clear she doesn't buy my denial. "I get it if you don't want to talk about it. And I don't want to make you talk. I'm just saying I understand bad days. Mine are different than yours. I don't have people watching me on TV, but I've had them at work and you've helped me through mine."

Ah, hell. She's right. She opened up to me. I'm shutting her down, and I know why.

I sigh then serve up a slice of vulnerability. "I want you to see what it's like to have an awesome boyfriend, not someone who's in a funk over a loss," I admit.

She presses her lips together and her eyes shine. Shit. I'm making her cry again.

"Rachel, I didn't want to upset you."

"I'm not upset," she says, a little wobbly, but she's also smiling? What the hell is going on?

"You're not upset?"

She shakes her head, adamant. "I'm happy you're telling me the truth. I want to know. I like it when you're open with me."

I should have let her in. I shouldn't have tried to be Mister Happy all the time. I should have told her the truth, even if it's boyfriend territory. "Sometimes I get moody when we lose," I admit, then shrug, a little helplessly, a little vulnerable.

Or maybe a lot. That's new for me too. Opening up like that about my feelings.

"That makes perfect sense. Sometimes I get moody when I have a bad day too," she says, then looks around at the nearby crowds. "And when I have a bad day, I don't want to be around *everyone*." She tips her forehead to the exit. "So, do you want to get out of here and make dinner?"

It's like a weight is lifted off me for real. A weight

I've felt since last night when I shut her down. Since I shut *me* down. "I do."

On the way out, I swing by a flower stall and buy her a bouquet of wildflowers. I hand them to her as we leave. "I love these," she says, smelling them.

"I know."

The look in her eyes says we both learned a little something from tonight's lesson.

* * *

We go to my place and make dinner—the sea urchin thingy, some eggplants and mushrooms, and some rotisserie chicken I picked up earlier. As we cook, I tell her more of what I didn't say earlier. "I didn't think you'd want to know," I admit.

"But I do want to know," she says.

She doesn't add *as your friend*.

I'm sure that's what she means though. And I'm sure I'm okay with it. Truly. I have to be.

When we're nearly done eating, my phone alarm beeps. *Ask Rachel about Halloween party.* I scan the screen.

Her eyes light up as she reads it. "A party?"

"You like to dress up?"

"I do," she says.

"Good. But once we're done eating, I'd like to undress you."

She sets her napkin next to the plate with a flourish. "What a coincidence. I'm done."

24

FACE TIME

Rachel

Three things I never thought I'd know.

1. Carter's bed is bigger than mine, and I'm going to be spending a lot of time in it on my back in the next hour.

2. His brown eyes go from warm to molten when he touches me.

3. Make that sizzling, as he's just discovered the last remnants of the mark he left on me last week.

We're standing near the foot of his bed. My shirt is off, and he runs his fingers around the border of the bruise above my breasts, staring at it, mesmerized, seeming proud of it. "This is beautiful on you," he murmurs in a voice that's deep and full of longing. He can't take his eyes off it.

"All week it felt like my secret," I confess.

He dips his face to it, kisses it a little reverently. "I can give you more secrets," he says, pulling back to regard the last traces of the mark on my flesh as he skims a hand over my white lace bralette. "But first, remember the other night when I said it's fun to ask for what you want in bed?"

How could I forget? It's one of the first lessons he taught me. Something I should have known at this point in my life. But something that wasn't part of my education. "I do."

With a satisfied smirk, he plucks at the fabric of his Henley. "Take my shirt off," he rasps out as he gives the instruction. "I like it when you strip me." There's a hint of vulnerability in his voice right along with heat.

Those are two things that feel brand new and wonderful to me—heat and vulnerability in a man.

With trembling but excited fingers, I reach for the hem and slowly peel it off, savoring the reveal of his muscles and his skin as I go. When it's off, he takes my hands and presses them against his chest then runs them down it, shuddering as I go.

I'm learning so much about him after dark. He's really into my hands on his chest and his stomach. He likes when I touch his shoulders, his pecs, his abs. And I'm the cartographer who likes mapping his body.

"There's something I like to do in bed," he says a little dreamily as I explore him more.

"What is it?"

He stops my exploration, holding my hands in his for a second. "I need to talk. I need to tell you the things I want to do to you. I want to work you up with words."

I knew that about him, but a pulse beats between my legs as he says it so plainly. "It's working. Keep going," I whisper.

"Good," he says, as he unbuttons the top button on my jeans then teases at the zipper. "Because I want to spread you out on my bed and spend a good long time with my face buried between your thighs. That work for you?"

I love his lessons so much. "Yes," I say, ever the eager student.

He tucks a finger under my chin, making me meet his gaze as he asks one more question: "Think you'd like that, sweetheart?"

He didn't ask if I *do* like it. He knows my past hasn't given me a lot of clues into my own likes and dislikes. But he wants to give me my fantasies. To make them real. And I want to discover what they are with him. So, taking a cue from him, I say invitingly, "Find out."

Carter grabs my chin a little rough, digging his thumb along my jawline. Hard. Like the way he bit my chest the other night. "Then I'm going to strip you naked right now, and eat you up," he says.

In a flurry my jeans are off, then my lacy bralette. He's backing me up to the bed, his hunger evident in his eyes, in his breath, even in his nipples.

They're hard.

Am I into his nipples? Is that a kink of mine? I think it might be.

But there's no time to contemplate kinks when he skims off my panties, pushes a hand to my stomach, and shoves me onto the bed.

A little aggressively, and I like it.

I scoot up the bed and he follows, stalking me. He catches me by my ankles, with narrowed eyes. Then he slides those big hands up my legs to the inside of my knees and spreads me wide open.

For a few suspended seconds, he doesn't move. Just gazes at my pussy as he groans. It's a little uncomfortable, his eyes on me like this. His gaze, so intense, so unforgiving. So different. No one has ever stared at me like this. He breaks the stare and dips his face to my thigh, brushing a soft kiss before he lifts his head again to meet my gaze. "You wanted to know how a man takes care of his woman?"

"Yes."

"I'm going to show you how *this* man takes care of you with his mouth."

I have no more words. I'm nothing but a raw, vibrating nerve of desire.

But it's been a while since a man went down on me and meant it. And I can't quite fully relax when Carter kisses the inside of my thighs. I'm still tense, even as he murmurs against my skin. My mind races with questions.

What do I do with all this want inside me? What if I

have too much desire? What if he doesn't receive it? What if—

"Oh god," I groan, unbidden, when he kisses my clit. The sound is chased by a gasp from the center of my soul.

I can feel him smiling wickedly against me. I feel his want completely now. And I relax into it.

In seconds, my hands are in his hair and he's French kissing my pussy. He's thorough, kissing and sucking, swirling and flicking. Lapping up all my wetness like it's his sustenance.

He goes down on a woman like he plays football. He holds nothing back. He leaves it all on the bed as he worships me with his lips and mouth and tongue.

His scruff scrapes my thigh, and his hands spread me wide open, holding my legs so that I have to submit to his mouth.

To his desire too.

I grip his hair, watching him eat me till he's groaning, gripping my ass hard, and…oh, god…he's so aroused he's humping the bed.

It's such a filthy, beautiful sight, his need. I'm rocking against his face, letting go of all the what ifs, giving in completely.

But abruptly, he stops and springs up to stand.

Tension slams back into me. I close my legs. "What? Is everything okay?"

"I need you to do something," he says as he shucks off his jeans in seconds, like he's entering a contest for clothing removal.

"Tell me." I sound desperate. I feel desperate to know we're okay.

"Sit on my face," he says.

Ohhh.

Oh, yes.

I pant out a yes as he pushes off his boxer briefs.

His dick is hard and throbbing. He gives it a tug. I nearly lose my mind. He prowls back onto the bed, grabs my hips, and jerks me on top of him. He's not gentle. He's rough and hungry. "Ride me, baby. Don't hold back."

I don't know if this is a sex lesson or a Carter demand, but I'll take either one. "I've never done it like this before," I whisper.

His smile is filthy. Full of pride too. "Give me that first. Give it to me now."

He smacks my ass hard, urging me closer to his mouth. For a second, I *think* about what I'm doing, and it's a little absurd—humping a man's face with my pussy.

But an order is an order.

I straddle him, and he yanks me down. I reach for the headboard, needing something to hold onto. As I rock against him, I look behind me, my gaze traveling the length of his hard body to his cock.

Thick, hungry, and leaking at the tip.

I ache, and I chase that ache on his face. Taking a page from his playbook, I don't hold back either. I use him—his mouth and his scruff and his lips until I'm tossing my head back and shouting his name. My world turns black and beautiful as I detonate, sinking into a land of chaotic, erotic bliss.

One I'd like to spend a lot more time in with him.

Somehow, the night gets even better when he grips my hips and gently moves me off him. With a dark intensity in his eyes, he drags me under him, staring hotly down at me as he straddles my belly. He strokes his hungry cock. "Let me fuck your tits."

There is only one answer. "Yes."

He looks like I just gave him the keys to the kingdom as he moves over me, straddling my chest, then sliding that big dick between my boobs as I push them together, creating a warm tunnel for his greedy cock.

"Ever since that day, I've wanted to play with them, touch them. *Fuck them*. Love your tits. Just fucking love them."

I don't know why, but I wasn't expecting *that* confession. I didn't think the sight of half-naked me had done it for him. I love being wrong so much that I whisper, "Fuck me hard."

"Yeah?" It's a rough scrape of a question.

"Do it. Use me."

"Oh, fuck, baby," he says. Then he pumps faster, one hand on the headboard, the other in my hair. As I squeeze my breasts closer together, giving him more friction as he goes, I gaze up at him and he's different...

In bed, he's Carter unleashed. He's raw and savage, and it's such a thrill to experience this side of him.

I stick out my tongue, as an offering. His whole body shakes. He stops thrusting and he rubs his cock against my lips. "Lick the tip, baby," he says, urging my mouth open more. "Tease me with your tongue."

His desperation is an aphrodisiac and I can feel myself gushing again, even though I just came. I swirl my tongue around the head, then say, "Next time, I want to learn how to suck your dick. I want you to teach me how to take it all the way. Will you? Can you?"

He shudders, his eyes squeezing shut. "Fuck yes," he mutters, and when he opens them he slides down me and drops his mouth to mine, lavishing a hungry kiss there. "I *have* to fuck you now."

Have to. He *has to*.

"Yes. You do," I say.

He grabs a condom from the nightstand, puts me on all fours, and lines up behind me.

If he's Carter unleashed, I think I'm Rachel unleashed. Because I'm saying things I've never said. Things I'm discovering I love saying. Like…"Fuck me."

"I'll fuck you so good," he says as he sinks into me.

I repeat it again and again as he thrusts. Like I'm addicted to saying it.

He seems addicted to hearing it.

He fucks me good and hard, and he slides a hand between my thighs, working me over till I'm this close to spinning out again. When I'm gasping, he bites my shoulder, sucking on my flesh and muttering against me a word that I want to tattoo into my dirty heart. *"Mine."*

I cry out, a loud, animalistic sound as I shatter while all our noises fill the room. Grunts, slaps, then a final roar as he comes inside me.

* * *

A few minutes later, I'm boneless, floating on an orgasm cloud on his bed. I turn to the sweaty man by my side, who's breathing hard too. I run a finger down his biceps. "I had no idea what you were like in bed," I say, speaking out loud something that was only in my head before.

It's a statement of the obvious. But I don't want to keep it inside me.

"Well, yeah," he says with a smile, then there's that vulnerability again as he adds, "But you like knowing."

My chest goes tingly. A little fluttery. "I feel like I have a good secret."

He kisses the blooming bruise on my shoulder. "You're learning my secrets too. Want another?"

I turn to my side. "Yes."

He cups my cheek. "I want you to stay the night."

It's half a command but half a request too. Like he knows a sleepover isn't a sure thing. Like he can't just demand it even though he wants me here.

"Is that the secret?" I ask.

"That I want you to stay over? Yeah. But my other secret is this," he says and takes a beat, holding my gaze as he drags a thumb along my chin. "How much I like fucking my best friend."

I shiver. It's a sex compliment, but it feels like there's something more to it. Like I'm a brand-new discovery to him too.

He nuzzles my neck, and this post-sex affection is addictive. "And I want to fuck you in the morning too."

Oh. So that's why he wants me to spend the night. Easy access to sex.

For a second, my chest feels heavy with that awareness.

But that's silly since this *is* a sex thing. We're ultra-sexing. *As friends.* Besides, I want all the orgasms too. "I want to stay," I say, and that's true.

I want more in the morning. I want as much as I can get before this arrangement comes to its inevitable end and we return to friendship only. That's the only guarantee, and I'd be wise to focus on that—friendship—since that's what will be left when we leave the bedroom.

After we clean up and get into bed, he tugs me close and curls an arm around my stomach, spooning me against his warm, naked skin.

Just like that, it doesn't feel as if I'm here for easy access, or for friendship for that matter—not as he spends a good, long time kissing my neck and my shoulder and my hair. Till he's yawning and murmuring, "Come with me to Jason and Beck's Halloween party."

"An un-date?"

"A date," he says sleepily, then drifts off.

I don't know if he meant to ask me on a date or an un-date, but either way, I'm saying yes.

25

DANGEROUS GROUND

Carter

This is boyfriend territory too—morning breath.

Mine's gone, since I just brushed my teeth. But what about Rachel?

Would she be insulted if I left an extra toothbrush out for her on the bathroom vanity? Or grateful? I stare into the mirror, dragging a hand through my messy bed hair.

Ah, screw it. Some things are just universal. No one is a unicorn with sparkly rainbow breath when they wake up.

I yank open a drawer, grab an extra toothbrush thanks to the gift bags from the dentist, then set it on the marble counter.

I adjust it a little bit. Hmm. What if I leave it by the cup? Yeah, that works.

I return to the darkened bedroom, the half-light of early dawn streaming through the windows. It's six and she's still sound asleep.

But I'm wide awake and itching to run. Before I go though, some sudden impulse in my chest tells me to head to her side of the bed.

To check on her.

Quietly, I pad over in my socks then look down at her, pausing to take in the surreal scene of Rachel in my bed. It's strange to see my friend like this, but also...wonderful at the same damn time. I never thought I'd see this. Never imagined she'd be here. Never knew I'd like it so much.

Now that she is here, these *newish* feelings jostle for space front and center in my head.

I really need to run to burn off some of these wild ideas. I glance at the door to the bedroom, leading out to the living room. I should go. I should stop looking at her like a creeper. But a few strands of her brown hair flutter across her lips. She blows on them in her sleep, a subtle but valiant effort to get them off her face.

My heart squeezes. Gently, I brush the strands away, my fingers barely dusting her soft cheek. I don't want to stop touching her face, but I have to. I let go, then swallow, like I can erase not only the moment but this thrumming in my body.

I'm about to turn around when I catch a glimpse of the bruise on her shoulder. A surge of pride rushes through me, chased by primal feelings of possession.

I did that to her. I left that there. And she loved it.

Before I think better of it, I lean down and kiss her bruise, hoping I don't wake her.

She stirs, but only for a second.

I loved giving this to her. I want to do it again and again. So much that I need to get out of here, stat.

I pop in my earbuds, grab my sneakers from the living room where I left them, then lace up. Once I'm out the door, I text her that I went for a run.

Then I do everything I can to burn off these newish desires.

* * *

Forty-five minutes later, I swing open the door. Endorphins race through me, sweat slides down my chest, and I am feeling good.

No.

Make that great. Since I'm in my body now, not in my head playing what-if games…

And look at the reward in my kitchen.

Wearing her black shirt and a pair of leopard-print panties, Rachel's standing at the counter, staring at the espresso machine like she's found a time capsule fifty years in the future and has no clue what to do with the foreign contents.

"What is this?" she asks, studying the Slayer. She doesn't say hi. She doesn't even say good morning. The normalcy of this morning-after moment—the sheer in medias res-ness—hooks into my heart.

This could be us.

I come up behind her and pluck at the back of her

panties. "I could ask you the same question. What is *this*?"

I can feel her roll her eyes rather than see it. "Cool new invention called underwear."

I press a kiss to the back of her neck. "These aren't the ones you wore last night," I say in a low voice, leading the sexy witness to reveal her secrets.

She shudders against my lips. "I know."

I kiss her again, murmuring against her skin. "You brought a change with you."

Why does this excite me so much? We clearly had an ultra-sex un-date scheduled, and she's clearly a panty planner, and yet the idea that she *knew* she'd need a change is doing that newish thing to me again.

"Had a feeling I'd need them."

I drag my nose along the side of her neck. She smells good with orange blossom. And, like now, without orange blossom. "Should have brought one more pair."

On a soft rumble in her throat, she turns around, her back to the counter now, her gaze meeting mine. It's the first time she's looked at me since I came in from my run. Her eyes pop as she checks me out. "You're sweaty."

She sounds…enchanted.

"I am."

"I just learned I like sweat," she whispers as she reaches for the bottom of my gray T-shirt.

Then my sexy friend yanks off my shirt, slides her hands up my chest, and pinches a nipple like she's testing that out.

I draw in a sharp breath.

She bites the corner of her lips, then, keeping her

gaze on me, she strays to the other side, pinching that one, too, then rubbing her thumb across it. I grit my teeth. She covers my pecs with her hands, lifting her chin, looking pleased.

Proud.

Excited.

"You like that," she says, as if she's discovered treasure.

My heart speeds up, right along with my dick, which is insistent and throbbing. "I do," I say, then I lift her up, letting her wrap her legs around my waist as I carry her to the bedroom.

I learn two things—that she used the toothbrush and that she comes fast first thing in the morning.

Oh, and here's a third—a run doesn't get her out of my system at all.

* * *

Twenty minutes later, I'm making her a cup of espresso in the kitchen as she twists her hair into a bun. She's fully dressed and about to take off.

But first, caffeine.

"You'll be addicted to my coffee in no time. Monroe is," I say, then hand her a little cup.

After a hearty inhale, she takes a thirsty sip, then nods approvingly. "You're a badass barista," she says, then sets down the cup and opens a cupboard.

"Help yourself," I tease as I work on making another espresso.

With an *I've got this* smile, she finds the cheese-grater

mug, fills it with water and heads to the window to feed Jane.

That warm, buzzy feeling is returning to my chest once again. It feels like sunlight as I watch Rachel do this little thing for me—water a plant.

When she returns to the kitchen, she sets down the mug in the sink and checks the time on her phone. "I should get out of here. I'll shower at home."

I wiggle my eyebrows. "Because if you got in the shower with me, you'd want to ride me again?"

"Yes," she answers with a smile. Not a smirk. Not a sly grin. Just a straightforward smile that doesn't feel friendly. It feels borderline...romantic. For a second, maybe more, I imagine days like this. Her and me, here together in the morning.

But then, she blinks off the soft look, like she's resetting.

That's a reminder. I ought to do the same.

I clear my throat as I pour the next cup. "How are things going at the store? Any better?"

"Business is starting to pick up. I think maybe it's the Date Night thing."

"Nice! I'm seriously stoked that this deal is working out for you. I'll be sure to get the new video up soon," I say, and that gives me something else to focus on rather than these pesky feelings. Something helpful and productive for her.

"You're the best," she says with a friendly smile.

Friendly.

That's what we are. Even if she flashes a romantic grin now and then. Even if we fuck like crazy. And even if mornings feel so damn good when we're together. No matter how nice this feels, it's ultimately just friendly for her. I might be craving more, but that doesn't matter. It's not in the plan.

She drains the rest of her cup when there's a knock on the door. Her brow knits. "You get visitors at this hour?"

I groan. "Just Monroe. Want me to not answer it?" I ask. I hadn't thought about what our friends would say if they found out we were messing around. "I can ignore him."

"I don't mind," she says, mostly upbeat, but I can't quite read the meaning behind her tone. Does it mean something that she doesn't mind? Or does it mean nothing? Then she adds, with a wince. "Juliet and Elodie know. Is that okay? I told them you made me, um, see stars."

Way to win over my dirty heart. "Next time it'll be galaxies."

"Think big, Carter. How about a parallel universe?"

I wink at her. "Done. And it's more than okay that they know," I say as Monroe raps again.

Rachel laughs. "He's persistent."

"And addicted to my brew," I say as she heads over to open the door for him.

On the other side, Monroe's fist is raised, and I swear he's about to say *what took you so long*. But in a second he rearranges his expression, nods to Rachel, and says, "That tracks."

She laughs and pats his shoulder. "Good to see you again too."

Ah, I get it now. She doesn't mind her friends or my friends knowing because…we're just friends who are fucking. Because there's nothing more to this. Because she's probably not up in her head, thinking about how nice it is to have a cup of coffee with me in the morning.

As Monroe strides up to the counter, I give him a chin nod in greeting. "The usual?"

"Yes, please."

As Rachel grabs the bouquet of wildflowers from the glass of water where she left them, Monroe parks himself on the stool and then turns to study Rachel. From the crease on his brow, something is ticking in that brain of his. "You two would make a really interesting case study for this new podcast I'm launching."

Rachel arches a brow as she waits by the door. "You're doing a podcast?"

Monroe has told me about it, but not many others. I wait for him to explain.

"It launches in a couple of weeks. 'The Matchmakers and The Heartbreakers.' It's about every stage of relationships, from cradle to grave. This whole how-to-date thing you're doing would be fascinating. Do you two want to come on and talk about it?"

She tilts her head, curious but clearly skeptical. "What exactly do you want us to discuss?"

Monroe's mind is a locomotive, and his answer is instantaneous. "What you learned during your five dates. Everyone wants to hear about the rules of dating because they're constantly changing. You're exploring them in an almost scientific way."

"So, we're a science experiment?" she asks, but her smile says she's clearly amused. It's her *friendly* smile.

"Yes."

She looks to me. "Do you want to, Carter?"

No reason not to help a friend. "I'm in."

"Me too, then," she says, but then she lifts a finger, staring sternly at Monroe. "But we're not going to talk about your *that tracks* comment."

He nods, resolute. "Fair enough."

When she shifts her gaze to me, her expression softens. Does she even realize how she's looking at me? What it's doing to me? "Bye," she says, quiet and personal.

There's a moment when I almost think she'll come over and give me a goodbye kiss to match her tone, her look.

But she doesn't. Maybe because Monroe's here. Or maybe because that's beyond girlfriend lessons.

"See ya," I say, in my most casual voice. The one that masks the thrumming in my heart.

"Bye, Rachel," Monroe adds, his eyes drifting to the flowers.

When she's gone, I shake off the buzzy feeling once more as I hand my friend the espresso. He takes it with a thanks, then says bluntly, "So you're pretending you're just friends?"

Of course he'd ask. Of course I'll be honest. "We are just friends."

"Friends who are sleeping together?" He asks like it's a follow-up, "just to clarify" question posed to a patient.

"We won't be the first. And we're not going to let it

ruin the friendship," I say, determined. Then, I take a drink before I say anything else. Because I'm treading on dangerous ground now.

Monroe nods and takes another long swallow. "But has that ever worked in the history of ever?"

It's a legit question asked with genuine concern. But I don't know that I want to ponder it too hard. "I haven't studied relationships. Why don't you tell me, doc?" I counter, as my guard rails go up.

"Look, you don't have to be honest with me," he says, then gives me a serious stare. "But you bought her flowers. So I need to ask—are you being honest with yourself?"

I don't gulp. I don't blanch. I keep on my best poker face as I say, "Yes."

"Good. That's key," he says, believing me.

When he leaves a little later, though, I turn his question over a few more times while I wipe down the espresso machine.

The more time I spend with Rachel like this, the more I realize it's stirring up wishes and wants that have been part of me for a long time.

Probably years.

These nights and mornings are making me look back on all the other moments when she fell asleep in my house.

Like when she woke up and made me cinnamon pancakes.

If I'm being honest with myself—like Monroe challenged me to be—I'm pretty sure that once upon a time,

I wanted those cinnamon pancakes to turn into something more.

What would've happened years ago if I'd confessed my uneasy feelings about Edward? Would she have called off the wedding? Would she have knocked on my door and asked me to kiss her like crazy and show her how it feels when a man wants her?

I'd have shown her and meant it then too.

Maybe I'd have had a chance to take her out before I met Sasha, Izzy, or Quinn. Before I became this jaded guy who doesn't believe romance works out.

When I set down the washcloth and finish my half-drunk cup of espresso, it's chased with regret.

That was then. This is now. We've both changed. I'm no longer a wide-eyed rookie when it comes to romance. I've been around the block and have the battle scars on my heart.

And Rachel? Well, she's recovering from a horrible marriage. She's barely divorced from a man who fathered three children in secret while married to her. Rachel's been honest with me from the start. She wants sex with someone she trusts, and she also wants to experience the *idea* of a good boyfriend.

Not the reality.

She deserves sex and kindness. Hell, she should be showered in foot rubs and enjoy a willing ear from someone who pours her a glass of wine at the end of the day and leaves all the bullshit of relationships at the door.

No, in the next freaking state.

I can give her what she wants for three more dates. I

can lavish her in orgasms and gifts like a fucking champ. I will make sure she feels nothing but bliss from this guy.

And, here's the reality. I'd be a selfish prick if I pushed my sexy, sweet, funny, wounded friend for romance just because my heart is a little achy for her. I'd leave a shitty review online for me if I did that.

I damn well know this isn't just ultra-sexing and undating *for me*. The way I looked at her this morning in my bed, the way I felt when she puttered around my home, the way I was desperate to tell her how I felt about the game last night—that tells me all I need to know.

But I also know *this*—you win some and you lose some.

These newish feelings might hurt me a little over the next three dates. But I can handle the pain, just like I can handle a hard tackle.

The thing I won't stand for is to let my feelings ruin our friendship. No way will I be that guy. I will swallow them down like the last dregs of a coffee and then motor on through the plan.

Starting now.

I grab my phone, search for cute leopard-print panties, and order a few pairs.

I send them to my home for express delivery. Then I forward her the email, adding a line: *For next time.*

It's a sex gift. That's all. Even though a new notification pops up on my phone—a calendar invite for this weekend.

Carter and Rachel decide upon costumes for the

Halloween party so they can claim top prize like the badasses they are.

I hit accept. I won't feel all warm and fuzzy about a reminder. I won't. I just fucking won't.

Then, with my renewed focus, I open my text app and start a message.

26

IF YOU GIVE A MOOSE A TO-DO LIST

Carter: What else is on your list?

Rachel: Besides showering?

Carter: Mental note made of showering.

Rachel: You're taking a note that I'm showering?

Carter: You took mental pictures of my shower. Fair's fair. But seriously. Your sex list. In bed last night, you mentioned you wanted me to show you how to do…a certain something.

Rachel: Are you actually afraid to say give a blow job?

Carter: Blow me.

Carter: Suck me.

Carter: Take that dick.

Carter: There. I was being fucking polite.

> Rachel: I'm so proud of you for using your words. But by list, I thought you meant a to-do list.

Carter: You thought I was texting you about your to-do list?

> Rachel: Well, yeah. And it was sort of sweet that you'd ask.

Carter: Now I have to know—do you really put shower on your to-do list?

> Rachel: Ummmmm.

Carter: Holy shit. You do???

> Rachel: Sometimes I get busy and then I'm doing fifty things and I'm behind on the day, and then all of a sudden, someone is coming over and I'm showering later than expected and then he shows up right when I'm answering the phone with my boobs flying!

Carter: DO NOT EVER PUT SHOWER ON YOUR TO-DO LIST WHEN I'M ON MY WAY OVER.

> Rachel: Glad to know you always want me to answer phone calls shirtless.

Carter: I always do. Anyway, so you have a sex list. Go on.

> Rachel: I don't actually have a sex list. But I have some ideas.

Carter: Sure, sure, same thing. Now, tell me your ideas.

> Rachel: Besides learning how to suck your secret dick?

Carter: And that nickname stuck.

> Rachel: In the back of my throat.

Carter: Well played.

> Rachel: Thank you. Thank you very much.

Carter: Anyway, I'm waiting for your naughty list. And make it very, very specific.

> Rachel: Fine. Here's an item. After the first time we had sex, when I was bringing cookies to the table, I was admiring your strong back. You were shirtless. I was ogling your back muscles. Then checking out your ass. And then I wondered how you'd look in the mirror fucking me. And then I decided I wanted to have sex in front of a mirror to watch you, um, rail me. So it was sort of an 'if you give a moose a muffin' train of thought.

Carter: Did you just quote a children's book to explain how you want to watch me fucking you?

> Rachel: I did.

Carter: There's only one thing on my to-do list now. And I will spend the rest of the day thinking about that.

> Rachel: Giving a moose a muffin, Carter?

Carter: Yes. Exactly.

> Rachel: What about you? Do you have a list?

Carter: Besides walking in on you playing with yourself? And, well, everything else?

> Rachel: Yes. Be specific, Carter.

Carter: I want to undress you slowly, put you on your stomach on my bed, kiss your shoulders, your back, the dip of your ass, those ass cheeks, your thighs, and your calves. Run my mouth all over your sweet orange-blossom skin till you're writhing, begging, and clawing at the sheets. And maybe then I'll finally satisfy the sweet ache between your legs. So yeah. There's that.

Carter: By the way, what else is on your to-do list today? Grocery shopping? Popping into the drugstore? Rotating your tires?

Carter: Rachel?

Carter: You still there?

> Rachel: Rachel is not here right now. Rachel was spending some time with her new toy. Rushing to work is now on her to-do list.

Carter: Along with talking about herself in the third person?

Rachel: Well, yes. I had an out-of-body experience from the O I just gave myself, so yeah, third person feels apropos. I might still be floating.

Rachel: By the way, I changed my panties again. Here's a pic of what I changed into.

Carter: Holy black-lace-I-want-to-rip-off-with-my-teeth. That's what you have on today?

Rachel: Yes. You like?

Carter: I like it so much I'm inviting myself over after work. Say yes, Rachel.

Rachel: Yes. You're on my to-do list tonight.

Carter: Same to you.

Rachel: And, if you give a girl a sex list, you just might get a couple orgasms.

27

THE LIFE DOCTOR

Rachel

That woman I just walked past on the street, the one chatting on her phone about her yoga class?

Does she know I'm having the time of my life?

What about that mom with the stroller I'm cruising by on Fillmore?

Can she sense that the woman strolling past her—me—is fueled by sunshine, the best dates ever, and oh, a bunch of mind-blowing orgasms?

I want to spread my arms and twirl in a field of flowers as I belt out a tune.

Climb every big dick, chase every O...

It'll be a chart-topper, I'm sure. Everyone should have a date at the farmers' market, a night of toe-curling sex, and a morning where you can just be yourself with another person. In fact, that gives me an idea.

As I walk, I tap out another text.

> Rachel: Hey! We could add Life Doctor to our doctor resumes. The Life Doctors prescribe…a date with your best friend and red-hot sex too.

> Carter: I'll take that medicine. Oh, wait—I am.

I'll take another several doses of it. Who knew girlfriend lessons would be like *this*? I'd thought I'd go to dating school and do some research on a distant, faraway romantic future for when I'm ready to dip my toes into the shark-infested dating waters. Instead, the professor is giving me special attention, and I like the extra credit very much.

So much that it's changing me. It's making me see myself in new ways. I see others through a new lens too.

Like…now.

I turn on the corner of Fillmore Street, onto the block of Haven Spa. I'm a little nervous heading into enemy territory, but I've got to do this. I have to take this important step. I'm clutching a gift, completely unsure of how it'll be received.

Taking a fueling breath, I march up the block, open the door to Haven Spa, and hope for the best. The thing about gifts is you don't know if they'll be wanted. But sometimes, you need to give them anyway, even if they might backfire.

I really hope this doesn't backfire.

At the front desk, a pair of placid-looking women in

matching lavender balloon pants look up in sync. A small fountain set on a stone table gurgles. A Zen garden sits next to it. Birds chirp overhead, but not actual birds. A soundtrack. But I wouldn't be surprised if Ava sailed out here with hummingbirds perched on her shoulders.

"Good morning. May I help you?" one of the lavender twins asks.

I kick my nerves to the curb, then I stride right up to the counter. "Good morning. You look lovely today. Is Ava here?"

"I am."

The serene voice of the wife of the man who thinks I'm a bitch greets me. I swivel around and there she is, floating from, I don't know, a session in the hydro pool where she probably glided in on a giant conch.

Chin up. Say it like you mean it. "I just wanted to say thank you, Ava," I begin, holding tight the gift I brought for her—brownies with peanut butter swirl. I baked them last night, before I saw Carter. I was going to bring all these to Fable as a thanks for being, well, for being Fable. But I squirreled some away in a Tupperware dish this morning for this purpose. "And to let you know I am feeling all the good vibes now. So here's a gift."

Whether I agree with the way she spoke to me or not doesn't matter. I was rude to a customer, and it had a boomerang effect. I need to do better for me. I need to be the kind of person I want to be. That's the kind of person who apologizes. Who takes responsibility for her mistakes.

With hopeful hands, I offer her the dish.

Head tilted, she stares at it, like it's as much a curiosity as I am. She says nothing. Maybe I wasn't clear enough? Apologetic enough? I hasten to fill the silence with a deeper explanation. "And you were right. I wasn't happy. I took that out on your husband, and by extension, you," I add, my gut churning with worry. Holy smokes, this be-a-better-person stuff is hard. Especially since she's so unreadable. But turning my attitude around can't only be about me. It has to be about others. How I treat them. "But I'm working to be happier. And I'm trying to feel all the vibes, all the goodness, all the energy."

She hums, still giving little away in her expression, but she takes the brownie container. "Thank you, but I should let you know, for the sake of transparency, that I don't eat brownies."

Um, why are you taking them then?

"Um, I do, I do!" a cheery voice calls out.

It's one of the lavender twins. Thank god. I was dreading crawling out of here with my tail between my legs and a container of rejected brownies in my paws.

"You can have it then, Cassandra," Ava says, like a generous benefactor, handing it to her minion who scurries over.

Ava turns to me, gives an ethereal nod, then says, "They smell good."

And that's better than expected. I'll take that as a step in the right direction. I don't say a word about her sending me business again, because that would make this payola rather than a gift.

Instead, I say something simple but surprisingly true. "I hope you have a great day."

I didn't feel that way about her a little more than two weeks ago. But I do now.

As the door swings shut behind me, I strut down the street on my good-vibe high. Life is better again. I've got three more dates with a guy who treats me like a queen. I have friends who I adore. And a business that—knock on wood—seems to be turning around.

Oh, and the icing? Tonight, I'm gonna have mirror sex. What does one wear to a mirror sex date? Well, besides nothing?

I run through my options of pretty things, as I unlock the store and pull open the door, ready to be a badass business babe today.

A few minutes later, Fable strides in with a yawn. "Damn, I am tired, and you look like you've been conquering the world."

"I've been climbing mountains and spreading goodwill," I say, then I reach into my canvas bag for another Tupperware container. "And for you, you goddess of jewelry-making and managerial awesomeness. Brownies with peanut butter swirl."

"Woman. Are you trying to win my loyalty for all time? Because let me just say—done. And gimme." She makes grabby hands, then bites into a brownie and moans. "You should sell jewelry with a side of brownies, Rachel."

It's not a bad idea.

A few minutes later, the first customer comes in, and I sell her two pairs of chandelier earrings.

Yup. I am Rachel 2.0, and I have Carter to thank.

Speaking of, I should send him a thank-you gift. He bought me undies after all. But what's a good thank-you gift for a guy? Is there an equivalent of boxer briefs? I imagine packs of briefs from TJ Maxx and Target. Not really in the same league as sexy panties.

What about aftershave? But does he wear it? Like it? I could get him a mug, but we've done that. I'd rather get him something more personal.

And something sexy like he got me.

Ooh! I know!

While there's a lull in traffic, I jump online, and order a new bodywash to send to his home. Then I add a note. *I wanted something that says I like you shirtless. And this seems to do the trick. To future showers.*

* * *

I rush around all morning, answering calls from suppliers, paying invoices, and checking in with Stella, the manager of the Venice location. She'd been managing the store like a pro for a few months, but lately she's been asking for more personal days. And now she tells me she wants me to make sure the employees are better trained for when she needs personal days. I don't tell her she's taken a lot recently, because what if she needs them? Instead, I tell her I'll visit the Venice store soon, then I return to the front of *this* store. Fable is chatting with a petite woman with a pixie cut. I recognize her as the owner of the cute dress shop.

"Oh, you run Better With Pockets," I say brightly.

"I do," the woman says.

"And Beatrix has some good news for you," Fable says with a big *get your ass over here* grin.

"We're doing an impromptu sidewalk block party and sale tonight. Do you want to include some of your necklaces—"

I say yes before she can even finish.

* * *

I dart into my office and call Carter during a quick lunch break. He answers with a "hey," then there's a loud clang of heavy metal hitting the ground.

He must be in the weight room. Mmm. That's a nice image. Carter pumping iron. It brings me more good vibes.

"Hey, I can't meet tonight. I'm sorry. But it's good. I swear," I say, feeling a little guilty for being so excited about a sidewalk sale instead of mirror sex. And all the things that come with mirror sex. Like laughter, and friendship, and…oh! We really need to do that puzzle. I really should add that to my to-do list.

"Oh," he says, with a tiny note of disappointment and a second or two of quiet.

What does that mean? Is he bummed? Edward was never bummed. Edward never seemed disappointed when something came up for me at the store. Even the time I had to cancel a dinner because the neighborhood business association in Venice called an impromptu meeting to discuss the prevalence of weed in the area.

But of course, Edward had other things to keep him busy. He'd just gone to Palm Springs to play papa.

"No big deal," Carter adds, all cheer now, like he shifted gears and is back to speed. "What's the good news?"

It takes me a second to shift gears because I'm strangely liking his disappointment. That's a sign he really wanted to see me tonight. *Well, he wanted to bang you.*

But you know what? Even if Carter's bummed about no banging, I'll take that as a victory because I *know* I'm the only one Carter's banging.

And that is a very good thing.

With that settled in my mind, I quickly explain that Bling and Baubles was invited to be part of a sidewalk block party with other businesses on Fillmore Street.

"Fuck yes," he says, and his enthusiasm is so genuine. It's another thing I *feel* for sure. Another thing I like being certain about. "I knew it."

"I'm so excited. I kind of can't believe it," I say.

"Things are happening for you. You deserve it."

Do I deserve it? I don't know that I believe people deserve good things. But I want to earn good things. Maybe my apology for my bad vibes set the stage for some good karma.

"I think it was the girlfriend lessons," I confess in a whisper.

"Explain."

"I think they're helping my mood. The dates and, well, the ultra-sexing too," I say, though I'm pretty sure spending time with someone I trust is the medicine. Someone I trust myself with.

"You're a life doctor, Rachel," he says.

"Evidently. Oh, and you can stop by if you want."

Quickly, he clears his throat. "Hey, I need to jump. Wilder is coming in."

"Oh, right. Go, go, go," I say, then hang up. I stare at his name on the phone a little longer, feeling bad that I won't see him tonight after all.

But I'm here in San Francisco to rebuild my life, my heart, my soul. And lately, my business. Tonight, I will be all-business Rachel.

Even if I'll miss Carter.

A lot.

28

MY, WHAT A BIG EGGPLANT YOU HAVE

Carter

There's no mistaking the precise echo of wingtips on the concrete floors in the training facility. People who work here wear sneakers—the guys on the team, the trainers, the coaches. If I'm hearing wingtips, it means either the owner or the general manager is on his way.

While I'm not scared of Wilder Blaine, per se, the boss is the boss is the boss. So when the man wearing the expensive shoes appears in the door to the weight room, looking like a billion bucks, I do what I would with anyone.

Parked on the weight bench, I curl the heavy weight one more time, then another, saying, "Nine hundred and ninety-nine, one thousand." I set down the weight and blow out a satisfied breath, turning to my buddy. "Hard to keep up with me, isn't it, Hamlin?"

From his spot at a nearby bench, my teammate

scoffs. "Never, Hendrix. I already ran eight miles," he says, before he turns to the man in charge. "Oh, hello, Mr. Blaine. Just getting a light workout in before I memorize all the new plays."

Wilder gives a small, humoring smile. "Competition. I like that."

He shifts his attention to me, his eyes a little...intense.

Oh, shit. I brace myself for some sort of comment about the Sunday game, a *try harder, do better* thing. Which is kind of ridiculous because Wilder doesn't indulge in that level of micromanagement. But then again, he doesn't usually stop by the weight room unless there's some kind of business to discuss.

"Everything's going well with Date Night, Carter?" he asks. It's more of a statement, though, letting me know he's on top of things.

I breathe a sigh of relief, grateful he's here about Date Night. No matter how long it's been since I was chewed out by an authority figure, I'm always on edge when a coach, a principal, a manager calls my name.

It's my own PTSD from being the kid who drifted off in class, the kid who couldn't sit still, the kid who talked out of turn, the kid who became too obsessed with a science project but then abandoned it for something shinier.

I'm older now. But old fears die hard.

I give Wilder my full attention. "I'm glad to hear you feel that way, sir. I know they're an important sponsor."

"They are. Our partnership is going great. Date Night helps us reach a different demographic. We're getting younger people to come to the games. That's important, marketing football to a new generation."

"It sure is," I say.

"And I'd be remiss if I didn't give you my suggestion for a great date."

Oh.

I wasn't expecting that. Rachel and I mapped out a lot of options for our next three dates, but of course, I'll switch it up for the boss. "Sure. Let me know what you have in mind."

He lifts a tattooed finger like he's going to make a very important point. "Mini golf makes for a great date. And you probably already know that my course has mini golf. I'd be happy to comp you."

I don't need the free date, but you don't turn the big man down. "Thank you. We'll do that."

"Terrific." He shifts his gaze to Hamlin. "I was thinking, Malik." He stops to rub his hand across his chin as if deep in thought. "Why don't you make sure to go run a few extra miles? Make it an even ten."

Hamlin's eyes pop. He swallows in obvious surprise. "Sure."

And on that mic drop, the man in charge walks away.

Once the sound of the shoes has faded and the boss is out of earshot, Hamlin turns to me and sing-songs, "Can I play mini golf with the owner too? Please? I want to suck up to him by the clowns on the golf course."

"Wilder Blaine is too classy for clowns."

"Maybe the two of you can discuss how classy he is by the windmills and the dinosaurs," Hamlin retorts.

I roll my eyes. "Dude didn't invite me to play mini golf with *him*. He just wants me to play at his fucking course instead of some other one. But I get it. You're jealous. That's understandable, Ham, since you've only got one ring."

He growls. Yeah, that shuts him down every time.

A throat clears. Is Wilder back? Shit. Did he hear us?

Cautiously, I turn to the door, and I'm relieved as fuck to see Beck. The quarterback stands against the doorframe, arms crossed, smirking. Where the hell did he come from?

"He wants you there at his golf course because of the eggplant," Beck says.

My brow knits. "What are you talking about?"

"Dude. You're a meme." Beck whips out his phone, and we gather around. He hits play on a three-second clip of Rachel at the farmers' market picking up the eggplant and mouthing, *"It's so big"* while she stares.

Right. At. Me.

29

RAIN CHECK

Rachel

Upbeat pop tunes give the sidewalk sale a party atmosphere. Crowds weave along the walkway, stopping at booths, checking out cute clothes from Better With Pockets, quirky gifts from Effing Stuff, cold brew from Doctor Insomnia's Tea and Coffee Emporium, and Fable's latest collection of "Treat Yourself" necklaces—sparkly sun, moon, and star pendants displayed on our table.

We've sold as many necklaces in the last few hours as we have in the last few days. I'll need to bring some brownies to Beatrix at the dress shop tomorrow to thank her for this opportunity.

Even though it's nearing nine, the event shows no sign of winding down. I tuck my phone back in my pocket as a woman in ripped jeans and a cropped sweatshirt walks past my table, then does a double take and hurries back to me.

"Hi," she says with a curious sort of grin. It seems like it's leading to something—something good—and I am here for it.

"Hey there," I say. "Can I help you with anything tonight?"

She tucks a strand of sleek black hair behind her ear, then lets out a relieved breath. "I just wanted to say your farmers' market advice is so good. I'm seeing a guy this weekend, and I was like *Do I research the farmers at the market? Do I ask if they use pesticide? Do I have to know all the different types of mushrooms?* My brain was spinning, and then your video made me realize, *Oh, I can just have fun.*"

I smile at her. "Dating is hard enough without having to memorize mushroom varieties."

Fable lifts an opinionated finger. "Chanterelles, honey. Those are the best."

"Good to know," the woman says, then turns back to me. "Also, you two are seriously the cutest."

I bump shoulders with Fable, proud of my talented friend. "Thanks. She's a goddess at jewelry-making."

My colleague snorts. "Rachel, I'm pretty sure she's talking about you and the hottie."

My cheeks heat. Oops. "Oh. Right."

"How long have you been together?" the woman asks.

I shake my head, dismissing that notion. I am definitely not trying to present myself as his girlfriend. I don't want anyone to think I'm trying to ride the coattails of his local sports fame. "We're just friends," I emphasize.

The woman snort-laughs.

That's...bold.

But okay, she can have her opinion. Rachel 2.0 isn't going to be a jerk anymore.

"Well, everyone is shipping you," she adds.

"They are?" That's news to me.

"Especially after the eggplant comment," she says.

Ah. That makes sense. Carter texted me earlier today. When I first opened it, his *I need to give you a heads-up about something* had me worried.

But then he'd sent the clip and added: *If they only knew what you plan on doing with my eggplant, just imagine the comments.*

Relieved, I'd laughed. Because even though I was making a dick joke, it was still a friendly one. I replied: *If they only knew how much you liked a pair of melons with eggplant, just imagine those comments.*

The woman pulls out her phone and shows me the latest.

He'd be the best boyfriend.

He is seriously boyfriend goals.

And you two are soooo adorbs.

My heart warms. He *is* the best. But it's not fair to him to let people presume we're together. So once more, I say, "We are *truly* great friends."

She grins. "Maybe he'd date me, then."

What??? I want to lunge at her.

No, he won't date you. He won't date anyone if he can't date me—don't you get it?

Whoa. Where did that nasty, green-eyed creature come from?

I try to shake off the jealousy. To accept that Carter's an unattached man. If I want to make it clear that we're just friends—friends with temporary benefits—I have to acknowledge that he's on the market.

"You never know," I say, hoping my breezy tone is believable. "But I hope your farmers' market date is great."

I hope it goes so well you marry the guy and have ten babies.

"Me too," she says, then her gaze snags on a sun pendant. "I think I'll take this necklace too."

"It's going to look great on your date," I say, *and you will tell your future children all about the night you met their dad.*

As I'm wrapping it up, she glances at her phone one more time, then at me with a thoughtful look. "You know, you should make an eggplant necklace."

When she leaves, I'm no longer strategizing how to tie her hands so she can never swipe right on Carter. I'm whipping my gaze to Fable, already picturing the purple veggie hanging on a silver chain. That's brilliant. That's like money-tree-level brilliant.

"Can you do that?" I whisper. The idea is too precious to say aloud.

"I'm on it," she says, then I hear a familiar voice.

"Looks like you two are up to trouble."

Warmth sizzles down my spine. "You came by," I say, a smile overtaking me when Carter strolls closer. Did my words come out kind of dreamy-sounding? I think they did.

"We were getting some ice cream," he says, nodding toward his teammate. Malik Hamlin's by his side.

"He treated me. Because I'm better than him," Malik deadpans.

"At what?" I ask, taking the bait.

"Everything," Malik says.

Carter laughs. "Whatever you tell yourself to sleep better."

Malik's gaze strays to our table and to some chains for men. "Oh, sweet. I need a new gold chain," he says.

"You'd look fine in this one," Fable says, tapping one for him.

He meets her gaze. "You think so?"

"I'm never wrong," she says.

There's a glint in Malik's eyes as he says, "I'll take it."

Damn. Easiest sale ever.

Carter shoots me a look that says *Damn, Malik moves fast.*

I give him one that says *I know!*

Then, I let my gaze linger on Carter a little longer. His forest-green T-shirt hugs his pecs and shows off his biceps. The ends of his hair are a little wet.

While Fable rings up Malik's purchase, Carter leans a little closer. "Thanks for the shirtless soap," he says in a low voice, just for me.

A tingle rushes down my chest. I feel fizzy and good in a way that's more than sexual, even though I know this thing between us is an experiment with an end date. Yes, I want mirror sex, but I also want to do something for him.

"Rain check on our plan tomorrow night? But it's for a lesson on my knees."

His eyes say *hell yes* as he nods. Maybe even growls.

Ha, take that. He's mine for a little longer.

30

THE LUCKY SPATULA

Carter

Guys with big dicks get no sympathy. I get it. It's a gold-plated problem. But here's what no one tells you about a large hammer.

Most girls don't want to suck the chrome off your bumper. And hey, no shade on the ladies. I'd be afraid my jaw would detach too.

So, I don't get my hopes up when I go to her home the next night. I'm more than happy however things go.

Rachel swings open the door, seductively licking a pink lollipop. And all my hopes rise along with my instant erection. Plus, she's wearing a white cami *with no bra*.

"Come in," she says after a long, sensual lick.

"Yeah, I think I just did." I step inside. An unfamiliar tune is playing from her mini speaker on the living room table. Sounds sexy, in an *eighties* kind of way. "What's that?"

"Mood music. 'Head' by Prince," she says.

Someone doesn't plan to back down. Bless her. Just fucking bless her. "Nice pick," I say, and this is all new.

The whole setup.

I'm used to doing the seducing. I've always taken the lead with sex. That's what I like, and that's what a lot of women I've been with have liked. But I've never walked into a woman's home with her ready to seduce me.

With her mouth.

The lights are low in the living room but not off. Fantastic. I want to watch her. There's a bottle of cherry-flavored lube on the coffee table and a hand towel. Right next to a large pink dildo.

I have questions, but I've got an answer to the most important one. It's yes. As in, yes, so far, I like being seduced by her.

She takes my hand and guides me to the couch. "Sit," she says. Immediately, she shakes her head, embarrassed. "Wait. Sorry. I should, um, get you ready with some foreplay."

Laughing, I close the distance between us and grab the back of her head. "Sweetheart, I was ready yesterday when you invited me over. I was more ready when I walked up the steps to your home. And I was the readiest when you opened the door sucking a lollipop." I take the candy from her hand and press a hello kiss to her lips, murmuring over the sugary sweetness of the sucker—she tastes like strawberry.

I break the kiss, setting the candy on a coaster on the

table. "There. One hundred percent ready and then some."

"I had it all planned. I practiced on Little Carter," she says, then gestures to the sex toy.

My brain is a fried egg on a hot sidewalk on a summer day. "You named a sex toy after me?"

She nods, eagerly. "Yes. Do I get an A plus?"

"You're a star student," I say, but I'm a star teacher too. I've learned a thing or two about what Rachel needs —some bossing around. "Now, listen, your teacher has a whole lesson for you. And it starts like this. Take off my shirt. Unzip my jeans. And get out my dick."

* * *

Five minutes later, I'm naked on her couch, legs spread like a king, and the sexiest woman I've ever known is kneeling between my thighs, running her hands up and down my legs.

I'm shivering.

Fucking shivering.

She drags her nails along my skin, making me hiss. Then she dips her face near my dick and presses a kiss right next to my cock.

Tease. Fucking tease. "Did you tease Little Carter too?"

She looks up and flashes me a sexy grin. "Maybe I did. Maybe he liked it."

"I bet he did," I murmur.

"Do you?"

I grip the base of my cock, pointing it toward her

Plays Well With Others

mouth, squeezing out a drop of arousal. "Yes. Now, treat me like a piece of candy."

She flicks her tongue across the drop and then hums. But my tease of a student is so defiant. She still doesn't take me between those pretty pink lips. She lets her lush chestnut locks fall like a silky curtain over my throbbing cock, then rubs her face against it.

Jesus. She's like a sex cat, rubbing her soft cheek on my dick, and I'm vibrating with lust. Finally, she flicks the tip of her tongue over the head. It's so good it's unholy. "Yessss," I moan.

She draws the crown past her lips, and my brain pops with excitement. Rachel learning how to suck me off is the hottest thing I've ever seen. I can hardly teach her when she's written her own lesson plan, and it involves licking the tip with abandon.

When she swirls her tongue under the head, my thighs shake. It's not just the motion of her tongue. It's the expression on her face. *Delight.* The way she sucks me like she loves it.

She's murmuring against my shaft as she draws me a little deeper. My internal temperature kicks up to thermonuclear.

"Fuck," I mutter.

I can feel her smile against my dick.

I'm honestly not sure she needs any instruction. She's clearly been practicing on Little Carter. She's done her homework. But there's one thing she could do. "Use your hands too, baby," I urge.

She blinks, then drops me from her mouth. "I

forgot," she says. "I was too excited. Thanks for the reminder."

Dear god.

It's a wonder I don't blow right now.

I reach past her to grab the lube. She holds open her hands, and I drizzle some into her palms.

"You're a two-hander." She says it like she's proud of my dick or maybe of her ability to take care of it. My eager girl is back on me with a throaty purr, her mouth a warm heaven, her hands a slick tunnel.

And I'm incinerated.

It's not the technique. It's not the placement of her hands. It's her—the sounds she makes. The enthusiasm she shares with me. The excitement that's palpable in her touch, in her body, in her eyes.

She wants this to be good for me.

She practiced on a silicone dildo to give me a blow job. If that doesn't say dedication, I don't know what does.

Her hands slide along the base, her tongue corkscrewing over the head.

Electricity crackles in me when she rolls her tongue down the underside of my shaft. I'm so damn sensitive there that I'm moaning, gasping, then just begging. "Finish me off, baby. I'm so fucking close."

In no time, her lips wrap tightly around me again, and everything is throbbing urgently. Her hands are slick and hot; her mouth is paradise. I grunt out an alert. "Coming," I mutter.

She swallows my release, then seconds later, as I'm

sighing and panting, she grabs the towel and wipes her hands.

"C'mere," I tell her. She climbs onto my lap, and I cup her face. She looks happier than I've ever seen her. I don't know what to make of that, except *these lessons are working on her.*

They're also working on me. Almost too well on me, but those are the risks. And I'm racing full speed ahead through them, no matter the danger.

Especially when I kiss her, tasting me, tasting cherry lube, and tasting *her*. I love all the tastes because the cocktail tastes like our private nights together.

When I break the kiss, I say, "I've never had a blow job like that."

Curious, she arches a brow. "What do you mean?"

"Like you really wanted to."

"Spoiler alert: I really wanted to."

"I could tell," I say, stroking her cheek.

"No one has ever…?" She doesn't finish the question, almost like she doesn't want to talk about other people or other blow jobs.

I don't really either, but I also want her to know what she did to me. "Not like that. Not with so much enthusiasm."

"Can I tell you something?" she asks, her eagerness to share pitching her tone higher.

"Anything."

"I like it. You taste really good," she says.

It's just sex. It's truly just sex. But goddamn, she makes me feel better than I knew was possible.

There's only one thing to do with all these feelings.

Give it to her good.

I strip off her top, tear off her panties, and then devour her pussy till she's writhing and screaming my name as she fucks my face. Seconds later, she's coming on my mouth.

When I wedge myself alongside her on the couch, my stomach rumbles.

Laughing, she sets a hand on my abs. "Let me make you something."

"Did you look that up in *How to be a Great Girlfriend?*"

She laughs. "No, Carter. I just know you. You like to eat. And despite your best efforts, you can't survive on me alone."

"But I can try," I say.

She rolls her eyes. "You need food. Not more pussy."

"I beg to differ," I say, since appearances and all.

But still, she does know me. And I like it too much, this knowing. These moments. This little cocoon of our private nights.

We get dressed and head to the kitchen where she grabs ingredients from the fridge with a focus that tells me she's planned for this. Then she confirms it as she says, "I went shopping for you."

"You did?"

"Well, I knew you were coming over, and I figured you'd be hungry. I wanted to have something to cook. Sort of the whole girlfriend experience."

She wants these days and nights together to be as good for me as they are for her. That blows my mind in a whole new way. I'm happier than I have a right to be as she appoints me her sous chef while she whips up lemon zucchini noodles with garlic chicken bites, telling me how she looked up recipes today at work, then shopped after she left the store. Hearing these little details of her to-do list tugs on my heart. This is another thing I like. Another thing I'll miss.

What would it be like if I were honest with her like I've tried to be with myself? Like Monroe asked me to be? Would I tell her how much I like hearing about her to-do list? How much I like cooking with her? Even chopping these orange peppers, as I'm doing now?

Done.

"Do you mind?"

What? Hold on. She just asked me something. Fuck. I have no clue what I do or don't mind. I hate that I drifted off while she was talking to me, even though I drifted to thoughts of her. "What did you say?" I ask, offering a guilty smile that ought to cover my sin.

She smiles warmly. "The olive oil. To your left. Do you mind handing it to me?"

I set down the knife, grab the bottle, and give it to her like a fucking champ of a sous chef who is in the zone all the time.

As she drizzles some in the pan, she asks gently, "Where'd you go? Were you replaying the game again?"

My heart squeezes at the question. Quinn never asked. No one I've dated really has. Everyone assumes I'm bored when I drift off. But she asks the question with genuine care and interest, as if she thinks I must have gone someplace important—like at the farmers' market when I was moody dwelling on the game. Now she's asked me to open up to her as part of the girlfriend lessons.

No fucking way am I going to blurt out that I was picturing a future I'll never have with her. So I omit that while still being as open as I can. "Just thinking about some plays we reviewed today. I'm going to do an extra workout tomorrow. Hey, you know what else I wanted to know?" I ask, doing a one-eighty back to our sexperiment. "What about the dildo? When did you buy that?"

She drops the chicken cubes in the sizzling pan and shoots me a playful look. "Last night after I left the sidewalk sale. There was a Good Vibes shop selling their wares, so I grabbed one."

I need a moment with that image. "Let me get this right. You walked home from the sidewalk sale with a dildo in your purse?"

"I took a Lyft," she corrects.

"Did you practice last night?"

"And this morning too."

My brain sticks on that image. Rachel in bed, or on the couch, or here at the counter, sucking on a schlong to get ready for me.

Now, that's an image I could get lost in, but I'm all focus now, so when she gestures to a drawer and asks, "Can you grab my lucky spatula?" I say *hell yes*.

"It's the red one," she adds.

I grab it. "Why is this spatula lucky?"

She stops to think. "Hmm. Good question. I think because I used it when my girlfriends came over for my 'you're free' dinner."

I regard the spatula with dirty deeds on my brain. "Want to find other ways to get lucky with it?"

* * *

Later, she's bent over the kitchen counter and I'm balls-deep in her, smacking her ass with the lucky spatula.

"Yes, mark me, Carter, please," she cries out.

"You love it when I mark you," I rasp out.

"I do," she says, nodding savagely, urging me on.

Another smack. Another moan.

Then a plea. "Harder."

I give it to her exactly how she wants it, and soon she's coming, and I'm following her there, my world blinking off for mind-numbing seconds of inimitable bliss inside my woman.

Only she's not mine.

Not really. She's only mine for a few more dates.

But I will savor them all. "Can I spend the night again?"

"For easy access?"

"No. Because I want to."

I can't see her smile, but I can sense it. I can feel it, too, in how she reaches back to touch my hip. "Me too."

I'll take that *me too* and keep it close for now.

31

SOMEDAY

Carter

"If you think about it, we're doing a public service with this How To Date series," I say to Rachel as I drive us to the mini golf course a few days later on Saturday afternoon. It's our bye week, so there's no football game tomorrow. I am so relaxed I'm beyond relaxed. Bye weeks are like mini vacations tucked into the middle of a ball-busting, back-breaking schedule. You can do whatever you want. Like, date on a Saturday. *Wild.* "We're going to help a whole generation of romantics embarking on first dates," I add.

"We've so got this. Four reasons why mini golf is an awesome first date," Rachel says, then we rattle off the reasons we picked already that we'll share on camera as we play.

"You know what to do with your hands," I begin. "You put them on the club, instead of having to endure awkward moments sitting across the table from each other at a coffee shop wondering *Do I put them on the table or keep them in my lap?"*

"Hands are so weird," she says, agreeing, then shifts to the next tip. "Two, it's a safe place for women. Lots of families and people are around, so that's a plus for the ladies," she adds as I flick on the blinker to turn right.

"And that's very important," I say, then take a beat. "Three, you can't hold a phone and a golf club at the same time."

"And four—anyone can play."

"We're brilliant. Do you think we might win an Emmy for our series?"

"Yes, and before you know it, we'll open up our own consulting service. We could teach classes on dating. The Date Doctors are here for you," she says in an infomercial voice.

"Yes, and people will come to us and ask questions like, *'Should I take out my phone during a date?'*" I continue as we near the course.

Rachel mimes slamming a hand on an imaginary buzzer. "Wrong, Bob. The correct answer is *pay attention to your damn date.*"

"Oh. So we're the Gordon Ramsay of date doctors," I say, as I turn into the course. "Got it."

"You think that's the wrong branding? I could try a different approach." She clears her throat, adopting the tone of a mob heavy. "Hey, Bob, if you take your phone out on your mini golf date, you might not get any pussy."

I crack up. I don't know why it's so funny to hear

Rachel say *pussy* outside of the bedroom. I just know that it is. Maybe that's a question someday for a Word Doctor or a Humor Doctor.

"That's some damn good advice, Rach," I say as I slide into a parking space.

Yup, bye weeks rock. This day is as good as it gets. But when I cut the engine, and turn to her, there's concern on her face. "Carter. We might need to share some *don'ts*."

"Okay?" I ask tentatively, unsure what she's getting at, and whether her tone is real or faux serious. "Like what?"

Her gaze lands on my big rings, then back on me. "Like...don't be a competitive beast."

Whoa. That's very specific. But I play along. "Hmm. Is that a general piece of advice?"

"Oh, c'mon. Don't you remember when we all went to mini golf earlier in the summer?"

Of course I do. She'd flown up from Los Angeles to scope out locations for her shop before she moved. "And you, Monroe, Juliet and I played a nice game of mini golf," I continue. I don't add that I won with a five under par. But I don't have to. Victory speaks for itself.

"And the whole time, you were dead focused on the game. *Only* the game. You were in the zone like it was a Sunday."

"I'm competitive. I literally have to be," I say, and I'm getting the feeling she's not teasing me anymore.

This is a real admonishment.

"And you kept checking the par for every hole, and

you were determined to be under par," she adds, and her memory is an iron cage.

"I like games," I say, defensively.

"I know." Her expression is gentle, but her reprimand is real. "But *maybe*, just maybe, cool the competitive drive."

She's being helpful. I get it. But I'm kind of annoyed. We've played all kinds of games together over the years —scavenger hunts, escape rooms, mini golf. She's never told me to cool it before. Why didn't she tell me sooner that I was being an asshole that day?

"Sure," I say, a little cold. Self-protection and all.

"Carter." There's a plea in her voice.

I hold up a stop sign hand. "Message received. I'll be chill."

She sighs, clearly worried this *don't* has gone south. Well, it has. "Don't get mad and pouty. I didn't mean it like that."

"Then how did you mean it?" I grab the door handle to get out of here. This car is suddenly too small. I need to go for a quick walk. Burn this off. This convo reminds me too much of Quinn. She got on my case about too many things. I didn't like it then, and I don't like it now.

Rachel reaches for my arm, wraps her hand around it. "I didn't mean it like a correction. It was more of a suggestion of how I like to play. I like it casual," she says, trying so hard to be upbeat and positive.

Unlike me.

"Sounded like a correction though," I grumble, but then I replay my words. Fuck, I sound like a little dick. I try to shake off this irritation. "Hey, it's no biggie. I'll be less competitive. Want to hit the links?"

She's quiet in a resigned sort of way. "Do you want to talk about this?"

"What's there to talk about?" I ask with a big smile. Fake it till you make it. I'll get this annoyance out of my system soon enough. All on my own.

"Carter, I don't mind your competitive side. I'm just not like that. And I don't know how to play that way. But please don't be mad at me," she says, and her voice is wobbly.

"I'm not mad at you, Rachel," I say, and soon, I swear I won't be pissed about this.

"You sound mad at me. I'm sorry I said it. It was no big deal. Just be yourself. I want you to just be yourself," she says, her tone urgent now as she tries to fix the situation.

I groan. Now she's walking it back. I pinch the bridge of my nose, trying to release my frustration. Trying to remember, too, why I was so damn competitive that day. I'm not normally like that. I *am* usually more chill. I save my competitive fire for the gridiron, where it counts.

I close my eyes, calling up the day. Rachel was getting divorced. She was telling us about her plans to move here, for the store, to see her family, her friends.

She was saying, *"This is a fresh start for me. To move on from the past."*

I should have been upbeat and encouraging, but all I'd wanted to say was *What did you ever see in that jerk?*

Only, I couldn't say it. She was hurting and yet trying to be hopeful. And I just couldn't be the prick who'd burst her tentative happiness bubble. So I channeled all my focus away from her and onto the game. I played like a competitive beast, so I wouldn't ask that terrible question.

"Carter, you're freaking me out. Talk to me."

I snap open my eyes. Her eyes are wide and guileless. I *am* hurting her now. But I just have to know. "What did you ever see in him?"

She blinks, confused. "Excuse me?"

"Edward. What did you see in him? He was such a colossal jackass," I say, holding nothing back.

Her lower lip quivers, and she jerks her gaze away from me, looking out the tinted passenger window.

Ah, fuck. This is why I should have shut up. I should never have given in to my own pointless urge to know something unknowable.

"Rachel, I'm sorry," I say, with genuine remorse.

She purses her lips, nods, then covers her mouth.

"Sweetheart. I mean it," I say, trying to right this sinking ship.

She drops her hand from her mouth, draws a breath, then meets my gaze again. Her eyes are vulnerable. "I ask myself that all the time. I feel so stupid for having fallen for him. So ridiculously stupid," she says, her voice breaking.

This was such a bad idea. I have to fix this situation now. I reach for her, tug her into my arms. "I'm sorry, baby. I didn't mean to make you cry. I just want the best for you. I want you to be happy. I want you to be with someone who treats you like the goddess you are. That's all," I say desperately, holding her close.

She sniffles against me. "I know."

"I didn't mean to upset you. I'm a dick."

"It just caught me off guard, because it had nothing to do with what we were talking about—mini golf and all," she says into my chest, and she has a point. She doesn't know that I was thinking about how I felt that day about her stupid ass of an ex.

"You're right. It didn't. It was just on my mind," I say, since that's true enough.

"But it's a legitimate question," she says softly.

"No. It's not fair. It's not right. We all make stupid relationship choices. Quinn was bad for me, and I stayed with her. She got on my case all the time, and I still stayed with her. I think I was just frustrated for you that day we played, because I've *always* wanted you to have everything you want," I tell her, finally admitting some of the truth.

Another sniffle. Another quiet sigh. Once more, she nods against me, then lifts her face, and swipes her cheek.

She looks down at my shirt. "No stain this time. Fewer tears. Progress?"

I shake my head. "It's not progress when I'm the one who made you cry."

She sets a hand on my chest, takes a shuddering breath. "If it makes you feel any better, I don't think there was anyone or anything that would have stopped me from marrying him. I was a girl who wanted romance. I grew up watching movies and shows with gallant heroes who swept the heroine away. That was Edward. That's what I saw in him. He was a fantasy. I was twenty-four when I met him, Carter. I was young and starry-eyed. And I said yes to the fantasy. And that's all it ever was. Not a single moment was ever real," she says, her tone emotional yet a touch detached. But in a good way. Like she's moving on. Like she's seeing her past for what it was.

My heart aches for her. I hate that she hasn't known what it's like when someone cares, truly cares about her. "I want you to have that someday," I say, meaning it, though it hurts to think of her with another man even in a someday far away.

Hurts like hell.

She gives a resigned shrug. "Me too. Someday," she says with a sad smile. Her smile turns warmer, and her hand presses harder against my chest. "But I know what I'm worth now. You're teaching me. You're showing me. I know what real is…because of you."

My throat tightens, swimming with emotions fighting to break the surface. But emotions that have no place in her presence. Or, likely, mine either.

"Someday, baby," I say, then, since we're still in this cocoon of a car with tinted windows and no one watching, I cup the back of her head and press a gentle kiss to her forehead.

Tender, caring, full of promise. And apologies too. Everything about this moment is so damn true for me.

When I break the kiss, she smiles again. "That felt real."

Solemnly I meet her gaze. "Good. Because it was."

Then, because she's been so honest, I give her some of the same treatment she's given me. "That's why I was a competitive beast that day. I needed to not focus on how much I hated your ex. So I played like that was all I cared about."

"Thanks for telling me," she says.

"I'll be casual today. I promise I won't be a beast," I say.

She lifts a brow. "Except in the bedroom?"

That's my girl. Finding a way to turn a moment around. "That's a promise."

* * *

We check in at the clubhouse, and the clerk hands us a scorecard and a pencil. "And everything is covered by Mr. Blaine," the guy says.

"I appreciate that," I say. It was wholly unnecessary, but far be it from me to tell Wilder Blaine how to run his business.

When we head to pick clubs from the rack, I hear the voice of the man himself a few feet away. "Of course. Things come up," he says, uber professional.

I glance over to see Wilder facing away from us, holding his daughter's hand while he talks on the phone.

"It's understandable. Take care of your mother. I'll be fine."

When he ends the call, he turns to his kid, putting on an *everything is fine* face. "Anya's mother is sick, and she needs to take her to urgent care."

Plays Well With Others

"Oh no! Will she be okay?"

"I think so. She just needs some meds." He checks his watch. His brow knits. "Want to come to play a round of nine with Daddy and some investors from Indonesia?"

His daughter shoots him a *you can't be serious* look. "That sounds boring. I'd rather play golf with Alice and Grace."

Wilder sighs, shaking his head. "Alice isn't working today. I'll cancel my game, honey."

No, he will not. I turn my gaze to Rachel. "The Babysitter Doctors?" I whisper.

She nods, one hundred percent on board. "We so are."

I clear my throat, and Wilder looks my way. "Mr. Blaine. Mac can play mini golf with us."

The man straightens his spine, meets my eyes, and then lets out a relieved breath. "Thank you. Her sitter can't make it. And I need to meet these investors…It's about this hotel."

I wave a hand. "We have a very chill game planned."

The tiny blonde stares at me with fierce eyes. "I'd like to see you try to beat me."

Oh well. It is on.

32

SMACK TALK LESSONS MELT MY HEART

Rachel

Someone should go on the PGA tour, and it's not Carter.

With an absurd amount of focus for anyone, let alone a fourth grader, Mac lines up at the fourteenth hole, staring intently at the windmill and then at the purple ball on the tee. With a steadying breath, she lifts the club, shifts her hips, and swings like a pro.

That purple ball is a soldier obeying a commanding officer's order as it rushes down a slope, under the spokes of the windmill, then…

I race down the green to track it, whooping in excitement as the ball rolls past my orange one, gliding gracefully into the hole.

"Hole in one, rock star!" I offer Mac a high-five as she runs down the green with a gleeful smile.

"Yay!" she calls out, smacking back when she reaches

me. Quickly, though, she erases the sunshine and pins me with a serious look. "But I can't get too excited. Daddy says it's not nice to showboat."

I give an approving nod. "Daddy is right."

"He usually is. But can I tell you something, Rachel? It's *hard* not to showboat sometimes. It's kind of fun."

"That's true too," I say, then stage-whisper, "But you know what else is super fun?"

"What?"

"Taunting your opponent. Watch this," I say, as Carter lines up at the other end. "Hey, Carter. You want to get the ball in this hole, *not* on the next hole."

He overswung earlier and sent it soaring to the waterwheel when we were on the pipe-drop hole.

Twenty feet away, Carter rolls his eyes. "Thanks for the tip. Just wanted to make sure you know the goal is to score *under* par, not *ten times* over it."

Oh, burn.

But I take my lumps like a big girl, especially because I don't care if I win. I turn to Mac. "See? That's not showboating. That's just trash talk. Are you allowed to trash talk?"

She taps her chin, considering my question, then nods. "Daddy didn't say anything about trash talk on the golf course," she says, and I rein in a snicker. Of course he didn't. Wilder Blaine probably doesn't play golf with people who would trash talk.

But when in Rome…

As Carter waggles his hips, getting ready to putt, Mac's brow knits like she's thinking hard about what to say, so I whisper a retort to use.

"Oh, that's funny," she says.

Carter taps the yellow ball, sending it down the slope, down the hill, and...oh, too bad...it whizzes right past the hole.

"Now," I urge.

She cups her mouth, then points to the hole. "Hey Carter, the hole is here," she says in the most innocently helpful tone.

The big, burly football player strides down the green, shaking his head in amusement. When he reaches us, he points his club from me to her. "You are a troublemaker."

"Me?" I ask, setting a hand on my chest as I flutter my lashes.

"Yeah, you."

"I don't think she's a troublemaker," Mac says, crossing her arms, and stepping closer to my side. "But whatever you tell yourself to sleep at night."

Holy shit. Someone is a fast study. I offer her a palm again.

With amusement in his eyes, Carter turns to me. "Did you want to take another swing, Rachel? We probably have time for your usual ten."

Mac laughs.

I scoff, then pat his shoulder before I turn to my apprentice. "Trash-talking rule number one. It *only* works on those who care. Me? I'm not competitive with sports. Baking is another story though."

I stride over to my orange ball, tap it once, then again, then one more time, shrugging like it's all no big deal, which is true. I officially suck at mini golf, but I don't care. It's still fun.

Which reminds me of our original mission today—the Date Night one.

I beckon for Carter's phone, and he hands it over. I turn on the camera. Keeping it on me and making sure Mac is off-screen, I add to the videos we already shot, saying, "Another big bennie of mini golf? Win or lose, even if you're terrible like me, the game is still fun."

Carter, the camera hog, sneaks into the shot, leaning in close, his face next to mine. "And it's more fun, too, for the other guy. I mean, winning *is* baller." He waggles his hand at the screen, showing off those well-earned rings.

"Gee, did you win a couple Big Games or something?" I deadpan.

"Just a few," he says.

I turn off the camera, nudging him with my elbow. "Show-off."

"More like suck-up. Mr. Blaine loves the rings. And I know he's watching the vids."

The sound of fabric rustling catches my attention, and I turn back to Mac, who's reaching into her peach-colored T-shirt, tugging on a chain, then pulling it out. "Look! I have one too," she says, proudly showing us her necklace —one of her father's rings dangles on the end of it.

Carter whistles. "That is some sweet hardware."

"Yeah, but it's heavy," Mac says, with a shrug, then taps the end of her club on the green. "Also, Carter, it's still your turn."

Tick tock.

"Yes. Yes, it is," he says, then moves behind the yellow ball.

As he lines up, Mac sighs like she's reminiscing. "I remember my first round of golf too."

I burst into laughter.

Carter stops mid swing, his gaze snapping to the kid's. "First you take me on in mini golf, now you're trying to school me in smack talk?"

"I'm just trying to help you improve your game," she says, already a master at the droll delivery.

Carter drops his head in his hand and cracks up. When he raises his face, he fights off a smile as he taps the ball. It falls into the hole with a plink.

He fists pumps, then fishes the ball from the hole.

Mac nods thoughtfully. "It must be nice to be excited about second place."

He growls playfully at her. "We have four holes left, Mac," he says, pointing as we head to the fifteenth hole.

"Maybe we should make a bet," Mac says, like she's musing on the possibilities while we wander down the path to the waterfall up ahead. She brightens, then skips. "How about...ice cream on *you* if *I* win?"

The question is delivered to Carter, but it gives me a good idea. "Do you like molten chocolate cake with ice cream?"

Mac's eyes widen. "I like anything."

She sounds hypnotized by sweets. That feeds the beast in me—the one that relishes watching her take him apart on the links. "Tell you what—if you can beat Carter, we can make this quick molten cake recipe at my house. It takes thirty-five minutes and is amazing with ice cream."

"*Everything* is amazing with ice cream," she corrects solemnly. She draws a deep breath, seeming to mull over my offer, then she nods resolutely. "All right. I'll do it. I'll beat him for ice cream."

As she marches to the tee, I hang back a few feet behind with Carter. "I figure Mr. Blaine's round of golf will take longer than ours," I say, using the formal name for the team owner since Carter always does. "So we'll need something to do after."

"I'll text him."

"Make sure she doesn't have any allergies or food restrictions," I add.

He smiles like that's the cutest thing I could have asked, then he takes out his phone and sends a message. When he puts it away, he bumps shoulders with me. "You just want to teach her more smack talk," he says with a smile. It's an easy, carefree grin. The man has rolled with this change of date plans so easily. That's new to me too—learning he has a good-with-anything attitude in these situations. And while I already knew he was a nice guy, to see him handle a babysitting date does next level things to my...well, to my...oh god, oh no...to my heart.

This is terrifying, but my heart is beating faster for him, especially as I see him with her. *With a kid.*

I feel warmer everywhere.

I set a hand on my chest, like that'll slow these new emotions swimming through my bloodstream, making me feel like...champagne.

I let him walk ahead of me and will my pulse to settle.

He's just a guy who's good with kids.

He's just a guy who wants the best for you.

He's just a guy who knows how to say he's sorry and mean it.

That doesn't mean we're going to be more than friends beyond our experiment, even though he's the guy I want to spend the rest of the day with. And the night too.

I talk back to the thrumming in my heart for the next four holes until Mac lifts her club in the air, victorious at the end. Carter comes up to her, extends a hand to shake, and says, "Good game."

"Yeah, well, I really like ice cream," she says, no showboating, no trash talk.

He ruffles her hair. "Me too."

And my heart flips one more time.

* * *

Mac has no interest in baking with me. The second Carter mentioned a raccoon jigsaw puzzle, she asked please, pretty please to do that instead. We swung by Carter's to grab it, and now Carter and Mac are parked on my living room rug, finishing the border.

While the oven's pre-heating, I have the best seat in the house to watch their game. As I whisk the melted chocolate in a bowl—we got the allergy all clear from Wilder—I steal glances at the pair across the room. Carter leans across the table and grabs a puzzle piece.

"This is the little stinker we've been hunting," he says, holding it up like discovered treasure.

"Yes!" She grabs it and slots it into place.

They high-five but don't waste much time patting themselves on the back. "Now, we need to work on this big raccoon. He's kind of plump," Mac says.

"Yup, and he's digging through the candy wrappers," Carter agrees. His phone beeps with an alert, and he pauses to quickly check it, then sets the device back down. The pair searches in quiet cooperation while I fold the chocolate into the egg mixture, along with the flour.

"Oh! Here's the rest of his tail," Mac calls out.

"You're a champ," says Carter. "And look. I found most of the pieces for his belly."

As I spoon the batter into floured and buttered ramekins, I listen to the soundtrack of their chatter like it's the best kind of song.

"There. Done. Should we work on the trash can?" Carter asks.

"I bet we can do it super fast," she says.

"No doubt. I bet we finish this whole thing in an hour."

"Whoa!" Mac gawks in amazement. "You can do a puzzle in an hour?"

"Usually I can do a five-hundred-piece in under two. I figured with you, we'll ace this in less than sixty minutes."

"My daddy has never finished a puzzle," she says, sounding awestruck.

Carter chuckles. "Your daddy has other skills."

"He's very good at reading books to me and braiding my hair," she declares as she hunts for more pieces, presumably the trash can.

Carter swings his gaze to me, tossing me a sly look. "Me too. Hair braiding, that is."

That warmth from earlier? It's hotter now. And tinglier too. It's stirring up thoughts and emotions that I've tried to tamp down for months. Feelings that arose when my marriage ended. Ones I don't want to think about today.

I shove those risky thoughts into a corner of my mind.

Mac tilts her head Carter's way. "Do you have a daughter?"

He shakes his head with a chuckle. "I have a little sister. Shelby's in the Galápagos Islands working on her biology fellowship."

"Sounds fancy. Does she braid her own hair?"

"Probably. But when we were kids, she made me learn how to do hers. And I have no regrets."

"I taught my daddy how to braid my hair. He can do French braids and reverse French braids," Mac says, then grabs another piece. "Why are you so fast at puzzles?"

"Because I have a good attention span for things I really like," he says easily, and I smile to myself. I know the full scope of his issues but appreciate the simplicity of his answer.

"Cool," she says, seeming satisfied too.

As they work on the puzzle, I fill the final ramekin, then wipe a hand on my mustache apron. After I set the ramekins in the oven, Carter's phone beeps again on the table. He flips it over and then offers a quick explanation to Mac. "It's a reminder of my schedule. Dinner with my agent tomorrow."

"What was your other one for?"

"I set a reminder to send Shelby an email later. I haven't emailed her in a while," he says.

"You set a lot of alerts," Mac says matter-of-factly as I clean up the counter.

"I do. Otherwise, I forget."

"My friend Charles is like that too. He has a watch that reminds him of things. It's kind of cool. The watch." And I bet I know why Charles has a smartwatch. I bet, too, that this curious kid will keep asking Carter questions.

"Why do you forget?" Mac asks.

Yup. Called it. But I feel certain Carter won't mind answering. Because of how she's asking. From a place of honesty, not judgment.

"I have ADHD," he says, equally matter-of-factly.

"Charles has that. His teacher didn't think it was real," she says, then frowns. "Which made no sense to me."

Carter frowns too. "I'm not surprised though. A lot of people don't think it's real."

"Why?"

He shrugs as he slides in another piece. "Don't know. I guess because some people think it's a convenient excuse. When I was younger, I had a football coach who didn't think it was a thing."

I stop cleaning the counter mid-swipe of chocolate. That's new to me. He never told me that before.

"Did you have to prove it was real?" Mac asks, clearly a little perturbed by this development.

"At first I tried to, especially with teachers and coaches who didn't get it. But then I learned it's not my job to prove it's real. The only thing I can do is live with it. There are always going to be people who say to me *just pay better attention*, or *how could you forget that*. But then you learn those aren't the people you want to be friends with." He takes a beat before adding, "Or date."

Did Quinn not believe him?

Mac seems to consider his answer for several seconds. "ADHD is real. It's not the tooth fairy."

"It sure isn't," he says, then snaps in another piece.

She slots in one more. "You're better at this than golf."

"Hey, now," he chides.

"You can't be good at everything," she says. "You're already good at football. Daddy said you're the best receiver he's ever had."

My spine straightens. Carter sits taller too. His smile is radiant.

I feel like I'm glowing from this secret nugget the owner's daughter has dropped.

"Yeah, I heard him say it to a friend," Mac continues, then imitates her dad. *"I never thought we'd find someone as good as Harlan Taylor,"* she says, naming the hall-of-fame receiver who retired a few years ago. *"But I've got Carter Hendrix now, and I've never been so glad to be wrong."*

My best friend fights off a well-earned grin. There's still pleased pride curving his lips when I join them a few minutes later with molten cakes and ice cream.

This Saturday is officially the most fun I've had in ages—maybe because I've seen all these new sides of Carter.

Maybe, too, because all his facets make me melt like this cake.

33

EYES ON ME

Rachel

He has to stop.

Seriously. My heart can't handle the sweetness.

Carter and I are braiding Mac's hair, and I am officially, one hundred percent dead from flutters.

The only thing keeping me alive is, well, the competition.

Mac challenged us. She said she wanted to see who could braid better. So we're giving her twin French braids. I'm right next to Carter on the couch as he weaves strands on the right side of Mac's head, and I do the left.

I try to concentrate on my mission—finishing this awesome braid. But I'm stealing glances at the man by my side, twisting and weaving blonde strands with those big hands, and that intense concentration in his brown eyes, and all I can think is *Why is it so damn swoony when a man does a kid's hair?*

You know why. You know what you want.

I lose my grip on a small chunk of Mac's hair.

Focus, Rachel.

I grab the fallen strands, then quickly finish the braid, tying it off. "There," I declare. "It's been a while since I've French braided, but check it out," I say, proud of my work.

Carter finishes, grabs the hair tie Mac is holding, and ends his braid. Before he can even survey his work, he peers at mine. "Mmm. Nice job, Rachel," he says, no teasing, no joking, just…praise.

My stomach flips—then cartwheels when he turns his face to me, his warm brown eyes locking with mine. "You're good at that," he says.

What is wrong with me? Do I have a *compliment my hair braiding* kink?

"Let me see how you did," Mac says.

"There's a mirror in my bedroom," I say, pointing.

The tiny human pops up from the floor, grabs her phone, and scampers to the bedroom.

And Carter comes in for a kiss.

Oh.

Wow.

That's surprising.

And nice.

I think I hum against his lips.

Yes, that's definitely a hum. His kiss is soft. Just lips. No tongue. No hands in my hair, or on my face. The only parts of us touching at all are our lips in the barest brush, the sweetest caress.

But somehow, it's making me want him even more than his heated possessive kisses do, than his filthy words, than his dirty stares.

This kiss is turning me inside out with its deceptive innocence.

When Mac's footsteps signal her return, Carter pulls away, saying nothing, just giving me a wolfish grin.

I'm practically a puddle. He went from a soft caress of a kiss to a filthy smile like that. *Just take me now.*

"I have a winner," Mac announces when she returns to the living room. "Both of you."

"Whoa," Carter says, his eyes widening. "A tie?"

"Ties are bad in football but sometimes okay in life," Mac says, waggling her phone. "That's what my daddy says. Oh! He's on his way. He just texted me."

That's good. Because I need to get Carter alone very, very soon.

Fifteen minutes later, Mac is rushing to the door I just opened. "Daddy, I beat Carter in golf, and Rachel made me cake, and Carter and I finished a puzzle in one hour and six minutes, and they both braided my hair."

"You've had a full day," he says.

She wraps her arms around him in a waist hug, and he scoops her up into his arms, pressing a kiss to the top of her head. "Those are some seriously impressive braids. Looks like my wide receiver might be trying to show me up," he says dryly.

Carter points his thumb at me. "No, sir. It was all her doing. Rachel is awesome at braids."

Mac tosses her head back, laughing. "Stop. You're good at hair. You said you were good at hair. Don't backtrack now," she says, and if that isn't a Wilder-ism, I don't know what is. This kid is full of Daddy's words of wisdom.

Wilder sets her down then turns to me, a sincere look in his eyes. "I can't thank you enough," he says, then to Carter, he adds, "I am truly grateful."

"We had a good time, Mr. Blaine," Carter says.

"Wilder."

Carter smiles, but his eyes say Wilder isn't winning this one. "Yes, Mr. Blaine."

I laugh, then take the man up on his offer. "You've got a great kid, Wilder. I hope your meeting went well."

"It was fantastic. Is there anything I can do for the two of you?" he asks, so earnestly wanting to repay us.

He truly doesn't need to, but how many times does a billionaire think he owes you a favor? Impulsively, I say, "Well, next time Carter helps win the Big Game, maybe my friend Fable can design your rings. She's a jewelry designer."

He smiles, looking pleased that I took him up on it. I bet he likes it when people operate in his sphere of understanding—trading favors for favors, deals for deals. "I'll keep that in mind," he says.

With another thank you, he turns to go, holding hands with Mac.

"Daddy, I learned to trash talk today," she says proudly.

I cringe. Oh shoot. Did all our goodwill just go down the drain?

"Is that so, sweetie?"

"Yeah. I'm pretty good at it too," she says.

I love this kid's confidence.

"Of course you are. You're pretty good at everything you do. Just remember—time and place."

"Time and place," she repeats, like it's their mantra, as they head down the stairs.

Leaving them to their daddy-daughter time at last, I push my door closed, then turn to Carter.

I'm ready for *my* alone time. Pretty sure he is, too, from the way the heat flares in his eyes.

"Your turn," he says, tipping his head toward the couch. "Time and place and all."

I swallow past the dry patch in my throat, then obey by walking to the couch with a pulse beating between my thighs.

I sit on the floor in front of it. He sits on the couch behind me and reaches for the hairbrush, wordlessly runs it through my hair. Closing my eyes, I try to sink back into the attention, to indulge in his caring touch.

But I'm not used to someone touching me with such focus and intention. I need to fill the silence so it doesn't overwhelm me. I return to something that stood out when Mac asked Carter about ADHD. "Quinn didn't think it was real?"

He pauses, letting the question register, then runs the brush one more time through my hair and sets it down. "No, she didn't."

Reaching for another hair tie, he loops it onto his wrist.

"Like, at all?" I ask.

Carter runs both thumbs through my hair near the crown of my head, gathering a chunk. "She said *It's just your excuse for everything.*"

Maybe because he asked earlier, I'm compelled to do the same. "Why did you stay with her so long?"

But what I really want to say is—*why did you propose?*

As he sorts my hair, he takes a deep breath. "There were things I liked," he says, but he sounds…evasive.

"It had to be more than things," I say, gently insistent. I want to understand him like he's understanding me.

I settle in deeper between the safe haven of his thighs, his knees framing me. Perhaps my touch reassures him because he tries again, saying, "I really like…" He blows out a big breath. "Ah, fuck."

I want to turn, check in with him, but I don't want to ruin his work, so I set a hand on his knee and ask with some concern, "What is it?"

As he gathers the next strand then loops it through, he sighs again. "I like being with someone," he says, and he sounds so damn sad.

There's a borderline embarrassment, too, like he's ashamed of his desire.

"You stayed with her because it was better than being alone?" You think you know everything about your best friends, but then you become intimate, and suddenly you're sharing stories and wishes and fears you never voiced. You see facets of them that you never expected.

He sighs, but it's a contemplative sound now. "I don't think I'm afraid of being alone. But I found I really enjoyed monogamy," he says, his voice as stripped bare as his admission of this *character flaw*. "I suppose my Achilles' heel is I like dating one person. I like being with one person. I really like having a girlfriend." He laughs lightly, a self-deprecating sound as he weaves in another strand of my hair. "And I love sex. On the reg."

I laugh too, grateful for the levity. "You're pretty good at it."

He kisses the top of my head. I close my eyes because the feeling in my chest is almost too much.

He pulls back, then keeps talking. "But I like it so much I stay too long. Even when things go south. I like the good things of relationships, so I ignore the bad things. I guess I should learn to like being alone more, because I keep staying too long, and then…shit happens. It goes south. I stayed with Quinn too long just because I like being with *someone*. Well, I enjoyed it until my fiancée took off with the ring and left me with nothing but a contract for five dates on an app," he deadpans, but there's a knife's edge to his voice.

A cutting reminder, too, of what these girlfriend lessons were born from—a deal he had to fulfill.

This is a deal between us. An exchange of goods and services, even when it feels like more.

But in the comfort of our exchange, I take more steps. I'm free to try things I wouldn't try. I rub my hand over his knee, perhaps to comfort him. Is he seeking comfort? I don't know. But I want to tell him with touch that I understand where he's been. "I understand, Carter. I'm sure that's why I stayed too," I say.

"I get it," he says quietly. "I was mad earlier, but I do get it."

A lump forms in my throat, but I'm not entirely sad. I'm just…emotional.

"And now, you're sort of…" I cast about for the right word. "Detoxing!"

He laughs as he reaches the nape of my neck. "Yeah, I suppose so."

"So this is an un-dating, ultra-sexing detox," I offer, because I don't want him to think I'm getting clingy.

Or needy.

Or all feels-y.

I don't want him to worry that I'm misunderstanding our exchange. He needs time to detox. He's a man who's trying to learn new patterns too. Just like me.

"I suppose so," he says, but his voice sounds a little far away as he finishes the braid, then loops a tie around the end. "Done."

"How does it look?" I ask, with a strange cocktail of nerves and hope in my voice. I want his *real* answer so badly. I want him to love the braid. I don't even know why. I just do.

He leans closer, slides his hands down my arms, reaches for my ass, and tugs me up, settling me between his legs…so he can press a kiss to the back of my neck. "Beautiful," he murmurs. "You're beautiful."

I feel beautiful for the first time in his arms.

He kisses my neck up to my ear, then says, "Remember in the car? When I kissed your forehead, and you said it felt real?"

I shiver from the tenderness of the memory. "Yes."

"You want to know what else is real? I can show you."

I shudder. I have no idea what he's getting at. But I say yes.

* * *

I've never felt so vulnerable or adored.

I'm naked on my stomach. Carter's shirtless, but still in jeans.

He's tied my wrists to the bed with my scarves. He checks to make sure the right one is secure, then he climbs over me. Straddles me right above my ass.

Is he going to give me a massage while I'm half tied up? Is that a thing? He doesn't tell me his plans, and I don't ask.

When his lips come down on my shoulder blade, I shiver.

He murmurs.

With one kiss, I'm already more aroused than I've ever been. His lips glide across my shoulder to my arm. "You should always feel beautiful," he whispers.

Something like bliss flows through my body, a warm gooey sensation. I can't answer with words. Just a needy sigh.

He moves to the back of my neck again, pushing the braid aside then laying kiss upon drugging kiss there.

I tremble.

"You should be adored," he adds as he travels down to my upper back, pressing a soft kiss there too.

His kisses become hungrier, more insistent as he journeys along my spine. Possessive, too, as his hands follow, sliding along my sides. "You should be worshiped," he says.

I want to answer him. But I can't. I just can't. I don't know what to say. This is so overwhelmingly exquisite. All I can do is sigh, and moan, and wriggle.

"Like this," he says, and when he reaches the top of my ass, he kisses the swell of my cheek, then he nips me with his teeth.

I gasp.

And…gush.

He slides his body down farther so he's kneeling between my legs, pushing them apart with big hands on the inside of my thighs. I'm naked, spread-eagled, and squirming.

He stops, hauls in a harsh breath. "Fuck, baby. Look at you. So fucking wet," he says. There's an urgency to his voice all of a sudden, like the switch flipped in him from seductive to carnal.

"I know," I say, sounding desperate. Feeling desperate for his touch.

"I fucking love turning you on," he says, then he presses a hungry kiss to the back of my thigh.

"I love that," I murmur.

"Because it's fucking real," he says, his lips roaming down my leg to behind my knee.

He doesn't owe me this after our argument. He definitely doesn't need to prove what *real* is. But his fierce desire to give it to me is making my heart swim with emotions and my body ache.

"Please," I pant.

He moves to my other knee, kisses it. "Please what?" he asks, back to his seductive tease.

"Please touch me," I beg.

"With what? My cock? My hands? My mouth?"

I lift my ass. "I don't care. I just need you."

His mouth comes down on me again, right at the bottom of my ass. He bites me, and my breath hitches. His mouth is so close to my center, and I have no idea where he's going, what he wants, what he's planned.

With my face pressed against the pillow and my hands tied, I'm at his mercy, and loving it.

He bestows another bite of a kiss to my flesh, then slides his hand between my spread thighs.

"Oh god," I groan when he makes contact.

"Fuck, baby," he says, as his fingers find all my slippery wetness. "You like it when a man treats you like a goddess."

"I like it when *you* do," I correct.

"Good answer," he says on a growl, then grazes his finger up and over my greedy clit.

I shake. Then try to grab at the pillows, the sheets, something, anything. "Please, Carter."

He reaches under me, scoops me up so my ass is in the air. I truly don't know what he's doing next.

But then...oh god.

His mouth is on my pussy, and he's eating me, and if I thought I'd never been more vulnerable before, that's nothing on how I feel now. Trussed up, ass in the air, soaked.

He goes down on me like a savage. Kissing and sucking and lapping me up.

I sound like an animal. Moaning and groaning, till finally, I know what I want. "Flip me over, tie me up again, and fuck me with my legs over your shoulders."

He freezes, but there's a welcoming fire in his tone when he says, "Well, that's specific."

"Yeah, it came to me in a flash," I say with a little laugh.

He laughs too, then smacks my ass and complies.

A minute later, his clothes are off, the condom is on, and I'm pinned on my back. But the difference is the view. "I like to look at you," I tell him as he positions his cock between my legs.

"Same fucking here," he says, then slides inside.

I howl in pleasure.

I'm stretched, and it's spectacular the way he fills me. What's even better is the dirty gleam in his eyes as he pushes up on my thighs, then hooks my legs over his shoulders.

And fucks me deep, passionate, with his eyes on mine the entire time.

If I wasn't chasing an orgasm, I might have thought harder on what this meant, how it felt, how it was different than every other time we'd fucked.

But the pleasure makes thinking impossible.

All I can do is feel the toe-curling, mind-bending pleasure of him taking me to the ends of the earth till I gasp out, "I'm close."

"Say my name when you come. Say it like a good girl," he commands.

A torrent of lust storms through me. Yes, I have a good-girl kink. Yes, I have a mark-me kink. Yes, I have a tie-me-up kink.

Mostly I have a Carter kink.

I shout his name as I shatter under him.

Seconds later, he follows me with a wild grunt, and then there are no more words.

Just sounds. Just sighs. Just…us.

34

PANCAKE FANTASIES

Carter

In the morning, as I water the rosemary, the basil, and Bob the Ficus, Rachel makes pancakes and we plan our final two dates.

Two more. That's it.

I try not to let the ticking clock bug me. When I'm on the field, I only focus on the play we're making in the moment not the one I'll need to execute in the next quarter.

I ought to do the same here.

As I pour water onto the soil, I toss her a question. "All right, Sunshine," I say, then stop my train of thought at the name. I haven't called her that in a while. I've called her sweetheart and baby. But she's still Sunshine too. I like the way it sounds.

As I glance over at her in the kitchen, she's fighting

off a smile that tells me she likes the return of Sunshine too.

"We've got two more dates. One should be this Halloween party, right?" I ask.

"Definitely," she says, as she spoons some batter into the pan. "But we should coordinate our costumes. Right? Well, you tell me. You're the one teaching me. But I'm guessing that's a girlfriend thing?"

I return to the kitchen, set the water bottle in the sink, then kiss the back of her neck. "Yes, the full boyfriend experience says we're coordinating our costumes. But we're not gonna be fucking M&Ms or cell phones or ghosts. Also, we're going to need to try to win. Because I won Best Costume a couple years ago at Jason's party."

"Oh, what was it?"

I square my shoulders. "I was the Big Game stripper."

Her brow knits in confusion.

"This dude ran onto the field during the game in black shorts and a bright pink mankini."

Her eyes pop. "You wore a bright pink mankini? You *own* a bright pink mankini?"

"I own it because I bought it for the party," I say, proudly. "And I looked hot in it."

She laughs, dipping her face. "You think so?"

I am shook. "What? You doubt me?"

She raises her face to meet my gaze with a knowing one of her own. "Carter, a pink mankini is not hot."

I scoff. "Have you seen me in one?"

"No, I have not."

"Then how do you know?"

"I guess you'll have to show me," she says, goading me.

"Challenge accepted," I say, then I grab my phone, scroll through past pics way back when and find one from that night, showing her the screen in victory.

Her lips part in an O. "I stand corrected. You are hot."

"Told you so, Sunshine," I say.

There's that smile again, and I just want to keep putting it there.

"Did you have fun at the party?" she adds.

"I did," I say, but then I'm quiet for a beat, thinking back. I would have had more fun if she'd been there. But she was in Los Angeles.

"It would have been nice to have gone," she says, a little wistful, clearly thinking the same thing too.

"Yeah, it would have."

She draws a deep breath, like she needs it for fuel. "I would have liked that."

She doesn't have to add if *I weren't married then*. Pretty sure we both know we're talking about an alternate reality.

In this world, we both go quiet, her finishing the pancakes, me grabbing some plates. As I move through the familiar choreography of a Sunday morning, I enjoy the silence a little too much, imagining that alternate reality.

One where I'd have made different choices. Objected *before* her wedding. Acted on the feelings I was having but hadn't named.

In that reality, she'd have been my date and I'd have saved her from heartache.

But our timing has always been a little off.

When she plates the pancakes, she asks with a tender sort of curiosity, "What are you thinking?"

The fact that she asks makes my heart thump harder.

"How good those pancakes look," I say with a smile.

It's true enough.

Even though she arches a playful brow. "Pancake fantasies?"

Well, yeah.

* * *

The next night, four alerts do the trick. Not only am I on time for dinner with Maddox and Zena, I am motherfucking early. My agent isn't at the restaurant yet. First time for everything.

It's Monday night and I wait at the bar for both of them. I'm so badass, I have to send my brother a text.

> Carter: Guess what I did? I arrived early to a meeting.

> Axel: Good. When I have my signing tomorrow night, will you come early to set up for me?

> Carter: You wish.

> Axel: Come on. You're the nice brother.

> Carter: Only because you set the bar so low.

> Axel: Fuck you and your early arrivals.

> Carter: Fuck you and your iron trap of a memory.

When Zena sweeps in a few seconds later, I type a hasty "**gotta go**," and put the phone away. The Date Night founder looks like San Francisco tech royalty in casual jeans and a sweater, blending in with the crowd. Such a California billionaire. There's not a speck of a designer label on her.

But there is nothing unassuming about her approach. She's a tenacious woman who goes after what she wants. When she spots me, wheels are turning in her eyes already.

Bet she's going to ask me for a favor. I can smell it like it's her perfume.

She power-walks to my side and extends a hand. "So good to see you, Carter. I only wish I'd signed you up for more than five videos. Our customers are going wild for you two."

She's not the only one. I kind of wish I owed them more than five, too, then I'd have an excuse to spend more time on Rachel's girlfriend lessons. There's so much I could still teach her. In bed, out of bed. Hell, we haven't gone on a bowling alley date. A proper dinner date. A workout date. An art gallery date. I haven't walked in on her fucking herself with a toy either.

Shame.

Yeah, several more dates would rock. Maybe we could extend this whole thing...indefinitely.

"I'm glad it's going so well for you," I say.

"It really is. And I think it could go even better. For both of us. I have a few ideas," she says, setting down her purse and gearing up for a big ask.

"Oh?" I ask offhand as I scan the doorway just over there for Maddox. I need my buffer, stat.

"Yes. Let me tell you more about what I envision," she says, not even giving a fuck that my agent isn't here yet, but when the door swings open and he's right on time, I'm infinitely relieved. She has the diplomacy of a snowplow. Maddox strides up to us and claps me on the shoulder. "Good to see you again."

"You too," I say.

Once he says hello to Zena, we all head to a table. After we order, Maddox guides the conversation through small talk and then Zena clears her throat, ready to do business.

She locks eyes with me. "So I wanted to tell you under NDA about a new feature we're rolling out," she begins, her chunky gold bracelet adding to her Wonder Woman vibe. "We're launching a new section of the app called *The Friend Zone*. We want to help people connect on all sorts of levels, including a friend level, and since you and Rachel are such good friends, we would love for you to host the kickoff event for us in a few weeks. It'll be a fun warehouse-type of party with music, games, photo booths, pool, board games—all sorts of friend-centric activities," she says.

Great. Just great. I'll forever be known as *the friend*.

But just because I want more with Rachel doesn't mean that more is on the menu. Besides, I'm trying to detox from girlfriends. I stay too long in toxic relationships because I like women too much, dating too much, romance too much.

I need to change my own habits. This expiration date with Rachel is healthy for me. It really, *really* is.

"And we'll invite influencers and some of our regular users in the area, and the media of course," Zena continues as I do my best to focus on the business side of her request.

Fortunately, Maddox jumps in and says, "What do you have in mind exactly? An extension of the deal? Will there be additional compensation?"

I love this guy. He does the hard stuff.

Zena smiles. "Of course. We'll pay you an appearance fee. And Rachel as well," she says, then shares a figure. "You'd both get it, of course."

Wow. I don't think Rachel's ever nabbed an appearance fee before, but I bet she'll be stoked.

"But I also had a special idea," Zena says, her tone suggesting she has an ace up her sleeve. "At the kickoff party, we'll have goodie bags for all the guests, and I thought perhaps we could have the bags branded with the name of Rachel's store. Would that work, too, for compensation?"

Zena looks to Maddox expectantly, but I've got this

covered. "I'll check with her tonight," I say, and I can't wait to tell Rachel.

* * *

After dinner, I walk home, calling Rachel along the way and updating her.

"Are you kidding me?" Her voice pitches up in obvious shock.

"Pretty cool, huh?"

"That's an understatement. An appearance fee? I'm... just a store owner. You're a star."

I laugh. "Guess you're a dating star now too."

"This is just beyond anything," she says. "I can use it to market the store more. And of course for savings. And I need to visit the Venice store soon, and maybe make some new hires because of the manager taking all these personal days, but I'll figure it all out. Still, I can't believe that this whole Date Night thing is turning my business around. It's still early days, but I'm so hopeful I can keep growing things," she says, obviously touched, and her emotions tug on my heart. "Carter, when I first came here and business was slow, I was beginning to doubt my decision. I thought I'd made a mistake fleeing to San Francisco and trying to open a second store while still running the Venice one. But then these last few weeks happened, and it makes me feel like I wasn't so crazy to escape."

I wince from the reminder. But hell, with the way I've been feeling lately, I need it.

Her escape from her ex was mere months ago.

That is all.

She came to San Francisco to get away from a five-year-lie. Not to find a new dude. Not to fall for her friend.

She has one goal here—to recover.

There is no way I could say to her *I'm falling for you* and have that be okay.

"Thank you so much," she adds. "I know I just said Date Night made this happen, but really, you made it happen, Carter."

"It was nothing," I say, deflecting.

"It's everything," she says, like she wants me to truly hear her, to know she means it.

And I do.

I just wish everything also included her and me.

Instead, I take what I can get. These little chances to make her happy. Because after two more dates, I won't be the one giving her girlfriend lessons.

* * *

The next night, I knock on Monroe's door so we can head over to An Open Book on Fillmore. Along the way, he tells me more details about the podcast he's launching and how the planning is going so far. He's working with a married couple as his counterpoint. "They're kind of disgustingly happy," he says dryly.

"I guess that means you're going to play the Eeyore?"

"If the shoe fits," he says, then shudders. "Relationships. Am I right?"

I laugh as we near the bookstore. "The shrink who

struggles with relationships," I say, shaking my head in amusement.

"The best friend who struggles with very unfriendly feelings," he says.

I flip him the bird. "Friends like you are such jackasses."

"But I'm a necessary jackass," he says.

"Yes, Monroe. Slap that on a name tag and wear it."

"Gladly," he says, chin up.

At An Open Book, I don't have to help set up because the bookstore manager does that. But I am required to heckle my brother. When Axel finishes reading a passage from his newest romantic thriller, in which his former-lawyer-turned-avenging-bounty-hunter hero outsmarts the bad guys in Vienna, then saunters into a nightclub and asks the sexy owner to make it a double, I raise a hand.

From the podium, Axel clearly tries not to roll his eyes. Truly he does. But he's terrible at veiling his sarcasm. "Yes, Carter?"

I smile, like a little dick. "Have you ever considered writing a hero who's a football player turned bounty hunter? Might make him even more attractive and a little more believable, too, when he outruns all the bad guys."

Axel smiles, the kind that says *I'm* a necessary jackass. "Gee, I hadn't," he says.

Monroe clears his throat, then goes next. "Or he could be a brilliant doctor turned shrink who recovers stolen artwork, all while winning the hearts and minds of wonderful women around the world."

Axel peers at the rest of the crowd here for the signing. "Does anyone else want to offer themselves up for a novel? Feel free."

All arms go up in the air.

* * *

When Axel finishes signing books for a long line of customers—I'm so damn proud of him for living his dream—the three of us grab a drink at The Spotted Zebra several blocks away. At the bar, Axel lifts his scotch and toasts to Monroe and me. "To you two amateurs, for trying and failing to knock me off my game."

Monroe clinks back with his tumbler of amber liquid. "To us continuing to try every single time."

"We will never stop. We will never surrender," I put in.

"I would expect nothing less," Axel says, but then he sets down his glass, his expression serious for a rare moment. "Thanks again for coming. I really appreciate it."

I slug his shoulder. "Thanks for writing books that don't suck."

He offers a smile. "I'm happy to entertain you."

Monroe takes a drink, then says, "Carter's pretty entertaining too. Wait till you hear what he's been up to. It's book fodder for sure."

From behind his glasses, Axel's eyes widen with curiosity. "This I must hear."

I groan, annoyed with Monroe for serving me up but mostly with myself for being fodder.

Axel sets his chin in his hand. "Tell me everything."

It was inevitable that I'd tell Axel. And I don't truly begrudge Monroe for stirring the pot. That's what we do. So I give Axel a quick debriefing on the situation with Rachel—and the situation in my stupid heart.

When I'm done, Axel whistles, low and long, the *sucks to be you* kind. But there's sympathy in his eyes too. He ought to understand my situation better than anyone. He's been there in many ways. "I always thought you had a thing for her," he says, with too much wisdom in his tone. I almost wish I didn't have a thing for Rachel. It would be so much easier if sex was just sex. If I could just fuck her and move on.

"Just like I always thought you had a thing for Hazel," I add.

There's no teasing or ribbing when he says, "And you were right."

But his happy ending with Hazel isn't proof that I'll have one. Our situation is different. Every romance is unique. Nothing is guaranteed, no matter how deeply you might long for another person.

Because now is the wrong time for romance for Rachel, and, likely, for me too. She's still escaping her painful past. We just don't have the timing on our side.

I know firsthand that when it comes to football, timing can be everything.

I'm learning now, it's pretty much the *only thing* in romance.

"But this isn't going to end the same way," I say, then for good measure, I add, "It's just not."

And my stupid heart is going to be okay with that. Even though I know I'll be drifting off later to pancake fantasies and other what ifs.

Which feels like the story of my relationship with Rachel.

35

MY UNREAL BOYFRIEND

Rachel

Well, this is going to be uncomfortable.

I mean, I know intrinsically that therapy is a little uncomfortable. But I don't want to dig deep today. So I'm careful as I open the door, as I say hi, as I sit on the couch, arranging myself for longer than I usually do. Purse here. Phone there. Legs crossed. Nope, uncrossed. Or maybe crossed after all.

It's a Tuesday, and this is the first time I've seen Elena since I started sleeping with Carter. Nervously, I glance around her office, fixing my gaze on that snow-covered cabin painting. What would it be like to be stuck in that cabin on a cold night, with a warm fire, and an honest man?

But that thought's not helpful today.

I can't think of *that* man while I'm with her.

I snap my gaze to Elena, pasting on a grin that I hope is believably *content*. That's the goal of therapy, I think. Contentment. Peace. I'm not there yet though.

I rub my palms along my jeans. She waits for me expectantly, a calm smile on her wise face.

A smile that says she's seen this fidgety behavior before. A smile that says, too, she can wait for me. Correction: she can *outwait* me.

I gulp. "So, how are you?"

Her smile brightens a bit. "I'm well. It's been a good few weeks for me."

I grab tight on the end of the rope she's offering. "Oh? In what way?" I ask, hoping she'll fill the time since I don't want to.

Elena is not one of those cipher shrinks. Granted, I don't know everything about her, but she's told me enough that I feel like I know who she is. She has two grandchildren, she's been in a committed relationship for twenty-five years, she likes to play pickleball, and she devours memoirs.

"My pickleball team won a tournament," she offers.

Boom. "Congrats," I say brightly. "Which one? What next? Did you get a pickle as a prize?"

She smiles pleasantly, then shakes her head. "Now, how about you?"

Well, somebody saw right through me.

I rub my hands along my jeans again while fishing for something to say. Something I *want* to say. "Things are better at work," I begin, and yeah, that'll do. I do want to chat about business. I dive right in and roll around in the shop conversation like it's a vat of gold I've stumbled into. Look at all the pretty coins. "And then I went back and I saw Ava and I apologized," I say after several minutes of work chatter.

Elena's nod says she's surprised but also impressed. "That does seem like growth, Rachel. I think it's great that you decided on your own to do that. That you felt it was important to you."

I beam from the therapist's praise. I like her praise. I want more of it. I want to make progress. I want to fucking heal. Isn't it time?

"Me too," I say, emotions rising up in me as I try to focus on the changes I have made—not the ones I haven't. "For a while, I felt like I was going through life with blinders on my face and I couldn't see what was happening to the side. All I could see was what was in front of me, and it just felt like more hurt and more pain. And then the blinders started to come off and I could see there was hope and possibility, and there were other ways for me to approach the world and people."

Her smile is full of grace. "I'm proud of you. That's a big step." Then, she wastes no time. "And what about Carter?"

I tense.

There it is. A simple question. One I knew was coming. One I don't even know how to address.

I'm not sure I want to face the inevitable scrutiny that would come from a licensed therapist over the reality of our girlfriend lessons, the way they've extended to the night, and to mornings waking up in his arms.

"He's great," I say and that's all true. "We're doing these five dates. These girlfriend lessons. I'm learning so much." I have to tell some of the truth because what if she's heard of my Date Night series? I quickly explain the girlfriend lessons bit, leaving off the sex. And the sleepovers. And, well, the bloom of feelings.

Her eyebrows rise. "That's interesting."

That's interesting is the kiss of death from a shrink.

It translates into—*holy shit, you're doing that???*

But I pretend to take her comment at face value, even though I know there's more to it. "It is interesting. I'm learning a lot," I say again, but my voice sounds so reedy, like I'm covering up the truth.

Well, you are.

She tilts her head thoughtfully. "Rachel, is there something you want to talk about?"

My stomach churns. With guilt. With worry. With a little bit of shame. A real therapist smoothie. Elena would know what to do with all of these feelings but really, what should I even say?

I'm in an unreal real relationship?

I'm in a real unreal one?

I'm pretending to be girlfriend/boyfriend with my best friend?

Except, it's not like we're fake dating, but it also kind of is. It's more like we're experimenting with dating. But that's just too personal for me to share, even with the one person who knows the deepest, darkest detail of my marriage. The one person I've shared something with that I've never told anyone else.

I trust her entirely and yet I still can't tell her *this*.

I don't even know what *this thing* with Carter is. And probably, if I tried to explain it, she'd question it too much. She'd ask if it was wise. If it was healthy. If I am truly moving on by pretending to be in a relationship that isn't real at all.

She might even ask if I'm making the same mistakes.

This relationship is not the same, but I'd sound foolish saying that. That blackness I felt when I left Edward darkens my heart again.

Sure, Carter is worlds different than Edward. I'm different than I was when I married Edward.

And yet, I am also the same woman who was fooled.

I am that girl who was hoodwinked for five years. I don't want to be the woman who's hoodwinked herself into believing that five dates and hot sex with my best friend could turn into a future.

The reality is this—I don't trust myself.

At last, I answer Elena. "We're just having a really good time," I say.

I tell her about Fable's eggplant necklaces and how we're starting to carry them in the store and that fills the rest of the hour.

* * *

Later that week, I meet Elodie for a punishing HIIT class. My thighs are on fire afterward, and it's all her fault. "You did this to me. My thighs are literally burning," I whimper as we leave the class.

My friend arches a brow. "Literally? They're literally burning?"

I point at my aching legs. "I see smoke. At least, I feel it," I say with a pout, but truthfully, this post-exercise burn feels good. Elodie suggested I take the class when I moved here, telling me exercise is a natural endorphin. She's somewhat religious about her exercise, but that's better than how she was about it years ago. Her attitude now is so much healthier.

"I'm proud of you for making it through," she says, patting me on the shoulder.

I raise my chin. "Me too. Because now it means we get to go shopping for costumes," I say, and I skip once, enthusiasm bouncing through me. "I do love Halloween. And when Carter and I planned our final two dates, we agreed to go with matching Halloween costumes."

Elodie bursts into laughter. "Do you even hear yourself?"

I knit my brow. "What do you mean?"

"You sound like you're infatuated," she says matter-of-factly.

I bristle. But not for long. Because...she's kind of right. I just didn't realize it was so obvious. And while I didn't want to talk about the situation with Elena for fear of judgment, I don't mind sharing with a friend.

Elodie's known about my zany plans from the start. She approved them with me that day we ate nachos and watched football. Still, I want to know *why* she's saying that, so I ask, "How so?"

"Carter and I are wearing matching Halloween costumes," she says, imitating me in a singsong tone.

And that's clear. "Is that really how I sound?"

She laughs. "You sure do, mon cheri. Like you can't

think of anything better than shopping for matching Halloween outfits to wear with him."

"Well, it does sound like fun," I say, defensively but with a giddy smile.

"It does." She takes a beat. "But it also sounds super couple-y."

My smile falters. Reality is such a bitch. The reality of my unreal boyfriend. "Well, it's just while we are doing this how-to-date thing," I say.

"Yeah, sounds like it's all about the *lessons*."

But it hardly feels that way lately with him. Impulsively, I grab her arm and blurt out, "I'm going to be sad when it's over."

I didn't really expect to say that, but I think I needed to voice it out loud, and now that I've opened the floodgates, more truth pours out. "We only have two more dates, and I feel like it's that halfway point in a vacation where you're happy and sad. When you have less time left. When every day, you're counting down till you board the plane and return to reality. You don't want it to end, but you can't stop it. We have the Halloween party—that'll be a sort of how-to-meet-the-friends date. Then we have one more and we're considering an art gallery, since I'm weird and I don't like going out to dinner."

"Right. Because Edward was Mister Let Me Impress You With New Restaurants," she says.

"Exactly. And then we have this party thing we're hosting for Date Night."

Elodie arches a brow. "That sounds like three more dates."

Fair point. "Yeah, it does," I say, a little hopeful, but I can't be too excited. We just extended our departure flight. We'll still be leaving Hawaii soon enough.

"But isn't that what you wanted in the first place?" Elodie asks thoughtfully as we turn onto the block with the costume shop. "You wanted girlfriend lessons. You wanted this experience. You're getting it."

We reach the costume shop and as we go inside, I weigh her words. At first, I did want lessons.

But now?

My heart flips and flops in my chest. "The thing is, I don't really know what I want," I admit, stopping at a rack of sexy angel, nurse, and witch costumes.

"I don't believe that," Elodie says, calling bullshit. "You've always been pretty decisive. You knew what you wanted to study in college. You go shopping and you pick out clothes easily. You go to a restaurant and you know what to order right away. How do you not know what you want with Carter?"

She's not wrong.

I do know what I want with Carter. The trouble is—I want the fantasy of these five dates to be real.

But I got married to a fantasy. "Because Carter's not mushroom risotto on a menu," I say.

Elodie gives a resigned smile. "Fair enough."

I flick through some costumes, giving her a deeper answer as I find just the right one. "I do feel infatuated. I'm all fluttery when I'm with him, and when I think about him too. It all feels good. But…that's dangerous. Everything felt good with Edward as well."

She sighs, understanding me completely. "What does Elena say?"

I wince.

Actually, it's a full-on cringe. Then comes my confession as we stand amidst the racy angels and the sexy devils. "I haven't told her." I bite off more of the truth. "I avoided it."

"Why do you think you avoided it?"

I laugh. "Now you sound like Elena."

Elodie sets a hand on the rack, leveling me with a piercing gaze. "Why do you think you avoided telling her?" she repeats, more forcefully this time.

My throat tightens. "I didn't want to tell her," I say in a soft voice.

Elodie's soft, too, when she answers. "Because you don't want it to end."

I shake my head, admitting this truth too. "I don't."

I want to stay in Hawaii with him.

* * *

After I pick and buy the costumes, we head out on the street, walking past a café, where the door slaps open.

Three young children rush out, followed by a thirty-something couple. Laughter surrounds them. My heart aches, and I jerk my gaze away before the hurt tunnels deeper into me.

Once we pass them, Elodie rubs my shoulder. "It's still hard, isn't it?"

A sob rises in my throat. "It is," I say meekly.

I wish it weren't. Some days, I think I'm doing

better. But then, there are times like now where I'm still living with this blackness inside me. This hardened sadness. This realization that what I had believed to be true for five years was all a lie. I only broke free of the lie a few months ago.

And yet the only way to heal from those lies is to live with the truth. I turn to Elodie and all that emotion rises higher in my throat, fighting to break free. "The month before I found out about his double life?" I say, quietly, needing to share this, even though it's the most embarrassing part of the story.

She nods.

I forge ahead, past the pain and the shame. "He'd taken me out to dinner. We'd been talking about having kids, Els," I say, admitting that terrible truth.

She frowns in sympathy.

"He'd wanted to for the last year. I told him I was finally ready. He took me out to dinner to celebrate," I say, my voice stretched thin with tears that I don't hold back anymore. "We were going to start trying the next month. I went off the pill and one month later, I discovered he already had two children and another on the way."

She hauls me in close for a protective embrace, her arms shielding me from all of San Francisco, as the tears fall. "I'm so glad you got out just in time."

"Me too," I say softly.

That was so hard to say, but as I head home, I feel a little lighter. Like some of the blackness is vanishing. Like maybe it doesn't have such a stronghold on me.

I'm glad I voiced it to someone besides Elena. It feels

freeing to let that final hard truth out into the universe.

Maybe to start to move beyond it.

I hope.

36

CARTER TIME

Rachel

I'm hooking closed a red lace bra when my phone rings on the bureau in my bedroom. I glance at the screen—it's Carter.

But he's not due to pick me up for the party for thirty more minutes. I hope he's not canceling. All the times that Edward canceled seem to flash before me all at once. My brain races away with worry. But then I talk to those fears before they steal my mental health.

Just because I've been hurt in the past doesn't mean I'll be hurt in the present. And, even if Carter's canceling, there's probably a good reason. Still, I answer the phone with a wary, "Hey, is everything okay?"

Way to show my fears.

"Everything is great. Did you think I was going to cancel?" he asks, busting me like that.

I hem and haw. "Well, not really."

"Rachel," he chides. "Trust me. This is good. I'm calling because I'm here now."

I blink. "Did I get the time wrong? Because Carter time is usually five minutes late, not thirty minutes early."

"That is true. But in Carter time, something amazing is probably happening thirty minutes before I was supposed to arrive. So I set an alarm for thirty minutes early and I'm really hoping I can walk in on you half-naked or all naked. Please say you're wearing next to nothing. Pretty fucking please."

I shiver from the sexy surprise of his early arrival. "Your timing is impeccable," I say, then stride across my living room, heading toward the door. "I'll buzz you in."

Fifteen seconds later, I've unhooked the bra so I can answer the door in my panties only, with the red lace bra dangling from my fingers.

He growls, slams the door closed, then cups my cheek and gives me a rough, almost brutal kiss.

The bra falls to the floor.

His mouth has a mission, and his lips are traveling down my neck to my tits. He's sucking on my nipples while kneading my flesh. When he presses his teeth to the flesh of my right breast, I'm so caught up in the moment that I urge him on. "Mark me."

His teeth come down on my skin, and I yelp, then shudder. A surge of pleasure rolls through me as he breaks the skin.

The intensity hurts so good that my bones are melting. When I open my eyes, I'm starving for him. "Please fuck me before we go."

In no time, he takes out a condom, bends me over the couch, and buries himself deep inside me. He palms my right cheek with one hand and slides his other hand up to my breasts, but he doesn't stop there. He travels to my neck, circling my throat, pressing the pads of his fingers around me.

Like that, he holds me in place, owning my pleasure, making me his. I cry out, coming hard and fast and breathlessly.

In seconds he's grunting, then shoving deep inside me, finishing on a feral growl. I'm still panting, still sighing while he wraps his arms around me, not wanting him to let go. He stays in me for a few more seconds, sweeping possessive kisses over the back of my neck, murmuring sweet nothings as he caresses me with his mouth. When he pulls out, he says in a sated rasp, "I'm gonna always be early from here on out."

I freeze at those words. *Always be early.*

Like we're doing this indefinitely. Like this vacation doesn't end.

That feels so surreal.

And yet, as I turn around in his arms, I say softly, "Good."

His lips curve up in a hopeful grin. "Yeah?"

That question tugs on my heart. "Yes," I say, and then, because I need some space from him and this storm of emotions, and since a girl has to clean up after sex, I grab my bra and head to the bathroom as an outrageously risky ray of hope shoots through me.

Could we do this? Would he want to? Could I handle

it? I didn't think so a few weeks ago, but I'm starting to wonder now if it's possible.

The questions don't terrify me anymore. They kind of...intrigue me.

Maybe even excite me.

I leave the bathroom, floating on possibilities as I find a fresh pair of red panties, then redo my lingerie. I zip up a short, tight nurse's uniform that lands in the middle of my thighs and shows off one of my assets that Carter loves best—I might as well be Nurse Tata.

I strut out to the living room to show him my costume.

He whistles his approval. I don't think we're going to win best costume.

But with my red lace bra peeking through and him as a sexy, shirtless doctor—in scrubs, a stethoscope, and an open lab coat that displays that absolutely fantastic canvas of a chest—it feels like our costumes are just for the two of us. A private commentary on our attraction for each other.

We head out. On the street, he opens the passenger door to his car, then loops an arm around me and presses a quick, firm kiss to my lips.

That's all new too. A public kiss.

Suddenly, this thing between us doesn't feel private anymore. Our after-hours affair doesn't seem like a secret.

My breath hitches in excitement.

I feel warm and fizzy everywhere. Hopeful, too, from this sort of public declaration. Especially when he says, "Glad you liked the surprise."

"I loved it," I say, breathy.

There's that warm gaze again, and it makes my heart pound. Carter doesn't say anything about the kiss or the change in PDA. He doesn't make it seem like it was a big deal.

Maybe it's not to him?

Or maybe it's just a natural next step.

He goes to the driver's side of his car and takes us to the party. I don't have any more answers as we head inside. In fact, I have so many more questions pinging through my mind. But striding up the steps to Jason and Beck's house together, dressed like this—like a couple, as Elodie said—feels like a natural next step too.

37

THE YOU EFFECT

Carter

When Beck swings open the door, he surveys my outfit, shaking his head in amusement. "You never miss a chance to be shirtless."

Before I can fashion a comeback, Rachel is on it with, "And he never should."

A smug smile takes over my face. I work hard for this body, and her appreciation of it makes every chest press, biceps curl, and crunch worthwhile.

Beck's husband, Jason, joins him at the door, dressed as a cowboy, complete with a ten-gallon hat and blade of hay in the corner of his mouth. Beck's wearing a fireman's turnouts. The pulsing beat of pop music from the house grows louder, while the dark lighting inside sets the spooky mood. Behind the hosts, zombies and devils dance and drink.

Jason surveys me, then my date, with obvious

costume approval. "Well, the doctor is in," he says, and turns to Rachel. "And I suspect you'll be treating all the boo-boos in the house."

I narrow my eyes, growling.

Jason cracks up. "You jealous fucker."

I growl some more, then we head inside in front of them. Rachel lifts a questioning brow. "Something stuck in your throat?"

"I swear, if any of my asshole teammates hit on you, I will rip them a new one," I grumble.

Where did that come from? Oh, just the depths of my caveman soul.

Rachel laughs in surprise. "Noted." She squeezes my arm again. "But I'm here with you. Why would they hit on me?"

She asks it so earnestly, but I know how straight dudes who make millions playing ball can act with women—like they can have anyone they want.

A minute later, our kicker weaves past us, stops, spins around, and meets Rachel's eyes. "I scraped my knee. Can you help me, nurse?"

Called it. "Fuck off," I say.

Hamlin appears next, in Black Panther gear, clearing his throat. "I have a sore throat, nurse. Will you look at my tongue?"

I bet Beck put the guys up to this to fuck with me.

"Sure. Stick it out," Rachel says.

Hamlin complies, and I have no choice but to smack him upside the head. *Gently.* Well, mostly. "Your tongue is fucking fine, Ham."

I tug her into the kitchen, hoping to get away from

pervy teammates. But the kitchen is swarming with teammates too. Well, it is a party.

"They're jackasses," I say to Rachel, apologizing in the crowded corner of the kitchen, by a tray of edible eyeballs.

Her smile says it's no big deal. "It's okay. They're your teammates. It doesn't bother me." She nibbles on the corner of her lips then raises her chin and takes a breath. "But why does it bother you so much?"

The question comes out like she's feeling me out. Like it's hard to ask, but like she really wants to know.

And after tonight and the way we crashed into each other with such need and desire, then the way I said *I'll always be early*, I'm starting to entertain new ideas.

Ideas that make me want to say something.

To tell her—*I am so infatuated with you, and I can't stand the thought of anyone else looking at you the way I do.*

But at a party? With loud music reverberating through speakers? And spiderweb nacho-spread and mummy jalapeño poppers and a hundred of our friends? A party where we're, for all intents and purposes, working? Where I have to make the second to last video in a contract that's been chasing me?

No. Now's not the time. You don't make a big play on first down. You just…move the ball.

So I answer her question with a question. "Did it bother you when I kissed you outside the car?"

Pretty sure it didn't. But I want to hear it in words, not just deeds. I was so caught up in the moment that I didn't think. I did something that could radically fuck with this whole *just friends* thing we've built at Date Night.

Something that Zena and app users and anyone could have a field day with.

But I loved kissing her freely. I want to know her toes were curling too.

She pins me with a heady gaze. "Couldn't you tell how much I didn't mind it?"

My dumb heart thumps.

Then my head does.

"Ouch!"

It's Hamlin smacking me. "Payback, bro," he says.

I roll my eyes. The moment is over, and I'd better focus on what we came to do. I whip out my phone and hit record.

* * *

After we capture some footage of us at the party meeting new friends, saying hi again to old friends, talking to the camera, and even dragging my brother and Hazel into the shot—much to Axel's chagrin—I finally hit *end*.

This series is fun, I suppose.

But what I like most are the moments when the cameras don't roll. When Rachel and I can be ourselves with each other and with friends.

Like when Hazel turns to Rachel and waggles a bottle of chardonnay at her. "Want to hang in the backyard, drink wine, and look at the stars as we debate who had the most clever costume?"

"I'm so there," Rachel says.

Is this some of what she's missed out on for the last five years too? A chance to be herself, the girl who likes cheap wine and fun costumes rather than pearls and snooty sommeliers?

Seems so, since she grabs her wine mug and shoves it Hazel's way. "But pour now. Don't wait another second."

I've seen Rachel hang out with friends before. But I'm staring at her holding a mug of white wine like it's fucking enchanting.

I don't even know why, except everything she does is.

And every time I see her, it's harder and harder for me to just be okay with the way things *were*.

When I want *this*.

I want all these guys to know they can't even pretend to hit on my girl. I want everyone in San Francisco to see me kiss her. I want her to feel what it's like when a man makes a declaration for you in public.

But what the fuck am I supposed to do with all these emotions bubbling up inside me? In a flash, that enchantment turns to irritation. To utter frustration.

"Fuck," I mutter to myself, then turn away from her to grab a beer from the cooler in the kitchen. After I open it, Axel joins me, clapping a hand on my shoulder as Hazel and Rachel motion that they're going to the backyard.

"Hey, just wondering if you wanted me to write your emotions on your sleeve," he deadpans as he surveys my open lab coat.

I turn to him in his cop uniform—with *Grammar Police* embroidered on the pocket—and sigh. "They already are," I admit.

"Yeah, no shit," he says, then lifts his beer and tips some back. "Here's a crazy idea. You could tell her how you feel."

I glance around the party. It's loud and hot and everyone's here. "Now's hardly the time."

"That's probably true, but you could, I dunno, find a time." Despite his joking words, he stares at me seriously. "Think about it, Carter. You don't have to do it tonight. But it's eating you up inside. And I know what that's like."

"What's it like?" I ask, sounding miserable and needing the corroboration.

"Like someone stuck a fist in your chest and twisted your heart. And the only thing worse is the worry she might not return the feelings," he says.

Leave it to a writer to use words to deliver a gut punch.

Shaking my head, I let out a mirthless laugh. "And on that note, I think I won't rush into it. I don't need to feel worse."

Right now, I still feel good. I still feel happy. I feel like something is stirring between us. Like maybe she's looking at me in new ways too.

Like she did earlier in her living room when we locked eyes and everything felt…possible.

But what if that was just a post-sex high?

I need more evidence before I hold up a boom box to her window. If you're going to do a John Cusack, you'd better be dead certain. There's no going back on a boom box serenade.

For now, though, I join her outside, setting a hand on her back—possessively. No one better go near her.

She dips her face and smiles.

Hazel lifts her wine glass and looks from Rachel to me. "So, Carter, how's everything going?"

There's so much more to her question. She means how are things going *with the two of us.*

"Everything is great," I say, meaning it. I've let go of that frustration, and I should focus on trying to read Rachel.

Axel joins us, and the four of us talk and drink and laugh. After three beers, I stop drinking, worried I'll blurt out a tipsy confession.

But I do want to get her naked all over again.

So after she finishes another mug of wine, I say, "Want to get on the horse?"

She reaches for my stethoscope and plays with it, speaking softly so no one else can hear. "Spoiler alert: I was thinking about banging you that night. When I looked at you at my breakup party, all I could think was *I want to sleep with him.*"

I go up in flames. I want her so damn much. "It's the shirtless effect," I say with a cocky shrug.

"It's the *you* effect," she corrects, in that same sweet voice she used post-sex. It wraps around me. It weaves through me. It lives inside my soul.

That's it. I call a Lyft and tell Beck I'll get my car tomorrow.

Sometimes when you take your date to a party, all you really want is to be alone with her.

* * *

We head up the steps to her place, both buzzed and handsy, kissing and laughing.

We've done this before, but it feels different tonight. Once she unlocks the door and we're inside, I reach for her hand, thread my fingers through hers, and meet her gaze, stripping away the laughter. "Let me take you to dinner for our fifth date."

I don't say *last date*.

She tenses. She hasn't wanted to go on a dinner date so far. "You want to go to a restaurant?"

"Doesn't have to be fancy," I assure her, linking our fingers more tightly. "I just want to show you how it feels. I want to erase all the bad memories you have. I want to take you out on a proper date to a restaurant so you can know what it's like to be with a guy who only has eyes for you."

Okay, that's not quite boom box territory. But it's getting closer.

She grabs the lapels of my coat, tugs on them with a particular intensity. "Yes. Take me out, Carter."

I want to take her out for all the days and nights.

For now, I take her and our buzz to the bedroom, open the closet door so the mirror is just so, then I strip her naked.

* * *

Her legs are wrapped around my ass, and she's watching our reflection. She can't tear her gaze away from the sight of me fucking her.

With all my strength, I drive into her, giving her what she wants.

"Like the view?" I grunt as I swivel my hips.

She whimpers a yes as she stares shamelessly at the mirror. "Love it," she adds on a staggered breath.

Let's see if she loves this more. I pause mid-thrust, taking a beat, then I sink into her so deep and so powerfully that she lets go of my shoulders, her head flopping down on the pillow with a wild moan.

She looks lost in bliss.

My breath quickens. Electricity crackles in my veins. And I feel like I'm succumbing to something…wild.

Something I never expected.

Something fierce and powerful all on its own—this connection between the two of us.

She wraps her arms around my neck, tugging me closer. But I tsk at her. "You're not watching me fuck you, baby," I admonish.

She cries out. "It's too good."

Her breath speeds up. Her moans shoot higher. She shudders. She's so damn close, and I love that I know all her signs.

"Watch us come," I demand.

I pull out, shift her from her back to her side and move behind her. I yank her against me, her back to my chest.

Lining up my cock, I slide back into her, groaning at the tight, hot feel of her welcoming me again.

In the mirror, I see her eyes flutter closed, but that won't do. I run a hand over her tits, right to her chin. With a firm grip, I push her face to the side. "Watch."

Her eyes open and she gasps. "We look so hot," she murmurs, like she's adoring the filthy movie in the mirror.

I wrap one arm around her, so I can play with her tits. The other skates over her hip, across her waist, down to her clit.

"I'll get you there, baby," I promise, whispering harshly in her ear. Her eyes lock with mine in the mirror.

Those amber eyes are wide and passionate. Emotional and vulnerable. Thrilled and hopeful.

And I'm devastated. I can't ever turn back. I'm so fucking crazy for her, I have to find a way to tell her. I have to find the right time. The right moment.

No matter the risk.

She screams, then shatters, panting, crying out, moaning.

When I'm *this* close, she watches me, and I crash over the edge too.

After a few heady, blissed out, post-sex minutes, she turns around in my arms. "That was the hottest thing I've ever seen," she says.

I can give that to you every night, I want to say.

But I'm pretty sure that's not how you ask your best friend to be your girlfriend.

38

THE ROMANCE PLAY

Carter

I wake up with a slew of ideas demanding attention and a restlessness in my muscles.

It's overwhelming, all these bumper cars in my brain and body, but in a good way. They get me up and out of bed. I leave at dawn, giving a sleeping Rachel a kiss goodbye, then I walk quickly to my home, energized by options for real dates, dictating some ideas into my phone so I don't lose the thread.

At my house, I change quickly into workout shorts and sneakers, and soon I'm out the door, hitting the streets for a run, working up a sweat as the fog rolls through the early November morning.

With my pump-me-up playlist blasting, I fly down a steep hill toward the looming Golden Gate Bridge. I cross the bridge, running romance plays while my sneakers slap against the stone path.

I don't want to move too fast with Rachel or too slow. Milliseconds make a difference in my job. And they matter in life too. My whole life is all about timing, on the field, and every damn day. My to-do list is a testament to how important tracking time is for me to function. I can't be sloppy. No mistakes, no missed passes, no dropped balls.

If I'm going to risk our friendship, I've got to find the right moment, the right wording, the right...*play.*

And boom, as I reach the end of the bridge, I'm pretty sure I've got it. *Yes, thank you, exercise. You always have my back.*

Back in Pacific Heights, I race to Beck's house, hop in my car, cranking up Taylor Swift as I drive. Except, wait. Nope. *Love you, T, but you're the breakup queen.* I switch back to my workout playlist, and the rock anthems suit my mood.

Yes, I am the fucking romance champion.

At my home, I slide into a spot out front, then bound up the steps, go inside, and take a quick shower. Once I'm out and dressed in—no surprise—shorts and a T-shirt, I take my ADHD pill, then fire up the bad boy of an espresso machine, singing as I go. *I am the romance champion of the world.*

As the machine hisses and the life-affirming brew fills a cup, Monroe knocks.

I yank open the door. "Talk about timing. Yours is sick," I say, impressed.

He smirks. "Yes, son. My timing is indeed...*sick.*"

And I walked into that one, but whatever. "Fuck off," I say, letting him in.

"But your timing? Let's talk about that. My coffee shop's been keeping weird hours lately," he remarks. "You're not here every morning."

"That must be hard for you," I say, finishing his cup and handing it to him.

"It is, admittedly, concerning." Monroe takes a pull, chasing it with a contented sigh. When he sets the cup down, he studies me quizzically as my espresso goes down the hatch. "Seems like you've had a couple cups of coffee already today."

I shake my head. "Just this one. But you know mornings and me," I say, washing my cup now, moving through my routine at lightning speed. There's so much to do.

He scoffs. "More like all day and you. You're naturally caffeinated," he says, but he looks pensive, unsatisfied with my answer. "So, your coffee shop hours. Are they going to return to normal after this fifth date with Rachel?"

I smile, a little cocky, but hopeful too. I'd like to keep him on his toes with my *coffee shop hours*. I'd like to be at Rachel's some mornings. I'd like her to be here some mornings. I'd like it all. "I hope not, actually."

"Oh?"

"Some jackass told me to be honest with myself," I say with a confident grin. "And so I was."

"Well, that ought to make my podcast interesting," he says.

Oh, shit. His fucking show. "When is that?" I ask, hunting for my phone to make a note.

With a warm smile, Monroe answers. "A couple weeks. I'll send you a reminder."

"Thanks," I say, setting the phone down, relieved he'll handle the reminder.

Once he's gone, I grab my keys and head out, but I stop at the door. Something's nagging at me. What the hell is it? Maybe it'll come to me later. I head down the steps to my car. But before I turn it on, my phone serves up a slew of alerts like a Vegas slot machine.

I read through them all.

Pick up Beck.

Easy. I'm nearly on my way.

Find a restaurant for the fifth date.

I'll ask Maddox. He's good with that.

Don't forget your meeting with Seductive in Las Vegas.

I snap my fingers. That's what I was forgetting. My cologne sponsor. I'm seeing them next week after my game against the Vegas Pioneers.

So much to do, but I don't want to lose track of my fifth date brainstorm this morning, so I add a new item to the calendar.

Get a mug.

I'll order that tonight.

Oh!

Chocolate. Yep. Rachel loves that. I'll stop by Elodie's and pick some up. Also, what the fuck with her ex? That jackass never took her on a chocolate shop date. Seriously. What kind of an asshat was he?

The kind I should have objected to at her wedding, that's what.

But he's history, and I'm the present.

I turn on the car, then drive, running the play as I go.

I'll take her out to a romantic dinner. It'll erase all her shitty memories of him. I'll show her that I'm the one guy who knows how to date her. That all these un-dates weren't just teaching her how a man should treat her in some distant *someday.*

These un-dates are for now.

I'll give her a brand-new mug, and I'll ask her to be mine. Five dates to a real date.

That's the play.

But when I reach Beck's house, I remember what I couldn't while standing at my door—Jane.

Dammit. I forgot to water the forget-my-tits ficus. I'll have to do it tonight, and in seconds, Jane is out of my mind.

Once Beck's in the car, we talk football. *Only football.* I shove romance out of my mind as we head to the Renegades facility. This Sunday in Las Vegas will be my first game since my bad catch cost us the last one.

I intend to do everything I can to win.

I don't do anything halfway—not football, and not romance.

39

DÉJÀ VU

Rachel

I am ready to rip out my hair.

"I can't take this game," I announce as I pace in my living room on Sunday night like a caged lion at a zoo, back and forth, staring at the tense action on the screen.

"We know, honey. Trust me, we all know," Fable calls from her spot on the couch. It's her first time here. I invited her over to watch the game, and it feels like she's already part of our regular crew. We've been brainstorming ideas with her during commercial breaks about how to get more stores to carry her jewelry. For now, though, I clutch my wine mug like it's a lifeline, but I can't take a drink because I'm too stressed. The game is tied.

It's one game. Just one regular season game. But it's not really *just one game*. It's a big one for my friend.

Carter won't say as much because he keeps things

to himself, but I know he's still beating himself up over the loss two weeks ago. While he's played flawlessly in Vegas tonight, the Renegades defense has struggled.

I cross my fingers and offer a prayer to the gods and goddesses of the gridiron.

Only a few minutes left, and offense is taking the field again after defense just gave up a touchdown to the Pioneers.

Carter runs across the grass, getting into the huddle.

I grip the back of the couch, staring at the pack of players like I can will the game to go the Renegades way.

"Go, Carter, come on. Make Rachel a happy girlfriend," Juliet catcalls at the screen.

I pinch my sister's shoulder. "I am not his girlfriend," I say, but secretly, I savor the sound of that.

She tosses me a sisterly glance that says I'm full of it. "Lies. Sweet little lies."

Well, I'm not his girlfriend *yet*. Maybe soon? But I can't even give voice to my *do you think that could actually happen*, or *maybe someday really, really soon*. Why? Because I want this win for him so badly. I want him to have all the good things. I want it so freaking badly that when Beck drops into the pocket, searches for an opening, then lobs a beautiful spiral Carter's way, I am about to chew off my arm as I wait.

"Come on, come on, come on, come on, come on, come on, come on, come on," I mutter at the screen as Carter chases it, arms outstretched. He leaps and hauls it close to his chest.

As he runs into the end zone, my heart explodes. "Yes, yes, yes, yes, yes, yes!"

My neighbors are going to hate me. But I'll live with their ire.

Powered by joy and adrenaline, I spin around and grab my phone from where I left it on the kitchen counter, tapping out a quick text to him. ***Amazing catch! You're incredible!***

Obviously he doesn't have his phone with him on the field. But I still want him to know I sent it now. That I am rooting for him in this moment.

My tension loosens enough for me to go to the couch and flop down between my friends. I blow out a breath that I've probably been holding forever. "I'm feeling better," I say, relieved.

Fable nods, patting my shoulder. "Yeah, it sounds like you just had an orgasm."

"She has them every time he plays," Juliet deadpans.

Elodie just peers at me with question marks in her eyes.

Questions I'll have to answer later.

Questions I want to answer.

* * *

Later, after the Renegades seal up a win, I send another text to Carter, full of exclamation points and confetti. Juliet and Fable ask if they can help clean up the party leftovers, but I wave them off. Elodie hangs behind, saying she has to pick up Amanda at a friend's place nearby soon.

But I don't think that's the only reason she's sticking around. There's a concerned but curious look in her eyes as we pick up glasses and plates. "How's everything since I saw you?" she asks.

I set the plates on the counter and meet her gaze, then speak from the heart. "You helped me a lot."

"Me? How?" She sounds shocked.

"By being my friend. By being a safe place. I hadn't said that to anyone but Elena. But then, telling you…" I stop to take a deep, fueling breath. Kind of an excited breath, too, because this realization feels big. "I think it was the last of my letting go," I admit in a hushed voice.

It feels fragile, the sentiment.

"Oh god," she says, sounding amazed as she beams at me and comes in for a hug. "I'm so happy for you, Rachel."

I choke up. "Me too."

When she lets go, she arches a mischievous brow, shifting gears as she asks, "So?"

I feel a little bubbly. A little daring. But a lot scared. I feel, too, like my future is wide open. Like my somedays aren't as far away as I'd thought they were. "I don't know, but maybe we can just keep on dating," I say.

It's an idea, one that has taken hold of me.

* * *

When I slide into bed, there's a text from him. ***Can't wait to see you tomorrow night.*** I'm giddy as I write back, ***Me too***.

He replies a few seconds later with, ***I sent the info to your calendar.***

I saw it there.

And it thrilled me, I want to add.

But I don't because I'd rather focus on him. ***You were amazing tonight! Great touchdown catch!***

His reply is instant. ***Your text made me happy.***

I squeeze the phone in excitement.

You make me happy, I want to say. But that might be too much. That might give my bruised heart away. I'll feel him out tomorrow. Make sure I'm not misinterpreting how things have felt on the last few dates. Better to be safe than stupid.

Tomorrow night, maybe I'll feel bold enough to say those four words: you make me happy.

For now, I send a smiley face and go to bed.

* * *

Monday is busier than usual. In the morning, I stop by some other shops in the city to check out the competition, then I have lunch with a supplier. Fable keeps the home fires burning at Bling and Baubles in the afternoon, while I meet with a PR firm about some social media initiatives for the store. Why not capitalize on the Date Night thing? I'm having my fifteen minutes of fame, so to speak, and I might as well use them.

After that meeting, I hustle over to the shop. It's already four o'clock, and I want to make sure everything is going well before I leave to get ready for my date. Carter should be landing any minute. Then he'll go home. I picture both of us getting ready, like in a movie montage, and I hope he's as nervous and excited as I am.

But I'm also scared of dinner.

Which is so stupid. It's a freaking meal. I eat at that damn time every day. But fancy restaurants remind me so much of my ex and his lies. They remind me, too, of the way Edward tried to smooth them over with his fancy meals and elaborate stories.

This is different.

Tonight will be different.

I'm ready to make new memories with my best friend. I'm ready to put the past behind me.

As I pass Sur La Table and its window display of utensils, a fun idea pops into my head. I dart into the shop and quickly find a red plastic spatula. It's silly, but so are we. I'll give this to him tonight and ask, "Can we keep a lucky spatula at your place too?"

Yes! That's what I'll say. That ought to make my intentions clear without putting too much pressure on him.

I buy the spatula, complete with a red bow. Once I leave, I fish my phone from my purse.

Whoa.

Three missed calls?

From Carter? That's odd. He never calls three times.

My smile erases itself.

Did something happen to him? Oh god, is he okay? Worry seizes me as I race to open my contacts while imagining the worst.

Something happened to him. He met someone else.

He's seeing another woman. He's canceling on me to see his other family.

Stop. Just stop.

This is Carter, and surely these three calls are nothing.

That's what I tell myself as I hit his name, but then a text pops up from him.

Call me when you see this. I have to cancel tonight.

I stop in my tracks, déjà vu knocking the breath out of me.

40

RAIN CHECK WOES

Rachel

"I'm sorry. I forgot," Carter says, contrition in his tone.

But still, as I trudge up Fillmore, my feet heavy and my gut twisted, I can't shake the awful familiarity lodged in me.

Even as he tries to reassure me. "I knew I had this photo shoot this morning, which is why I didn't fly back with the team last night," he says, explaining himself. Practically over-explaining himself as he adds, "But I completely forgot that I'd also committed to do this dinner with Seductive tonight and then a golf game for charity tomorrow, and I just totally fucked up, Rachel. I am so sorry."

"It's fine," I say, swallowing down my disappointment. This isn't about me.

It's just one date. One *un-date*. What's the big deal?

I have to find a way to put my past aside. I can't let it

get in the way of our friendship. Besides, he's so earnest, and I can tell he's beating himself up over one little moment, so clearly this is not the moment to fly my "I fell for you and here's a lucky spatula" flag.

"I get it. I do," I say, so cheery, so chipper, so upbeat. I refuse to let on that I am disappointed. I don't want to be like his ex-girlfriends who gave him a hard time about his focus, his attention, his time management. They aren't in his life. And dammit, I'm going to be in his life no matter what. So, I add, "I'm your pal. I totally get it."

"Rachel, I feel like shit," he says, so genuinely remorseful that my heart hurts for him. "I never want you to think you don't matter. Can we have a rain check?"

Oh.

Oh, no.

My head rings with that word.

I stop in my tracks, setting a hand against the brick wall of Better With Pockets.

Rain check is what I said when I rescheduled the mirror sex because of the sidewalk sale opportunity.

He's doing the same. *Understandably.*

But holy smokes. He's following the same rules. The rules we effectively established for our five dates of girlfriend lessons—sex and education and then we stay friends.

That. Is. All.

I am such a fool. I've read everything wrong. I took every sweet moment, every sexy moment, every dirty moment, every soulful look, and I twisted them around to assume he was falling in love with me too.

What an idiot I am.

He's not falling in love with me. He's doing exactly what I asked him to do—giving me girlfriend lessons. He said he'd be the best boyfriend ever. And he has been, and he still is—right now.

He's showing me how it feels to be treated well. And he's doing it because he is my best friend. Not because he feels the same ridiculous, romantic way I do.

My throat tightens, and a sob tries to fight free. I swallow it immediately, since I don't want him to hear the catch in my voice. The catch that says all these flutters and swoons were only in *my* head.

I am so glad I saw the truth before I said something stupidly romantic that could have harmed our lifelong friendship.

Those times when I'd asked him to open up? When he'd sometimes drift off? I'd hoped he was thinking about me. But he was probably being honest then, too, when he'd said he was thinking about football. Even when I'd asked him about the Halloween party I didn't go to, and we'd both gotten a little wistful—I'd been so sure we were both wondering what might have been if I had gone. If I'd made better choices five years ago. I was so sure we were thinking about *each other*.

He was just thinking about friendship.

God, I'm so clueless. I can never read a man correctly. But at least Carter never lied to me. He never betrayed me. And I never ever want to lose him in my life. I will save our friendship no matter what.

I won't become an Izzy, or Sasha, or Quinn. I won't be a friend who became a lover and is now out of the picture.

I am going to keep this man in my life for all time. How? By being a great friend. I start walking again, and as I do, I circle back to his rain check comment. "A rain check sounds fab. Don't even think twice about it," I add with so much pep and sunshine you could bottle it.

I will show him I learned friend lessons too.

"But I wanted to…" he begins, except there's so much noise where he is. Voices chattering. Someone saying *play a hand before dinner*. The sound of payouts on slot machines. "I wanted to be a better boyfriend."

Wanted.

Past tense. As part of our lessons. As part of this pretend relationship. Because he values our friendship.

That. Is. All.

I have to exonerate him from his guilt. I can't let him feel it a second longer over a simple mistake. Hell, I forget things too, and I don't have ADHD. "You are a great pretend boyfriend, and our friendship means everything to me," I say, gentle and caring as I reach the block with my store.

"Rachel, that's not what I'm—"

But someone cuts him off, and his voice is muffled as he says, "Be right there" to whoever he's with. When he comes back with a "Hey, so I was saying," I'm quick to jump on the problem and fix it.

"Listen, when you come back, we'll do our last undate and call it good. The girlfriend lessons will be all done. Now go," I say, with a bright smile in my voice that shows I am the supportive girlfriend he taught me to be. So I'll be ready to be one for my maybe-someday down the road.

"Look, that's not what I'm saying. But I really have to go. I'll call you later and explain better."

I don't want him to see me as that fragile. I don't want him to think I need that much attention. "Carter, I'm fine. Don't worry. It's not like I'm your real girlfriend," I say with a forced laugh, like *how ridiculous is that*. "We're just friends."

He's starkly silent for several long seconds. He lets out a weighty, "Right." A sigh. "I have to go."

And so do I. I'm at the shop, and someone is waiting outside the door for me.

It's Ava and her perfectly coiffed blonde hair is tied up in an unkempt, unruly bun. She's wearing jeans and a hooded sweatshirt. She looks nothing like the woman who floated into my shop a few weeks ago. Neither does she look like the woman I apologized to two weeks ago.

She looks everything like me when I learned the truth of my marriage.

When she spots me, we lock eyes. Hers fill with tears and apology, and she says, "You were right."

My heart goes out to her. "Oh, honey."

I bring her into my arms for a hug and do the only thing I can. I ask Fable to close up the shop, and I take Ava to my home, open a bottle of wine, and I listen as she pours out her heart for the next few hours.

41

JUST EVERYTHING

Carter

I'm standing in the middle of the blackjack tables at The Extravagant, my phone in my hand, the call over, wondering why my hands feel clammy, and my heart feels leaden.

Did she just break up with me before we even started?

I drag a hand through my hair, trying to sort out that bizarre phone call.

But Amar from Seductive is waiting for me at the poker tables, and so is his second-in-command, Naveen. They're cool dudes, and I like my sponsors, but I wish I weren't here right now. I wish I were in San Francisco so I could go bang on the door to Rachel's house.

Show up at her store.

Ask for a do-over of that phone call.

Hell, it happens in football.

I motion to the guys that I'll be right with them, then I turn and weave through the crowds, past the roulette games and the craps table, past the Aladdin and AC/DC slots, walking and thinking.

Doing my own instant replay.

If I were an official in this game, what would I see if I watched that scene in slo-mo, checking out every frame?

I'd see a woman who was overly friendly.

Who told me everything was fine.

Who said not to worry.

But you know what? I am fucking worried. About her. Because she thinks something that's all wrong. She clearly thinks I just want to be friends with her. Hell, I've let her believe this. I believed it once upon a time too. I told her when we started that I didn't want to go anywhere near a real date, and then I went and told her before we had sex that I didn't want to ruin our friendship.

I groan to the ends of the earth. No wonder she redrew the friendship line in the sand on that call.

This is all my fault.

I laid down the friendship rules in the first place, and all she did today was follow them. But I've already broken them. I don't want to be just friends with her. I want to be just everything.

But she won't know that till I, spoiler alert: say it. And say it with all the feelings.

I grab my phone, duck into a hallway near the restrooms, and dial her. She doesn't answer. I try again a few minutes later. It goes straight to voicemail.

"Fuck," I mutter.

Maybe she thinks something is wrong, but I *did* do something wrong. And it's not forgetting I had a whole damn dinner tonight and golf game tomorrow.

It's that I waited for the perfect moment. I tried to set up a perfect date. I tried to execute a perfect play.

But sometimes you have to call an audible. There is no perfect timing in football, or in life. Sometimes you have to make your chances.

Maybe I can have it both ways. As I return to the guys, I google flights. Perhaps I can fly home late tonight after dinner, see her and explain, then get back out here in the morning for the golf game.

Yeah. That's what a fucking awesome boyfriend would do.

And that's who I am.

I check the flights. But then I groan. The earliest flight that could get back here would be landing at seven. And we have an eight a.m. tee time.

If the flight is late, I'm fucked.

It's fine. It's totally fine. I'll just see her tomorrow. I put the phone away and deal with the here and now.

* * *

When I return to my room later that evening, I try her again. Voicemail. Fucking voicemail. I grip the phone, wanting to chuck it at the wall. I'm really going to have to fix this shit big time.

I move my afternoon flight tomorrow a couple

hours earlier, then I order her flowers to arrive first thing tomorrow morning.

Her favorite—wildflowers.

Then I add chocolates too.

* * *

I wake up to an email from the flower company saying the vase was left in the foyer since no one was home.

Where the hell is Rachel?

I try her one more time. It's the crack of dawn, and I hear it in her voice when she answers. "Hey, what's up?"

"Where are you? I sent you flowers?"

She yawns. "There were some problems with the Los Angeles store. My manager quit, so I flew here late last night. I'm staying at Ellie's house," she says, barely awake. "But I should get up and head to the store. I have an interview with a possible new manager soon. I'll be back tomorrow night."

Jesus. Now I've woken her up. And she's having business problems. She mentioned the trouble with the manager. My timing could not be any worse.

But tomorrow night is too long to wait. I say goodbye and I do the thing I didn't do yesterday.

I'm done waiting.

42

EMPOWERED ME

Rachel

"It's fine. I'm fine. Everything is totally fine," I say with a stiff upper lip as I chat with Ellie's little Chihuahua, Gigi, once I'm dressed and ready for the day. The pipsqueak blonde cutie follows me to the kitchen. Ellie's still sleeping since she had a late night on her show, and her fiancé, Gabe, is out running.

Like Carter does in the mornings.

Stay strong. Don't think of him.

But that's near impossible.

Still, I have to try, so I talk quietly with Gigi. It's just the dog and me as I grab a sesame bagel Ellie left for me on the kitchen counter. Gigi wags her tail, staring relentlessly at the food.

I give her a sad smile as I pluck a piece off. "I mean, relationships suck, people cheat, and employees quit with no notice. But hey, as long as you have friends and bagels, right?"

Her little tail thumps. And a tear slides down my cheek.

What the hell? I'm crying because a dog is wagging her tail?

No, I'm crying because Carter makes me happy but I can't be with him because everything sucks.

But the last time I thought everything sucked, I told off a customer and then I stained Carter's shirt with my mascara, and I am *not* backtracking. I take one more bite of the bagel, then I kiss the dog and go.

I still need to be a better me even if I can't have *everything* I want. I need to be the me who invited Ava over last night. The me who brings good vibes to the block. The me who cares about her friends, her employees, her family.

I need to be Empowered Me. I have enough. I have a new life. I have great friends.

Most of all, I'm free.

So there.

Ellie lives a mile from the main drag in Venice where my store is. I walk to work and along the way, I make an important call. I don't expect Elena to answer, since shrinks don't usually answer the phone, but she picks up on the second ring. "Elena Lopez."

"Oh, hi," I say. "It's Rachel. I wasn't expecting you."

She laughs softly. "Then why did you call? Or were you hoping to leave a voice message confessional rather than talking to me?"

I gulp. Totally busted. "I guess I'm not the only patient to do that?"

"You're not even the only patient to do that this week," she says, then clears her throat and adopts a thoroughly professional tone. "What can I help you with? I do have another session in a few minutes, but when I saw you calling, I thought it might be important."

Is this important? It feels vitally important to me, but I'm not sure it'll be important to her. Sounds pretty foolish to say *I played pretend girlfriend with my best friend, but I fell for him for real, and now I'm kind of sad, but I'm mostly calling because I lied to you about it.*

But I say it anyway, even if it's embarrassing. "I wasn't honest with you at our last session. With this whole five dates thing I've been doing with Carter. Yes, I told you we were doing girlfriend lessons, but we also started sleeping together and it's amazing. But so are the girlfriend lessons. Each time we go on a date. He shows me how a man should treat a woman. And that probably sounds absolutely ridiculous, like we've been playing at being boyfriend and girlfriend. I guess in some ways we have, especially since I stupidly fell in love with him, and I didn't want to tell you that because I was embarrassed."

To her credit, she doesn't laugh. Doesn't scoff. She asks without agenda, "Why were you embarrassed?"

"Because I thought you'd say it wasn't healthy. That it was the opposite of what I should be doing. That I should be having *adult relationships*."

"It certainly sounds like you're having adult relations," she deadpans.

I laugh at her joke. "That's true."

"Why did you think I would say it was unhealthy? What about it feels unhealthy to you?"

That's a good question. As I walk into the Los Angeles morning, the sun warming my shoulders, I ask myself that too, and I only find one good answer: "Because it wasn't entirely real."

But is that even the right answer anymore?

"Were you honest with each other?" Elena asks.

"Absolutely."

"Did he treat you with respect?"

"All the time." *Even when he bit me, spanked me, and almost choked me.*

"Were you truthful with each other?"

I hesitate. "I think so."

"You're not sure?"

"Well, I didn't tell him I fell in love with him. I didn't want to ruin the friendship."

She hums thoughtfully. "Do you think your friendship is strong enough to withstand that piece of information?"

The hair on my arms stands on end.

That's the right question. That's the one I never asked myself. I just assumed the truth would ruin our friendship. But maybe we're strong enough. "I don't know," I say, but my voice climbs up. With new hope.

"You've been friends for fifteen years. You tell me if it's strong enough."

I have chills. Good chills. Excited chills.

Maybe our friendship is strong enough. Maybe I haven't been giving it the credit it deserves. Maybe I haven't been giving myself the credit *I* deserve. Maybe I need to trust my own heart more. Maybe I need to go out on a limb.

I thank her and walk into my store feeling excited about this new possibility. But also feeling a lot of pressure to find a new manager soon.

Because I want to be in San Francisco, rather than here.

First, I conduct a job interview, then I help the employees, doing my best to stay in the moment. Around lunchtime, I send them out, and a few minutes later, someone I know far too well walks through the door.

My ex-husband.

I don't think he notices me, even though I'm the only one in the store right now. He's busy perusing necklaces, and it's the strangest thing to see him. It's... surreal. From behind the counter, I study his handsome face, his tailored suit, his shaven jaw, his expensive watch.

And I feel nothing.

I don't feel shame.

I don't feel anger.

I don't even feel hurt anymore.

If I feel anything, it's gratitude that I got out in the nick of time.

But I still don't want that asshole in my store.

I clear my throat and since there aren't any

customers here this second either, I don't mince words when I say, "What are you doing here?"

He looks up and smiles pleasantly. He doesn't even act surprised. This is how he fooled me. His poker face.

But I'm over it and over him.

"Good to see you, Rachel. I was just buying a necklace," he says, like I care.

Ha. As if I'd sell to him. I point to the door. "No, you're not."

He blinks. Now he's surprised. Good. There's more where that came from—the heart of Empowered Me. "Excuse me?" he asks.

"No, there is no excuse for what you did," I say, like I'm the judge in a courtroom—strong, tough, no-nonsense. Someone you can't talk over, you can't trick. Someone who gives you a piece of her mind. "You can't walk into my store like you did into our marriage—so cavalier, so indifferent. You can't trick me ever again, and you certainly can't trick me with a *necklace*. You don't get to be a customer. You don't get to show up and take what you want with money. I know who you are now. I found out *in this very store*. You're a lying, cheating bastard who stole my trust for five years and stomped all over it...gleefully. You're the worst kind of person. I gave you my heart and you gave me lie after lie, night after night, while you went behind my back and led a second life with another woman and children," I say, coldly, clinically, reading off a list of crimes that don't hurt me anymore but that cut so deep back then. "You don't deserve nice things ever. From anyone. And you are most definitely not ever welcome here. Leave. *Now.*"

His lips twitch. He's not used to people telling him no. He doesn't move for a second. Just studies me.

Until another voice booms through the store. "You heard her. Get the hell out."

I gasp. Carter's standing in the doorway, and my heart gallops with joy.

43

I OBJECT

Carter

That guy.

I swear. If I never see him again, it would be too soon.

And yet, there is something I both *want* and *need* to say to the perfectly polished man in a three-piece suit who looks my way with a careless smirk. "And who are you?"

Edward says it like a gentleman.

A gentleman snake.

He doesn't even remember meeting me, and I went to his wedding and a couple of birthday parties for Rachel. Plus I've no doubt she would have mentioned me to him before. How many childhood friends who play for the Renegades does she have?

Still, I'm not surprised by this guy's douchiness.

"I'm the guy who should have objected more than five years ago," I say as I advance toward him.

His expression is still blank, but his reaction isn't the point. You don't get a lot of do-overs. I've learned that the hard way on the field. But every now and then, life serves one up and you better seize it while you have the chance.

I turn to the woman I adore, and my god, I am overcome with emotions for her. She's worth every canceled golf game, every last-minute trip. She's worth everything. "I'm here for you, Sunshine. But I need to deal with *this* first."

"Do it," she says, her eyes wide and sparkling, as if she's eating popcorn in the front-row seat.

I turn back to the guy in the way. "Now, Rachel was perfectly clear. But maybe you need to hear it from someone who could snap you in half." I flash him a closed-mouth smile. Edward blinks, steps back. Good. "But I won't do that because I'm the good guy in this story."

He holds up the chain in his hand, stammering, "I was just…going to buy a necklace for my wife."

"The fuck you are," I say with a sneer, then I finish what I wanted to do years ago. "Let's do this again, Edward. Rachel objects to you, like I object to you, like I should have done at your wedding. You never deserved her. *Ever.* And I am not missing my chance again." I point to the door just as she did a minute ago. "Nobody wants your business."

With a stoic huff, he sets down the necklace. "I'll shop elsewhere," he says.

"Brilliant fucking idea," I say with a slow clap.

He slinks out with his tail between his legs.

Good riddance. With him in the rearview mirror, I turn to Rachel, my Rachel, my woman, my best friend, and the love of my life.

She's ten feet away, staring at me from behind the counter with wonder and wild hope on her face.

I close the distance between us a few steps. When I arrive at the counter, I cup her cheeks. God, it feels great to touch her again.

"Rachel, I have one regret in life and it's that I didn't realize sooner that you were the one. I didn't say anything then because I wasn't sure what I felt. I had no idea that my feelings were the start of *this*. But I'm dead sure now. I've been falling for you since we first met in high school. I've been falling a little harder every day, but I didn't know it till our first date at the chocolate shop. But once I knew, let me tell you, I *knew*. I don't want to be just your friend anymore. I came down here to ask you if you'll go out with me on a real date."

She gasps and nods at the same time. Several times. "Yes, yes, yes," she blurts out, then adds, "You make me happy."

My heart floods with joy. That's all I've ever wanted. My pulse beats harder, faster, powered by adrenaline and a wide-open future with my best friend. "Sunshine, you're the one."

I lean over the counter and kiss her, and it feels like forever since I've touched these lush lips. I never want to go this long without kissing her again. But it's a first kiss too—the first after I've spoken the truth of my heart and soul—that after all these years and four un-dates, it's always been her.

When I break the kiss, she whispers, "Wow."

She sounds mesmerized. Intoxicated. Blissed out.

Join the club.

But then she knits her brow. "Wait, did you actually fly down here to ask me on a date?"

I smile. Proud and utterly un-remorseful. "I sure did. After we talked this morning, I called my agent and asked him to cancel my golf game so I could catch the next flight out of Vegas."

"The one with your sponsor? The one for charity?" She sounds shocked.

"Yeah, the one that I forgot about when I canceled on you."

She sets a hand on her chest like she needs the double confirmation. "You canceled it? For me?"

"Don't you get it? I'd do anything for you." It feels so damn good to finally tell her, to set all these feelings free so we can share them.

She beams, then in a trembling voice, she says, "I'm so in love with you, Carter Hendrix."

I couldn't be happier to hear that four-letter word falling from her lips, even if she beat me to it.

I capture her mouth in another kiss, and when I let go, I say, "I canceled it because that's how a man should treat the woman he's fallen in love with."

"I love your girlfriend lessons," she says as she rushes out from behind the counter, throws her arms around me, and kisses me once more, her whole body aligned with mine. This kiss is tender and gentle, like her voice when she surfaces to whisper again, "I'm so in love with you."

Like it's fragile and breakable. And it is. That's why you have to treat it with care.

I plan to.

But I also need to jet. "I could kiss you all day. But I have a plane to catch. I'll make a reservation for dinner tomorrow night, then you can invite me over."

"You have to leave?"

"Well, I canceled my golf game, but I do have practice this afternoon."

She bursts into laughter. "You flew down here *just* to ask me out?"

I stare at her, completely serious. "I sure did."

That earns me a kiss that makes me want to miss all my practices.

When we separate, there's a customer meandering around the store, a woman about our age who shoots us a knowing look and smiles like she has a secret. "You two are that Date Night couple?"

I wrap an arm around Rachel. "We are."

She wags a finger. "I always knew you weren't just friends."

Rachel smiles. "You were right."

When I settle into my flight a little later, I send her a calendar invite for tomorrow night. *Dinner with Plays Well With Others.*

And *Seeking Pro Baller Who Loves Chocolate* accepts.

44

IN OTHER WORDS

Carter

Jocundity is the word of the day. It means merriment, jocularity, extreme happiness.

I shake my head at the calendar as I crumple up the page and toss it in the recycling bin the next morning. During my run across the bridge, I try to use the word in a sentence, but it's just too douchey. Who could possibly say that and mean it?

I shift mental gears as I power up the thigh-burning hills of San Francisco, reviewing the day ahead and everything on my to-do list.

Like my first real date with Rachel.

All day, I am aware of time. As I shower after my run. As I pick up Beck. As we review the game film from Vegas. As we work out and go over the playbook for the home game this coming Sunday.

Rachel will be in the stands. I can't wait to kiss my girl on the sidelines after we win.

But first, there's tonight.

And later that evening, I check the ticking clock as I get ready to see her at the restaurant in an hour.

I leave my place with a brand-new kind of excitement in my step. It's not jocundity though. Nor is it the thrill of a date, though I'm definitely thrilled. And it's not the excitement over sex tonight, but fuck yes, I want to make her come so many times.

This feeling powering me is all new. Maybe I'll figure out a better word for it by the end of the date.

Once I shut the door behind me, I turn around to find Monroe standing on his deck, holding a tumbler of scotch. He eyes me up and down then sighs in resignation. "From the looks of it, the coffee shop is closed tomorrow."

I knock fists with him. "Yes, bro."

He lifts his glass. "I'll drink to you then."

I say goodbye then head to an *it* place that Maddox helped me pick. He wasn't stoked that I canceled on Seductive, but he's a good agent who goes to bat for me, so he handled it and set up another charity golf game with Naveen and Amar. I've promised him I won't cancel that one. I've already set the reminder. Well, five reminders.

I drive down to the Marina to a Mediterranean restaurant that's getting all the raves. Rachel had a quick appointment with a supplier after her flight, so she's meeting me here any second now.

After I park, I grab a gift bag I brought along, and I

fly inside, excitement pushing me on. When I pull open the door, she's already at the bar. My heart stutters and I give a low whistle of appreciation as I reach her. "Hey, Sunshine."

"Hi...*friend*." She sounds nervous.

Like me.

But excited.

Also like me.

She wears a dark red dress that hugs her curves and shows off some skin. It's the right kind of short and the perfect kind of tight. She's wearing a couple necklaces. One with stars. One with hearts. She looks bright, upbeat, happy.

She rises to give me a peck on the cheek. I turn my face and capture her lips. She sighs happily against me.

As the hostess guides us to our table, I set a hand on Rachel's back so everyone knows she's mine.

Once we're alone, I say, "I missed you."

It feels good to say that. It's such a relief and a joy to talk to her like this at last.

"I've missed you too," she says, dipping her face, a little shy. It's too cute. Too sexy.

After we check out the menu and order, I ask about her day, and she tells me about her flight and the meetings she had about marketing Fable's eggplant necklaces. I smile, knowing those came from our un-date at the farmers' market.

"Oh, that reminds me," I say with a groan.

"What's wrong?"

"Just that I have to record this date. Can I tell you

how happy I'll be when this recording is over? I can't wait to date you camera-free."

"Same here, but I don't regret a thing about our un-dates."

Reaching across the table, I run a thumb along her jaw. "I don't either."

I do the responsible thing and shoot a few minutes of how to take the woman you love out to dinner. How to romance her. How to make her feel like she's the only one.

Finally, I turn off the camera and hand her the gift bag. "So, I got you this mug. I was going to give it to you Monday night at the date I canceled. I had this whole thing planned where I'd ask you to keep seeing me with this mug."

She opens the bag, and takes out the custom-ordered cup that says *The Doctor Is In*. "I was going to say I thought you could keep it at my house to use whenever," I tell her, and while that would have been a nice way to ask her to be mine, flying to Los Angeles to ask her out was worlds better.

She holds it close to her chest. "Ah. It's the commemorative every-night-is-a-sleepover mug."

I crack up. This woman. She just fucking gets me, and she always has. She nibbles on the corner of her lips before she says, "I got something for you too."

She reaches into her purse and takes out a red plastic spatula, tied with a bow.

And I laugh even harder as I take the gift and mime spanking her. "This is absolutely my lucky spatula. And

I see it's a two-fer," I say, fingering the silky ribbon. "I can tie you up and spank you."

"Yes. Yes, you can. I was going to give it to you on Monday night and see if you wanted to keep doing this."

I guess our timing wasn't so off, after all. "I'm going to use it on you every single night," I say in a husky tone, lowering my voice. "Because you are my dirty girl."

She shrugs coquettishly. "You bet I am."

We eat and laugh and talk and touch, and when I've paid the bill, she meets my gaze and says contentedly, "I think I like restaurants now."

"No. You just like me," I say.

"That's true."

When we leave, I can't wait to finally get her alone. I'm frisky as we're heading up the stairs of her place, my hand sliding down her back, over her ass. As she unlocks the door, I kiss her neck, a rumble working its way up my chest.

When the door slams shut, we're off to the races, touching and kissing, unzipping and stumbling to the couch. I pull up her dress to her waist and yank off her blue lace panties. She undoes my jeans and straddles me. We had the talk at dinner. We've both been tested. So for the first time, she sinks onto me.

Bare.

I groan in bliss. In joy. In exuberance. In ecstasy. But not in fucking jocundity.

Sometimes the word of the day should be a much simpler one. One you can use easily in a sentence.

Maybe even while you're doing two things at once, like talking and loving.

So I do as I thrust up, saying, "I'm so happy when I'm with you."

She moans as she grinds down on me. "You make *me* happy."

Those are my four favorite words of the day. Or, really, of all my days.

45

THE FRIEND ZONE IS THE BEST ZONE

Rachel

"Welcome to the first episode of Heartbreakers and Matchmakers. I am your host, Monroe Blackstone."

We're in the podcast studio the next week, along with Monroe's cohosts, who he introduces next. "And this is Jack and Vanessa Larkin. They're—wait for it—happily married."

Vanessa smiles then says into the mic, "And Monroe's—wait for it—happily unmarried."

"And perennially jaded," Monroe adds, and I smile sadly, but not too sadly. Monroe has mostly accepted the unraveling of his marriage. "And that's the point of this show. You'll get all our perspectives on romance."

His attention shifts to Carter and me, parked across the table from the podcast hosts. When Monroe invited us on a few weeks ago, I'd said yes, thinking we'd talk about our "dating experiment." At the time, that was all it was. I don't think I had fully processed, even then, what was happening in my heart. It took me a while to see what was in front of me all along.

Now, here we are, together, and it feels so right.

Monroe tosses out the first question. "So, you did this series for an app on how to go on dates. Basically, a tips-for-dating show, which is something a lot of people are eager to find out about. But I'm thinking we maybe ought to retitle that...How to Date Your Best Friend?"

"Or Five Un-Dates to a Real Date?" Carter suggests.

"Or Girlfriend Lessons to a Real Girlfriend," I offer.

"Let's talk about how it all started," Monroe says.

My guy looks at me with a glint in his warm brown eyes. "Well, it all started when I met Rachel Dumont in high school..."

* * *

A few days later, we're at a warehouse in the Dogpatch district. Pop music plays while some guests stuff themselves into photo booths to snap pics while others battle it out with retro board games like Clue.

Carter and I survey the scene from a corner near the stage. It's a fiesta of possibilities. And my romantic heart —full of all the good vibes now—can't help but imagine the new couplings starting tonight.

"What's your bet on how many of these friends will end up just like us?" I say to my guy.

"Depends on how lucky they are," he says, looping an arm around my waist and kissing my cheek.

My man is so affectionate. So possessive. He loves to

touch me when we're alone, but he loves to touch me in public too. Pretty sure he wants the world to know I belong to him.

And judging from the way he kissed me at his football game last week—a toe-curling, knee-weakening kiss in the stands—the world does know.

Which works for me.

"Good point," I say, then I spot Fable and Elodie near the entrance, handing out gift bags that include Fable's eggplant necklaces and Elodie's chocolates.

But that's not the most interesting part. What's more intriguing is that Wilder Blaine has just arrived at the door.

"I didn't expect to see him," I whisper.

"I didn't either," Carter says, sounding a little surprised too.

From our vantage point, I study the charismatic man, and for a few seconds, I swear he's looking at Fable with a spark in his eyes.

Or wait, is it Elodie? Because now he's talking to her.

Maybe he knows them both? I have no idea, but I'll have to ask my friends later.

For now, my boyfriend and I head to the stage to host this kickoff party for The Friend Zone.

At first, I wasn't sure we'd be such good hosts anymore, since we're no longer *just friends*.

But the thing is—we *are* still friends.

We're best friends.

We're just more now.

Sometimes friends become lovers—like we did when

I learned to trust my heart. And to trust the strength of our friendship.

I guess it's a good thing I accidentally flashed him my boobs one fine day. Later tonight, when we're home alone, I'll do it on purpose.

EPILOGUE
HOW TO HOLI-DATE

Rachel

I'm dreaming of a foggy Christmas doesn't quite have the same ring to it, but does it ever work for this evening. As I peer through the window of my jewelry shop at the misty night sky, I remember why returning home was the best decision I ever made.

When I moved here from Los Angeles several months ago, I was hoping I'd lick my wounds, see my friends, and start over away from the painful memories.

Now, I have so much more, including regular customers, and as a new business owner on busy Fillmore Street, I'll take that any day.

The Date Night series rejuvenated my business, and the customers keep coming, both here and in Venice, where I have a new, very loyal, very punctual manager. I couldn't be happier.

The bell above the door tinkles, and Ava comes in, looking stylish in a black coat and black boots.

"Hey, you." I greet her warmly, hoping this is one of her good days.

As she unloops her scarf, she meets my gaze with a sparkle in her eyes. Yes, it's a good day for sure. "Hey to you too. Got anything for a gal who's moving on?"

"I sure do," I say, smiling, grateful to hear she's healing too.

"Something that says *I have good vibes about my future*," she adds.

"Of course you do," I say. We're not best friends. I don't think we ever will be. But we support each other as women who've been through the same thing, and as female entrepreneurs, regularly sending business to each other.

I've referred her to Elena too. Paying it forward, I suppose.

Ava peers around the little shop, checking out my display of trendy, artsy jewelry—boho necklaces, chunky bracelets, and cool rings—but I point her to Fable's "Treat Yourself" line, then spot the perfect one for Ava. I show her a silver chain that has a B hanging on it.

She arches a brow in curiosity. "Is the B for badass?"

"You know it," I say.

"I'll take it," she says, then slips her phone from her coat pocket to pay.

"Your money is no good here," I say. Then I hand her a little silvery bag with the necklace in it. "You deserve it."

"Thank you. And there's a free massage for you anytime you want," she says.

"I won't turn that down," I say, but I don't know if I'll use it soon. A certain football player has very strong hands and loves to work out the kinks in my neck each night.

Well, he loves to work out all my kinks.

We've explored many others. Scarves, blindfolds, and handcuffs now and then. And all sorts of spatulas. Sidenote: a shoehorn leaves wonderful marks. Big, beautiful bruises that make me feel…wanted.

Everything he does makes me feel that way.

Especially the fact that we decided to keep doing our How to Date series after all. We're not doing the series out of obligation. We don't do it for money. We do it for fun, when we want to, sharing with others how a real relationship feels. What it's like to hit the town with someone you love who loves you back the same, big, beautiful buoyant way.

We like to share what the real thing looks like.

I guess we're sort of like romance doctors. It's our thing.

Tonight, as I'm walking down the street in the foggy evening, silver and gold lights twinkling on the shop windows, the real thing looks like the most handsome, big-hearted person I've ever known waiting for me outside The Spotted Zebra.

Carter

. . .

She's a Christmas gift.

Just look at my Rachel walking toward me, the way she wears those jeans that hug her long legs and snuggle against her fantastic hips. Check out that chestnut hair curling over her shoulders. And how about that smile tilting her pretty lips, the twinkle in her eyes, and the radiance of all her upbeat...Rachel-ness.

Yup. It only gets better, falling for your best friend.

Especially when she's wearing the fuck out of a cute pink knit hat with a snowflake design. I swear, it's almost as sexy as lingerie, the way it's tugged down over her hair, letting those soft brown strands curl around her shoulders. Lip gloss shines on her lips. I want to kiss it off. And do other bad things to her.

When she reaches me, I pull her in for a kiss. "Mmm. Missed these lips," I say.

"You kissed me this morning when I left," she teases.

"Doesn't matter. Kissing you is my favorite thing," I say. But wait. "Well, that's not completely true. I have a lot of favorite things I do with you...Fucking you, hanging out with you, spending the night with you."

"What do you know? Those are my favorite things too."

When I let go, I catch the scent of her hair. *Orange blossoms.* I told her how much that scent turned me on, and I don't think she's stopped wearing it since.

Works for me.

"Now tell me what's so special about The Spotted Zebra tonight?" she asks eagerly. I told her the bar had something different planned, but I didn't tell her what.

That's part of how to romance your woman. A little intrigue goes a long way.

"You'll find out soon," I tell her, then we head inside the bar, ready for a little "how to date at Christmas."

I can't get enough of the holidays, from the lights to the music to the decorations. It's a feast for the senses.

We head inside to record this special edition of the How to Date series. I admit, this isn't entirely altruistic. There are benefits for me, too, like an excuse to impress my girl as often as I can.

The sign over the bar proclaims *Hot Cocoa Tasting*, and when Rachel sees it, she spins around with a beaming smile and a hand over her heart. "You so get me." Another tally in the "win" column.

We amble closer to where the bar is offering spiked cocoa with names like *Lick My Lips, Melt in My Mouth*, and *With Extra Cream*.

"This is giving me all sorts of ideas," I say.

"Oh, you already had those ideas," she says.

"That is true."

And one of those ideas involves mistletoe. Just wait till she sees.

* * *

Thirty minutes later, I'm camped out on the chichi black-and-white-striped couch in the corner, enjoying a mug of cinnamon hot chocolate spiked with Irish Cream, and time with Rachel. As she sets down her mug of Lick My Lips, she tells me about the store and how well it's going this holiday season.

Such a welcome change from how she felt a few months ago.

Another welcome change? The Renegades' record is no longer solid. It's stellar, and knock on wood, we're likely to snag a playoff spot.

"I think you're my good-luck charm," I tell her. "We haven't lost at home since I made you mine."

"Then I'd better keep coming to your games," she says.

"And coming," I say.

But before I get too caught up in innuendo, I want to show the world—or really, the world of Date Night—how to have an awesome holi-date.

I take out my phone, then tell her to turn to the bar. Yeah, I like to impress my girl.

Rachel

The bartender in the Santa hat calls out from behind the bar, "Time for a mistletoe moment for charity. If you want to raise money for rescue animals, be sure to look up and see if there's a mistletoe near you, and if there is, feel free to have a kiss for the pets."

A mischievous smile curves her lips as the bartender turns toward us, then lifts a red bucket on the counter. On the side of the bucket, words in white say: *Singles for Kisses.*

Carter's gaze drifts up. There's a sprig of mistletoe above us.

My breath catches.

How did I miss it? The mistletoe? Maybe because I was so caught up in talking to him. Not that I need an excuse to kiss my guy, but I will take it. Oh yes, I will.

With the phone recording, Carter says to the camera, "Now listen, I've maybe, possibly, kissed her a few times, but this is a reminder to all of you. At Christmas time, mistletoe is your best friend. It's a better lubricant than alcohol. So use it."

The other patrons chant: "Kiss her, kiss her, kiss her."

He doesn't need their incentive, but I can tell he loves it because I do. I love his declarations. He makes them over and over for me. In private, yes, but in public, too, at games and in moments like this. Letting the world know I'm taken.

By him. *Only* by him.

He leans closer, taking his time. My heart speeds up. My skin tingles. I've kissed him a million times, and every time I want more.

He reaches me, brushes his lips to mine. His are lush, full, and I want to taste them deeply. But this is a kiss for the camera. It's chaste. Borderline sweet. A whisper of a kiss, and still, I don't want it to end. Even as the crowd claps and cheers, their voices barely register.

I'm too swept up in this kiss and what it might lead to later.

When Carter breaks it, he turns off the camera. "You know, Rachel, I'd like to know if you've been naughty or nice this season."

"Which one do you want me to be?" I ask, breathless, turned on, and *so* ready.

"A good boyfriend would show you rather than tell you," he says with a glint in his eyes.

We're out of there faster than Santa's sleigh.

Carter

In no time, we're in her home, hastily shutting the door. I tug off that knit cap, then hold her face. "That hat is almost better than lingerie," I admit in a husky voice.

"But you haven't seen what lingerie I'm wearing tonight," she says coyly.

"Doesn't matter. You have been turning me on ever since we met at the bar," I say. I press my body against hers so she can feel the truth of my words and my desire. I love showing her how much I want her. I *never* want her to doubt my desire or my love. Both are boundless.

When I drop my lips onto hers, I kiss her in a way I wouldn't on camera. It's hot and deep. It thrums through me everywhere, buzzing under my skin, racing through my veins, settling deep into my bones. But most of all, I feel it in the beating of my heart. Strong, passionate. And all for her. Every night.

We kiss for several minutes in a consuming, hungry way, with hands and bodies, sighs and groans.

Her fingers travel up my chest, exploring me, pinching my nipples. Fuck, she has my number.

But I have hers too. I know what she likes. I hoist her up, toss her over my shoulder, and carry her to the bed. "Gonna spread you out on the bed and taste you till you're coming on my lips. Then I'll fuck you good and hard."

She lets out a long, happy sigh, chased with a purr. "Merry Christmas to me."

* * *

Stretched out on her big bed, Rachel looks like a holiday angel, all long legs and smooth skin. And the best part of all is—she wears lacy panties and a see-through bra.

Red and white. Like a Christmas treat for this guy.

"Mmm. You win," I tell her as I unhook that bra, freeing her tits. "Better than the hat."

"Told you so," she says.

I kiss my way down her soft belly, swirling my tongue around her belly button, then I tug at the top of her panties with my teeth.

"I'm in the mood to tease the hell out of you," I tell my woman who likes words. Lots of dirty words. I slide between her legs, wrap my hands around her ass, and kiss her sweetness. I bury my face between her legs, rubbing my scruff against her thighs, then devote my lips to her sweet center.

Soon, I'm drawing chants and moans from her that make my dick harder than granite. "Yes, yes, yes," she calls out.

She is a dirty, delicious gift in bed.

And she's so damn close. I stop for a brief second only to issue a command. "Say my name."

She bucks against me. "Oh god, Carter," she calls out, and then my name breaks apart, spiraling into incoherent shouts of pleasure.

Yes, fucking yes.

When her cries turn into soft whimpers, I stop, drag a hand across my face, then sit on my knees and give my dick a tug. "Be nice and get on your hands and knees like the naughty girl you are."

She scrambles to all fours, lifting that beautiful ass high in the air.

"Damn, woman. You're too fucking sexy," I praise as I kneel behind her, notching the head of my cock against her slick opening.

Like that, I fill her and fuck her. I slide a hand between her legs, stroking her until she's shuddering, then crying out beneath me, cresting the hill once again. With a loud, carnal grunt of *coming*, I follow her there.

We collapse together in a hot, sweaty, very happy mess. I pull her close, savoring her orange-blossom scent mixed with sex, mixed with *us*. When I recover the power of speech, I say, "Confession: I love Christmas and Christmas dirty talk."

She wriggles against me. "You should give me more dirty girl lessons."

"I will." But there's something else I want. Maybe it's too soon. Maybe it's too much. But maybe I'm no longer afraid to make a big play.

I stroke her hair. "Know what I want for Christmas?"

She shakes her head. "I already got you a self-watering pot for Jane, so nope."

I meet her gaze, turn serious, and I just go for it. "I want to share a home with you. Will you move in with me?"

Her lips part. Her eyes widen. And for one long, tense moment, I fear I've asked for too much.

That my timing is all wrong.

But then she smiles, brighter than I've ever seen. "I will. Home is you and me."

Yes, yes it is.

THE END

I loved writing Rachel's and Carter's romance so much that I wasn't ready to say goodbye! Scroll below for access to an exclusive bonus scene of their life together, but first be sure to find out how Hazel's and Axel's love story unfolded in their spicy, enemies-to-lovers romance My So-Called Sex Life. That only one bed in the room standalone with a feisty heroine and a grumpy hero is available right now for FREE in KU! If you've read it, then grab my spicy, top-five Amazon bestselling, hockey romance DOUBLE PUCKED for free in KU! That rom com is filled with sweet revenge, heat and lots of shenanigans!

* * *

Click here for the Plays Well With Others Bonus Epilogue! Or scan the QR code!

* * *

My So-Called Sex Life Excerpt

Hazel

I glance out the window, enjoying the nighttime view.

It's dark. The train lights illuminate the path as we curve along a bend in the tracks. But neither one of us slams into the other.

"See? We didn't just fall and land in each other's laps, lips pressed together, like we would have in a book." Though, a lot of things that happen in my romance novels haven't happened in my real sex life. Like, say, great sex. Maybe someday I'll have what my heroines are having.

"How does that even happen in stories? We never wrote an accidental kiss," he says.

"I haven't in my solo books either," I say.

"I don't understand how a kiss could be anything but

intentional. Even if they're in a cab, and the cabbie slams on the brakes and they wind up in each other's arms, the thing that happens next is always intentional."

"Kisses are deliberate," I say, relieved that finally we're talking again—like yesterday. But also like we did once upon a time, before our blow-up.

"And they should be," he adds as the train swings around another curve.

Faster than I expected.

Before I'm even aware of what's happening, I'm sliding closer to him, my hip slamming against his hip. He grabs my upper arm, holding me tight.

I laugh briefly from the surprise, then look at the shaved distance between us. "See? We're closer. But we're still not accidentally kissing."

Even though I kind of want to be. Even though my heart is beating faster than it was before.

When Axel looks at me, his eyes are darker than I'm used to. "Because someone always has to make the first move," he says.

"Even if there's an accidental-on-purpose kiss," I add.

"Like in a book," he says as he curls his hand a little tighter around my arm. I hope he doesn't let me go.

Since I'm letting go of reason, I let go of the past too. In this moment, I want an accidental-on-purpose kiss.

"Sort of like this?" I ask, then lean in and give him a swift peck on the cheek. I catch the fading scent of the forest after it rains. I let out a tiny gasp.

His breath catches.

I pull back from his cheek, meet his eyes. They're

wild. Hungry. Then my gaze strays to his lips. They're plush, pillowy soft.

"Or maybe…" I lean in, and I don't accidentally kiss him. I kiss him on purpose. A soft, barely-there sweep of my lips. "…like this."

Keep reading for hot sex on a train, witty banter and wild escapades in: MY SO-CALLED SEX LIFE

And sign up for my newsletter for details on more stories from this cast of characters…

DEAR READER

Carter's experience living with ADHD is based on extensive research into ADHD, as well as insight and interviews from people living their best lives with ADHD. Ultimately, everyone's experience of ADHD is unique to the individual as are their choices for managing it. Carter's choices as they relate to medication are uniquely informed by his job. Adderall is indeed a banned substance in the NFL, and that is why Carter takes non-stimulant ADHD medication. Any decision about medication should be discussed with a doctor or medical professional. Carter's time management strategies are informed by my conversations with people living with ADHD, as well as his intrigue, passion and focus for certain things, such as jigsaw puzzles and exercise. The occasional forgetfulness and ways to manage it also stem from conversations with those individuals. I am grateful to my sensitivity readers for combing over this manuscript and helping me to present this side of his character authentically. Thank you deeply to Kayti, Jen, and Steph. Any mistakes are entirely my own. My goal was *not* to write a story about someone learning to live with ADHD, or learning to love in spite of it. My goal was to show positive representation and write a love story that happened to have a hero with ADHD in it. I hope I succeeded, and I thank you for taking the time to read this story!

Lauren

BE A LOVELY

Want to be the first to know of sales, new releases, special deals and giveaways? Sign up for my newsletter today!

Want to be part of a fun, feel-good place to talk about books and romance, and get sneak peeks of covers and advance copies of my books? Be a Lovely!

MORE BOOKS BY LAUREN

I've written more than 100 books! **All of these titles below are FREE in Kindle Unlimited**!

Double Pucked

A sexy, outrageous MFM hockey romantic comedy!

The Virgin Society Series

Meet the Virgin Society – great friends who'd do anything for each other. Indulge in these forbidden, emotionally-charged, and wildly sexy age-gap romances!

The RSVP

The Tryst

The Tease

The Dating Games Series

A fun, sexy romantic comedy series about friends in the city and their dating mishaps!

The Virgin Next Door

Two A Day

The Good Guy Challenge

How To Date Series (New and ongoing)

Four great friends. Four chances to learn how to date again. Four standalone romantic comedies full of love, sex and meet-cute shenanigans.

My So-Called Sex Life

Plays Well With Others

The Anti-Romantic

Blown Away

Boyfriend Material

Four fabulous heroines. Four outrageous proposals. Four chances at love in this sexy rom-com series!

Asking For a Friend

Sex and Other Shiny Objects

One Night Stand-In

Overnight Service

Big Rock Series

My #1 New York Times Bestselling sexy as sin, irreverent, male-POV romantic comedy!

Big Rock

Mister O

Well Hung

Full Package

Joy Ride

Hard Wood

Happy Endings Series

Romance starts with a bang in this series of standalones following a group of friends seeking and avoiding love!

Come Again

Shut Up and Kiss Me

Kismet

My Single-Versary

Ballers And Babes

Sexy sports romance standalones guaranteed to make you hot!

Most Valuable Playboy

Most Likely to Score

A Wild Card Kiss

Rules of Love Series

Athlete, virgins and weddings!

The Virgin Rule Book

The Virgin Game Plan

The Virgin Replay

The Virgin Scorecard

The Extravagant Series

Bodyguards, billionaires and hoteliers in this sexy, high-stakes series of standalones!

One Night Only

One Exquisite Touch

My One-Week Husband

The Guys Who Got Away Series

Friends in New York City and California fall in love in this fun and hot rom-com series!

Birthday Suit

Dear Sexy Ex-Boyfriend

The What If Guy

Thanks for Last Night

The Dream Guy Next Door

Always Satisfied Series

A group of friends in New York City find love and laughter in this series of sexy standalones!

Satisfaction Guaranteed

Never Have I Ever

Instant Gratification

PS It's Always Been You

The Gift Series

An after dark series of standalones! Explore your fantasies!

The Engagement Gift

The Virgin Gift

The Decadent Gift

The Heartbreakers Series

Three brothers. Three rockers. Three standalone sexy romantic comedies.

Once Upon a Real Good Time

Once Upon a Sure Thing

Once Upon a Wild Fling

Sinful Men

A high-stakes, high-octane, sexy-as-sin romantic suspense series!

My Sinful Nights

My Sinful Desire

My Sinful Longing

My Sinful Love

My Sinful Temptation

From Paris With Love

Swoony, sweeping romances set in Paris!

Wanderlust

Part-Time Lover

One Love Series

A group of friends in New York falls in love one by one in this sexy rom-com series!

The Sexy One

The Hot One

The Knocked Up Plan

Come As You Are

Lucky In Love Series

A small town romance full of heat and blue collar heroes and sexy heroines!

Best Laid Plans

The Feel Good Factor

Nobody Does It Better

Unzipped

No Regrets

An angsty, sexy, emotional, new adult trilogy about one young couple fighting to break free of their pasts!

The Start of Us

The Thrill of It

Every Second With You

The Caught Up in Love Series

A group of friends finds love!

The Pretending Plot

The Dating Proposal

The Second Chance Plan

The Private Rehearsal

Seductive Nights Series

A high heat series full of danger and spice!

Night After Night

After This Night

One More Night

A Wildly Seductive Night

Joy Delivered Duet

A high-heat, wickedly sexy series of standalones that will set your sheets on fire!

Nights With Him

Forbidden Nights

Unbreak My Heart

A standalone second chance emotional roller coaster of a romance

The Muse

A magical realism romance set in Paris

Good Love Series of sexy rom-coms co-written with Lili Valente!

I also write MM romance under the name L. Blakely!

Hopelessly Bromantic Duet (MM)

Roomies to lovers to enemies to fake boyfriends

Hopelessly Bromantic

Here Comes My Man

Men of Summer Series (MM)

Two baseball players on the same team fall in love in a forbidden romance spanning five epic years

Scoring With Him

Winning With Him

All In With Him

MM Standalone Novels

A Guy Walks Into My Bar

The Bromance Zone

One Time Only

The Best Men (Co-written with Sarina Bowen)

Winner Takes All Series (MM)

A series of emotionally-charged and irresistibly sexy standalone MM sports romances!

The Boyfriend Comeback

Turn Me On

A Very Filthy Game

Limited Edition Husband

Manhandled

If you want a personalized recommendation, email me at laurenblakelybooks@gmail.com!

CONTACT

You can find Lauren on Twitter at LaurenBlakely3, Instagram at LaurenBlakelyBooks, Facebook at LaurenBlakelyBooks, or online at LaurenBlakely.com. You can also email her at laurenblakelybooks@gmail.com

Printed in Great Britain
by Amazon